SONIC™
THE HEDGEHOG

THE CHASE

WELCOME TO SONIC'S COMIC BOOK ADVENTURES -- A WORLD UNIQUE AND BEYOND WHAT YOU KNOW FROM THE SEGA GAMES! WHERE SONIC AND HIS FRIENDS WORK TO SAVE THE WORLD FROM THE FORCES OF EVIL!

SONIC THE HEDGEHOG

THE CHASE

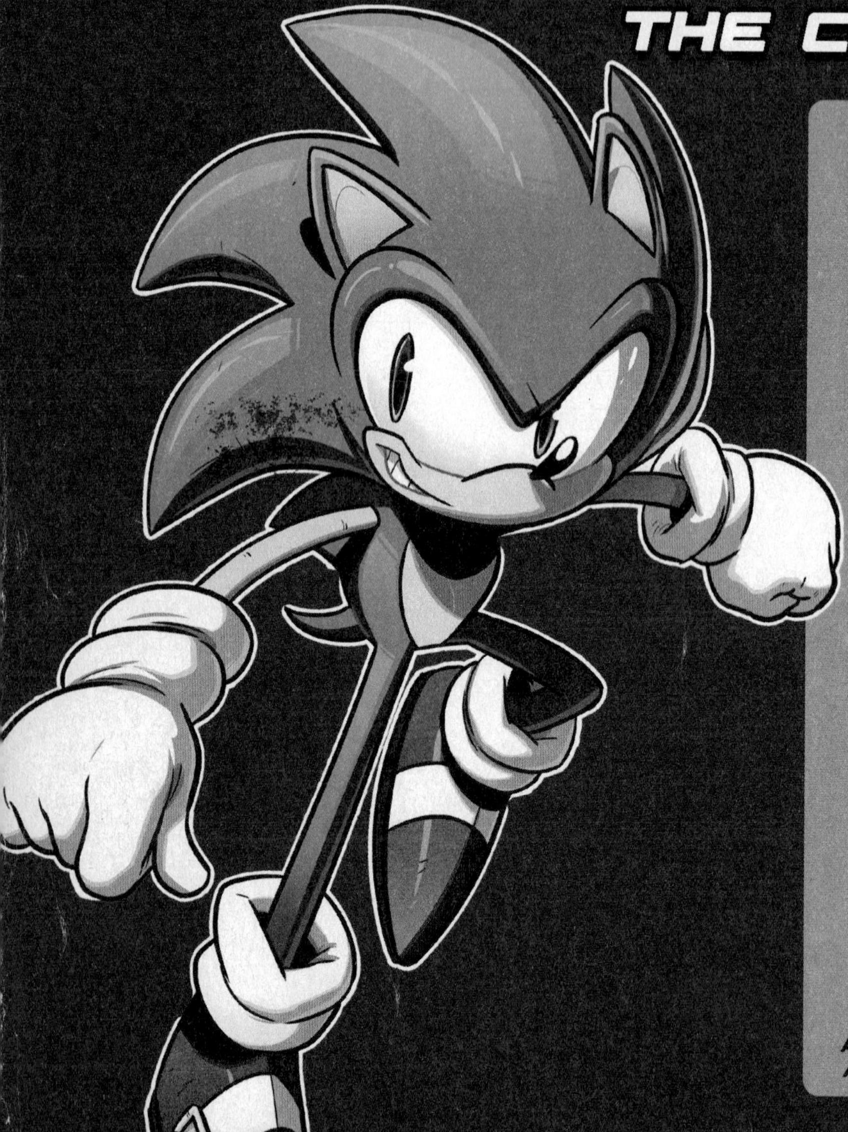

IAN FLYNN
SCRIPT

EVAN STANLEY
SONIC THE HEDGEHOG #257-259
TRACY YARDLEY
SONIC THE HEDGEHOG #259
(PENCIL BREAKDOWNS)
LAMAR WELLS
SONIC COMIC ORIGINS #1-4
PENCILS

TERRY AUSTIN
SONIC THE HEDGEHOG #257-259
GARY MARTIN
SONIC COMIC ORIGINS #1
RICK BRYANT
SONIC COMIC ORIGINS #2-4
INKS

STEVE DOWNER
SONIC THE HEDGEHOG #257-259
MATT HERMS
SONIC COMIC ORIGINS #1-4
COLORS

JOHN WORKMAN
SONIC THE HEDGEHOG #257-259
JACK MORELLI
SONIC COMIC ORIGINS #1-4
LETTERS

COVER BY
TRACY YARDLEY

SPECIAL THANKS TO
TYLER HAM &
ANTHONY GACCIONE
AT SEGA LICENSING

ARCHIE COMIC PUBLICATIONS, INC.
JON GOLDWATER, publisher/co-ceo
NANCY SILBERKLEIT, co-ceo
MIKE PELLERITO, president
VICTOR GORELICK, co-president, e-i-c
ROBERTO AGUIRRE-SACASA, chief creative officer
JIM SOKOLOWSKI, senior vice president of sales and business development
HAROLD BUCHHOLZ, senior vice president of publishing and operations
ALEX SEGURA, senior vice president of publicity and marketing
PAUL KAMINSKI, exec. director of editorial/compilation editor
VINCENT LOVALLO, assistant editor
STEPHEN OSWALD, production manager
JAMIE LEE ROTANTE, editorial assistant/proofreader

SONIC THE HEDGEHOG, Book Two: The Chase, 2014. Printed in Canada. Published by Archie Comic Publications, Inc., 325 Fayette Avenue, Mamaroneck, NY 10543-2318. Originally published in single magazine form in Sonic the Hedgehog # 257-259, Sonic Super Special Magazine #11 and Sonic Super Digest #7-9.
ISBN: 978-1-62738-928-0

TABLE OF CONTENTS

CHAPTER 1: DAMAGE CONTROL .... PG. 7

CHAPTER 2: THE CHASE PT 1 .... PG. 28

CHAPTER 3: THE CHASE PT 2 .... PG. 49

CHAPTER 4: SONIC COMIC ORIGINS PT 1 .... PG. 71

CHAPTER 5: SONIC COMIC ORIGINS PT 2 .... PG. 77

CHAPTER 6: SONIC COMIC ORIGINS PT 3 .... PG. 83

CHAPTER 7: SONIC COMIC ORIGINS PT 4 .... PG. 89

SPECIAL FEATURES .... PG. 94

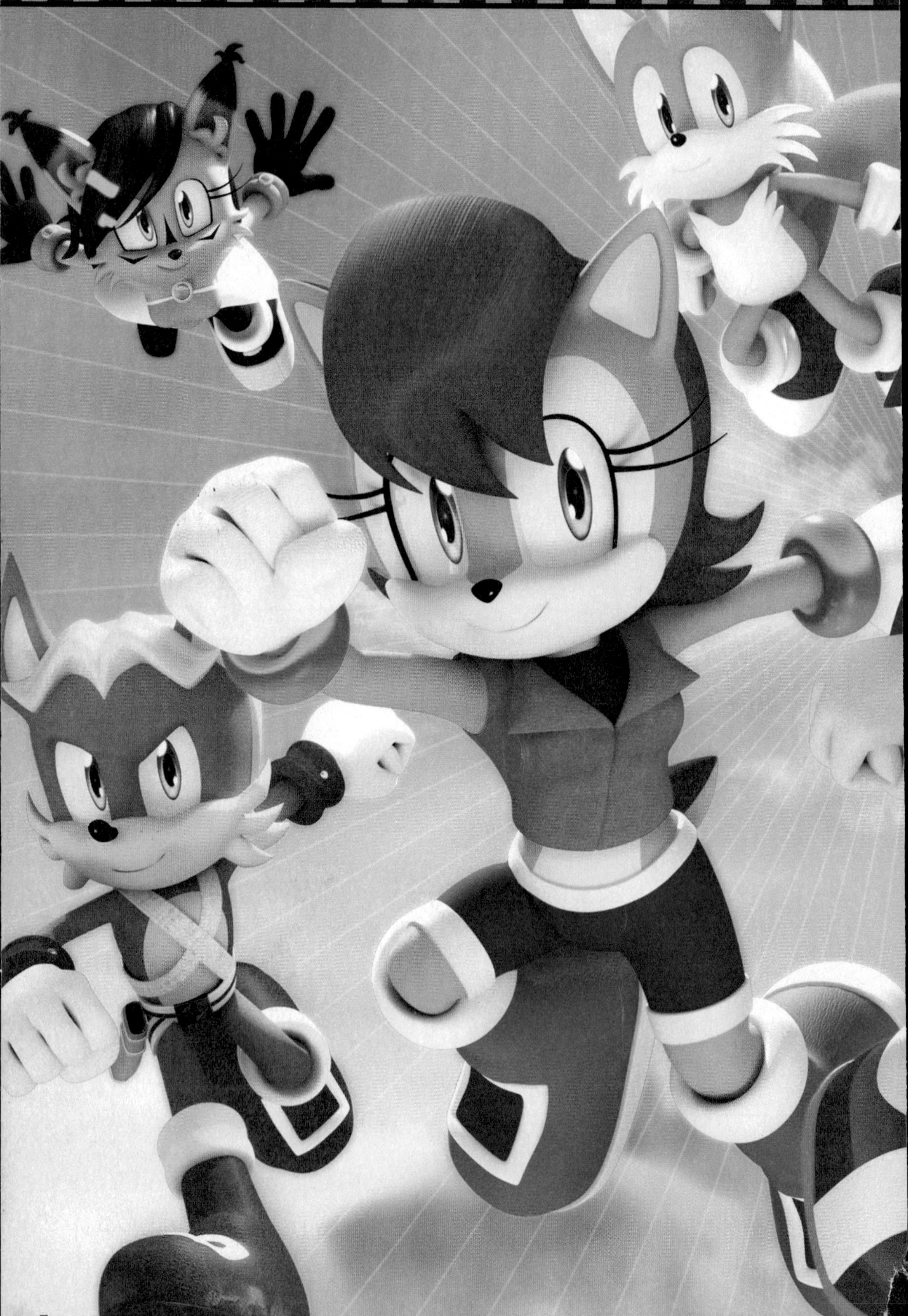

CHAPTER 1

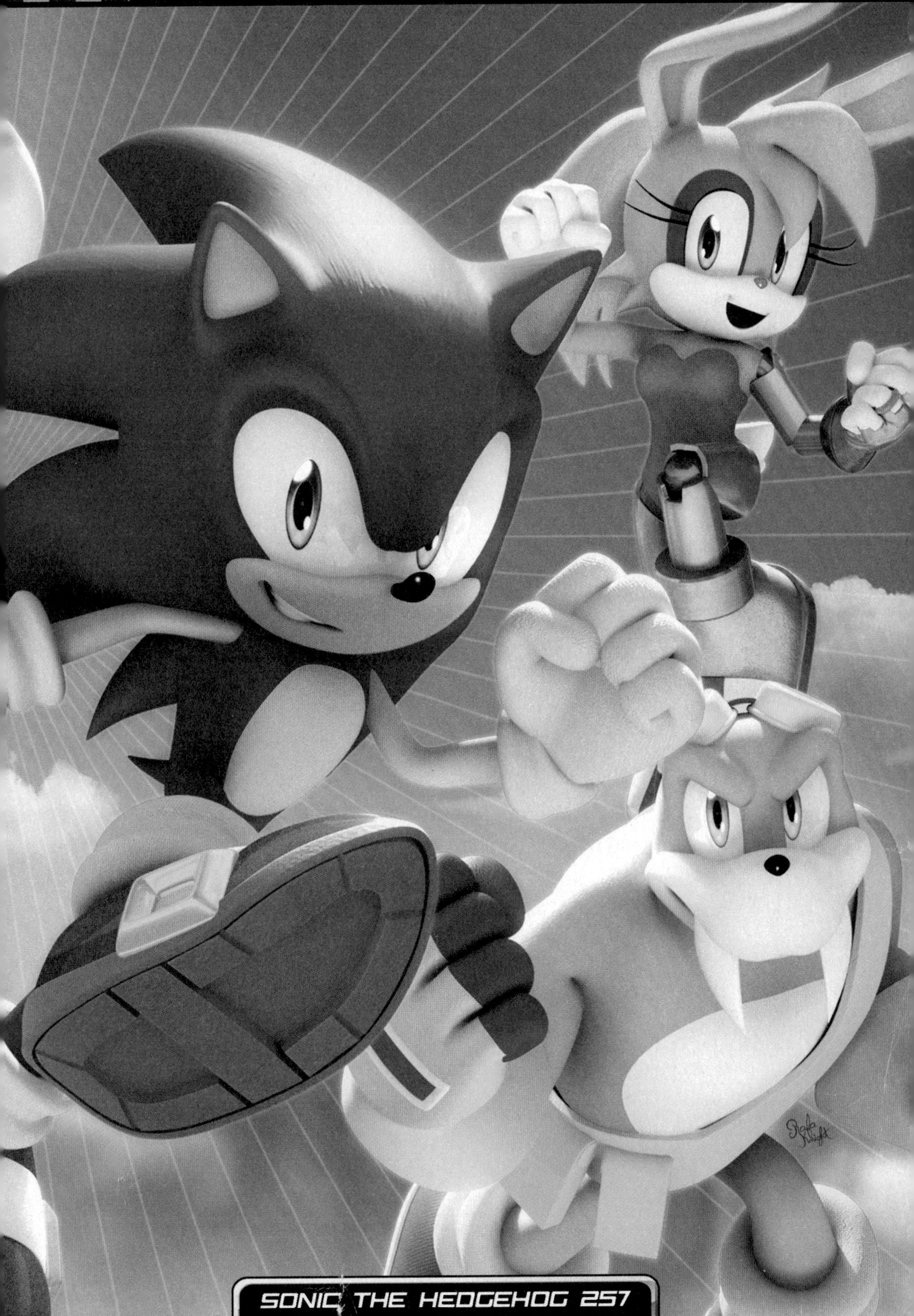
Rafa Knight

SONIC THE HEDGEHOG 257
COVER BY RAFA KNIGHT

PREVIOUSLY...

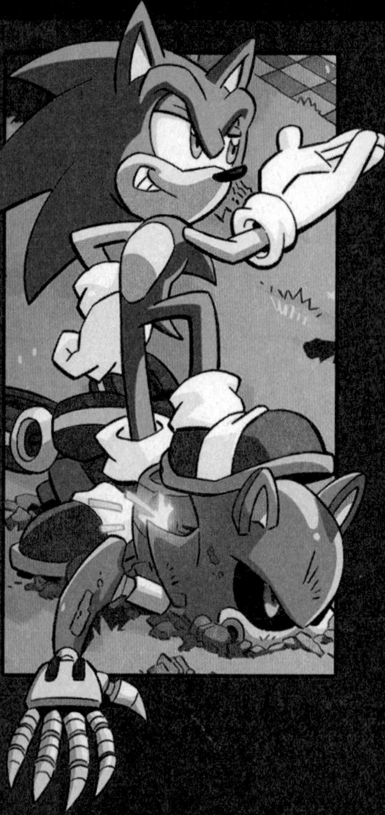

SONIC'S WORLD: IN PERIL!

Sonic the Hedgehog and his heroic Freedom Fighter friends have saved the world countless times over. Now they might be out of their league.

Thanks to a short-sighted and spiteful attack by Dr. Eggman, reality has been irreversibly changed. The chaotic energies at play pushed the world to the breaking point – and beyond!

Now hero and villain alike look on as the planet rips itself apart before their eyes. Fighting regional Egg Bosses is one thing, but the scale of this problem is larger than anything Sonic or Dr. Eggman have ever faced.

Our heroes better get ready, because the shattered world crisis has only just begun...

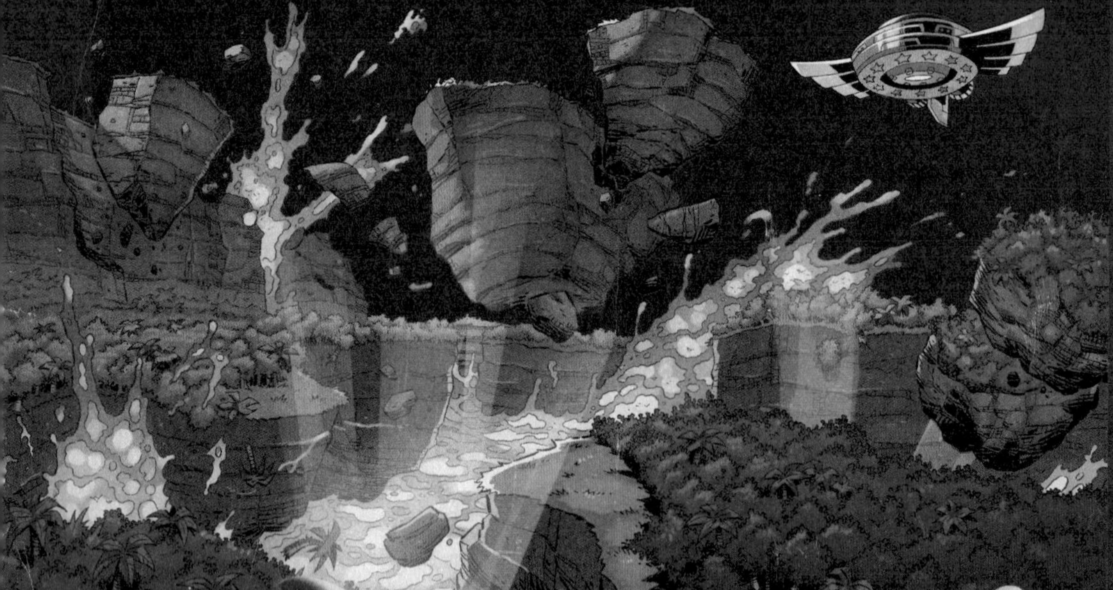

WHO'S WHO

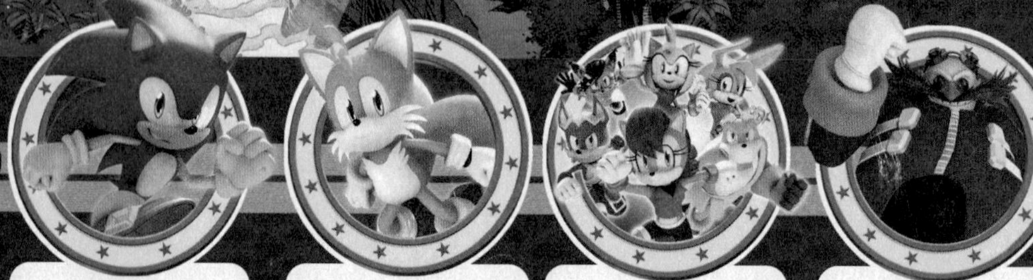

SONIC THE HEDGEHOG
WORLD HERO

MILES "TAILS" PROWER
SONIC'S BEST FRIEND

THE FREEDOM FIGHTERS
SALLY, ANTOINE, NICOLE, AMY, BUNNIE & ROTOR

DR. EGGMAN
MAD SCIENTIST

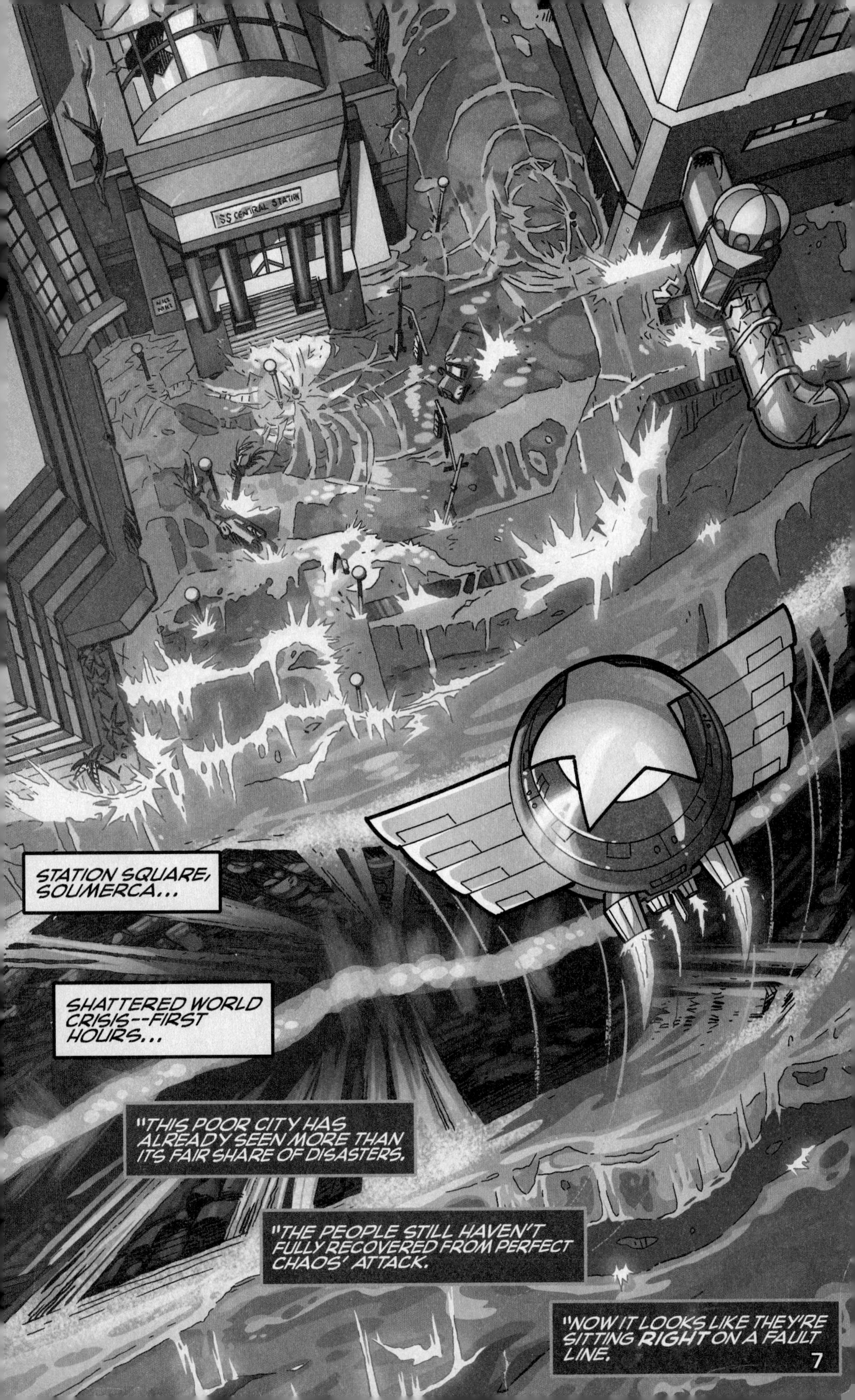
SS CENTRAL STATION
STATION SQUARE, SOUMERCA...
SHATTERED WORLD CRISIS--FIRST HOURS...
"THIS POOR CITY HAS ALREADY SEEN MORE THAN ITS FAIR SHARE OF DISASTERS.
"THE PEOPLE STILL HAVEN'T FULLY RECOVERED FROM PERFECT CHAOS' ATTACK.
"NOW IT LOOKS LIKE THEY'RE SITTING RIGHT ON A FAULT LINE.

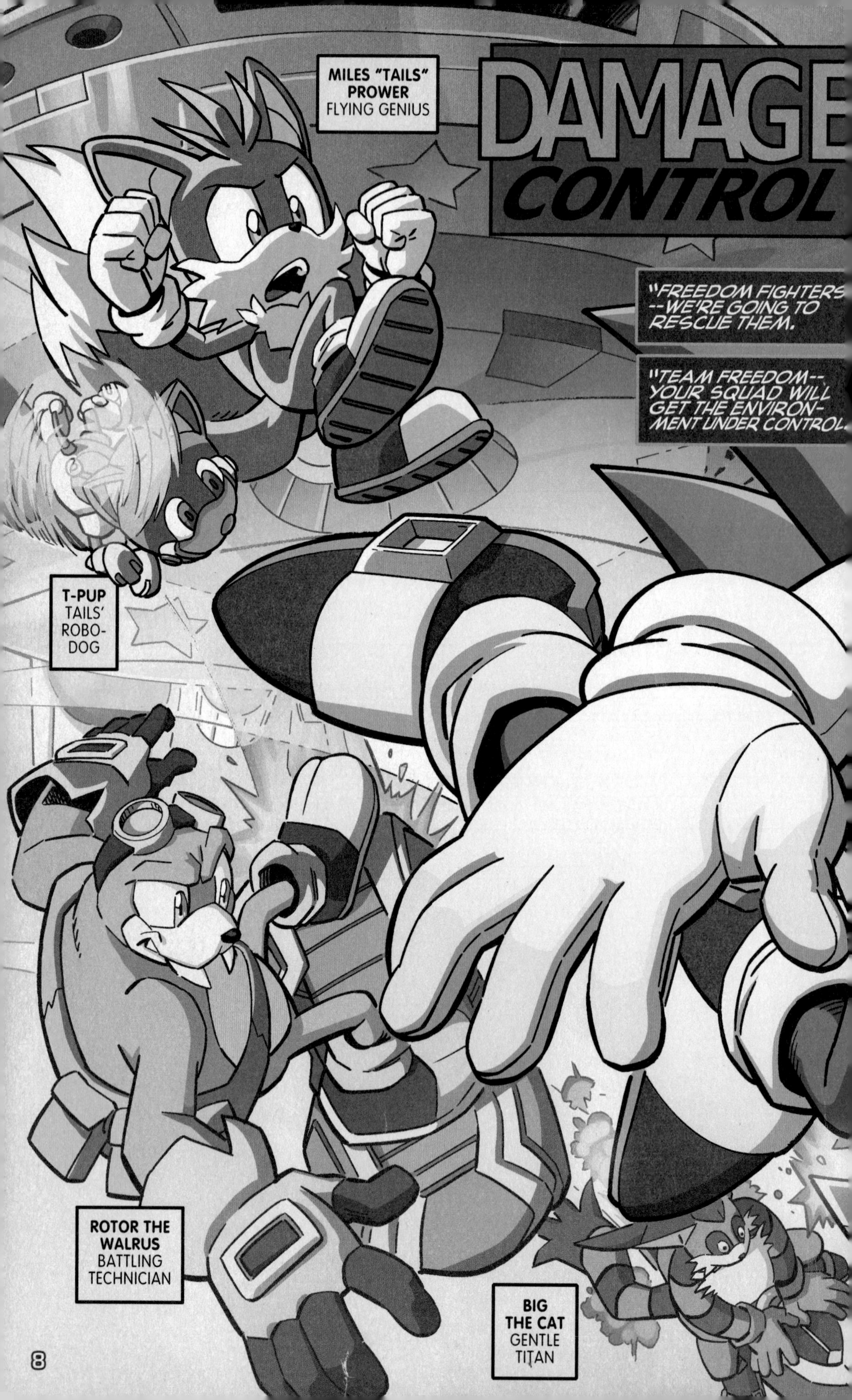
DAMAGE CONTROL
MILES "TAILS" PROWER FLYING GENIUS
"FREEDOM FIGHTERS --WE'RE GOING TO RESCUE THEM.
"TEAM FREEDOM-- YOUR SQUAD WILL GET THE ENVIRON-MENT UNDER CONTROL
T-PUP TAILS' ROBO-DOG
ROTOR THE WALRUS BATTLING TECHNICIAN
BIG THE CAT GENTLE TITAN

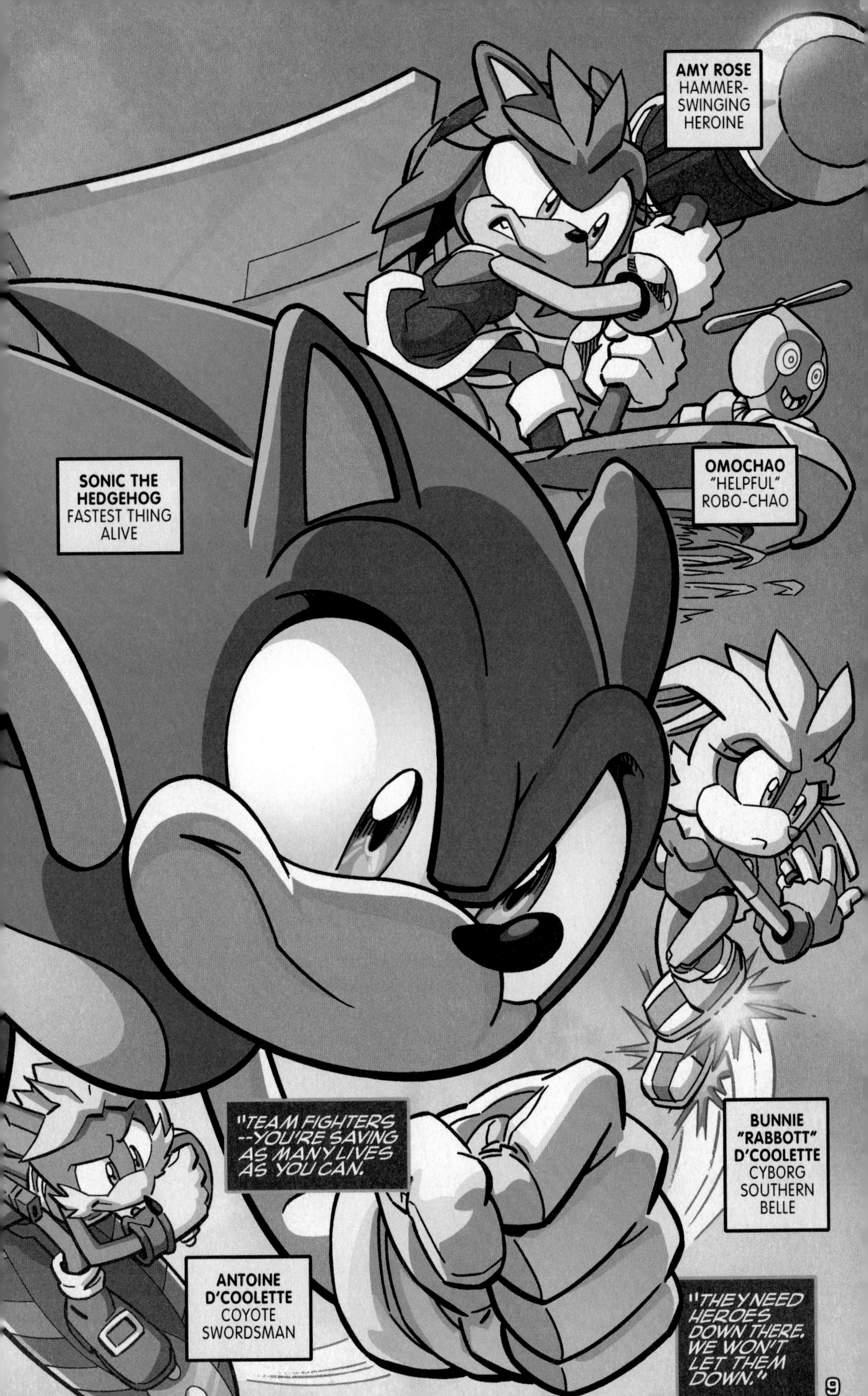
AMY ROSE HAMMER-SWINGING HEROINE
SONIC THE HEDGEHOG FASTEST THING ALIVE
OMOCHAO "HELPFUL" ROBO-CHAO
BUNNIE "RABBOTT" D'COOLETTE CYBORG SOUTHERN BELLE
"TEAM FIGHTERS --YOU'RE SAVING AS MANY LIVES AS YOU CAN.
ANTOINE D'COOLETTE COYOTE SWORDSMAN
"THEY NEED HEROES DOWN THERE. WE WON'T LET THEM DOWN."

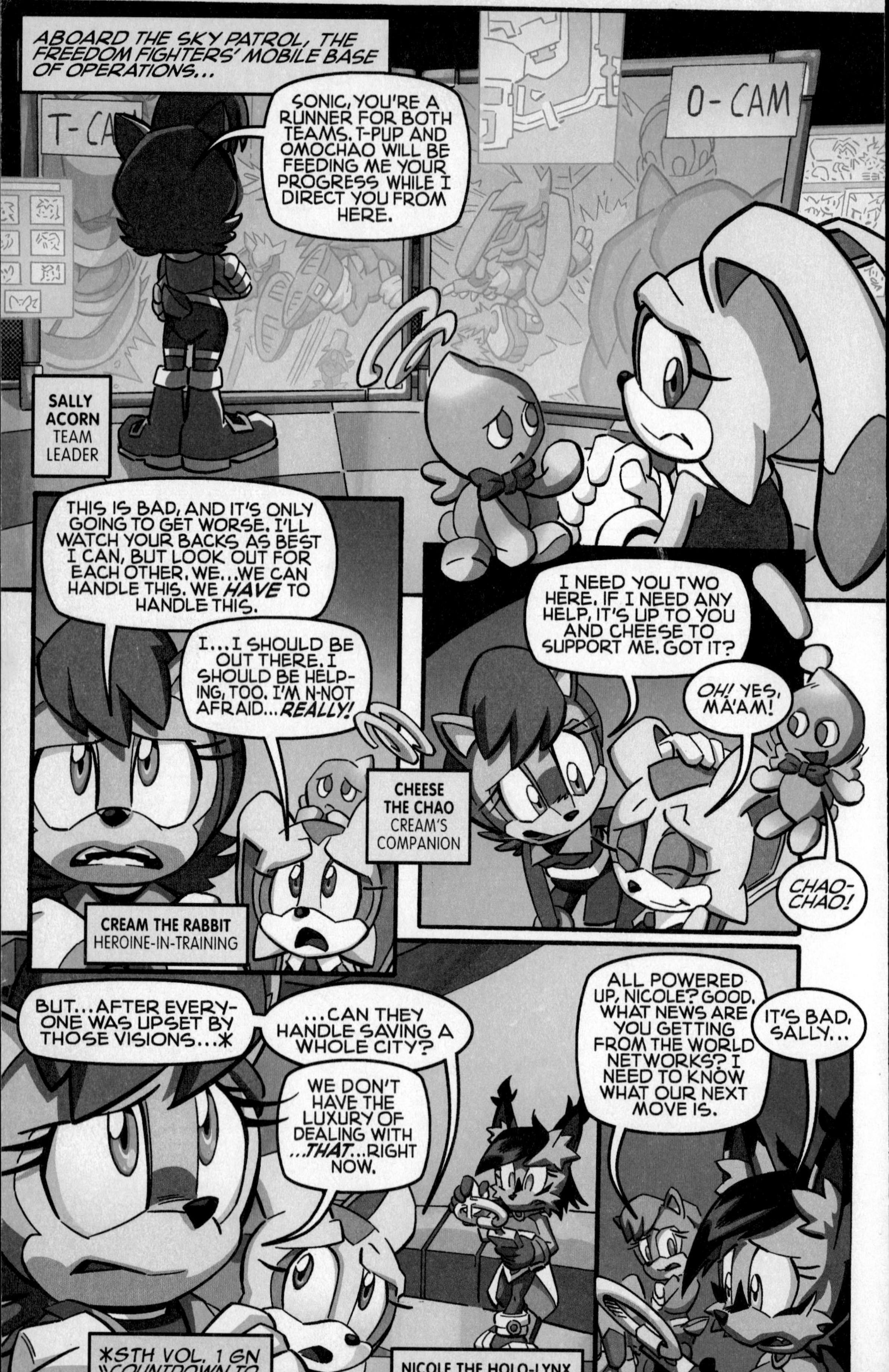
ABOARD THE SKY PATROL, THE FREEDOM FIGHTERS' MOBILE BASE OF OPERATIONS...
SONIC, YOU'RE A RUNNER FOR BOTH TEAMS. T-PUP AND OMOCHAO WILL BE FEEDING ME YOUR PROGRESS WHILE I DIRECT YOU FROM HERE.
O-CAM
SALLY ACORN TEAM LEADER
THIS IS BAD, AND IT'S ONLY GOING TO GET WORSE. I'LL WATCH YOUR BACKS AS BEST I CAN, BUT LOOK OUT FOR EACH OTHER. WE...WE CAN HANDLE THIS. WE *HAVE* TO HANDLE THIS.
I...I SHOULD BE OUT THERE. I SHOULD BE HELPING, TOO. I'M N-NOT AFRAID...*REALLY!*
CHEESE THE CHAO CREAM'S COMPANION
CREAM THE RABBIT HEROINE-IN-TRAINING
I NEED YOU TWO HERE. IF I NEED ANY HELP, IT'S UP TO YOU AND CHEESE TO SUPPORT ME. GOT IT?
OH! YES, MA'AM!
CHAO-CHAO!
BUT...AFTER EVERYONE WAS UPSET BY THOSE VISIONS...*
...CAN THEY HANDLE SAVING A WHOLE CITY?
WE DON'T HAVE THE LUXURY OF DEALING WITH ...*THAT*...RIGHT NOW.
*STH VOL. 1 GN "COUNTDOWN TO CHAOS."
NICOLE THE HOLO-LYNX LIVING COMPUTER
ALL POWERED UP, NICOLE? GOOD. WHAT NEWS ARE YOU GETTING FROM THE WORLD NETWORKS? I NEED TO KNOW WHAT OUR NEXT MOVE IS.
IT'S BAD, SALLY...

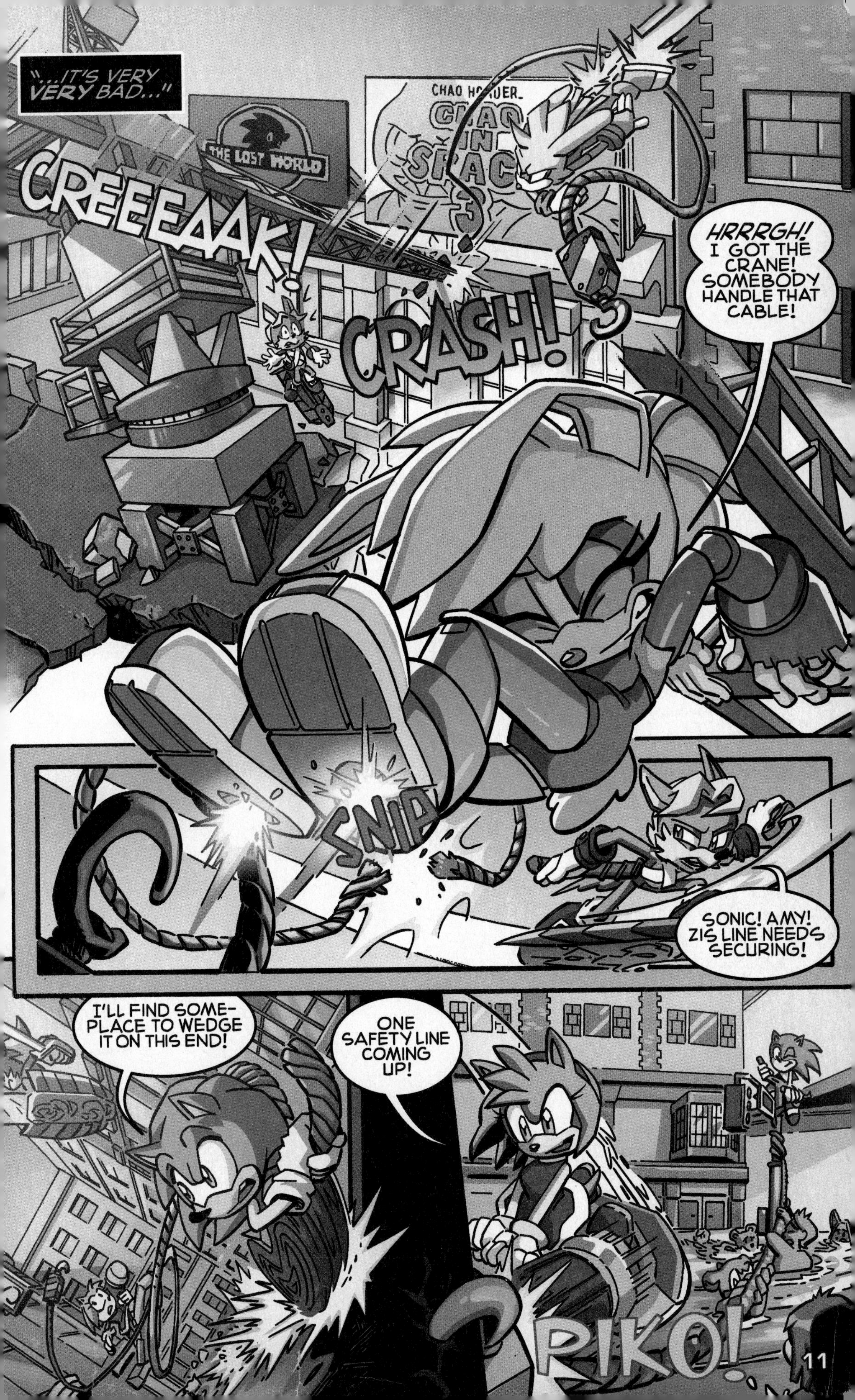
"...IT'S VERY VERY BAD..."
THE LOST WORLD
CREEEAAK!
CRASH!
HRRRGH! I GOT THE CRANE! SOMEBODY HANDLE THAT CABLE!
SNIP
SONIC! AMY! ZIS LINE NEEDS SECURING!
I'LL FIND SOME-PLACE TO WEDGE IT ON THIS END!
ONE SAFETY LINE COMING UP!
PIKO!

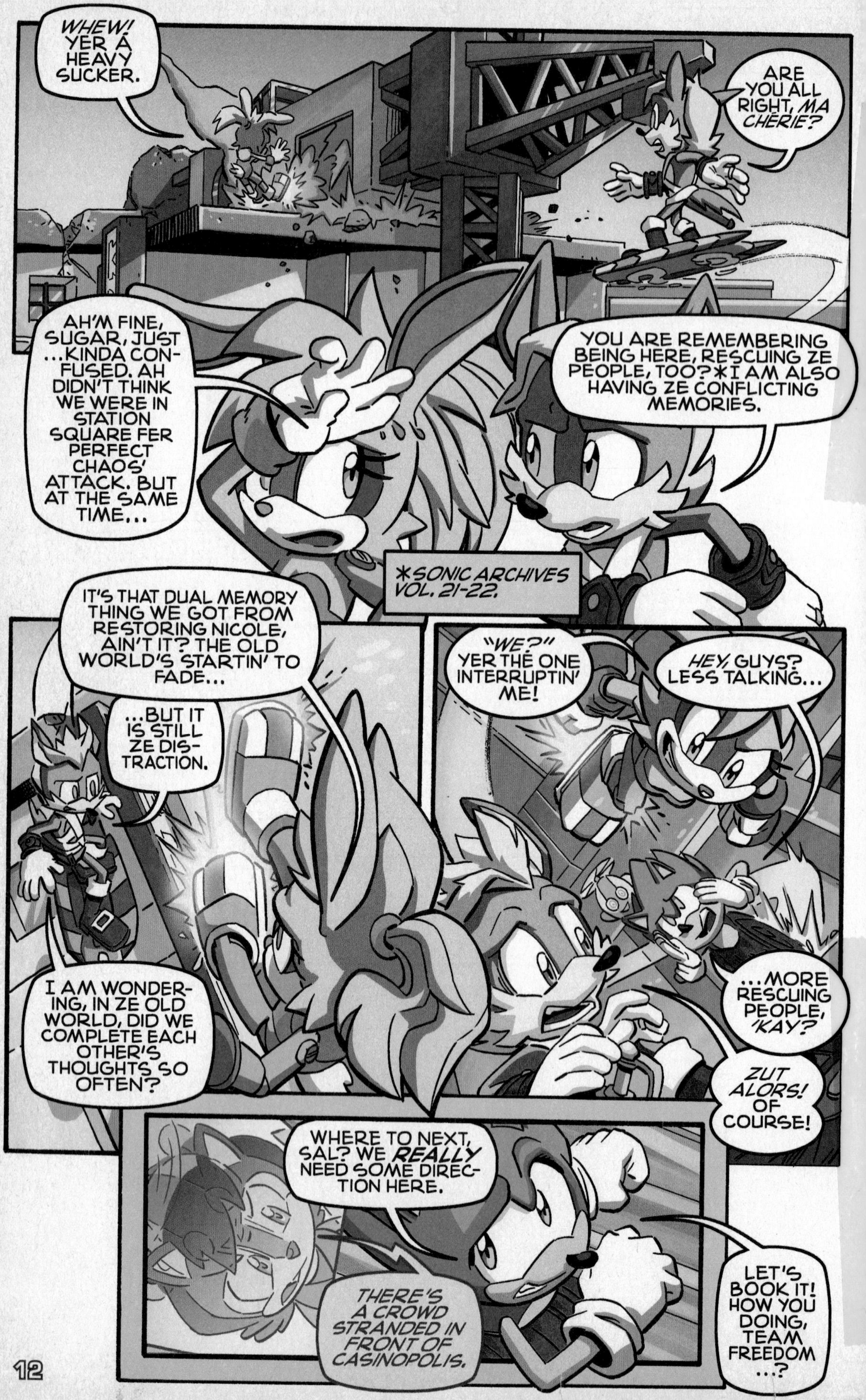

WHEW! YER A HEAVY SUCKER.
ARE YOU ALL RIGHT, MA CHÉRIE?
AH'M FINE, SUGAR, JUST ...KINDA CONFUSED. AH DIDN'T THINK WE WERE IN STATION SQUARE FER PERFECT CHAOS' ATTACK. BUT AT THE SAME TIME...
YOU ARE REMEMBERING BEING HERE, RESCUING ZE PEOPLE, TOO?* I AM ALSO HAVING ZE CONFLICTING MEMORIES.
*SONIC ARCHIVES VOL. 21-22.
IT'S THAT DUAL MEMORY THING WE GOT FROM RESTORING NICOLE, AIN'T IT? THE OLD WORLD'S STARTIN' TO FADE...
...BUT IT IS STILL ZE DISTRACTION.
I AM WONDERING, IN ZE OLD WORLD, DID WE COMPLETE EACH OTHER'S THOUGHTS SO OFTEN?
"WE?" YER THE ONE INTERRUPTIN' ME!
HEY, GUYS? LESS TALKING...
...MORE RESCUING PEOPLE, 'KAY?
ZUT ALORS! OF COURSE!
WHERE TO NEXT, SAL? WE REALLY NEED SOME DIRECTION HERE.
THERE'S A CROWD STRANDED IN FRONT OF CASINOPOLIS.
LET'S BOOK IT! HOW YOU DOING, TEAM FREEDOM ...?

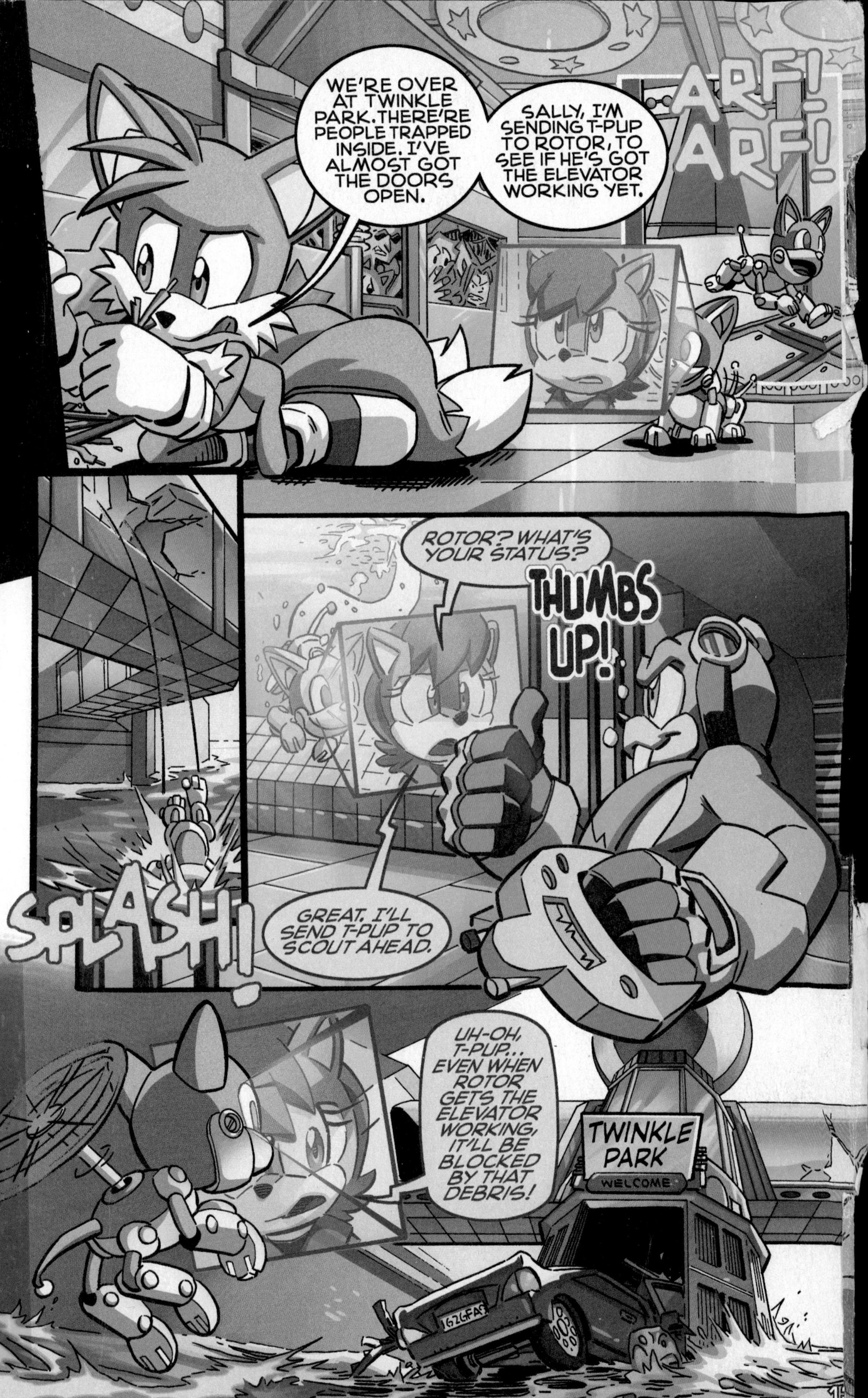
WE'RE OVER AT TWINKLE PARK. THERE'RE PEOPLE TRAPPED INSIDE. I'VE ALMOST GOT THE DOORS OPEN.
SALLY, I'M SENDING T-PUP TO ROTOR, TO SEE IF HE'S GOT THE ELEVATOR WORKING YET.
ARF! ARF!
SPLASH!
ROTOR? WHAT'S YOUR STATUS?
THUMBS UP!
GREAT. I'LL SEND T-PUP TO SCOUT AHEAD.
UH-OH, T-PUP... EVEN WHEN ROTOR GETS THE ELEVATOR WORKING, IT'LL BE BLOCKED BY THAT DEBRIS!
TWINKLE PARK
WELCOME
626FAS

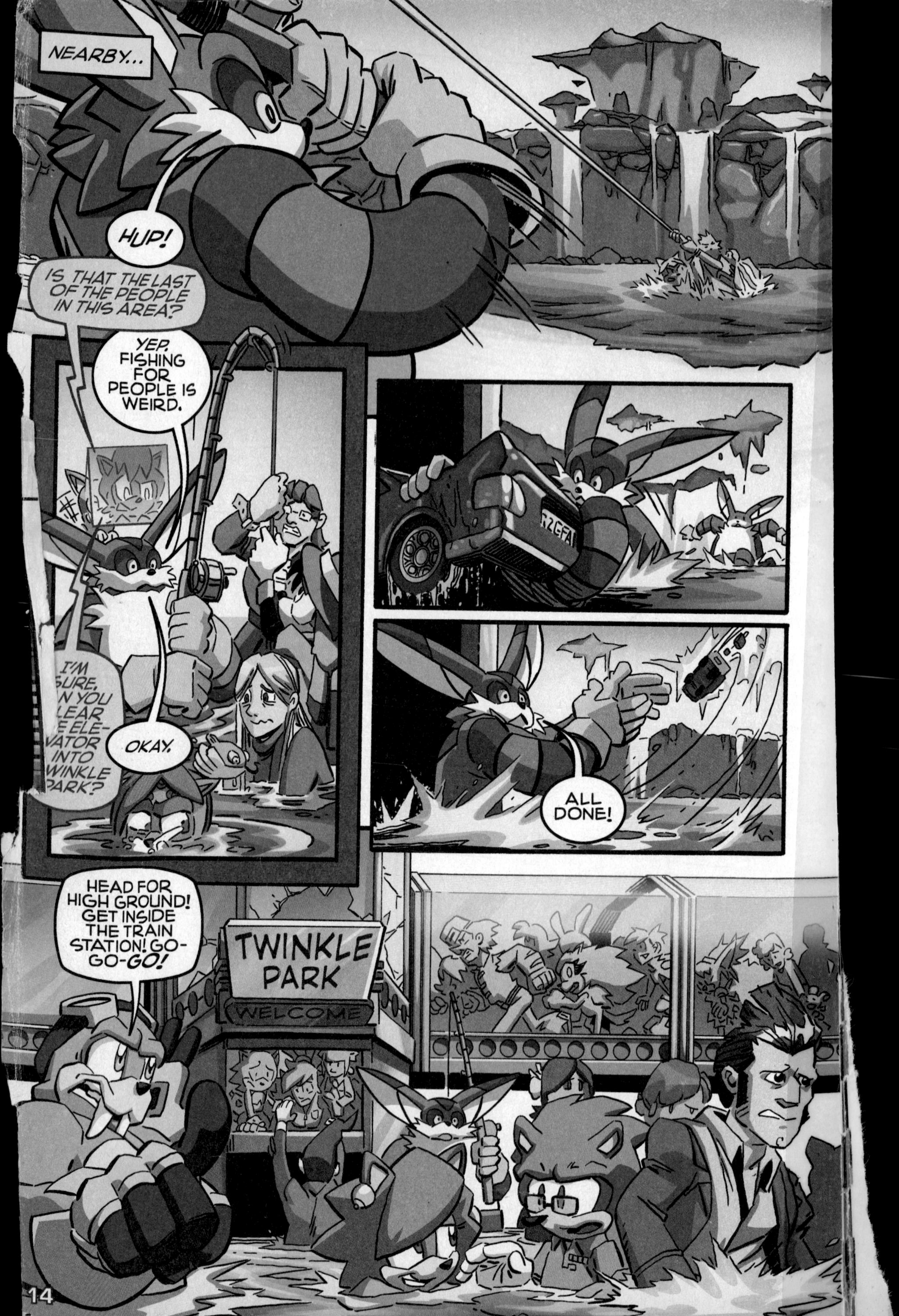
NEARBY...
HUP!
IS THAT THE LAST OF THE PEOPLE IN THIS AREA?
YEP. FISHING FOR PEOPLE IS WEIRD.
I'M SURE. ...N YOU ...LEAR ...E ELE-VATOR INTO ...WINKLE ...PARK?
OKAY.
ALL DONE!
HEAD FOR HIGH GROUND! GET INSIDE THE TRAIN STATION! GO-GO-GO!
TWINKLE PARK
WELCOME

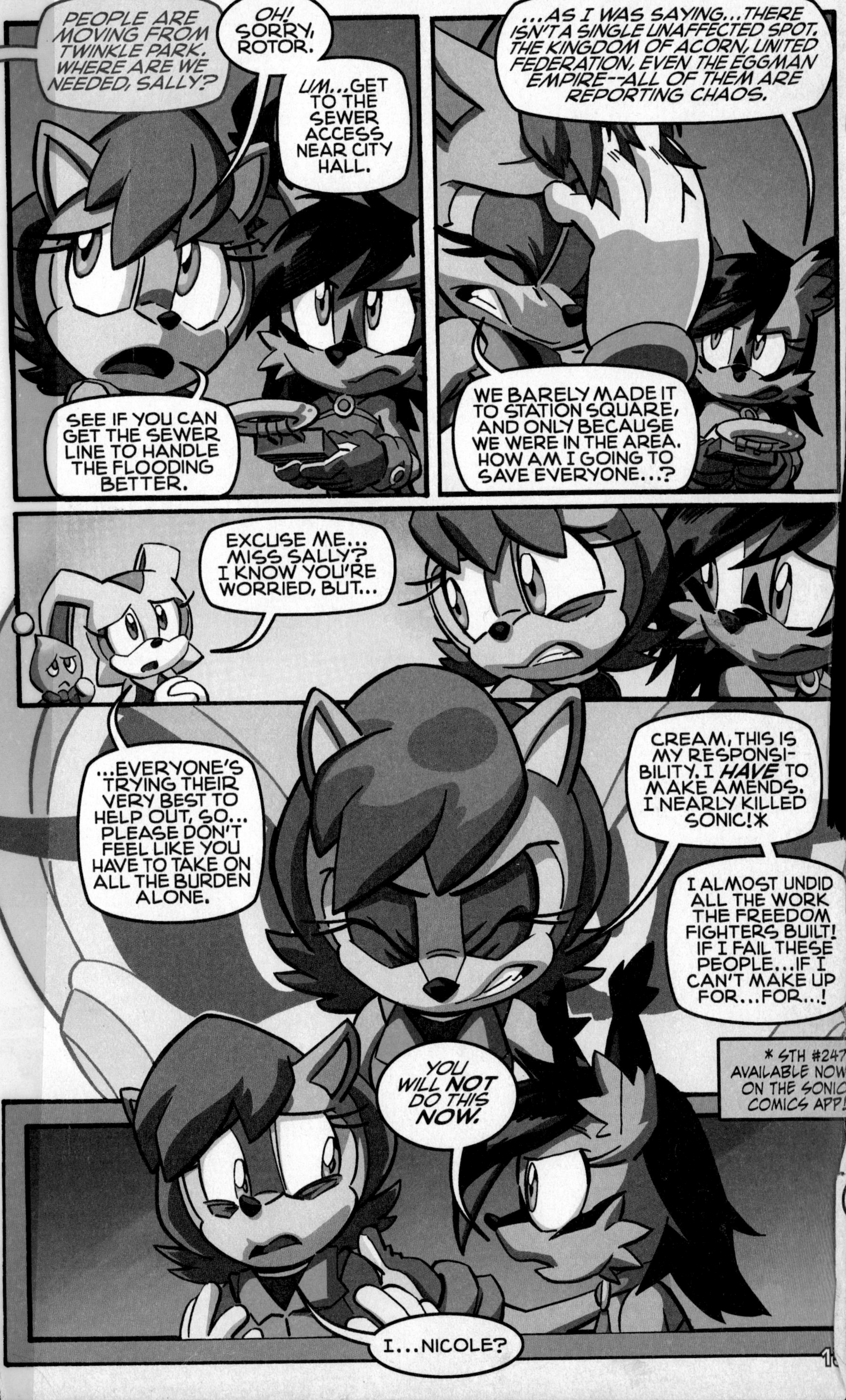

PEOPLE ARE MOVING FROM TWINKLE PARK. WHERE ARE WE NEEDED, SALLY?
OH! SORRY, ROTOR.
UM...GET TO THE SEWER ACCESS NEAR CITY HALL.
SEE IF YOU CAN GET THE SEWER LINE TO HANDLE THE FLOODING BETTER.
...AS I WAS SAYING...THERE ISN'T A SINGLE UNAFFECTED SPOT. THE KINGDOM OF ACORN, UNITED FEDERATION, EVEN THE EGGMAN EMPIRE--ALL OF THEM ARE REPORTING CHAOS.
WE BARELY MADE IT TO STATION SQUARE, AND ONLY BECAUSE WE WERE IN THE AREA. HOW AM I GOING TO SAVE EVERYONE...?
EXCUSE ME... MISS SALLY? I KNOW YOU'RE WORRIED, BUT...
...EVERYONE'S TRYING THEIR VERY BEST TO HELP OUT, SO... PLEASE DON'T FEEL LIKE YOU HAVE TO TAKE ON ALL THE BURDEN ALONE.
CREAM, THIS IS MY RESPONSI-BILITY. I HAVE TO MAKE AMENDS. I NEARLY KILLED SONIC!*
I ALMOST UNDID ALL THE WORK THE FREEDOM FIGHTERS BUILT! IF I FAIL THESE PEOPLE...IF I CAN'T MAKE UP FOR...FOR...!
* STH #247 AVAILABLE NOW ON THE SONIC COMICS APP!
YOU WILL NOT DO THIS NOW.
I...NICOLE?

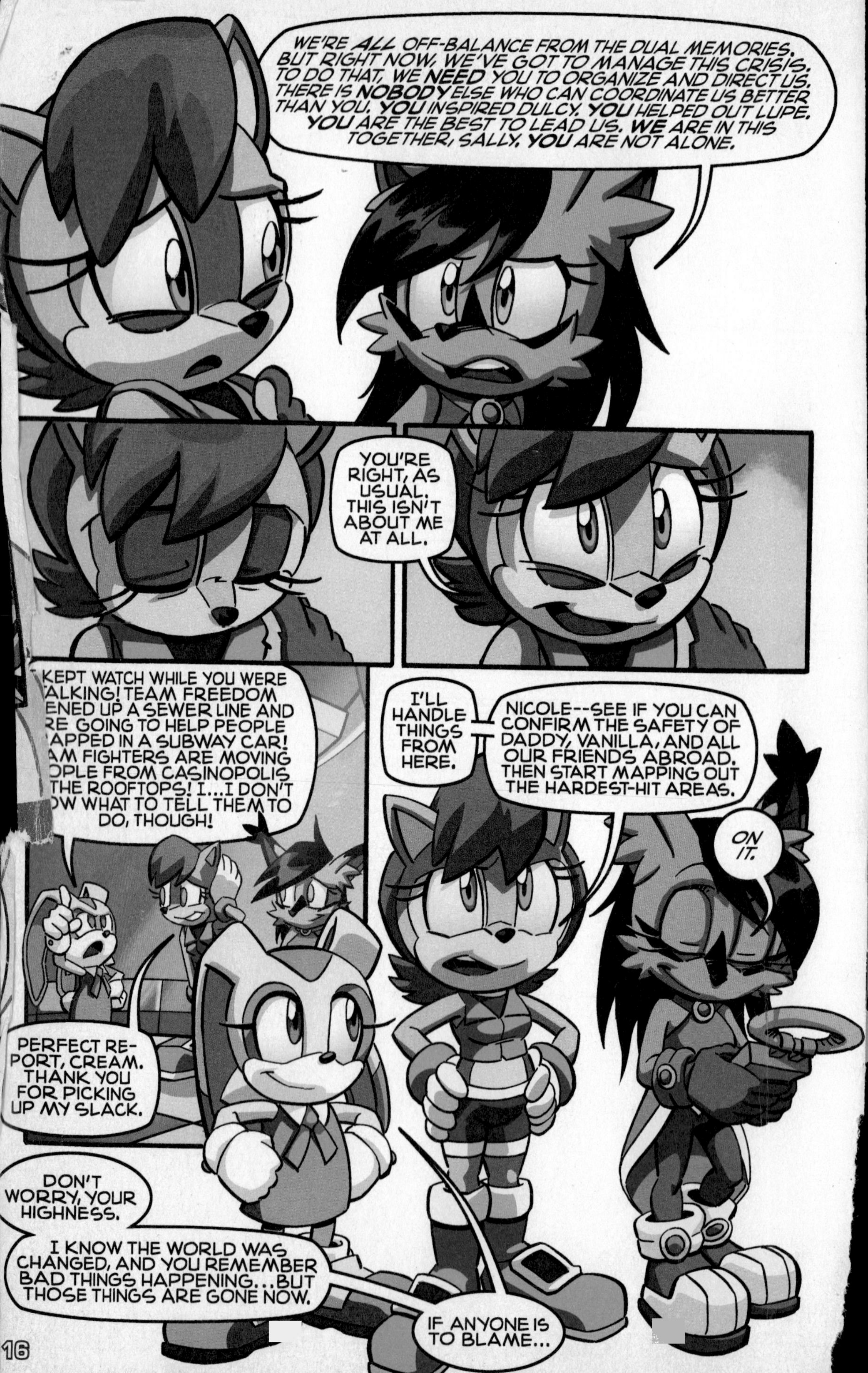
WE'RE ALL OFF-BALANCE FROM THE DUAL MEMORIES. BUT RIGHT NOW, WE'VE GOT TO MANAGE THIS CRISIS. TO DO THAT, WE NEED YOU TO ORGANIZE AND DIRECT US. THERE IS NOBODY ELSE WHO CAN COORDINATE US BETTER THAN YOU. YOU INSPIRED DULCY. YOU HELPED OUT LUPE. YOU ARE THE BEST TO LEAD US. WE ARE IN THIS TOGETHER, SALLY. YOU ARE NOT ALONE.
YOU'RE RIGHT, AS USUAL. THIS ISN'T ABOUT ME AT ALL.
KEPT WATCH WHILE YOU WERE ALKING! TEAM FREEDOM ENED UP A SEWER LINE AND RE GOING TO HELP PEOPLE APPED IN A SUBWAY CAR! AM FIGHTERS ARE MOVING OPLE FROM CASINOPOLIS THE ROOFTOPS! I...I DON'T OW WHAT TO TELL THEM TO DO, THOUGH!
I'LL HANDLE THINGS FROM HERE.
NICOLE--SEE IF YOU CAN CONFIRM THE SAFETY OF DADDY, VANILLA, AND ALL OUR FRIENDS ABROAD. THEN START MAPPING OUT THE HARDEST-HIT AREAS.
ON IT.
PERFECT RE-PORT, CREAM. THANK YOU FOR PICKING UP MY SLACK.
DON'T WORRY, YOUR HIGHNESS.
I KNOW THE WORLD WAS CHANGED, AND YOU REMEMBER BAD THINGS HAPPENING. . .BUT THOSE THINGS ARE GONE NOW.
IF ANYONE IS TO BLAME...

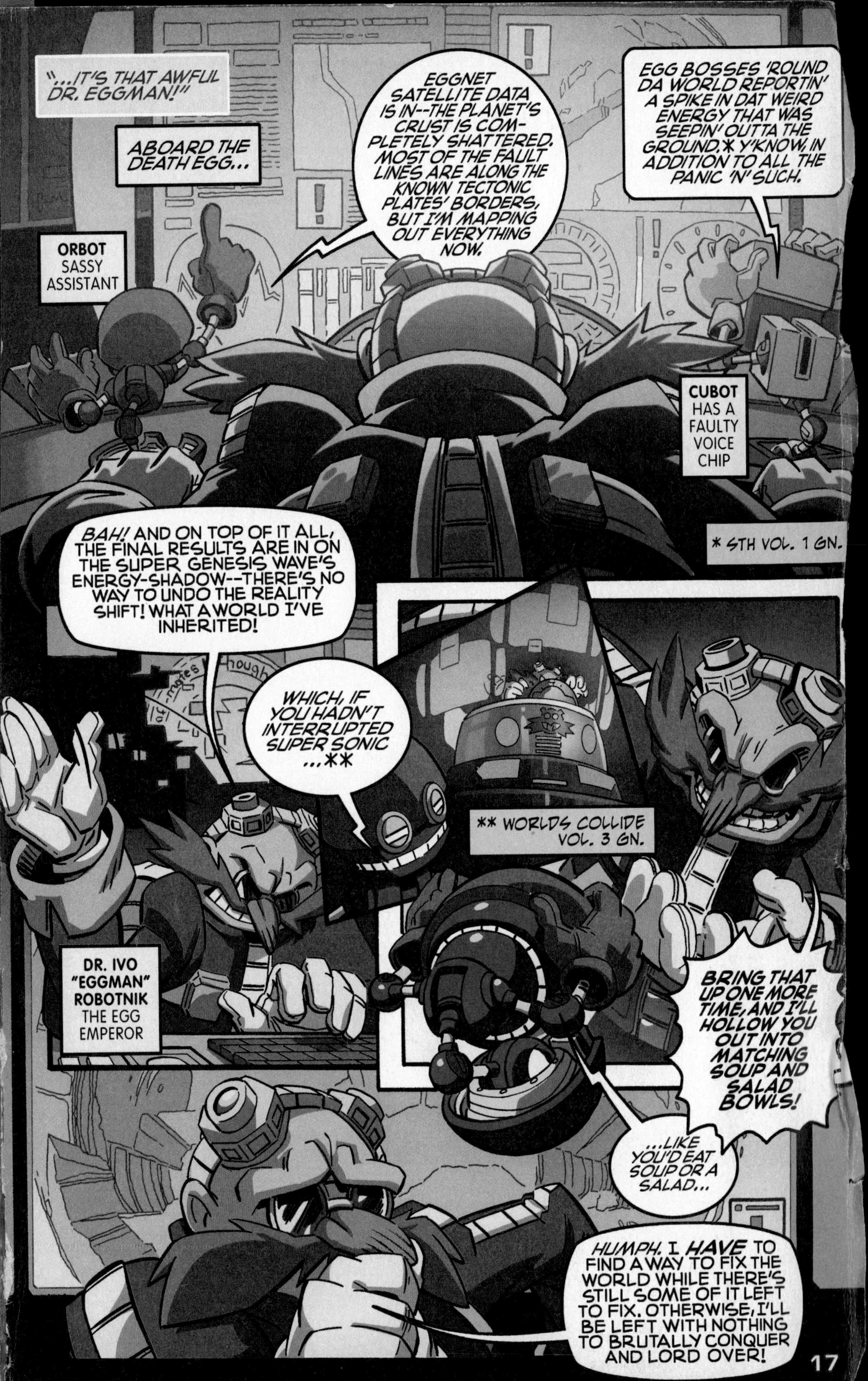
"...IT'S THAT AWFUL DR. EGGMAN!"
ABOARD THE DEATH EGG...
EGGNET SATELLITE DATA IS IN--THE PLANET'S CRUST IS COMPLETELY SHATTERED. MOST OF THE FAULT LINES ARE ALONG THE KNOWN TECTONIC PLATES' BORDERS, BUT I'M MAPPING OUT EVERYTHING NOW.
EGG BOSSES 'ROUND DA WORLD REPORTIN' A SPIKE IN DAT WEIRD ENERGY THAT WAS SEEPIN' OUTTA THE GROUND.* Y'KNOW, IN ADDITION TO ALL THE PANIC 'N' SUCH.
ORBOT SASSY ASSISTANT
CUBOT HAS A FAULTY VOICE CHIP
* STH VOL. 1 GN.
BAH! AND ON TOP OF IT ALL, THE FINAL RESULTS ARE IN ON THE SUPER GENESIS WAVE'S ENERGY-SHADOW--THERE'S NO WAY TO UNDO THE REALITY SHIFT! WHAT A WORLD I'VE INHERITED!
WHICH, IF YOU HADN'T INTERRUPTED SUPER SONIC ...**
** WORLDS COLLIDE VOL. 3 GN.
DR. IVO "EGGMAN" ROBOTNIK THE EGG EMPEROR
BRING THAT UP ONE MORE TIME, AND I'LL HOLLOW YOU OUT INTO MATCHING SOUP AND SALAD BOWLS!
...LIKE YOU'D EAT SOUP OR A SALAD...
HUMPH. I HAVE TO FIND A WAY TO FIX THE WORLD WHILE THERE'S STILL SOME OF IT LEFT TO FIX. OTHERWISE, I'LL BE LEFT WITH NOTHING TO BRUTALLY CONQUER AND LORD OVER!

EGG1

EGGWIKI

EGGNET

EGGLE

FULL DATA MINE! EGGNET, UNITED FEDERATION, G.U.N.--ALL OF THEM, SECURE OR OTHERWISE. SEARCH FOR *ANYTHING* ASSOCIATED WITH MASSIVE TECTONIC SHIFTS, STRANGE ENERGY SIGNATURES ...DOOMSDAY SCENARIOS...

SORT BY RELEVANCE, AAAAAND... THAT'S IT? *HMM*...

"RENOWNED ARCHAEOLOGIST AND HISTORICAL ANTHROPOLOGIST PROF. DILLON PICKLE HAS BEGUN TO DECIPHER THE ANCIENT GAIA MANUSCRIPTS."

PROFESSOR PICKLE

PROFESSOR BEGINS UNCODING THE GAIA MANUSCRIPTS

YADDA-YADDA-YADDA-- "...WHICH, ACCORDING TO PICKLE, CHRONICLE A CYCLICAL WORLD DESTRUCTION-AND-REBIRTH COSMOLOGY..." *HMM*...

ARE ANY EGG ARMY UNITS FREE NEAR SPAGONIA?

NO, BOSS, THEY'RE ALL BUSY SECURING THEIR TERRITORIES. I DON'T KNOW IF YOU'VE HEARD, BUT THE WORLD HAS SHATTERED APART.

SHUT UP! WHAT ABOUT BADNIK HORDES?

E-107 ETA'S UNIT IS THE NEAREST.

GOOD. SEND THAT UNIT TO SPAGONIA UNIVERSITY. HAVE THEM GRAB ANYTHING AND *ANYONE* REMOTELY RELATED TO PROF. PICKLE'S RESEARCH AND BRING THEM TO ME.

IT'S NOT MUCH, BUT SINCE IT'S MY *ONLY* LEAD, I NEED TO BE THOROUGH. THERE *HAS* TO BE A WAY TO MANAGE THIS CRISIS.

18

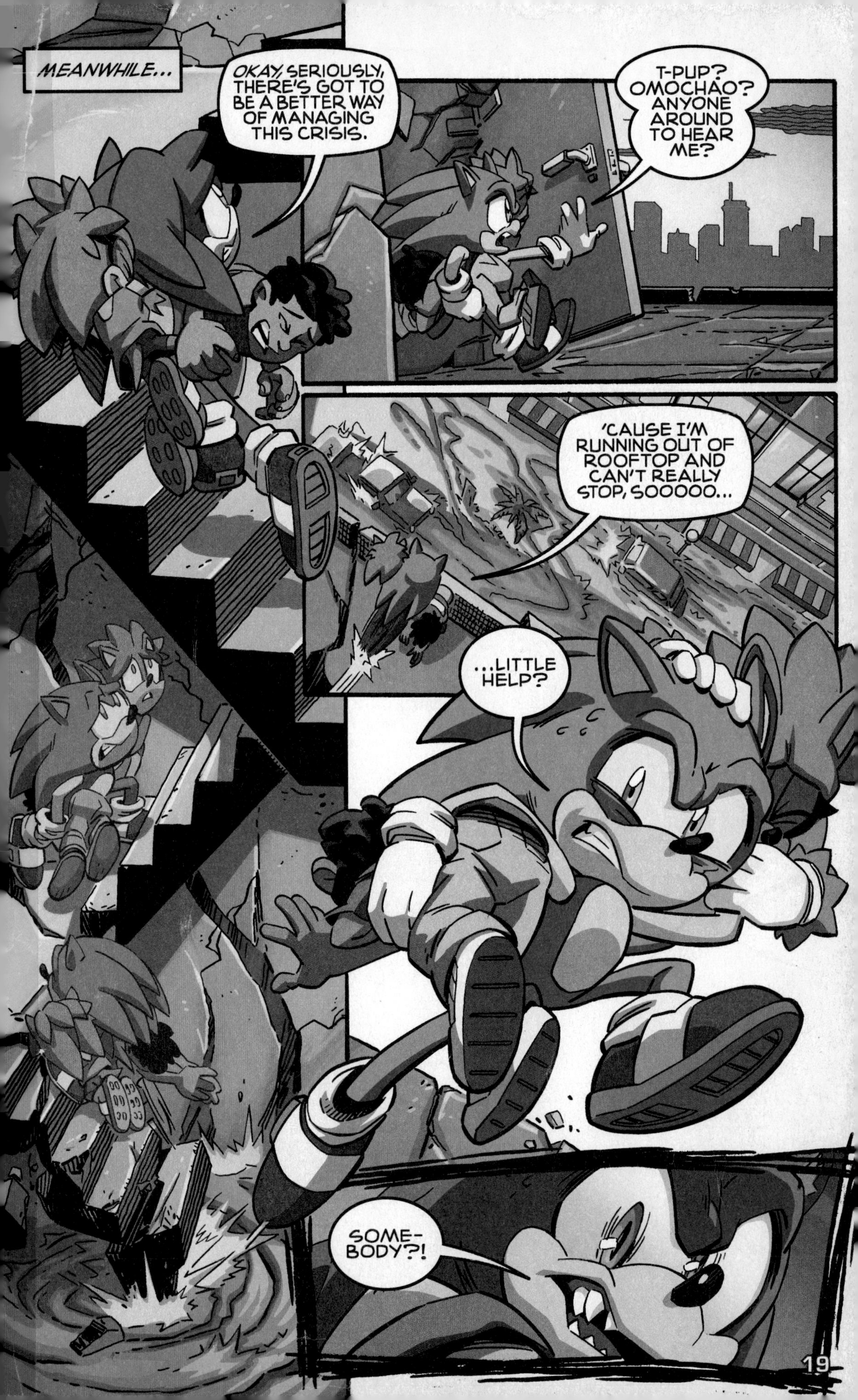
MEANWHILE...
OKAY, SERIOUSLY, THERE'S GOT TO BE A BETTER WAY OF MANAGING THIS CRISIS.
T-PUP? OMOCHAO? ANYONE AROUND TO HEAR ME?
'CAUSE I'M RUNNING OUT OF ROOFTOP AND CAN'T REALLY STOP, SOOOOO...
...LITTLE HELP?
SOME-BODY?!

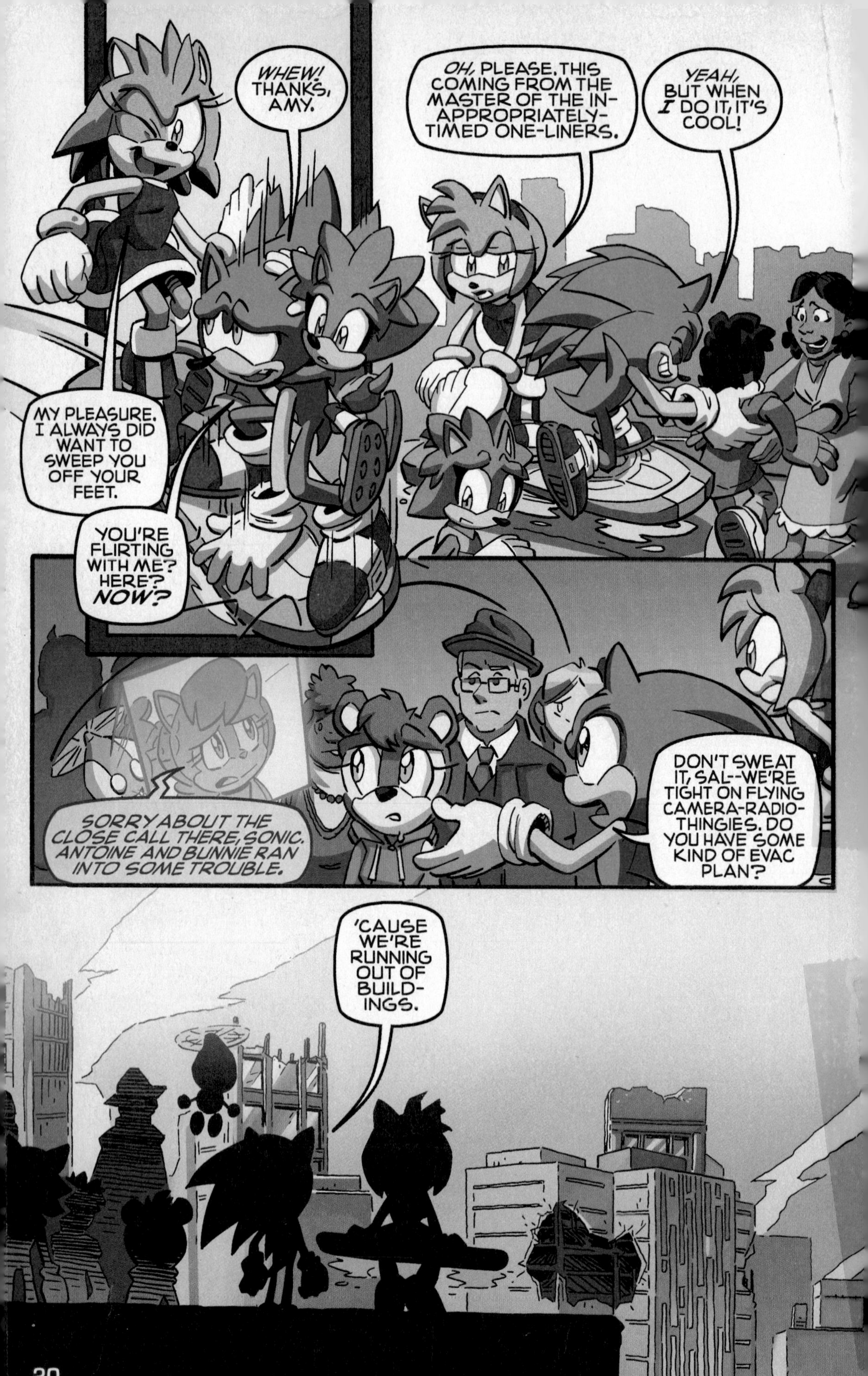
WHEW! THANKS, AMY.
MY PLEASURE. I ALWAYS DID WANT TO SWEEP YOU OFF YOUR FEET.
YOU'RE FLIRTING WITH ME? HERE? NOW?
OH, PLEASE. THIS COMING FROM THE MASTER OF THE IN-APPROPRIATELY-TIMED ONE-LINERS.
YEAH, BUT WHEN I DO IT, IT'S COOL!
SORRY ABOUT THE CLOSE CALL THERE, SONIC. ANTOINE AND BUNNIE RAN INTO SOME TROUBLE.
DON'T SWEAT IT, SAL--WE'RE TIGHT ON FLYING CAMERA-RADIO-THINGIES. DO YOU HAVE SOME KIND OF EVAC PLAN?
'CAUSE WE'RE RUNNING OUT OF BUILD-INGS.

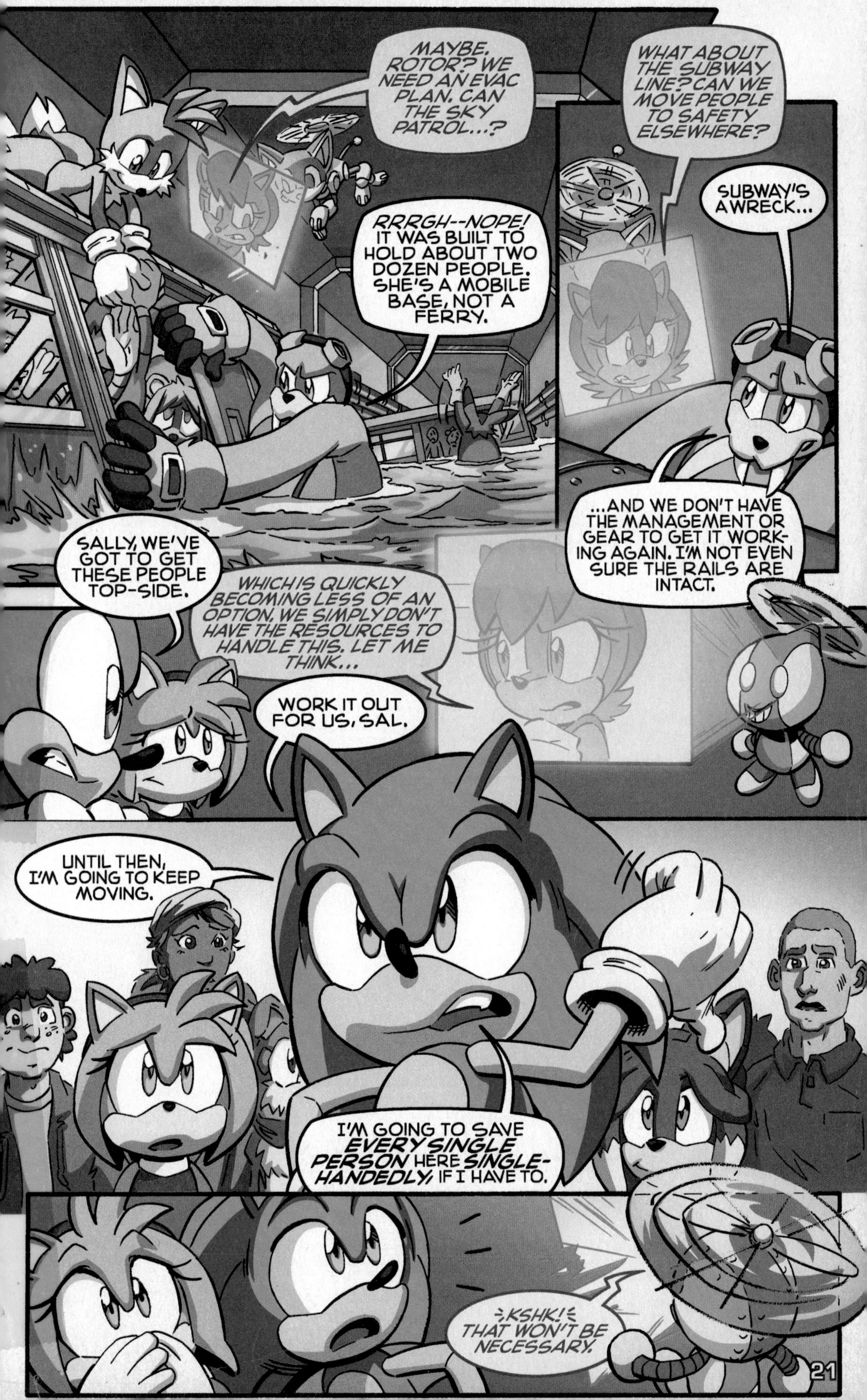
MAYBE. ROTOR? WE NEED AN EVAC PLAN. CAN THE SKY PATROL...?
RRRGH--NOPE! IT WAS BUILT TO HOLD ABOUT TWO DOZEN PEOPLE. SHE'S A MOBILE BASE, NOT A FERRY.
WHAT ABOUT THE SUBWAY LINE? CAN WE MOVE PEOPLE TO SAFETY ELSEWHERE?
SUBWAY'S A WRECK...
...AND WE DON'T HAVE THE MANAGEMENT OR GEAR TO GET IT WORKING AGAIN. I'M NOT EVEN SURE THE RAILS ARE INTACT.
SALLY, WE'VE GOT TO GET THESE PEOPLE TOP-SIDE.
WHICH IS QUICKLY BECOMING LESS OF AN OPTION. WE SIMPLY DON'T HAVE THE RESOURCES TO HANDLE THIS. LET ME THINK...
WORK IT OUT FOR US, SAL.
UNTIL THEN, I'M GOING TO KEEP MOVING.
I'M GOING TO SAVE EVERY SINGLE PERSON HERE SINGLE-HANDEDLY, IF I HAVE TO.
KSHK! THAT WON'T BE NECESSARY.

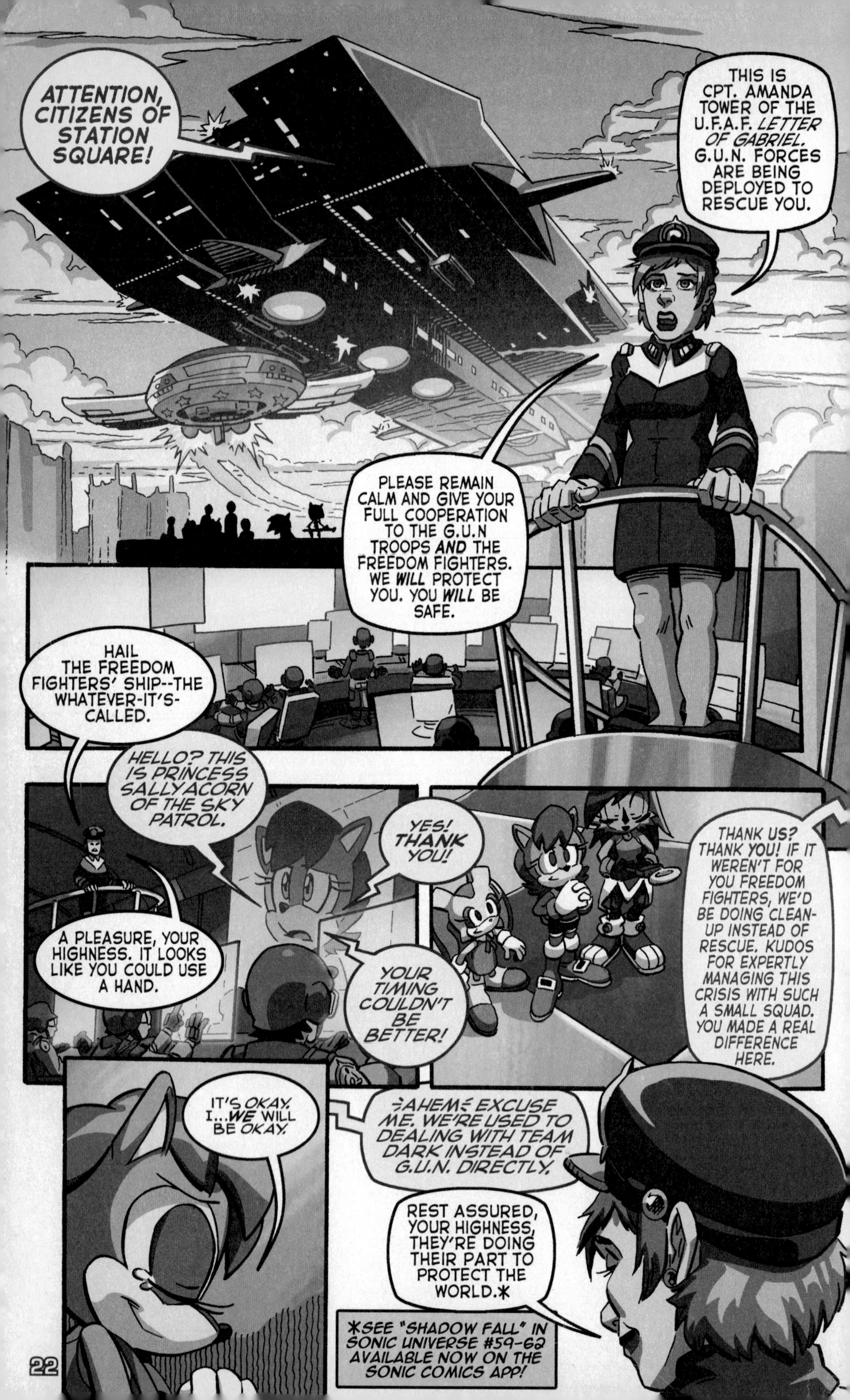
ATTENTION, CITIZENS OF STATION SQUARE!
THIS IS CPT. AMANDA TOWER OF THE U.F.A.F. LETTER OF GABRIEL. G.U.N. FORCES ARE BEING DEPLOYED TO RESCUE YOU.
PLEASE REMAIN CALM AND GIVE YOUR FULL COOPERATION TO THE G.U.N TROOPS AND THE FREEDOM FIGHTERS. WE WILL PROTECT YOU. YOU WILL BE SAFE.
HAIL THE FREEDOM FIGHTERS' SHIP--THE WHATEVER-IT'S-CALLED.
HELLO? THIS IS PRINCESS SALLY ACORN OF THE SKY PATROL.
A PLEASURE, YOUR HIGHNESS. IT LOOKS LIKE YOU COULD USE A HAND.
YES! THANK YOU!
YOUR TIMING COULDN'T BE BETTER!
THANK US? THANK YOU! IF IT WEREN'T FOR YOU FREEDOM FIGHTERS, WE'D BE DOING CLEAN-UP INSTEAD OF RESCUE. KUDOS FOR EXPERTLY MANAGING THIS CRISIS WITH SUCH A SMALL SQUAD. YOU MADE A REAL DIFFERENCE HERE.
IT'S OKAY. I...WE WILL BE OKAY.
=AHEM= EXCUSE ME. WE'RE USED TO DEALING WITH TEAM DARK INSTEAD OF G.U.N. DIRECTLY.
REST ASSURED, YOUR HIGHNESS, THEY'RE DOING THEIR PART TO PROTECT THE WORLD.*
*SEE "SHADOW FALL" IN SONIC UNIVERSE #59-62 AVAILABLE NOW ON THE SONIC COMICS APP!
22

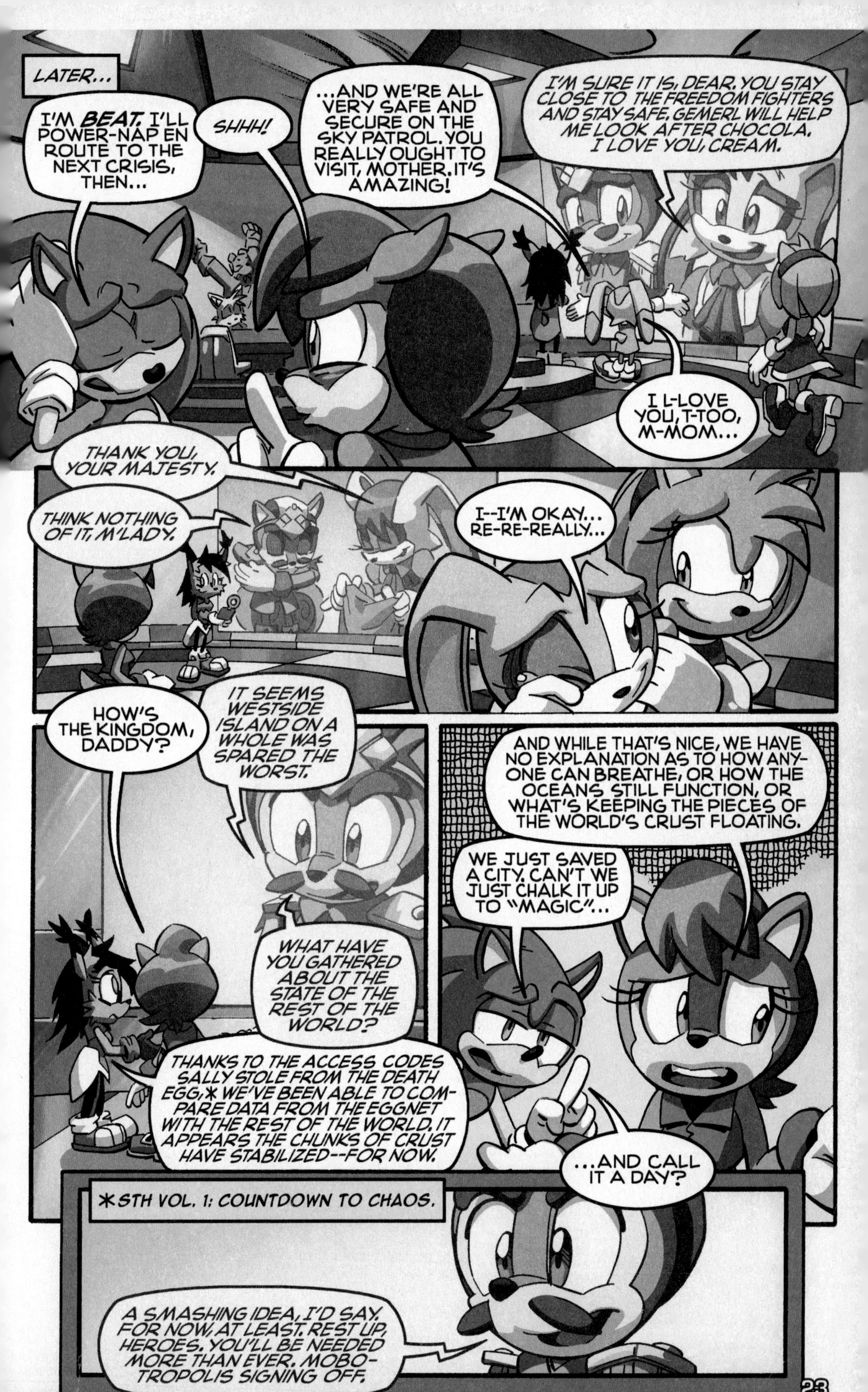
LATER...
I'M BEAT. I'LL POWER-NAP EN ROUTE TO THE NEXT CRISIS, THEN...
SHHH!
...AND WE'RE ALL VERY SAFE AND SECURE ON THE SKY PATROL. YOU REALLY OUGHT TO VISIT, MOTHER. IT'S AMAZING!
I'M SURE IT IS, DEAR. YOU STAY CLOSE TO THE FREEDOM FIGHTERS AND STAY SAFE. GEMERL WILL HELP ME LOOK AFTER CHOCOLA. I LOVE YOU, CREAM.
I L-LOVE YOU, T-TOO, M-MOM...
THANK YOU, YOUR MAJESTY.
THINK NOTHING OF IT, M'LADY.
I--I'M OKAY... RE-RE-REALLY...
HOW'S THE KINGDOM, DADDY?
IT SEEMS WESTSIDE ISLAND ON A WHOLE WAS SPARED THE WORST.
WHAT HAVE YOU GATHERED ABOUT THE STATE OF THE REST OF THE WORLD?
THANKS TO THE ACCESS CODES SALLY STOLE FROM THE DEATH EGG,* WE'VE BEEN ABLE TO COMPARE DATA FROM THE EGGNET WITH THE REST OF THE WORLD. IT APPEARS THE CHUNKS OF CRUST HAVE STABILIZED--FOR NOW.
AND WHILE THAT'S NICE, WE HAVE NO EXPLANATION AS TO HOW ANYONE CAN BREATHE, OR HOW THE OCEANS STILL FUNCTION, OR WHAT'S KEEPING THE PIECES OF THE WORLD'S CRUST FLOATING.
WE JUST SAVED A CITY. CAN'T WE JUST CHALK IT UP TO "MAGIC"...
...AND CALL IT A DAY?
*STH VOL. 1: COUNTDOWN TO CHAOS.
A SMASHING IDEA, I'D SAY. FOR NOW, AT LEAST. REST UP, HEROES. YOU'LL BE NEEDED MORE THAN EVER. MOBOTROPOLIS SIGNING OFF.

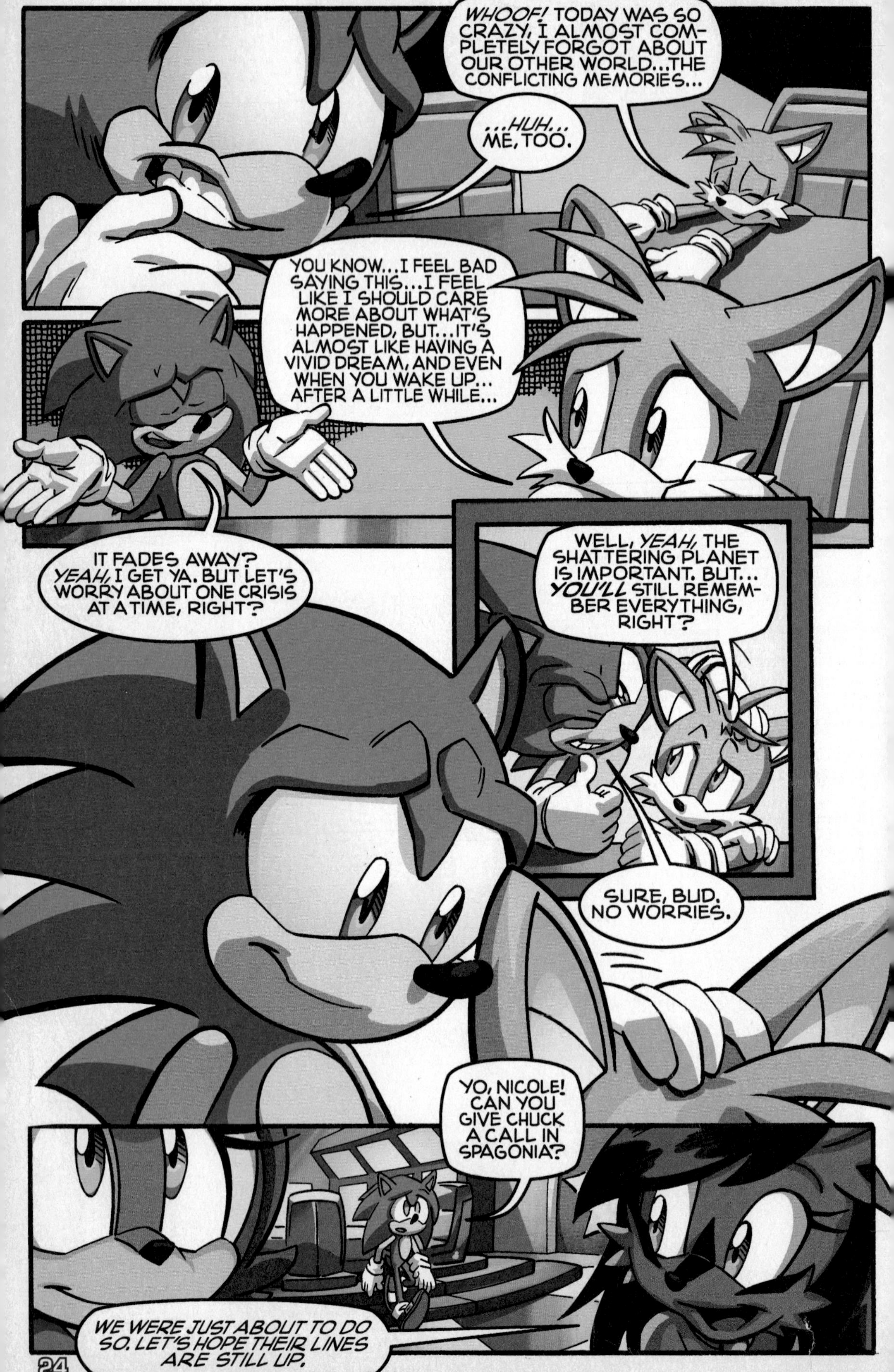
WHOOF! TODAY WAS SO CRAZY, I ALMOST COMPLETELY FORGOT ABOUT OUR OTHER WORLD...THE CONFLICTING MEMORIES...
...HUH... ME, TOO.
YOU KNOW...I FEEL BAD SAYING THIS...I FEEL LIKE I SHOULD CARE MORE ABOUT WHAT'S HAPPENED, BUT...IT'S ALMOST LIKE HAVING A VIVID DREAM, AND EVEN WHEN YOU WAKE UP... AFTER A LITTLE WHILE...
IT FADES AWAY? YEAH, I GET YA. BUT LET'S WORRY ABOUT ONE CRISIS AT A TIME, RIGHT?
WELL, YEAH, THE SHATTERING PLANET IS IMPORTANT. BUT... YOU'LL STILL REMEMBER EVERYTHING, RIGHT?
SURE, BUD. NO WORRIES.
YO, NICOLE! CAN YOU GIVE CHUCK A CALL IN SPAGONIA?
WE WERE JUST ABOUT TO DO SO. LET'S HOPE THEIR LINES ARE STILL UP.

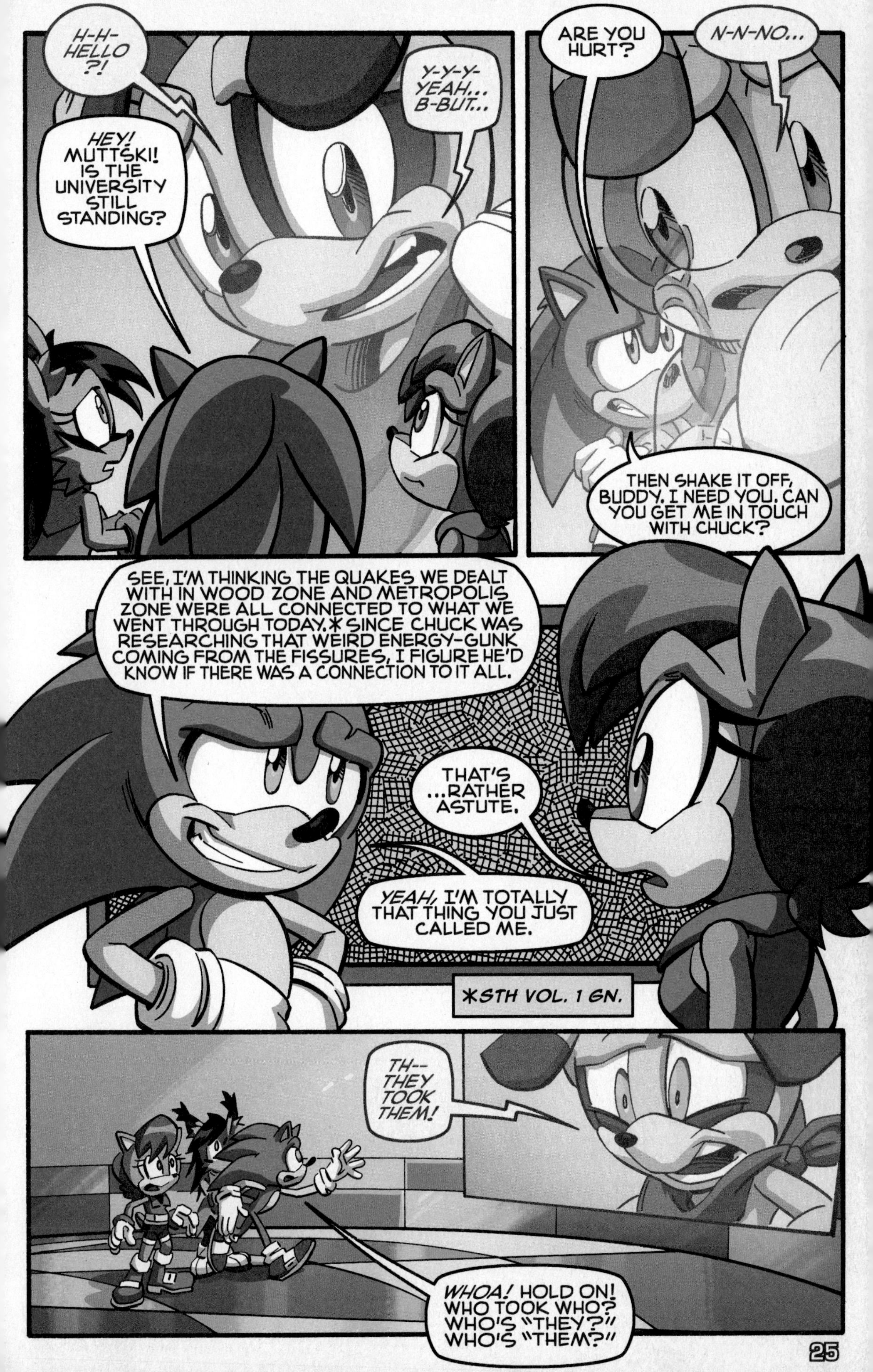
H-H-HELLO?!
HEY! MUTTSKI! IS THE UNIVERSITY STILL STANDING?
Y-Y-Y-YEAH... B-BUT...
ARE YOU HURT?
N-N-NO...
THEN SHAKE IT OFF, BUDDY. I NEED YOU. CAN YOU GET ME IN TOUCH WITH CHUCK?
SEE, I'M THINKING THE QUAKES WE DEALT WITH IN WOOD ZONE AND METROPOLIS ZONE WERE ALL CONNECTED TO WHAT WE WENT THROUGH TODAY.* SINCE CHUCK WAS RESEARCHING THAT WEIRD ENERGY-GUNK COMING FROM THE FISSURES, I FIGURE HE'D KNOW IF THERE WAS A CONNECTION TO IT ALL.
THAT'S ...RATHER ASTUTE.
YEAH, I'M TOTALLY THAT THING YOU JUST CALLED ME.
*STH VOL. 1 GN.
TH-- THEY TOOK THEM!
WHOA! HOLD ON! WHO TOOK WHO? WHO'S "THEY?" WHO'S "THEM?"

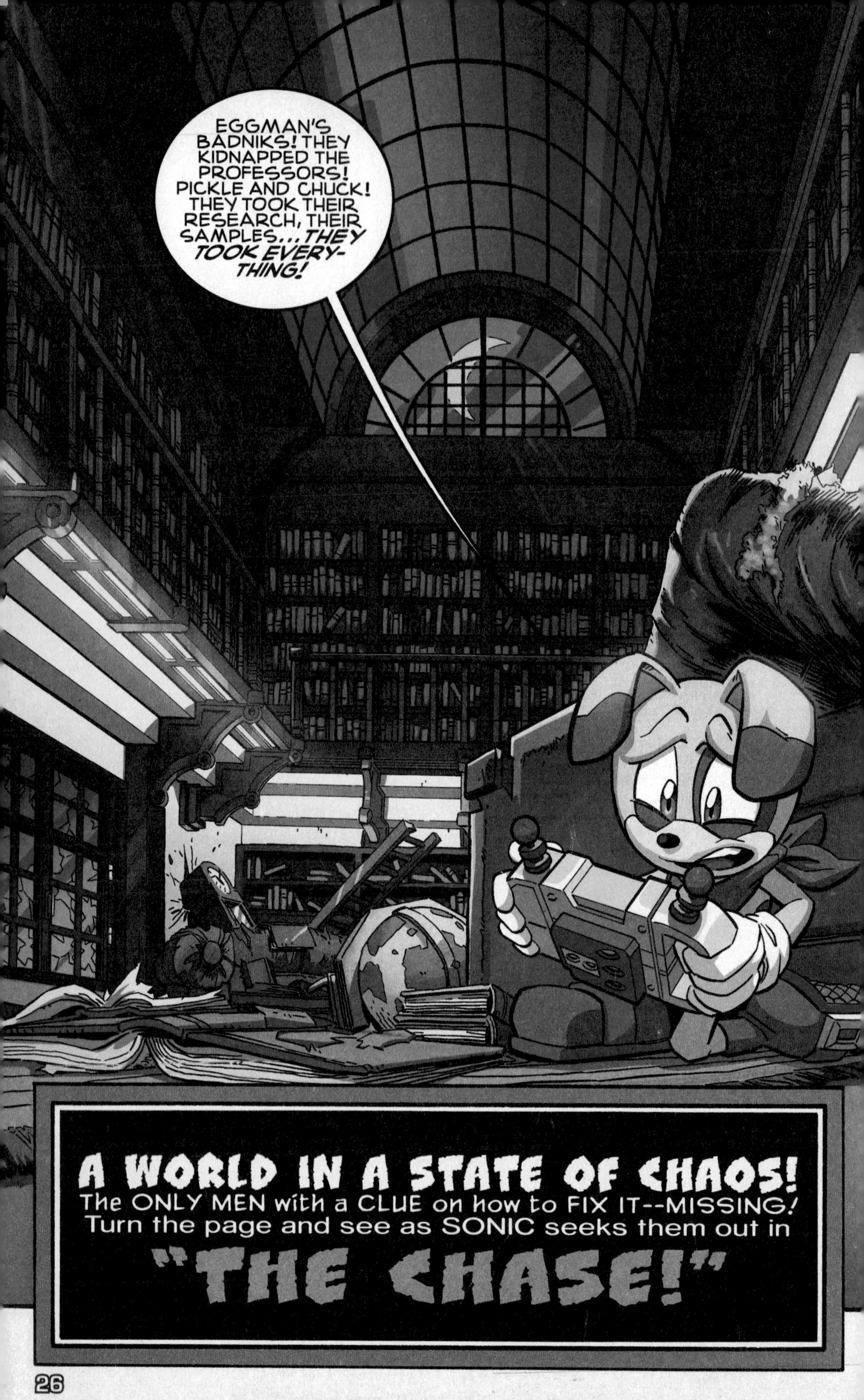
EGGMAN'S BADNIKS! THEY KIDNAPPED THE PROFESSORS! PICKLE AND CHUCK! THEY TOOK THEIR RESEARCH, THEIR SAMPLES... *THEY TOOK EVERY-THING!*
A WORLD IN A STATE OF CHAOS!
The ONLY MEN with a CLUE on how to FIX IT--MISSING!
Turn the page and see as SONIC seeks them out in
"THE CHASE!"

CHAPTER 2

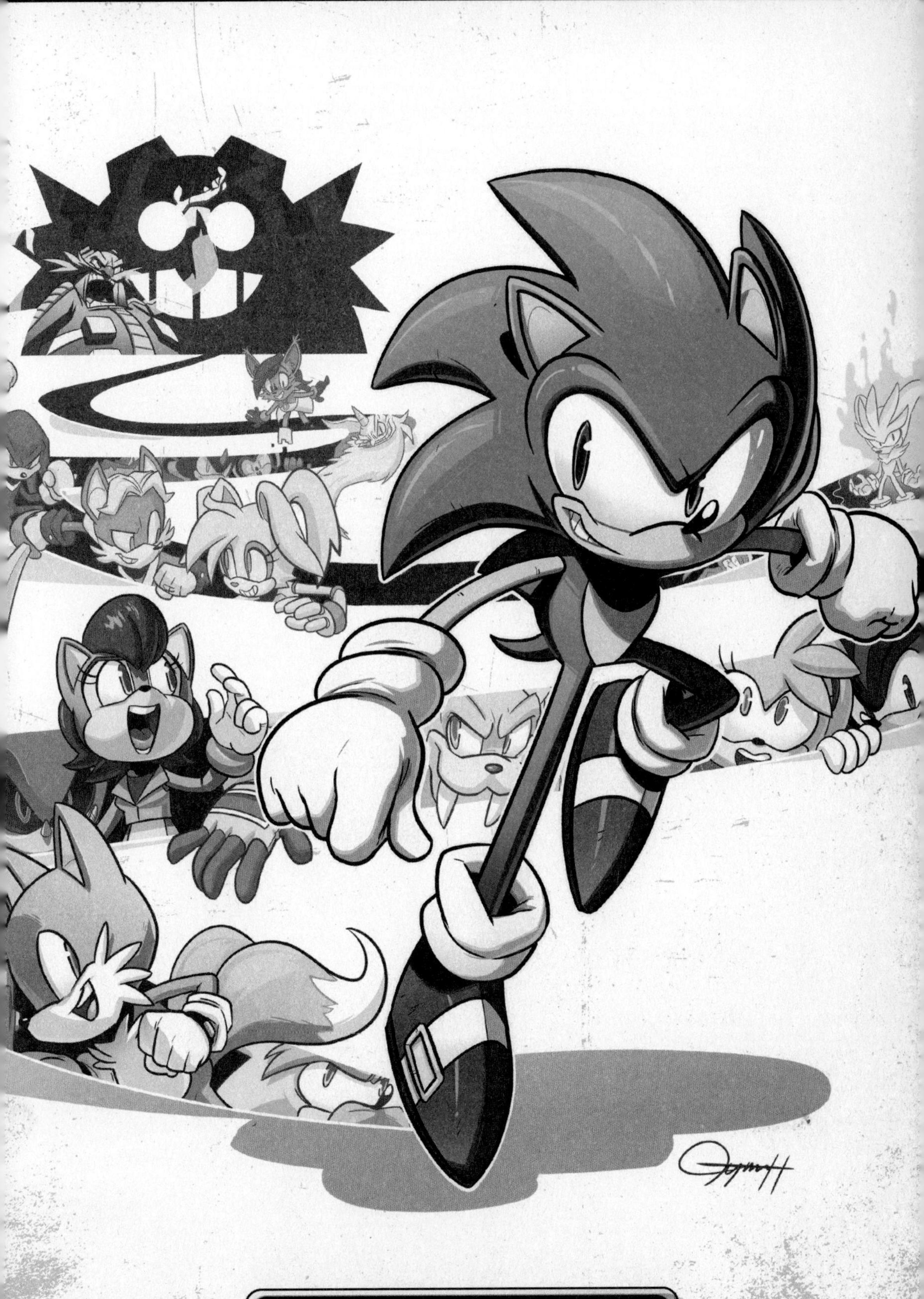

SONIC THE HEDGEHOG 258
COVER BY TYSON HESSE

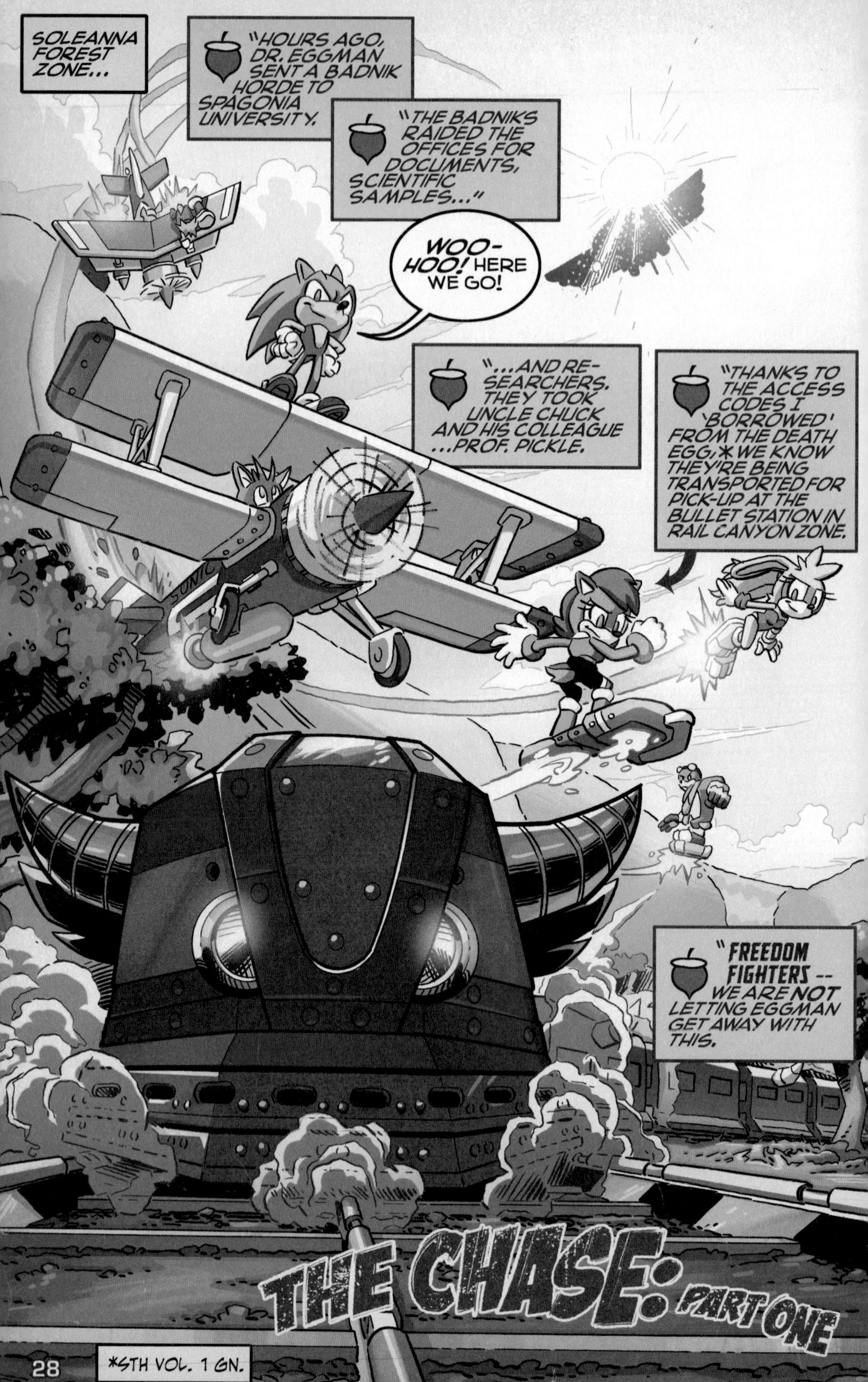

SOLEANNA FOREST ZONE...
"HOURS AGO, DR. EGGMAN SENT A BADNIK HORDE TO SPAGONIA UNIVERSITY.
"THE BADNIKS RAIDED THE OFFICES FOR DOCUMENTS, SCIENTIFIC SAMPLES..."
WOO-HOO! HERE WE GO!
"...AND RE-SEARCHERS. THEY TOOK UNCLE CHUCK AND HIS COLLEAGUE ...PROF. PICKLE.
"THANKS TO THE ACCESS CODES I 'BORROWED' FROM THE DEATH EGG,* WE KNOW THEY'RE BEING TRANSPORTED FOR PICK-UP AT THE BULLET STATION IN RAIL CANYON ZONE.
SONIC
"FREEDOM FIGHTERS -- WE ARE NOT LETTING EGGMAN GET AWAY WITH THIS.
THE CHASE: PART ONE
*STH VOL. 1 GN.

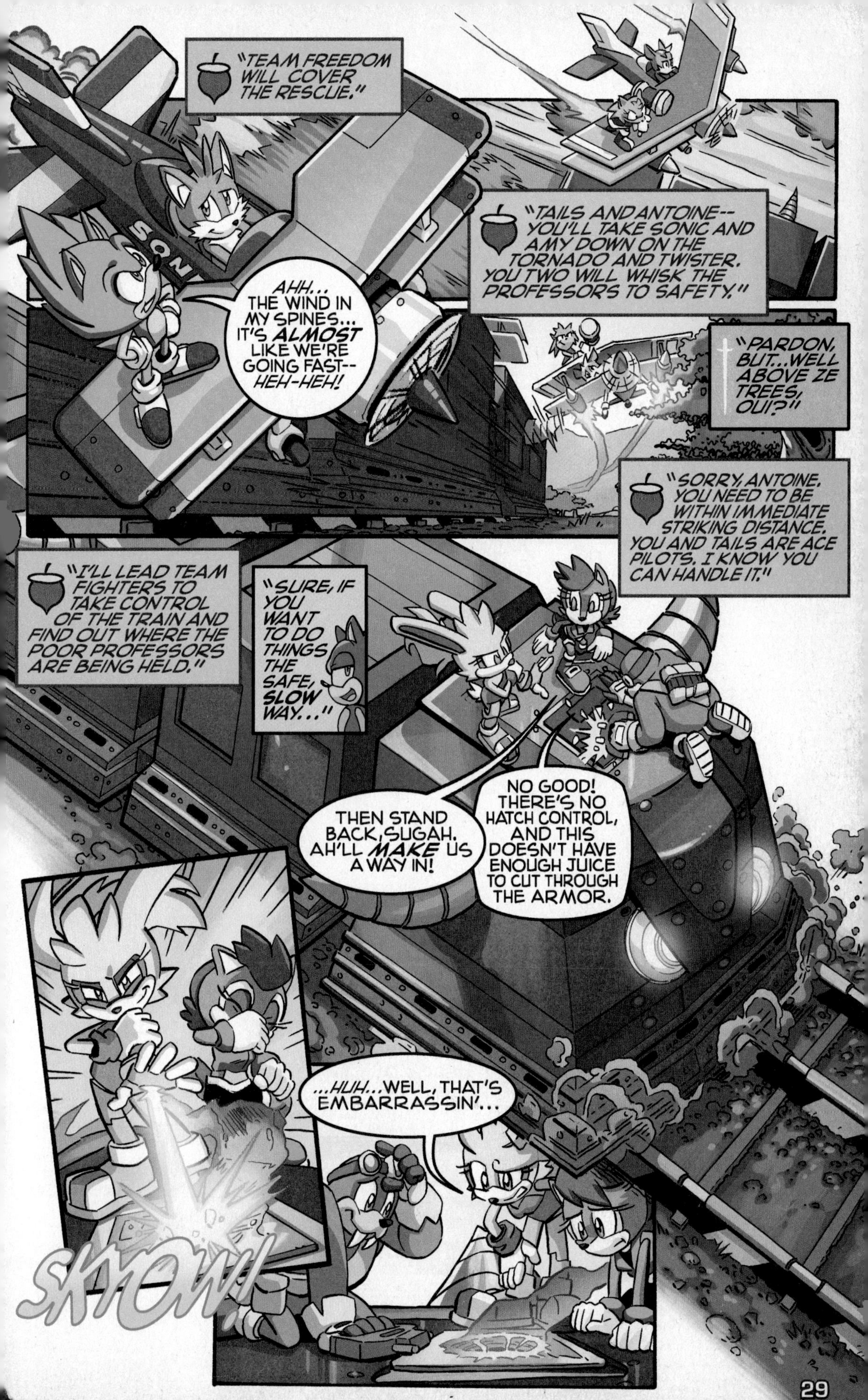
"TEAM FREEDOM WILL COVER THE RESCUE."
"TAILS AND ANTOINE-- YOU'LL TAKE SONIC AND AMY DOWN ON THE TORNADO AND TWISTER. YOU TWO WILL WHISK THE PROFESSORS TO SAFETY."
AHH... THE WIND IN MY SPINES... IT'S *ALMOST* LIKE WE'RE GOING FAST-- HEH-HEH!
"PARDON, BUT...WELL ABOVE ZE TREES, OUI?"
"SORRY, ANTOINE, YOU NEED TO BE WITHIN IMMEDIATE STRIKING DISTANCE. YOU AND TAILS ARE ACE PILOTS. I KNOW YOU CAN HANDLE IT."
"I'LL LEAD TEAM FIGHTERS TO TAKE CONTROL OF THE TRAIN AND FIND OUT WHERE THE POOR PROFESSORS ARE BEING HELD."
"SURE, IF YOU WANT TO DO THINGS THE SAFE, *SLOW* WAY..."
NO GOOD! THERE'S NO HATCH CONTROL, AND THIS DOESN'T HAVE ENOUGH JUICE TO CUT THROUGH THE ARMOR.
THEN STAND BACK, SUGAH. AH'LL *MAKE* US A WAY IN!
SKYOW!
...HUH...WELL, THAT'S EMBARRASSIN'...

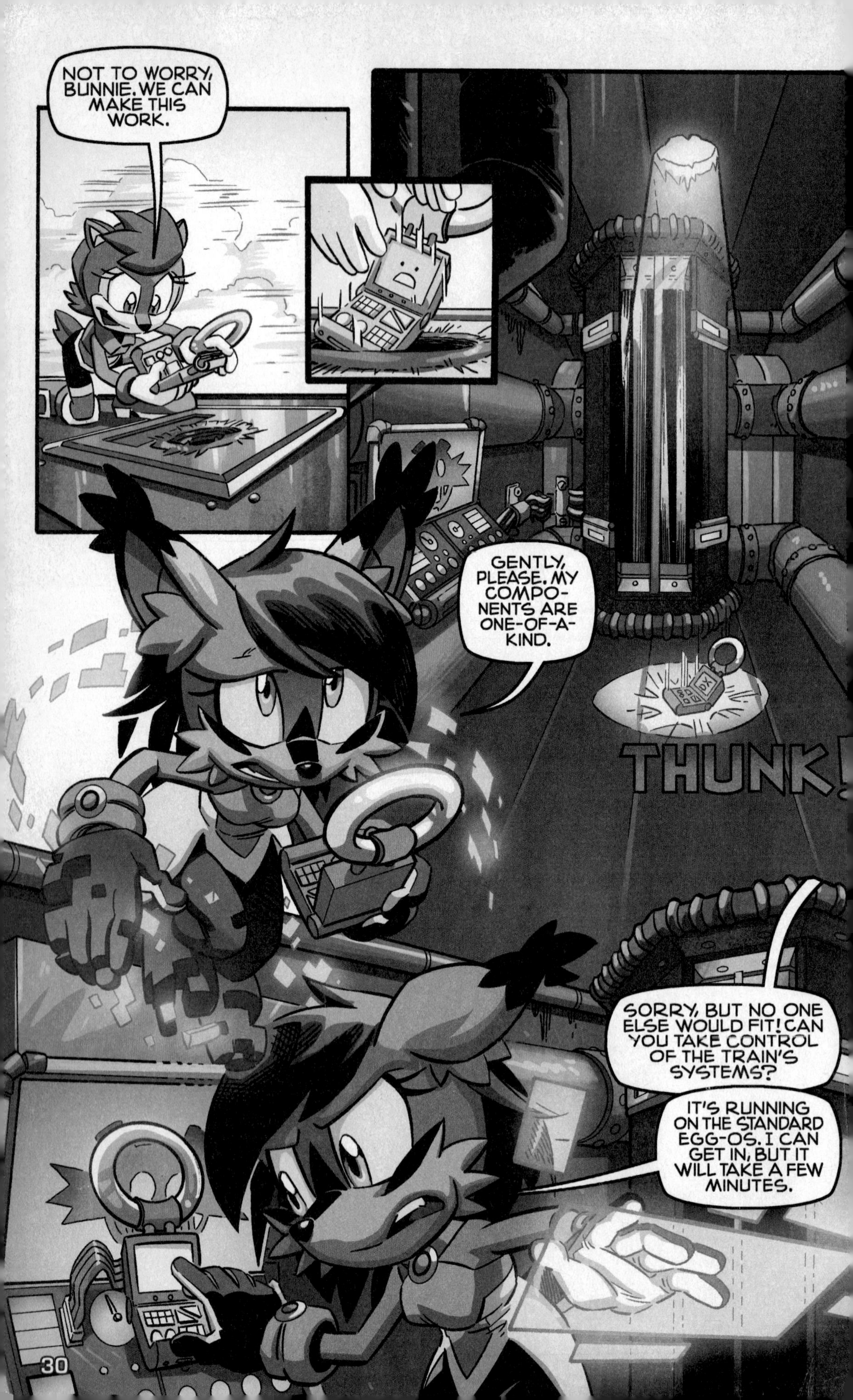

NOT TO WORRY, BUNNIE. WE CAN MAKE THIS WORK.
GENTLY, PLEASE. MY COMPONENTS ARE ONE-OF-A-KIND.
THUNK!
SORRY, BUT NO ONE ELSE WOULD FIT! CAN YOU TAKE CONTROL OF THE TRAIN'S SYSTEMS?
IT'S RUNNING ON THE STANDARD EGG-OS. I CAN GET IN, BUT IT WILL TAKE A FEW MINUTES.

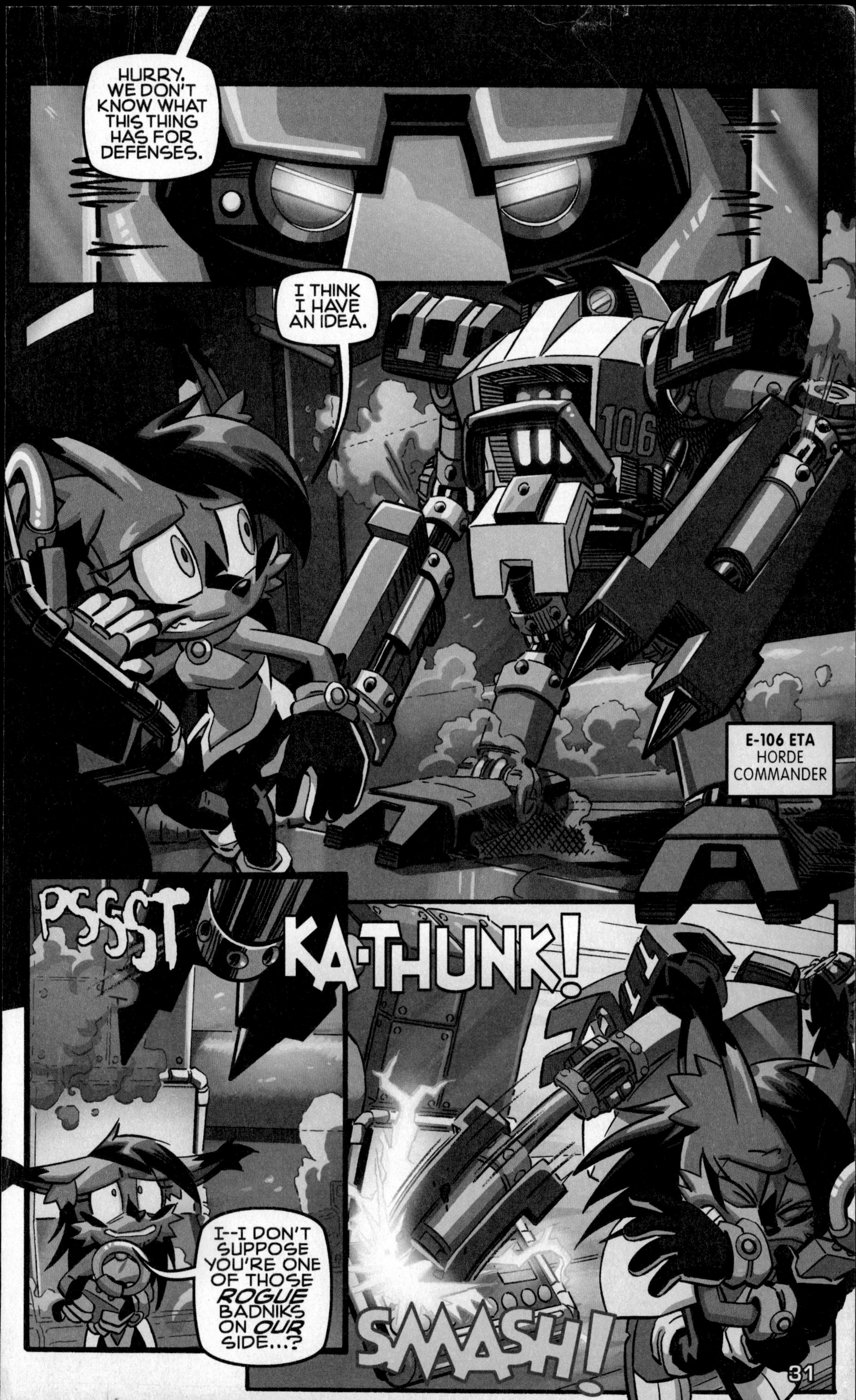
HURRY. WE DON'T KNOW WHAT THIS THING HAS FOR DEFENSES.
I THINK I HAVE AN IDEA.
E-106 ETA
HORDE COMMANDER
PSSST
KA-THUNK!
I--I DON'T SUPPOSE YOU'RE ONE OF THOSE *ROGUE* BADNIKS ON *OUR* SIDE...?
SMASH!

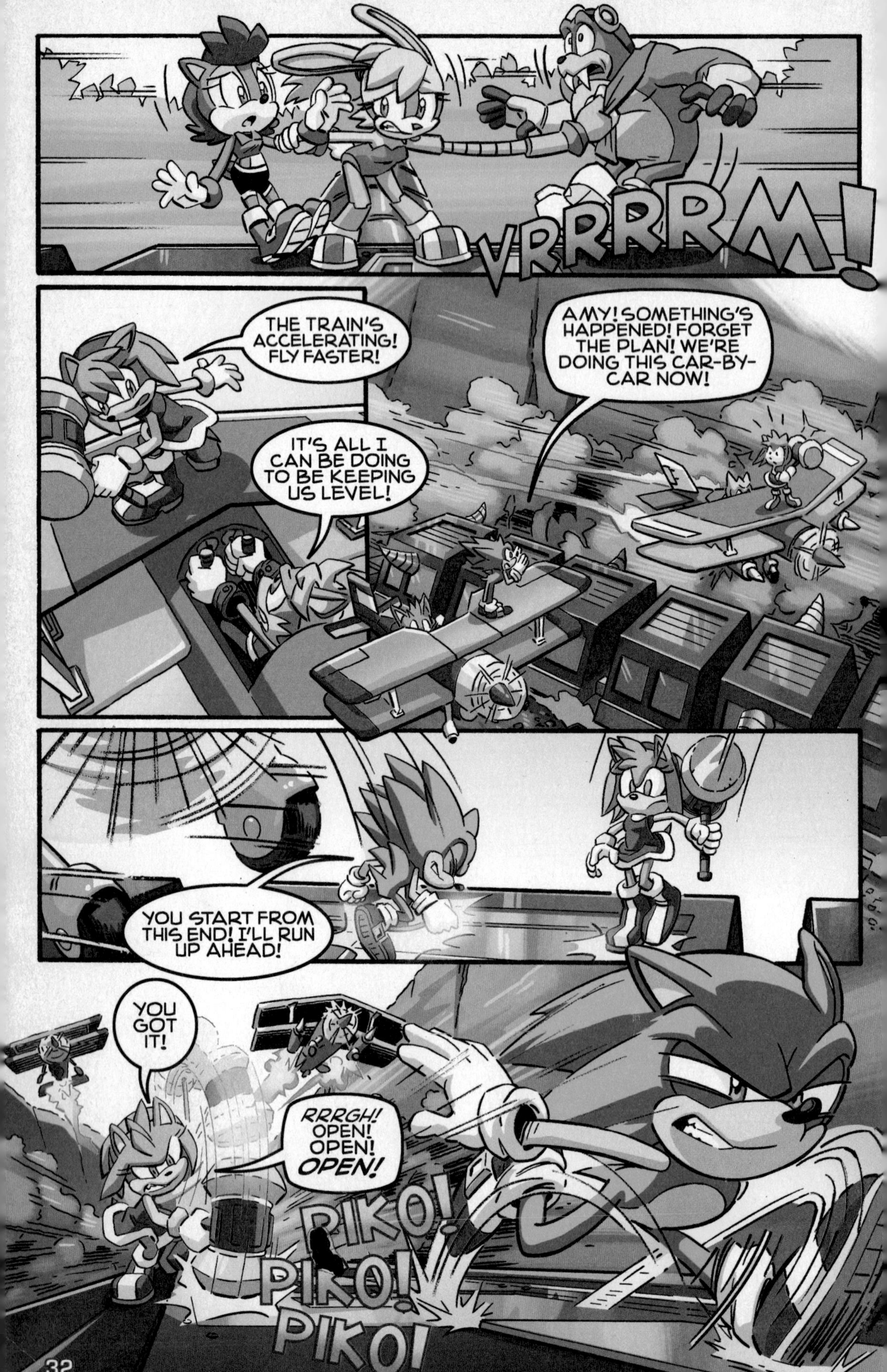
VRRRRM!
THE TRAIN'S ACCELERATING! FLY FASTER!
AMY! SOMETHING'S HAPPENED! FORGET THE PLAN! WE'RE DOING THIS CAR-BY-CAR NOW!
IT'S ALL I CAN BE DOING TO BE KEEPING US LEVEL!
YOU START FROM THIS END! I'LL RUN UP AHEAD!
YOU GOT IT!
RRRGH! OPEN! OPEN! OPEN!
PIKO! PIKO! PIKO!

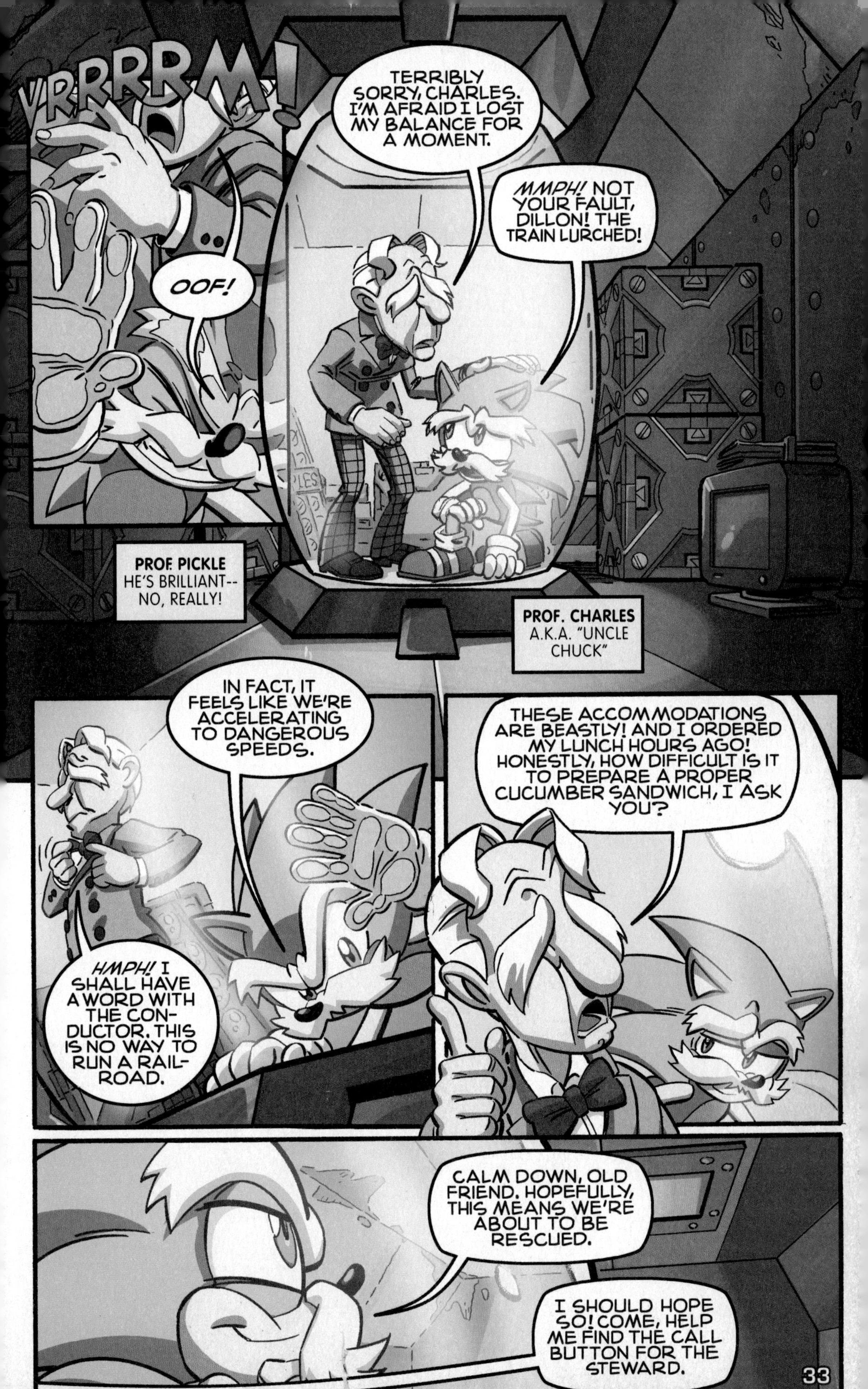
VRRRRM!
TERRIBLY SORRY, CHARLES. I'M AFRAID I LOST MY BALANCE FOR A MOMENT.
MMPH! NOT YOUR FAULT, DILLON! THE TRAIN LURCHED!
OOF!
PROF. PICKLE HE'S BRILLIANT-- NO, REALLY!
PROF. CHARLES A.K.A. "UNCLE CHUCK"
IN FACT, IT FEELS LIKE WE'RE ACCELERATING TO DANGEROUS SPEEDS.
HMPH! I SHALL HAVE A WORD WITH THE CON-DUCTOR. THIS IS NO WAY TO RUN A RAIL-ROAD.
THESE ACCOMMODATIONS ARE BEASTLY! AND I ORDERED MY LUNCH HOURS AGO! HONESTLY, HOW DIFFICULT IS IT TO PREPARE A PROPER CUCUMBER SANDWICH, I ASK YOU?
CALM DOWN, OLD FRIEND. HOPEFULLY, THIS MEANS WE'RE ABOUT TO BE RESCUED.
I SHOULD HOPE SO! COME, HELP ME FIND THE CALL BUTTON FOR THE STEWARD.

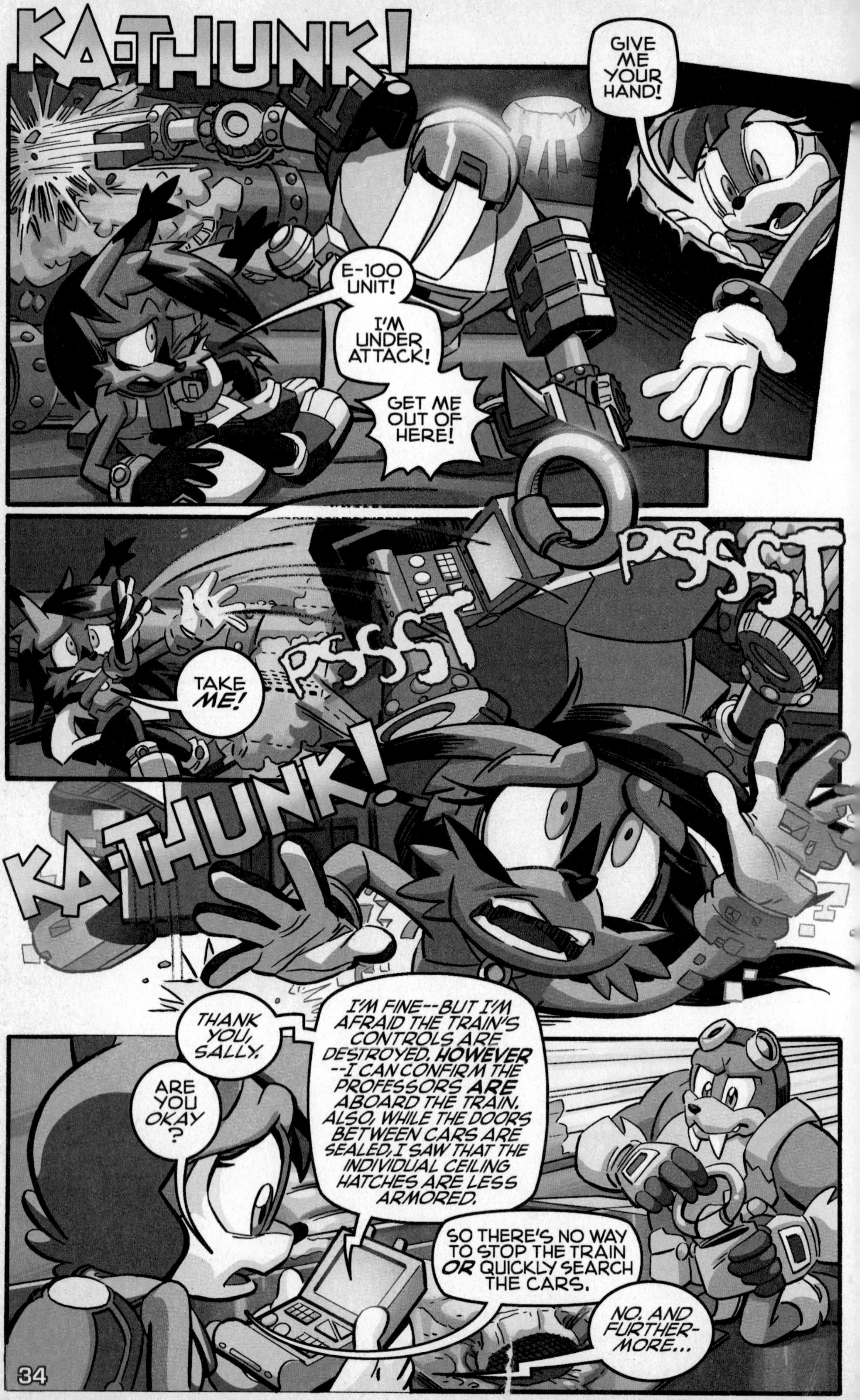
KA-THUNK!
GIVE ME YOUR HAND!
E-100 UNIT!
I'M UNDER ATTACK!
GET ME OUT OF HERE!
PSSST
PSSST
TAKE *ME!*
KA-THUNK!
THANK YOU, SALLY.
ARE YOU OKAY?
I'M FINE--BUT I'M AFRAID THE TRAIN'S CONTROLS ARE DESTROYED. **HOWEVER** --I CAN CONFIRM THE PROFESSORS **ARE** ABOARD THE TRAIN. ALSO, WHILE THE DOORS BETWEEN CARS ARE SEALED, I SAW THAT THE INDIVIDUAL CEILING HATCHES ARE LESS ARMORED.
SO THERE'S NO WAY TO STOP THE TRAIN **OR** QUICKLY SEARCH THE CARS.
NO. AND FURTHER-MORE...

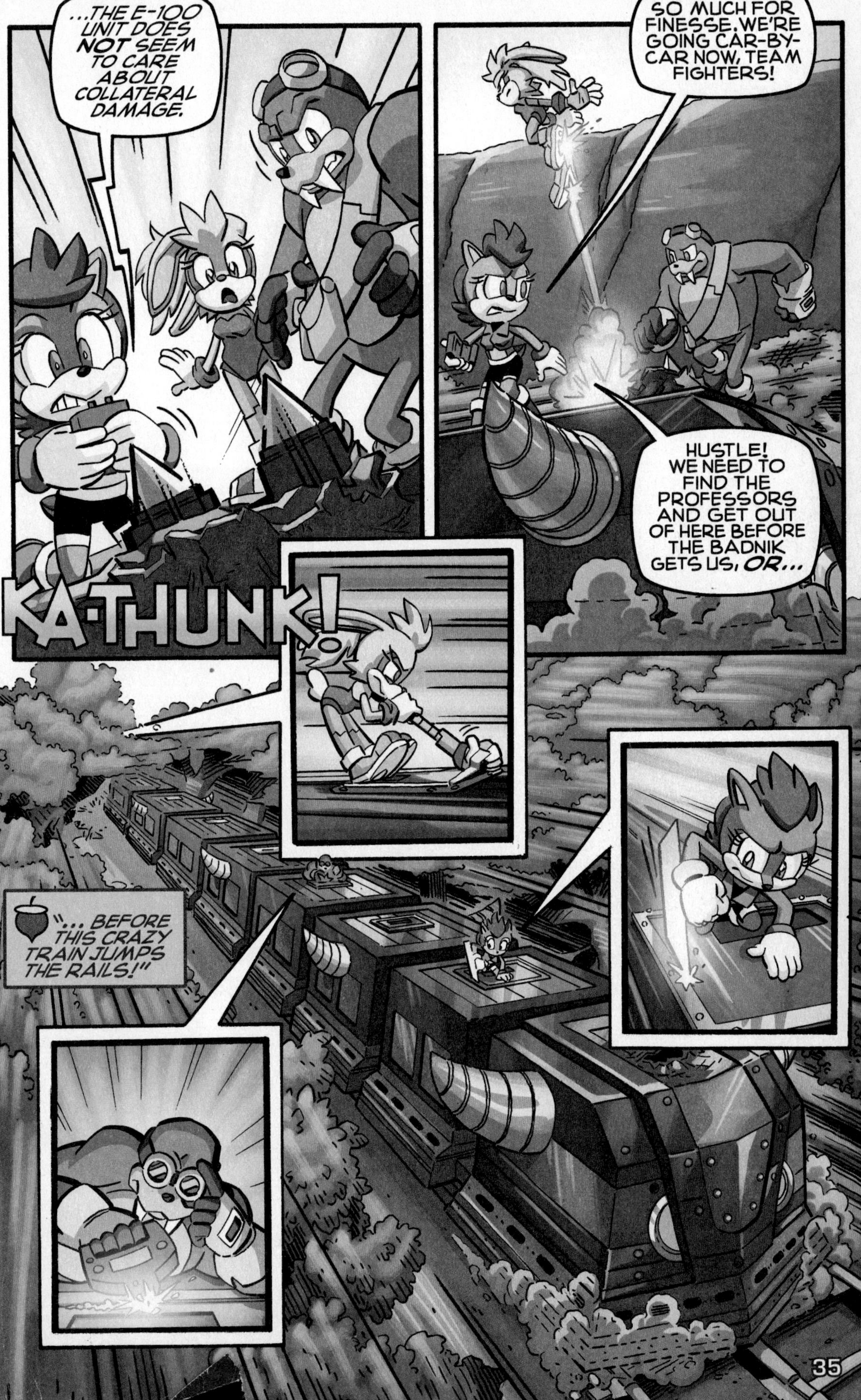
...THE E-100 UNIT DOES NOT SEEM TO CARE ABOUT COLLATERAL DAMAGE.
SO MUCH FOR FINESSE. WE'RE GOING CAR-BY-CAR NOW, TEAM FIGHTERS!
HUSTLE! WE NEED TO FIND THE PROFESSORS AND GET OUT OF HERE BEFORE THE BADNIK GETS US, OR...
KA-THUNK!
"... BEFORE THIS CRAZY TRAIN JUMPS THE RAILS!"

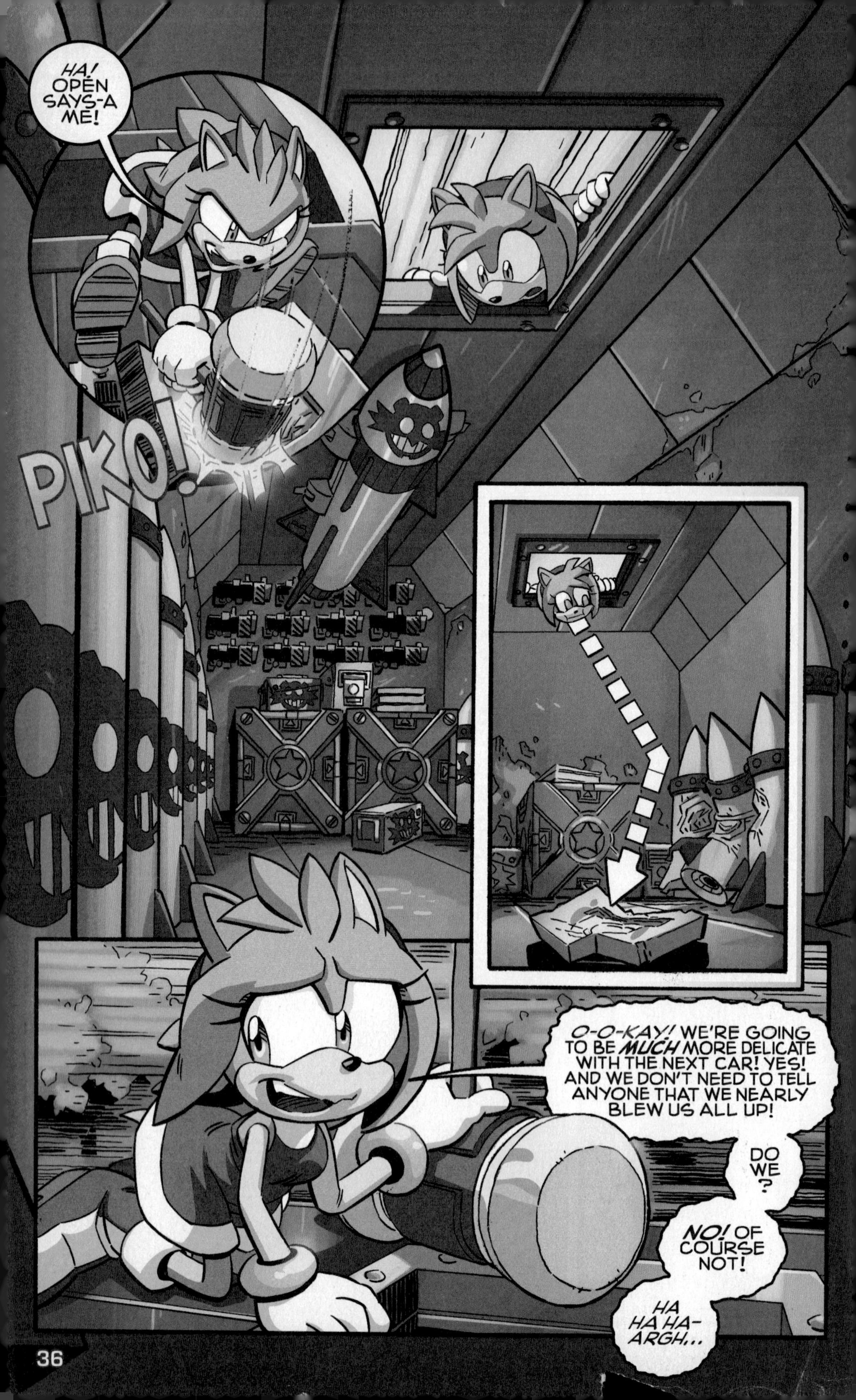
HA! OPEN SAYS-A ME!
PIKO!
O-O-KAY! WE'RE GOING TO BE MUCH MORE DELICATE WITH THE NEXT CAR! YES! AND WE DON'T NEED TO TELL ANYONE THAT WE NEARLY BLEW US ALL UP!
DO WE?
NO! OF COURSE NOT!
HA HA HA-ARGH...

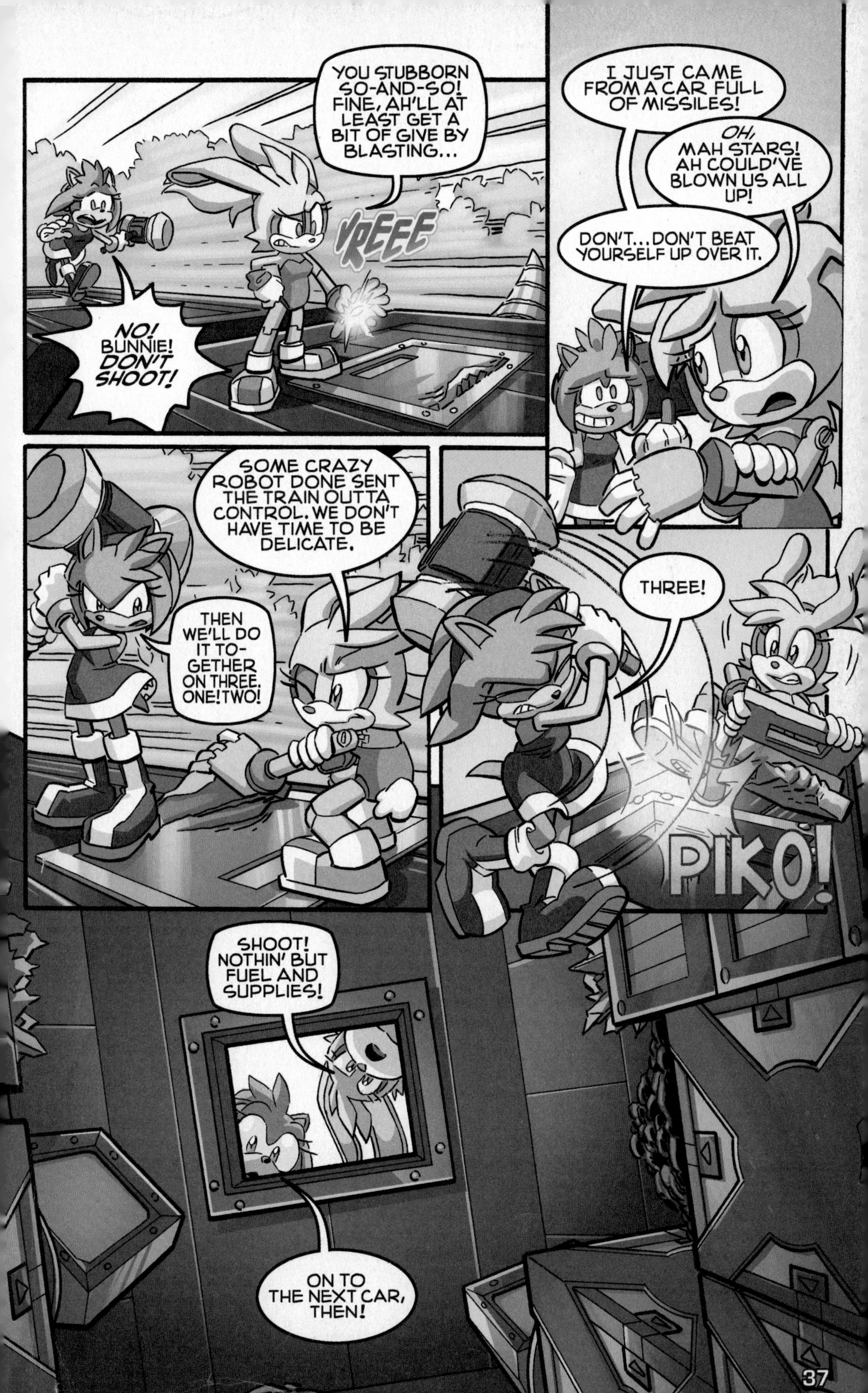
YOU STUBBORN SO-AND-SO! FINE, AH'LL AT LEAST GET A BIT OF GIVE BY BLASTING...
VREEE
NO! BUNNIE! DON'T SHOOT!
I JUST CAME FROM A CAR FULL OF MISSILES!
OH, MAH STARS! AH COULD'VE BLOWN US ALL UP!
DON'T... DON'T BEAT YOURSELF UP OVER IT.
SOME CRAZY ROBOT DONE SENT THE TRAIN OUTTA CONTROL. WE DON'T HAVE TIME TO BE DELICATE.
THEN WE'LL DO IT TO-GETHER ON THREE. ONE! TWO!
THREE!
PIKO!
SHOOT! NOTHIN' BUT FUEL AND SUPPLIES!
ON TO THE NEXT CAR, THEN!

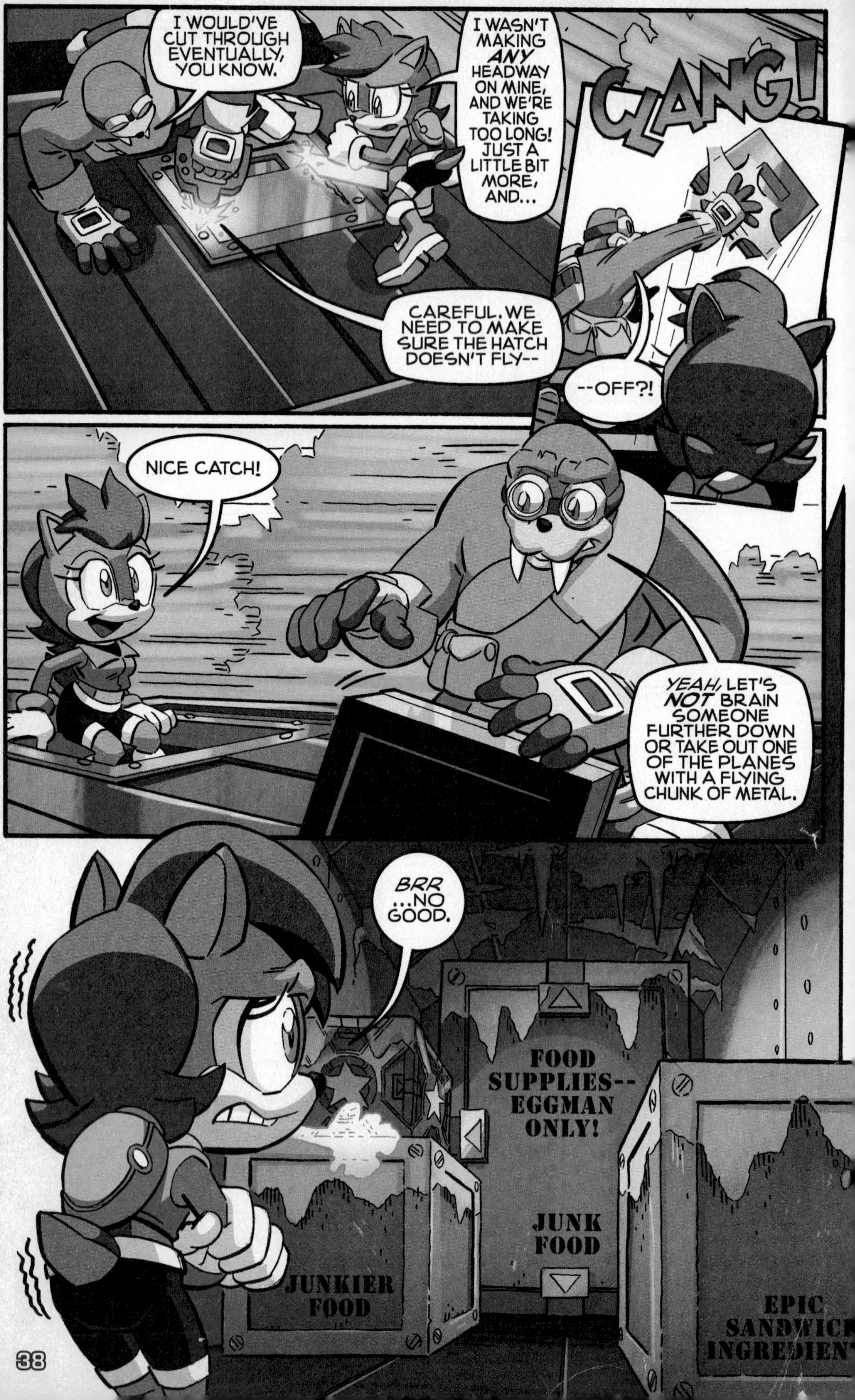
I WOULD'VE CUT THROUGH EVENTUALLY, YOU KNOW.
I WASN'T MAKING ANY HEADWAY ON MINE, AND WE'RE TAKING TOO LONG! JUST A LITTLE BIT MORE, AND...
CAREFUL. WE NEED TO MAKE SURE THE HATCH DOESN'T FLY--
CLANG!
--OFF?!
NICE CATCH!
YEAH, LET'S NOT BRAIN SOMEONE FURTHER DOWN OR TAKE OUT ONE OF THE PLANES WITH A FLYING CHUNK OF METAL.
BRR ...NO GOOD.
FOOD SUPPLIES-- EGGMAN ONLY!
JUNK FOOD
JUNKIER FOOD
EPIC SANDWICH INGREDIENTS

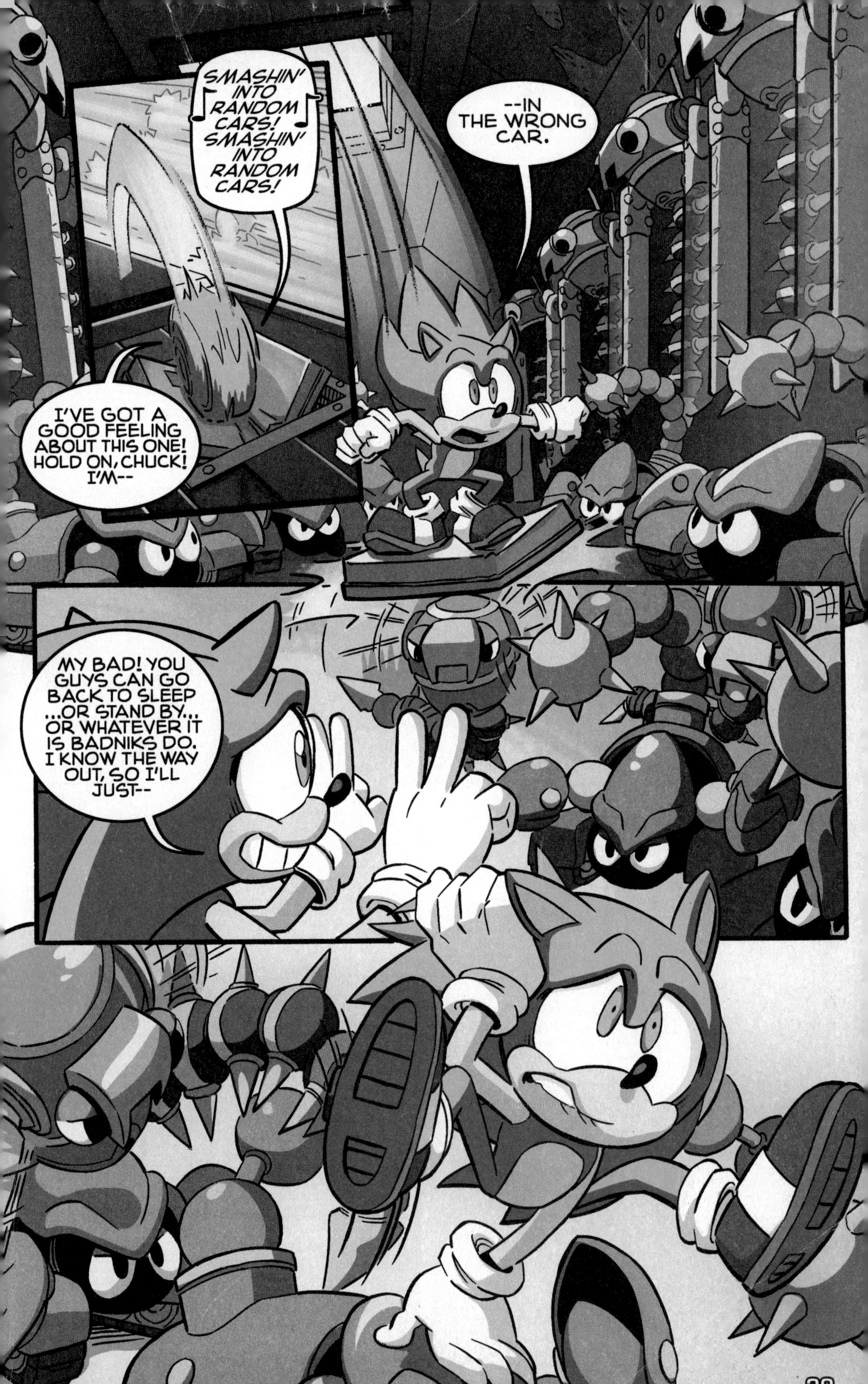
SMASHIN' INTO RANDOM CARS! SMASHIN' INTO RANDOM CARS!
I'VE GOT A GOOD FEELING ABOUT THIS ONE! HOLD ON, CHUCK! I'M--
--IN THE WRONG CAR.
MY BAD! YOU GUYS CAN GO BACK TO SLEEP ...OR STAND BY... OR WHATEVER IT IS BADNIKS DO. I KNOW THE WAY OUT, SO I'LL JUST--

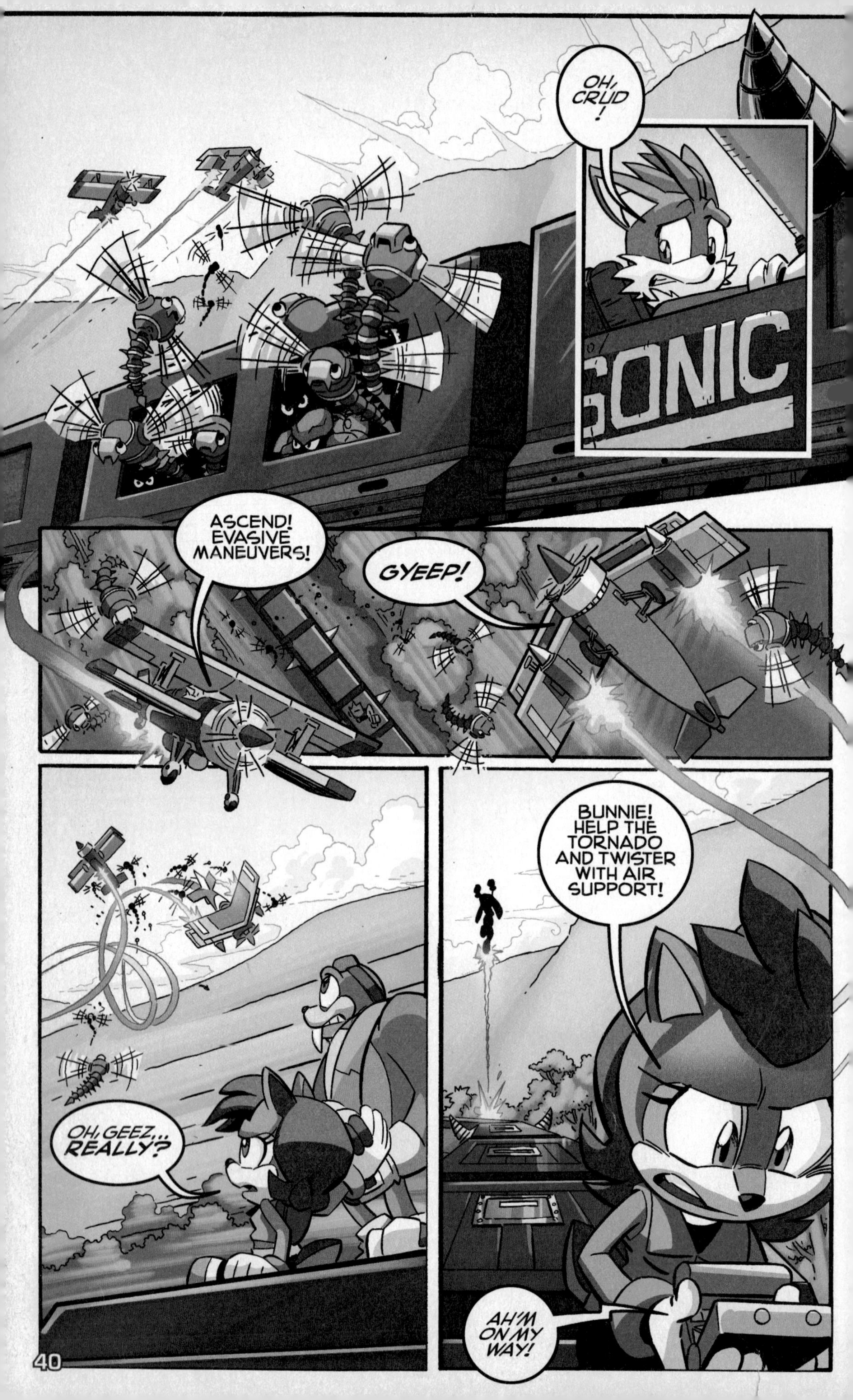

OH, CRUD!
SONIC
ASCEND! EVASIVE MANEUVERS!
GYEEP!
OH, GEEZ... REALLY?
BUNNIE! HELP THE TORNADO AND TWISTER WITH AIR SUPPORT!
AH'M ON MY WAY!

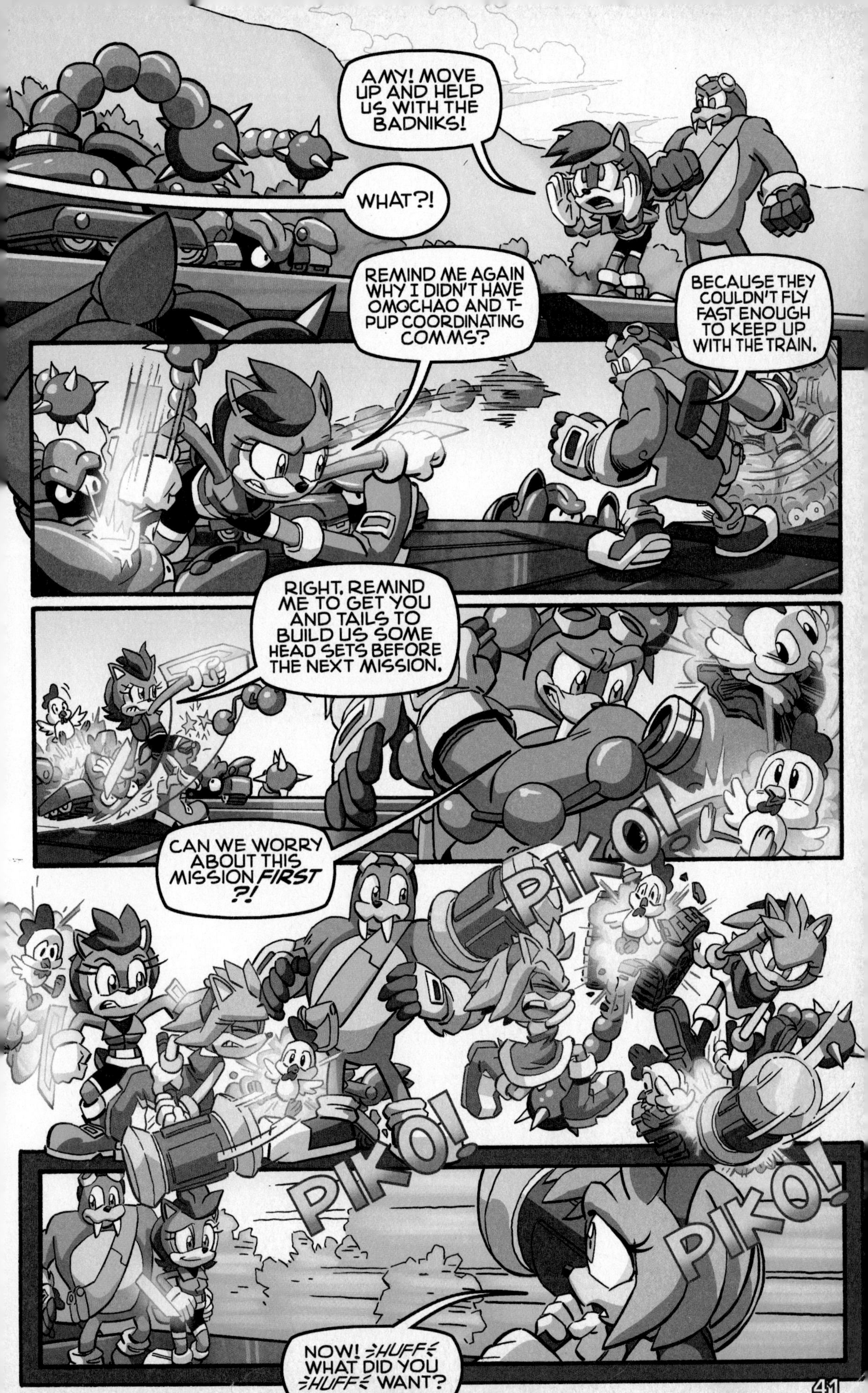
AMY! MOVE UP AND HELP US WITH THE BADNIKS!
WHAT?!
REMIND ME AGAIN WHY I DIDN'T HAVE OMOCHAO AND T-PUP COORDINATING COMMS?
BECAUSE THEY COULDN'T FLY FAST ENOUGH TO KEEP UP WITH THE TRAIN.
RIGHT. REMIND ME TO GET YOU AND TAILS TO BUILD US SOME HEAD SETS BEFORE THE NEXT MISSION.
CAN WE WORRY ABOUT THIS MISSION FIRST ?!
PIKO!
PIKO!
PIKO!
PIKO!
NOW! HUFF WHAT DID YOU HUFF WANT?

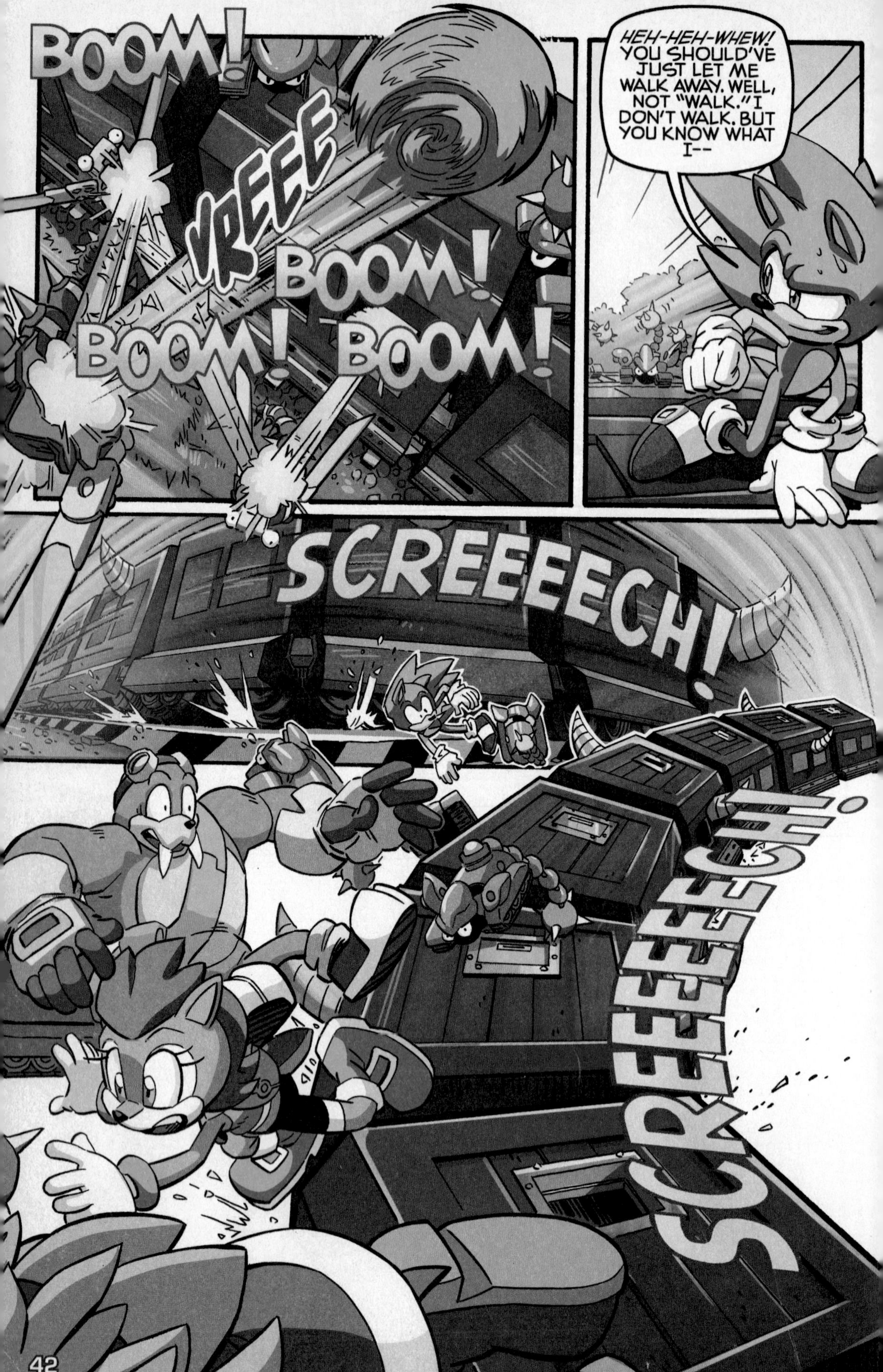
BOOM!
VREEE
BOOM!
BOOM! BOOM!
HEH-HEH-WHEW! YOU SHOULD'VE JUST LET ME WALK AWAY. WELL, NOT "WALK." I DON'T WALK. BUT YOU KNOW WHAT I--
SCREEEECH!
SCREEEECH!

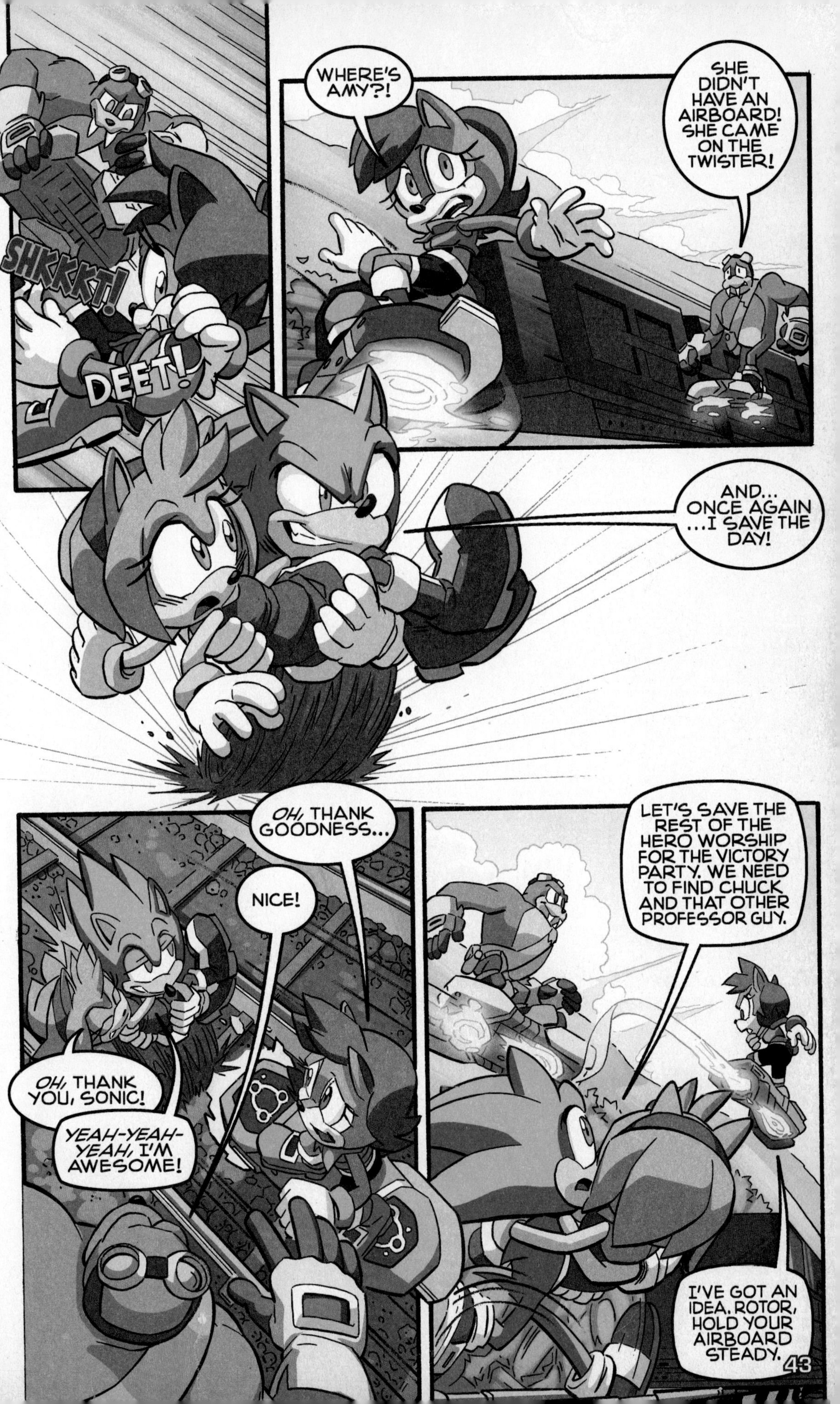
SHKKKT!
DEET!
WHERE'S AMY?!
SHE DIDN'T HAVE AN AIRBOARD! SHE CAME ON THE TWISTER!
AND... ONCE AGAIN ...I SAVE THE DAY!
OH, THANK GOODNESS...
NICE!
OH, THANK YOU, SONIC!
YEAH-YEAH-YEAH, I'M AWESOME!
LET'S SAVE THE REST OF THE HERO WORSHIP FOR THE VICTORY PARTY. WE NEED TO FIND CHUCK AND THAT OTHER PROFESSOR GUY.
I'VE GOT AN IDEA. ROTOR, HOLD YOUR AIRBOARD STEADY.

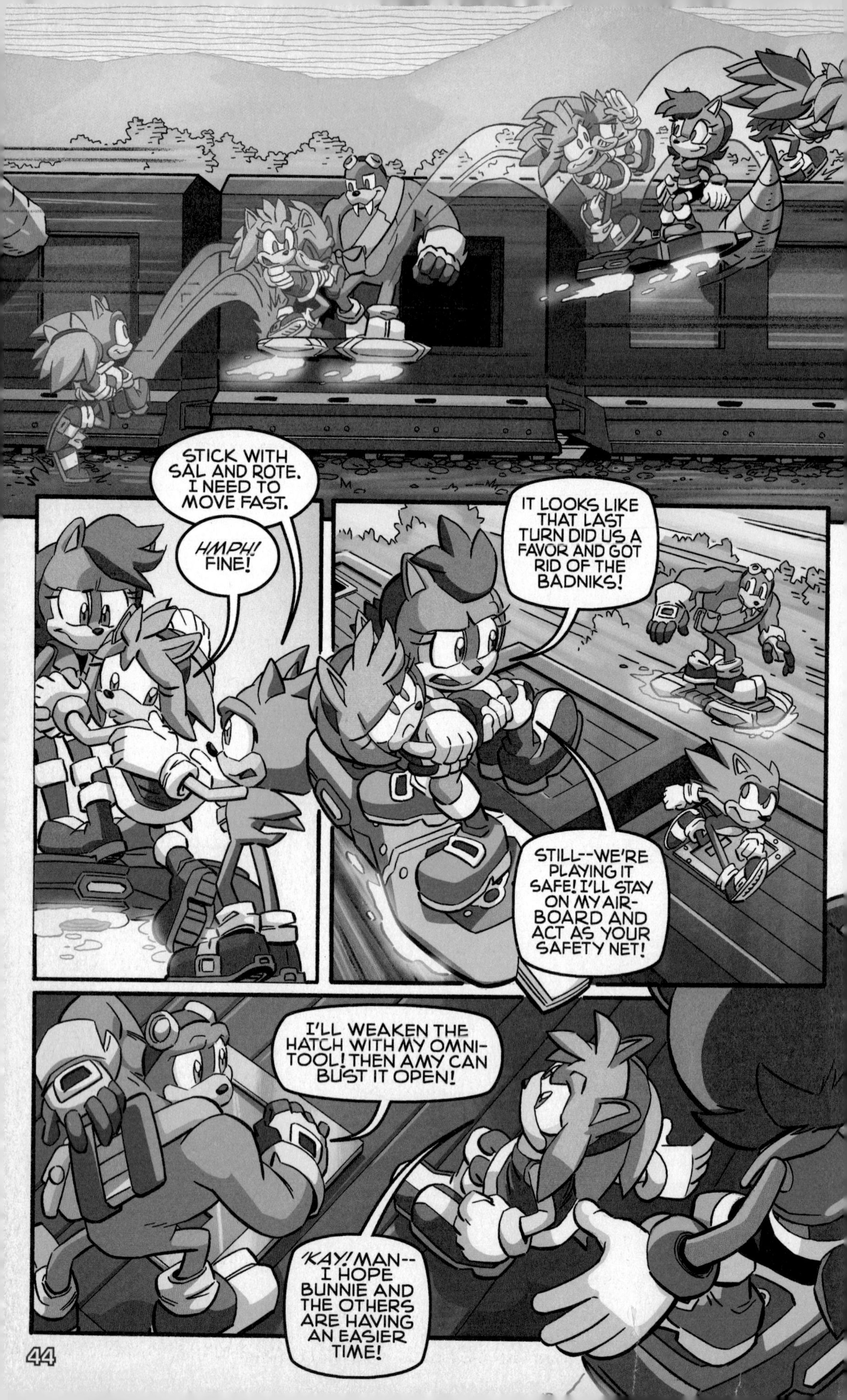
STICK WITH SAL AND ROTE. I NEED TO MOVE FAST.
HMPH! FINE!
IT LOOKS LIKE THAT LAST TURN DID US A FAVOR AND GOT RID OF THE BADNIKS!
STILL--WE'RE PLAYING IT SAFE! I'LL STAY ON MY AIR-BOARD AND ACT AS YOUR SAFETY NET!
I'LL WEAKEN THE HATCH WITH MY OMNI-TOOL! THEN AMY CAN BUST IT OPEN!
'KAY! MAN-- I HOPE BUNNIE AND THE OTHERS ARE HAVING AN EASIER TIME!

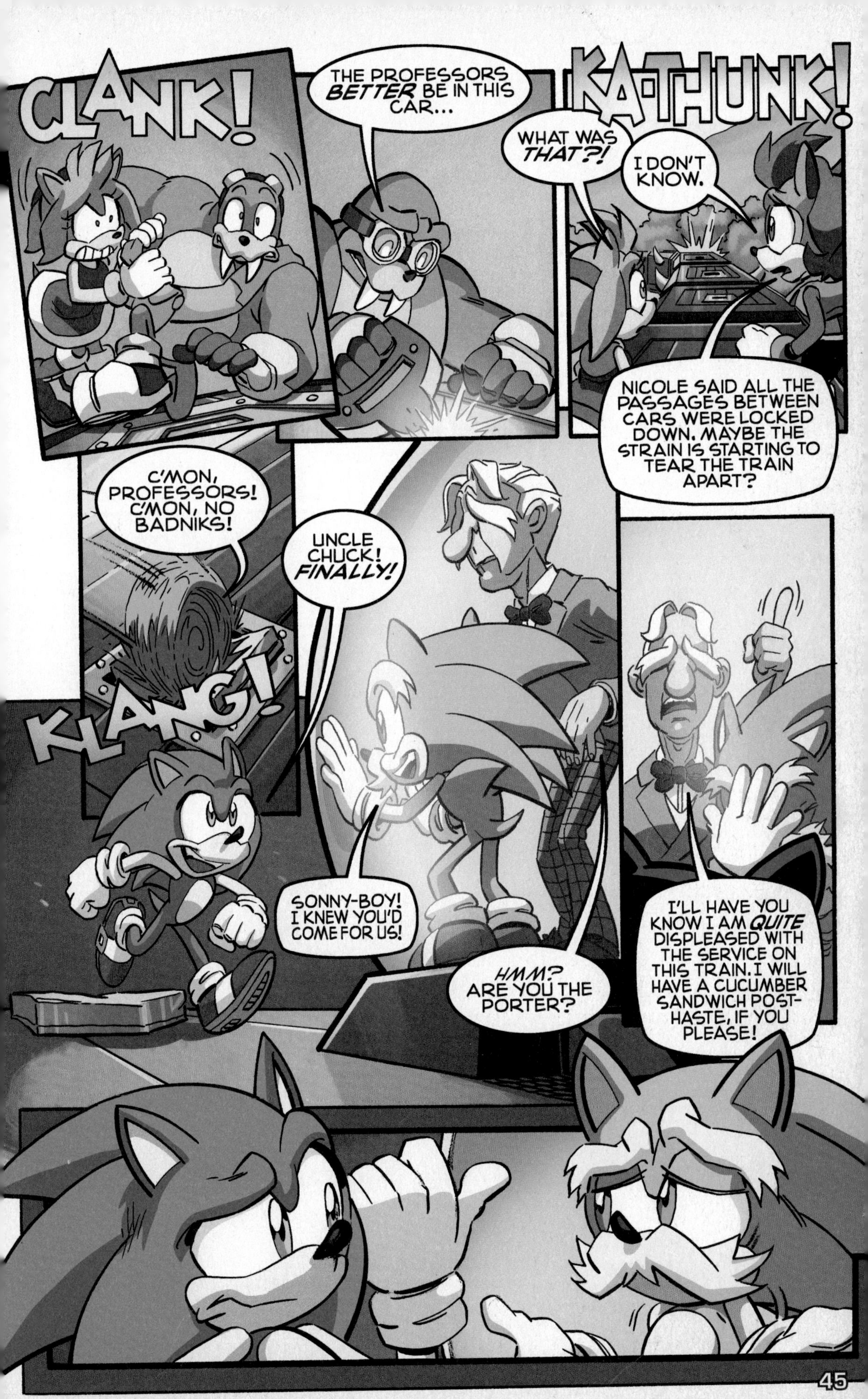
CLANK!
THE PROFESSORS BETTER BE IN THIS CAR...
KA-THUNK!
WHAT WAS THAT?!
I DON'T KNOW.
NICOLE SAID ALL THE PASSAGES BETWEEN CARS WERE LOCKED DOWN. MAYBE THE STRAIN IS STARTING TO TEAR THE TRAIN APART?
C'MON, PROFESSORS! C'MON, NO BADNIKS!
KLANG!
UNCLE CHUCK! FINALLY!
SONNY-BOY! I KNEW YOU'D COME FOR US!
HMM? ARE YOU THE PORTER?
I'LL HAVE YOU KNOW I AM QUITE DISPLEASED WITH THE SERVICE ON THIS TRAIN. I WILL HAVE A CUCUMBER SANDWICH POST-HASTE, IF YOU PLEASE!

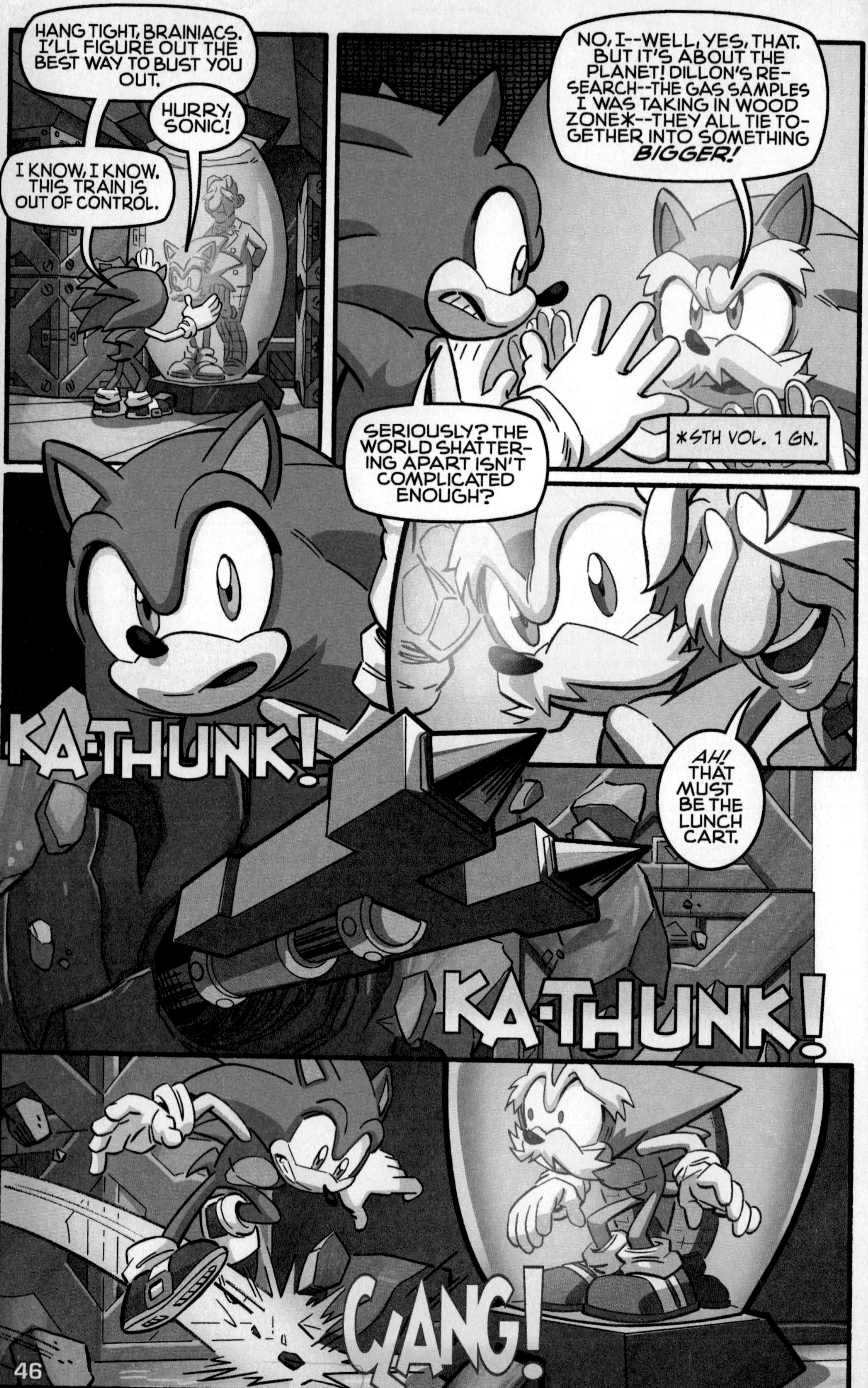
HANG TIGHT, BRAINIACS. I'LL FIGURE OUT THE BEST WAY TO BUST YOU OUT.
HURRY, SONIC!
I KNOW, I KNOW. THIS TRAIN IS OUT OF CONTROL.
NO, I--WELL, YES, THAT. BUT IT'S ABOUT THE PLANET! DILLON'S RE-SEARCH--THE GAS SAMPLES I WAS TAKING IN WOOD ZONE*--THEY ALL TIE TO-GETHER INTO SOMETHING BIGGER!
*STH VOL. 1 GN.
SERIOUSLY? THE WORLD SHATTER-ING APART ISN'T COMPLICATED ENOUGH?
KA-THUNK!
AH! THAT MUST BE THE LUNCH CART.
KA-THUNK!
CLANG!

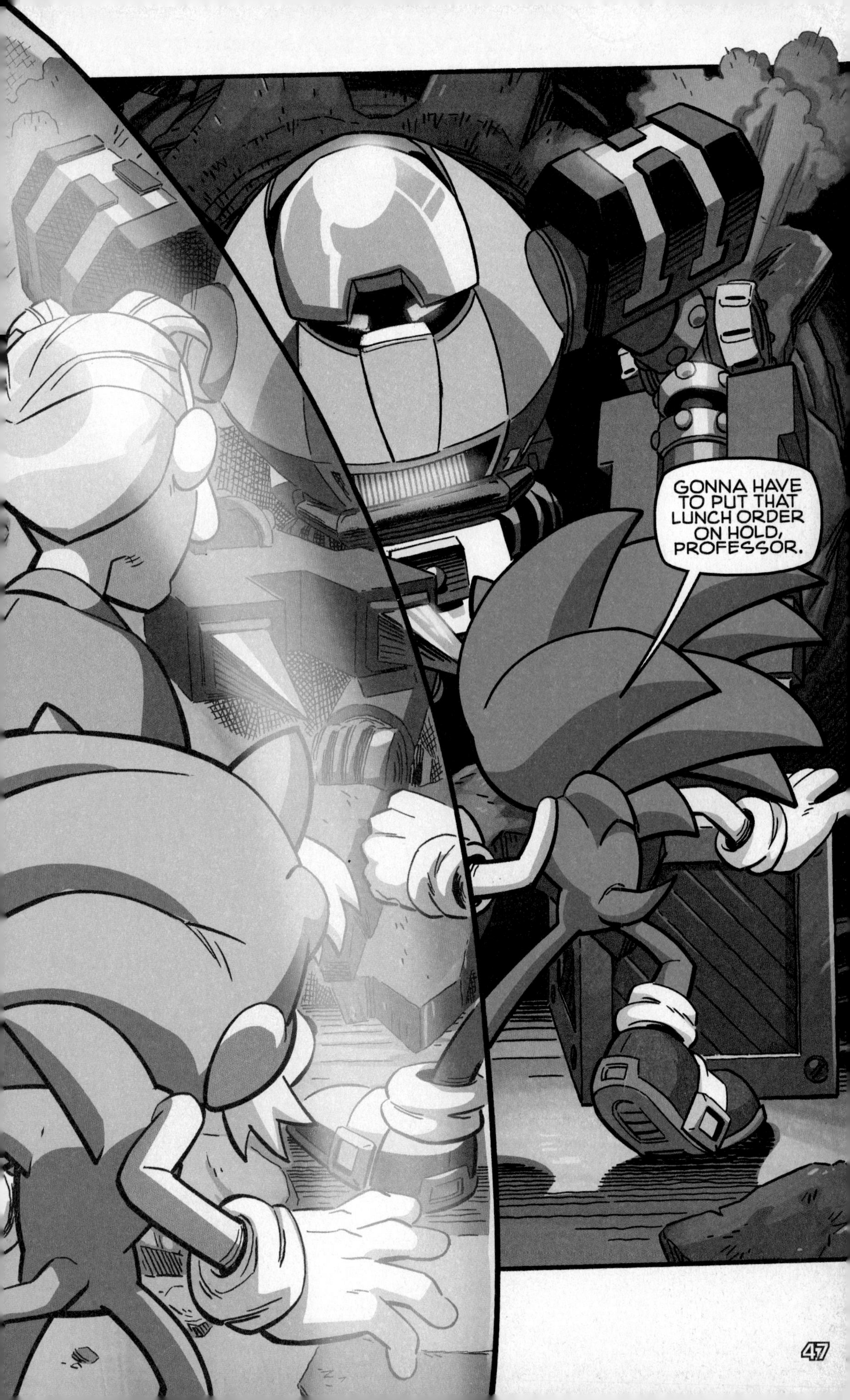
GONNA HAVE TO PUT THAT LUNCH ORDER ON HOLD, PROFESSOR.

CHAPTER 3

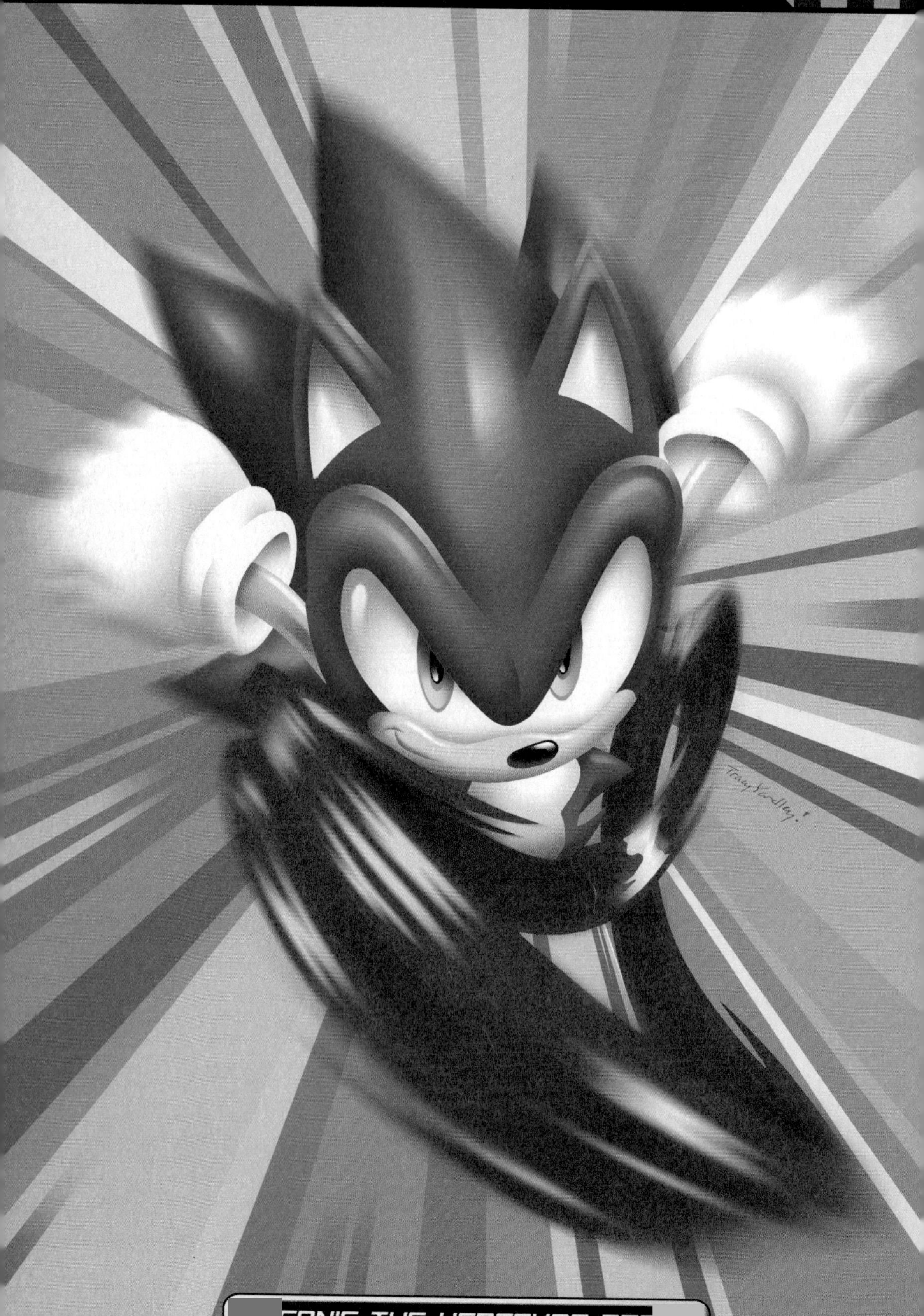
Tracy Yardley!

SONIC THE HEDGEHOG 259
COVER BY TRACY YARDLEY

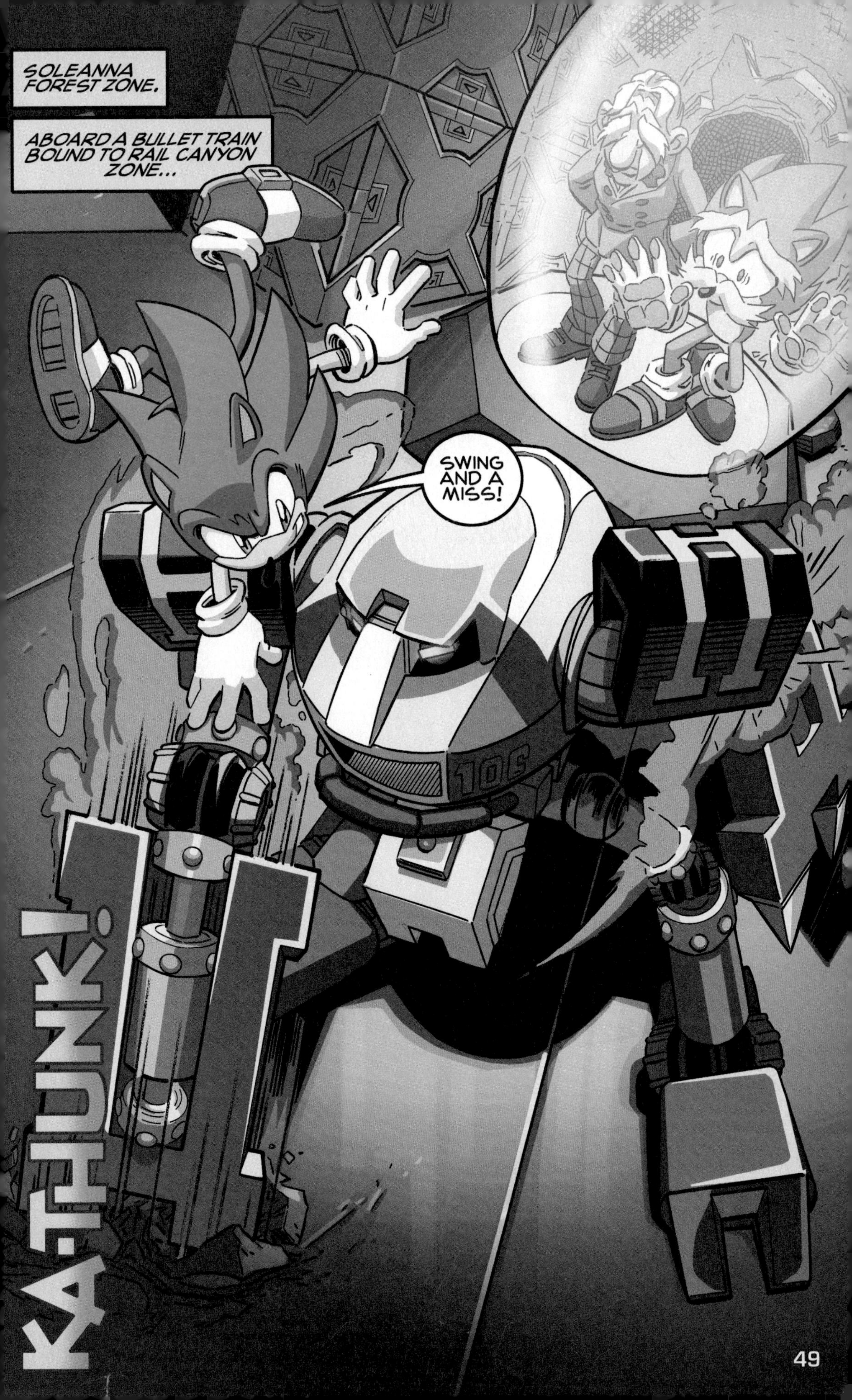
SOLEANNA FOREST ZONE.
ABOARD A BULLET TRAIN BOUND TO RAIL CANYON ZONE...
SWING AND A MISS!
KA-THUNK!

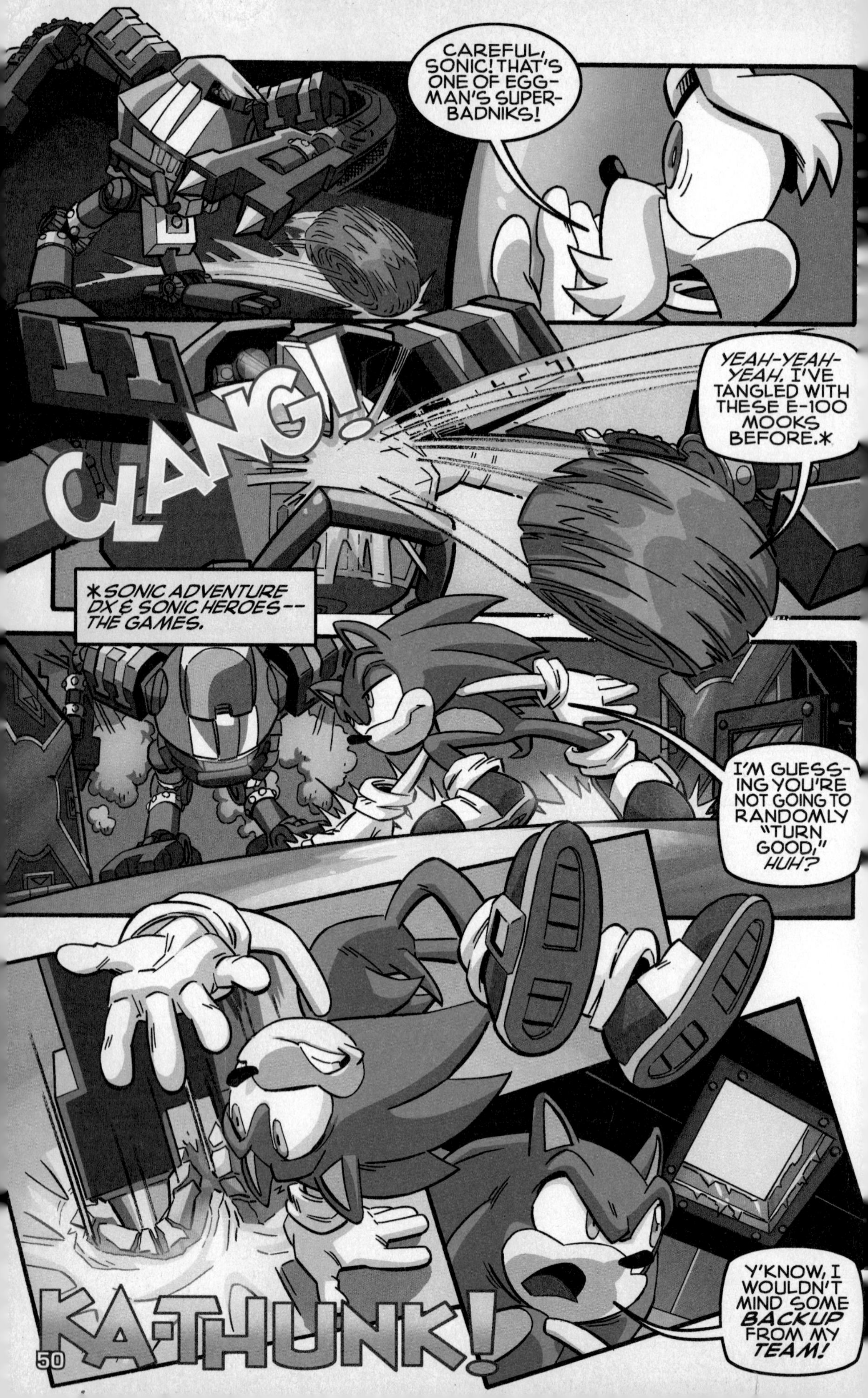

CAREFUL, SONIC! THAT'S ONE OF EGG-MAN'S SUPER-BADNIKS!
CLANG!
YEAH-YEAH-YEAH. I'VE TANGLED WITH THESE E-100 MOOKS BEFORE.*
*SONIC ADVENTURE DX & SONIC HEROES--THE GAMES.
I'M GUESSING YOU'RE NOT GOING TO RANDOMLY "TURN GOOD," HUH?
KA-THUNK!
Y'KNOW, I WOULDN'T MIND SOME BACKUP FROM MY TEAM!

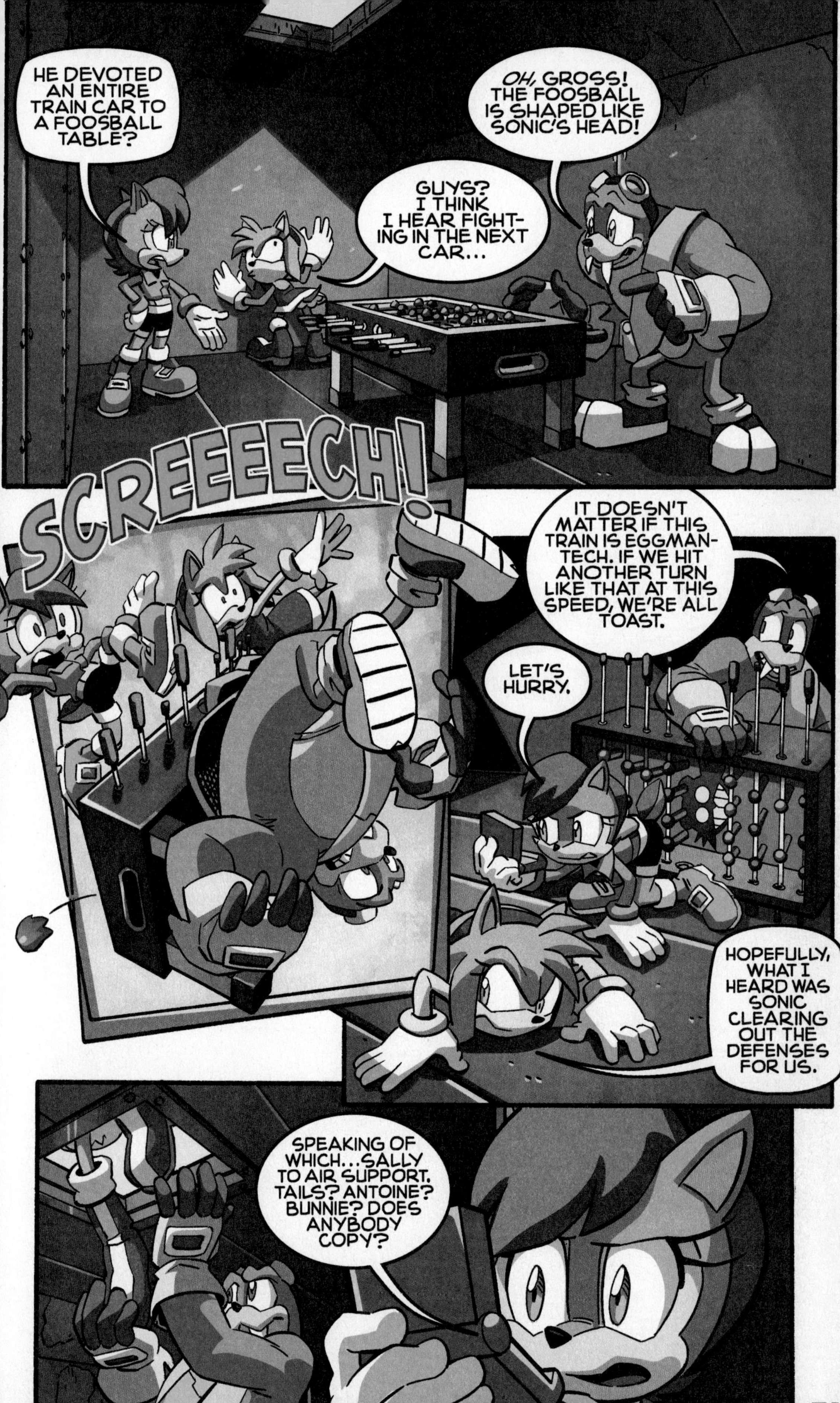
HE DEVOTED AN ENTIRE TRAIN CAR TO A FOOSBALL TABLE?
GUYS? I THINK I HEAR FIGHTING IN THE NEXT CAR...
OH, GROSS! THE FOOSBALL IS SHAPED LIKE SONIC'S HEAD!
SCREEEECH!
IT DOESN'T MATTER IF THIS TRAIN IS EGGMAN-TECH. IF WE HIT ANOTHER TURN LIKE THAT AT THIS SPEED, WE'RE ALL TOAST.
LET'S HURRY.
HOPEFULLY, WHAT I HEARD WAS SONIC CLEARING OUT THE DEFENSES FOR US.
SPEAKING OF WHICH...SALLY TO AIR SUPPORT. TAILS? ANTOINE? BUNNIE? DOES ANYBODY COPY?

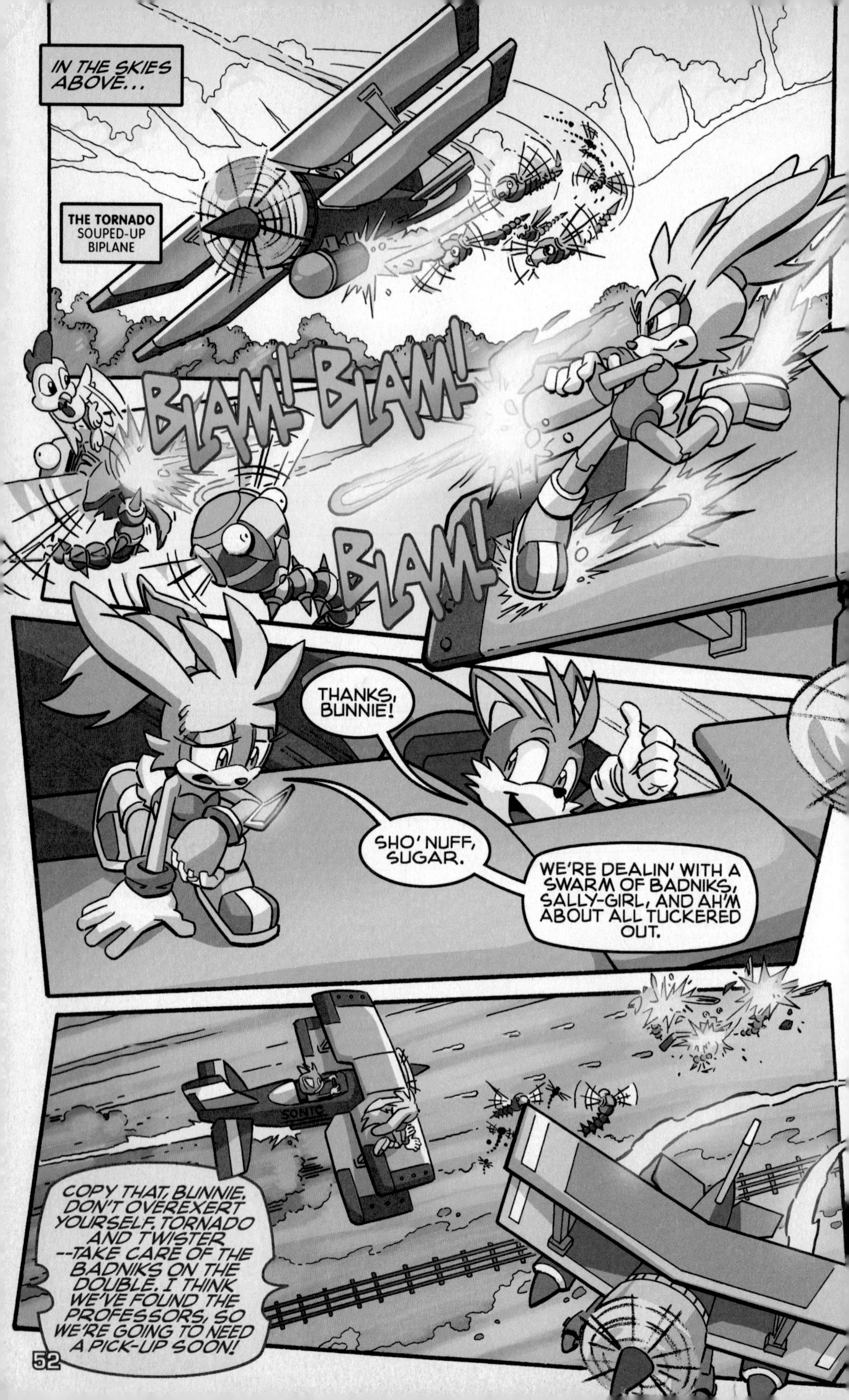
IN THE SKIES ABOVE...
THE TORNADO SOUPED-UP BIPLANE
BLAM! BLAM!
BLAM!
THANKS, BUNNIE!
SHO' NUFF, SUGAR.
WE'RE DEALIN' WITH A SWARM OF BADNIKS, SALLY-GIRL, AND AH'M ABOUT ALL TUCKERED OUT.
SONIC
COPY THAT, BUNNIE. DON'T OVEREXERT YOURSELF. TORNADO AND TWISTER --TAKE CARE OF THE BADNIKS ON THE DOUBLE. I THINK WE'VE FOUND THE PROFESSORS, SO WE'RE GOING TO NEED A PICK-UP SOON!

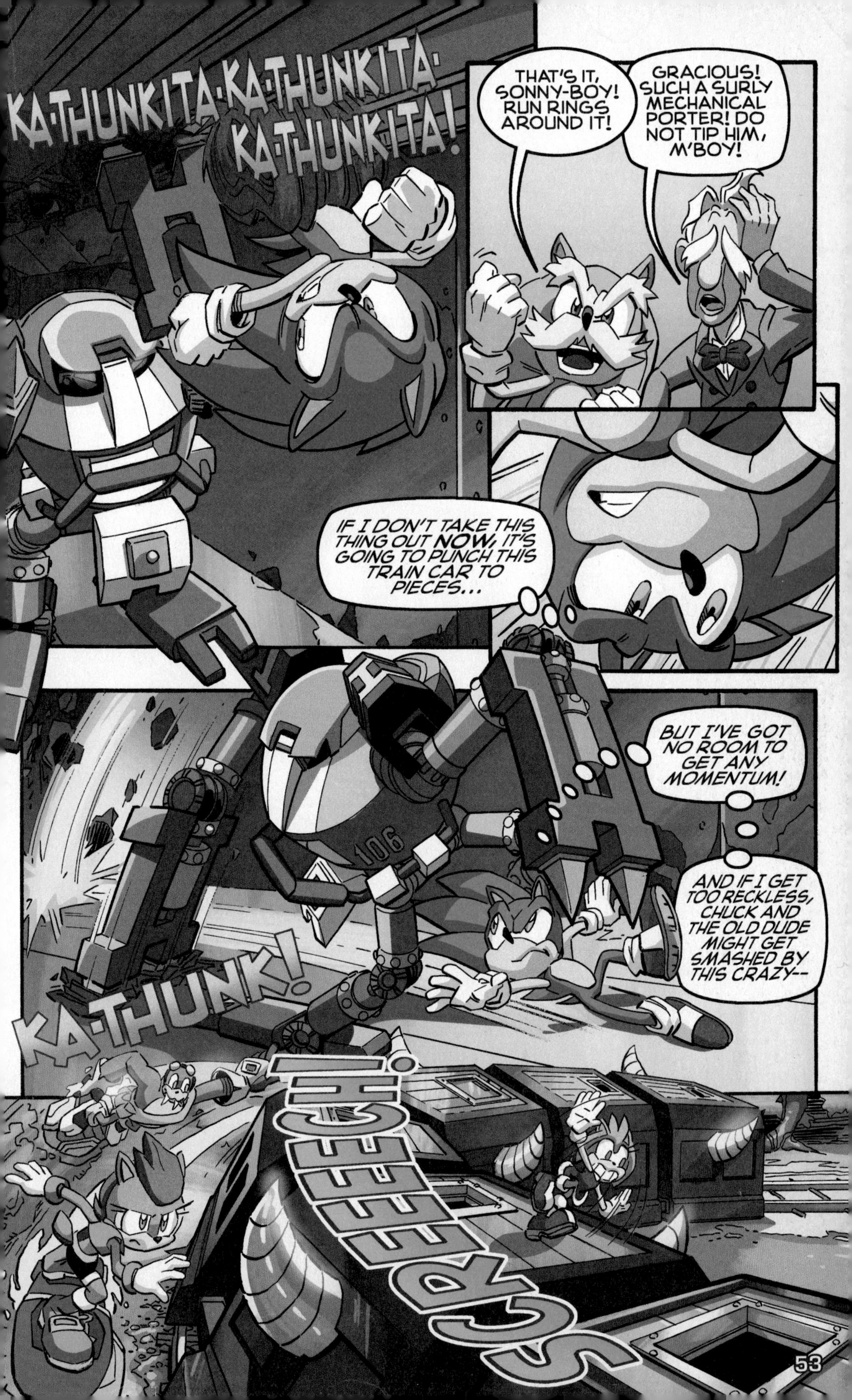
KA-THUNKITA-KA-THUNKITA-
KA-THUNKITA!
THAT'S IT, SONNY-BOY! RUN RINGS AROUND IT!
GRACIOUS! SUCH A SURLY MECHANICAL PORTER! DO NOT TIP HIM, M'BOY!
IF I DON'T TAKE THIS THING OUT NOW, IT'S GOING TO PUNCH THIS TRAIN CAR TO PIECES...
BUT I'VE GOT NO ROOM TO GET ANY MOMENTUM!
AND IF I GET TOO RECKLESS, CHUCK AND THE OLD DUDE MIGHT GET SMASHED BY THIS CRAZY--
106
KA-THUNK!
SCREEEECH!

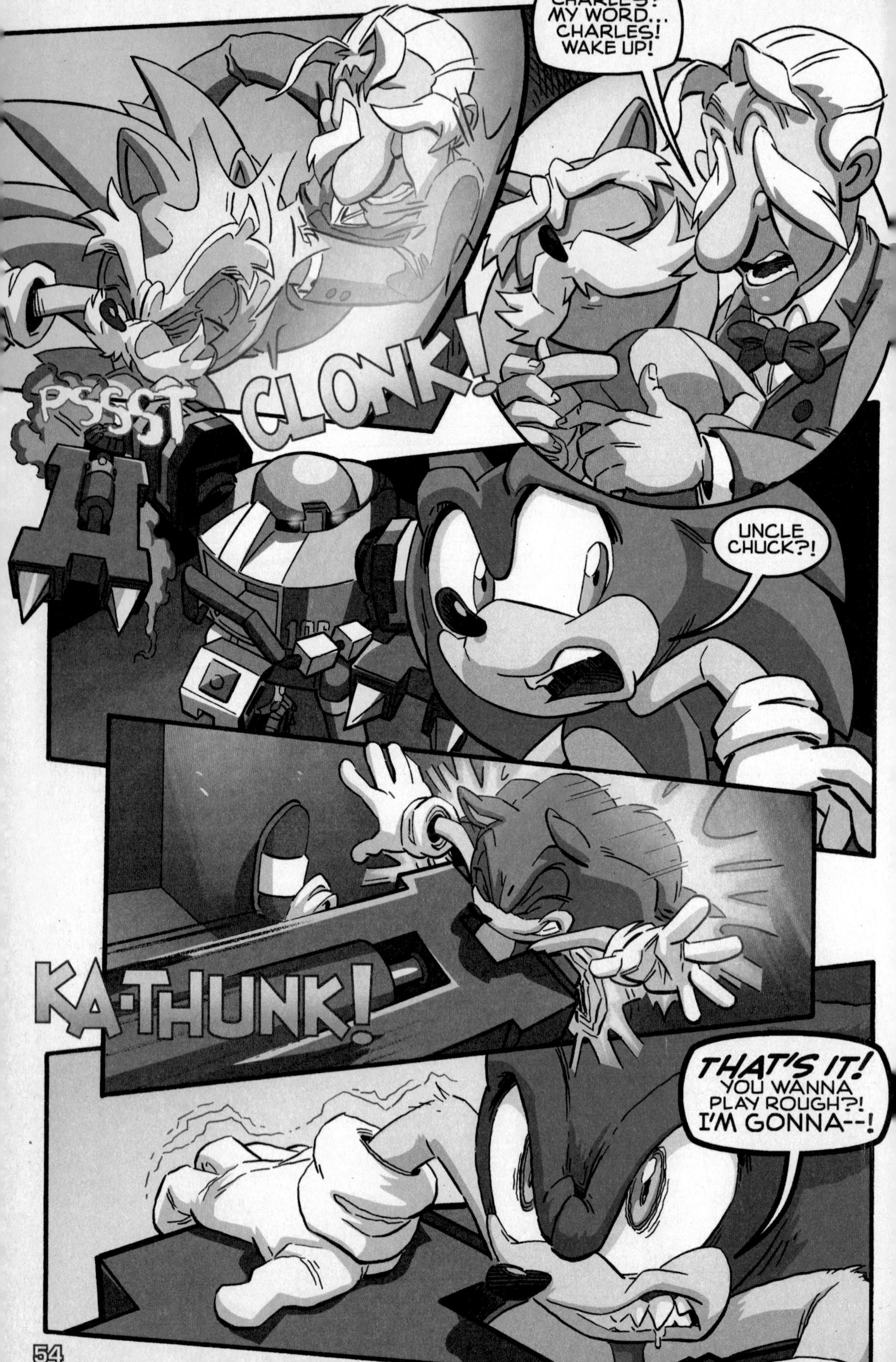

CHARLES? MY WORD... CHARLES! WAKE UP!
PSSST
CLONK!
UNCLE CHUCK?!
KA-THUNK!
THAT'S IT! YOU WANNA PLAY ROUGH?! I'M GONNA--!

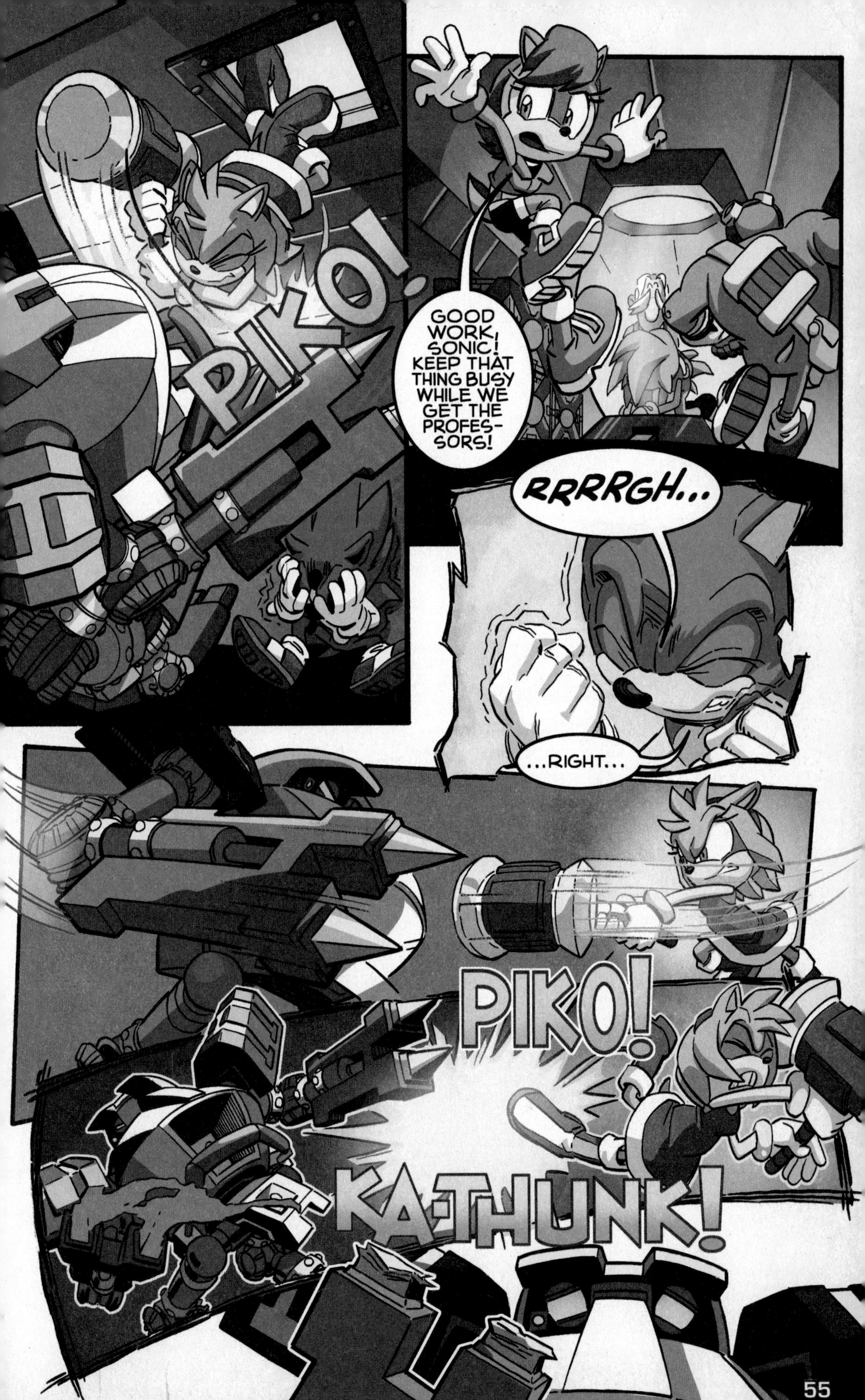
PIKO!
GOOD WORK, SONIC! KEEP THAT THING BUSY WHILE WE GET THE PROFESSORS!
RRRRGH...
...RIGHT...
PIKO!
KA-THUNK!

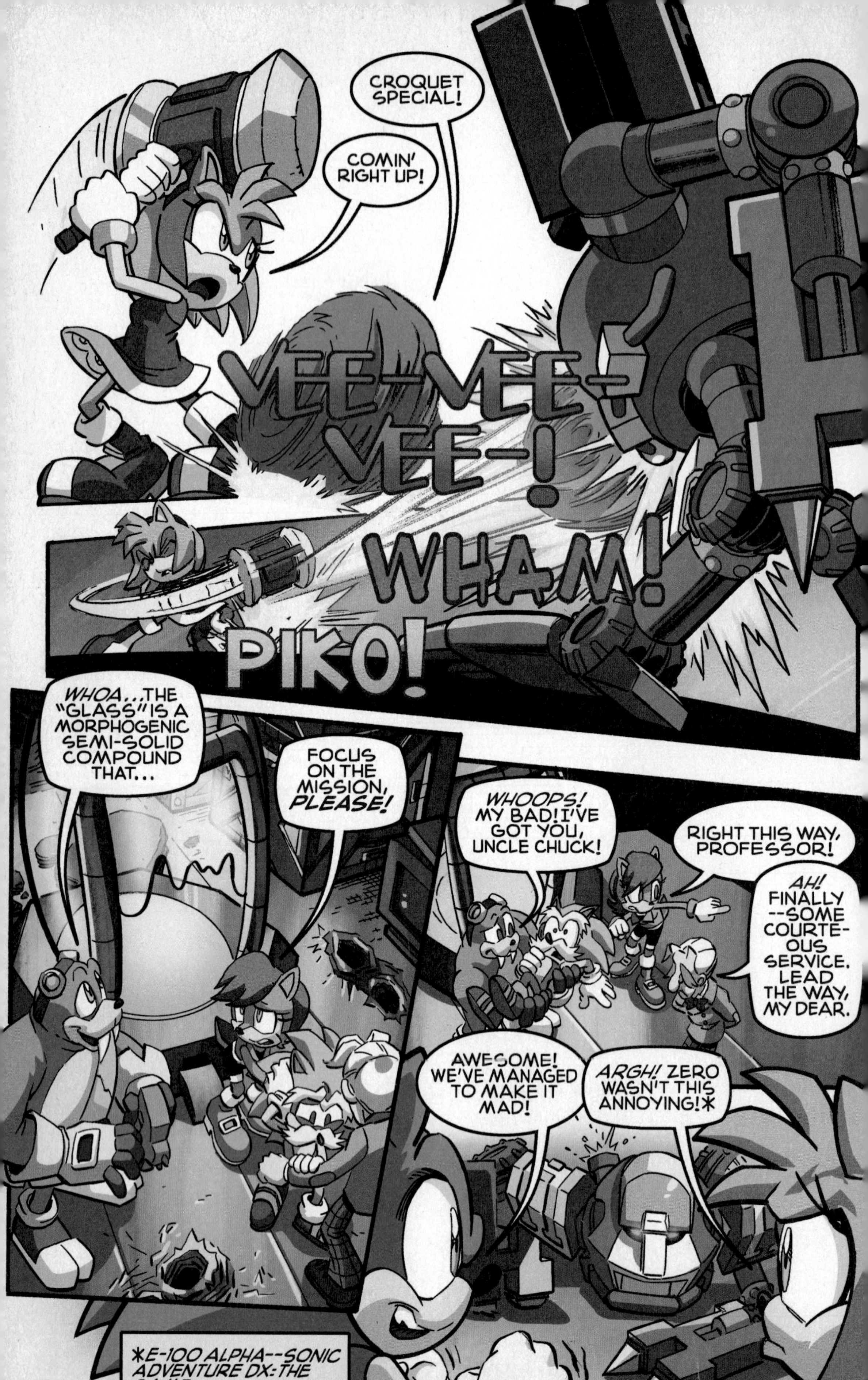

CROQUET SPECIAL!
COMIN' RIGHT UP!
VEE-VEE-VEE-!
WHAM!
PIKO!
WHOA...THE "GLASS" IS A MORPHOGENIC SEMI-SOLID COMPOUND THAT...
FOCUS ON THE MISSION, PLEASE!
WHOOPS! MY BAD! I'VE GOT YOU, UNCLE CHUCK!
RIGHT THIS WAY, PROFESSOR!
AH! FINALLY --SOME COURTE-OUS SERVICE. LEAD THE WAY, MY DEAR.
AWESOME! WE'VE MANAGED TO MAKE IT MAD!
ARGH! ZERO WASN'T THIS ANNOYING!*
*E-100 ALPHA--SONIC ADVENTURE DX: THE GAME.

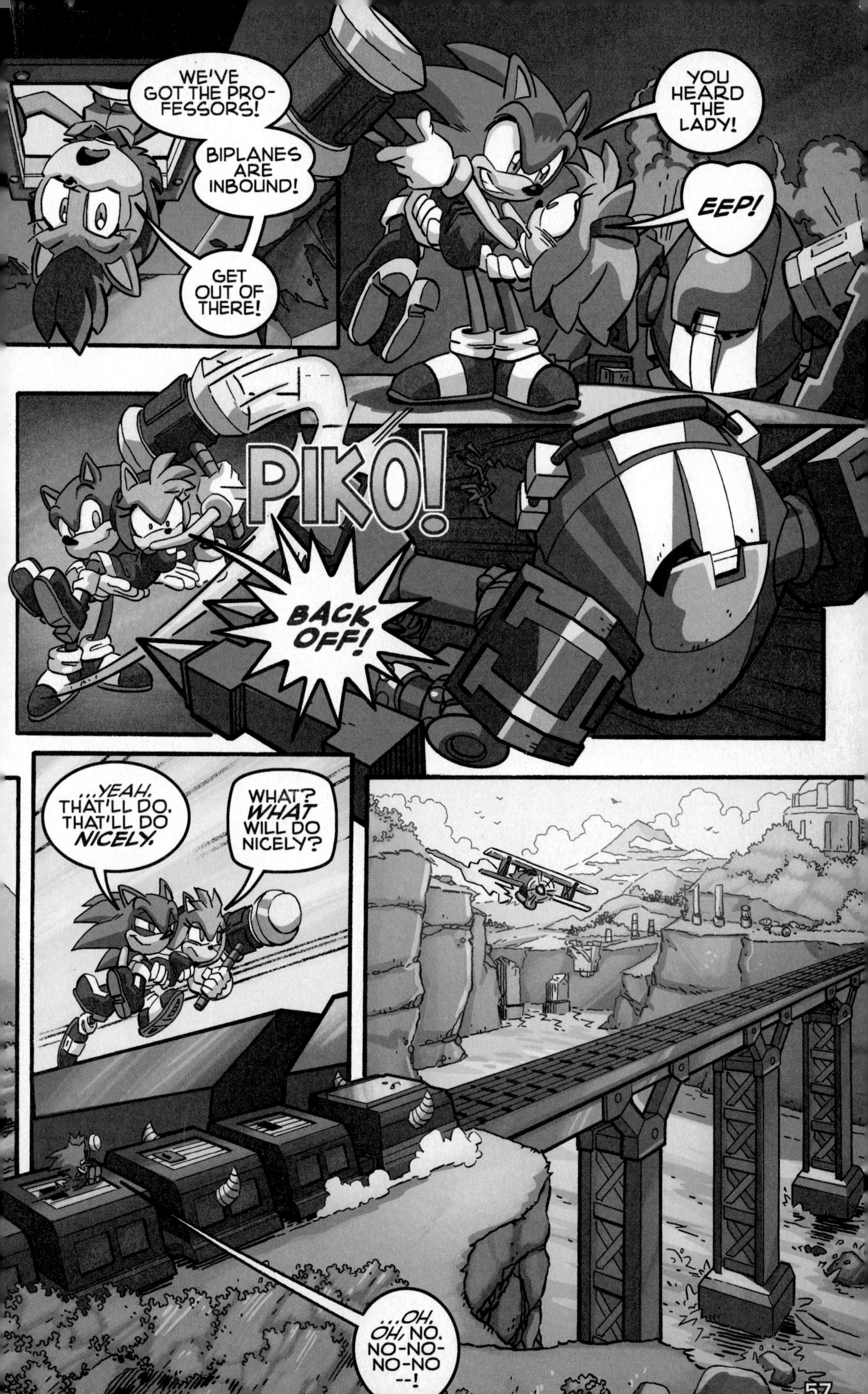
WE'VE GOT THE PRO- FESSORS!
BIPLANES ARE INBOUND!
GET OUT OF THERE!
YOU HEARD THE LADY!
EEP!
PIKO!
BACK OFF!
...YEAH. THAT'LL DO. THAT'LL DO NICELY.
WHAT? WHAT WILL DO NICELY?
...OH, OH, NO. NO-NO- NO-NO --!

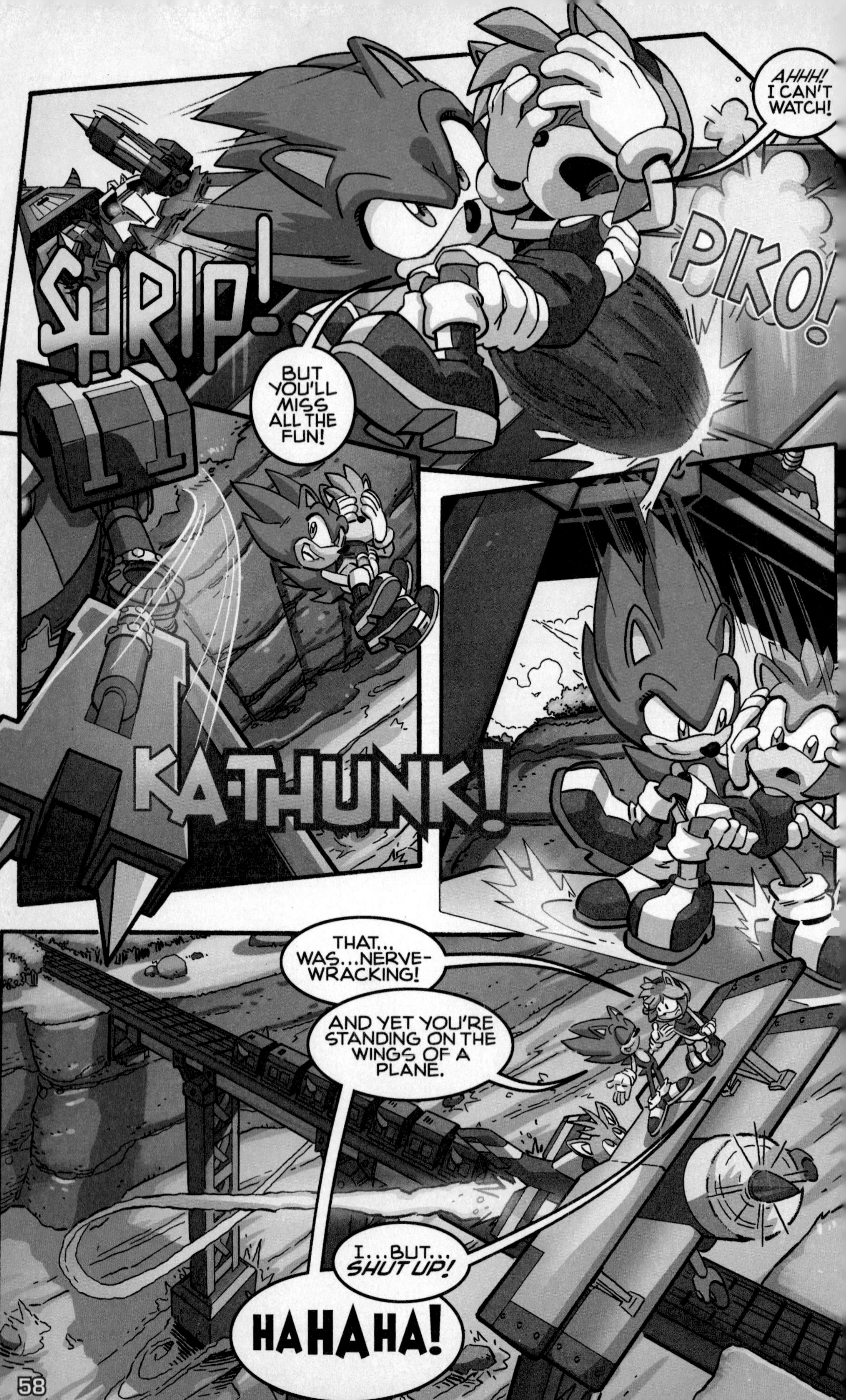
AHHH! I CAN'T WATCH!
SHRIP!
PIKO!
BUT YOU'LL MISS ALL THE FUN!
KA-THUNK!
THAT... WAS...NERVE-WRACKING!
AND YET YOU'RE STANDING ON THE WINGS OF A PLANE.
I...BUT... SHUT UP!
HAHAHA!

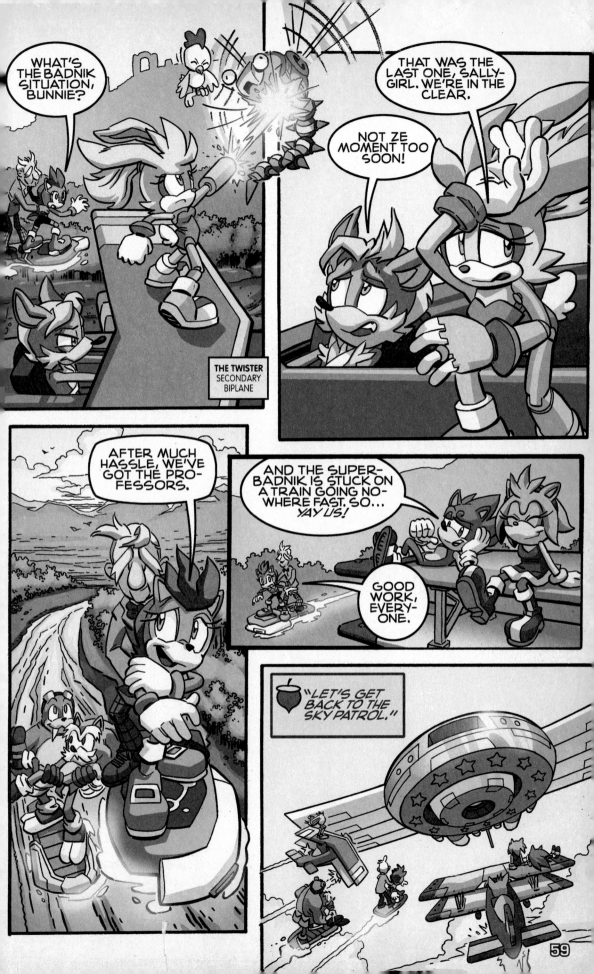

WHAT'S THE BADNIK SITUATION, BUNNIE?

THE TWISTER
SECONDARY BIPLANE

THAT WAS THE LAST ONE, SALLY-GIRL. WE'RE IN THE CLEAR.

NOT ZE MOMENT TOO SOON!

AFTER MUCH HASSLE, WE'VE GOT THE PROFESSORS.

AND THE SUPER-BADNIK IS STUCK ON A TRAIN GOING NOWHERE FAST, SO... YAY US!

GOOD WORK, EVERYONE.

"LET'S GET BACK TO THE SKY PATROL."

WHAT DO YOU MEAN, "WE LOST YOUR STUFF"?!

PRECISELY WHAT I SAID, M'BOY.

YOU FAILED TO RECOVER ALL THE RESEARCH MATERIAL I'D ACQUIRED, AS WELL AS ALL THE SAMPLES CHARLES HAD COLLECTED.

OH, SO YOU DIDN'T THINK TO BRING IT UP WHILE I WAS BUSY SAVING YOUR *LIVES*?!

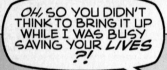

YOU WERE QUITE INVOLVED WITH YOUR FISTICUFFS. IT WOULD'VE BEEN RUDE TO INTERRUPT. FROM THERE, IT MUST HAVE... *MMM*, SLIPPED MY MIND.

MY EXCUSE IS THAT I WAS UNCON-SCIOUS.

AND THIS GUY'S SUPPOSED TO BE A "GENIUS," FOLKS...

SONIC.

PROFESSOR PICKLE --WHAT WAS IT YOU WERE RESEARCHING? WHAT DID DR. EGGMAN WANT WITH YOU?

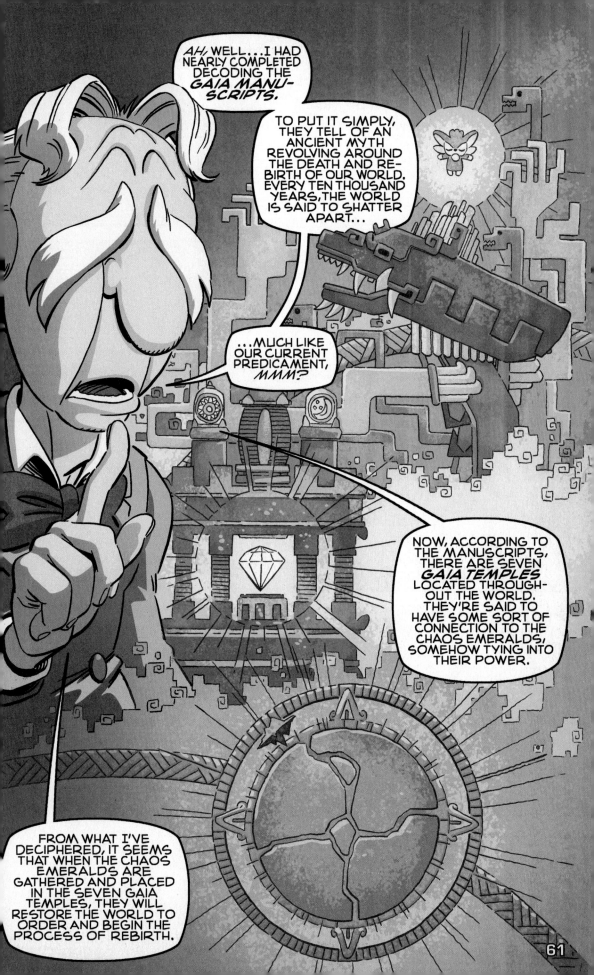

AH, WELL...I HAD NEARLY COMPLETED DECODING THE *GAIA MANU-SCRIPTS.*

TO PUT IT SIMPLY, THEY TELL OF AN ANCIENT MYTH REVOLVING AROUND THE DEATH AND RE-BIRTH OF OUR WORLD. EVERY TEN THOUSAND YEARS, THE WORLD IS SAID TO SHATTER APART...

...MUCH LIKE OUR CURRENT PREDICAMENT, *MMM?*

NOW, ACCORDING TO THE MANUSCRIPTS, THERE ARE SEVEN *GAIA TEMPLES* LOCATED THROUGH-OUT THE WORLD. THEY'RE SAID TO HAVE SOME SORT OF CONNECTION TO THE CHAOS EMERALDS, SOMEHOW TYING INTO THEIR POWER.

FROM WHAT I'VE DECIPHERED, IT SEEMS THAT WHEN THE CHAOS EMERALDS ARE GATHERED AND PLACED IN THE SEVEN GAIA TEMPLES, THEY WILL RESTORE THE WORLD TO ORDER AND BEGIN THE PROCESS OF REBIRTH.

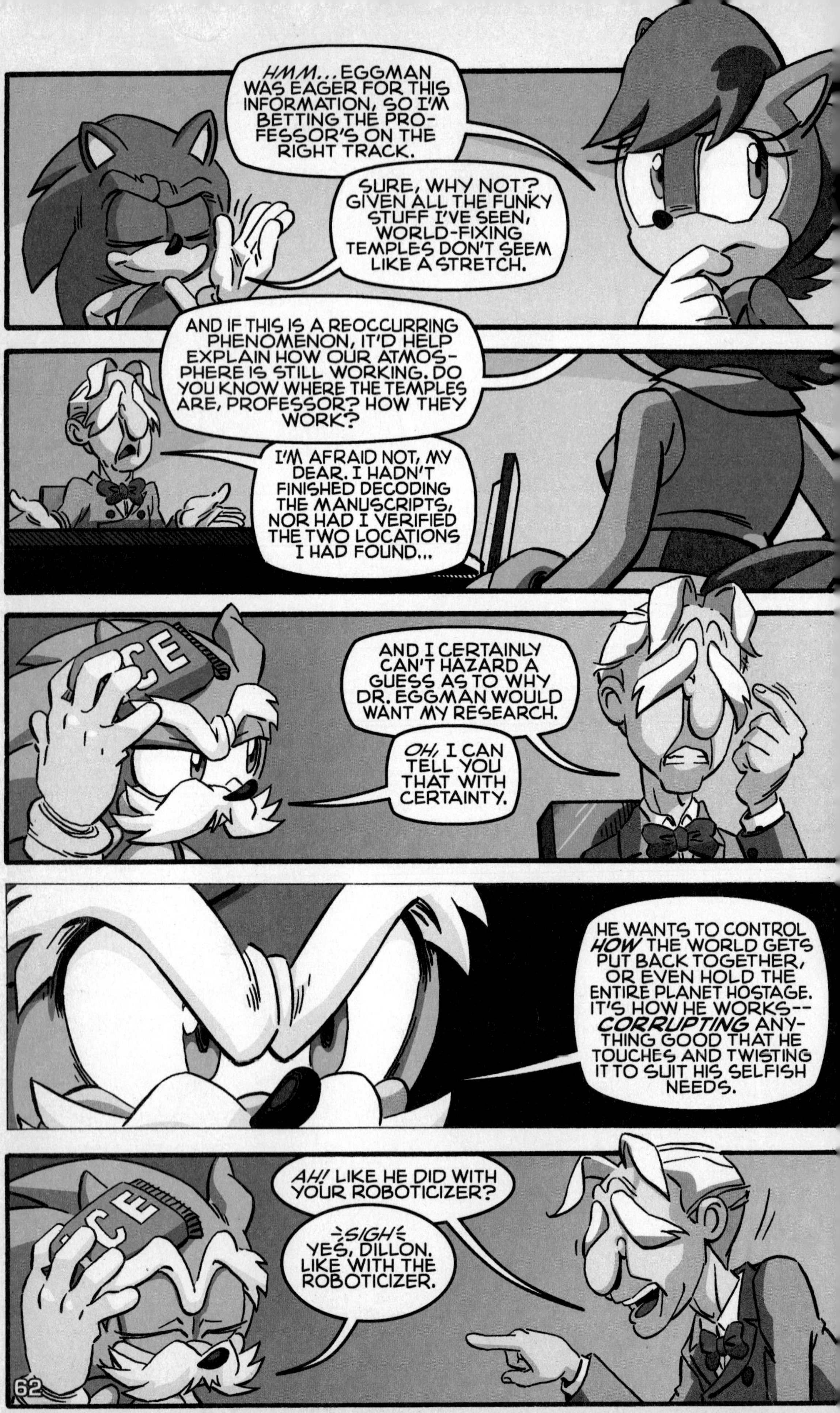
HMM... EGGMAN WAS EAGER FOR THIS INFORMATION, SO I'M BETTING THE PROFESSOR'S ON THE RIGHT TRACK.
SURE, WHY NOT? GIVEN ALL THE FUNKY STUFF I'VE SEEN, WORLD-FIXING TEMPLES DON'T SEEM LIKE A STRETCH.
AND IF THIS IS A REOCCURRING PHENOMENON, IT'D HELP EXPLAIN HOW OUR ATMOSPHERE IS STILL WORKING. DO YOU KNOW WHERE THE TEMPLES ARE, PROFESSOR? HOW THEY WORK?
I'M AFRAID NOT, MY DEAR. I HADN'T FINISHED DECODING THE MANUSCRIPTS, NOR HAD I VERIFIED THE TWO LOCATIONS I HAD FOUND...
AND I CERTAINLY CAN'T HAZARD A GUESS AS TO WHY DR. EGGMAN WOULD WANT MY RESEARCH.
OH, I CAN TELL YOU THAT WITH CERTAINTY.
HE WANTS TO CONTROL HOW THE WORLD GETS PUT BACK TOGETHER, OR EVEN HOLD THE ENTIRE PLANET HOSTAGE. IT'S HOW HE WORKS-- CORRUPTING ANYTHING GOOD THAT HE TOUCHES AND TWISTING IT TO SUIT HIS SELFISH NEEDS.
AH! LIKE HE DID WITH YOUR ROBOTICIZER?
SIGH
YES, DILLON. LIKE WITH THE ROBOTICIZER.

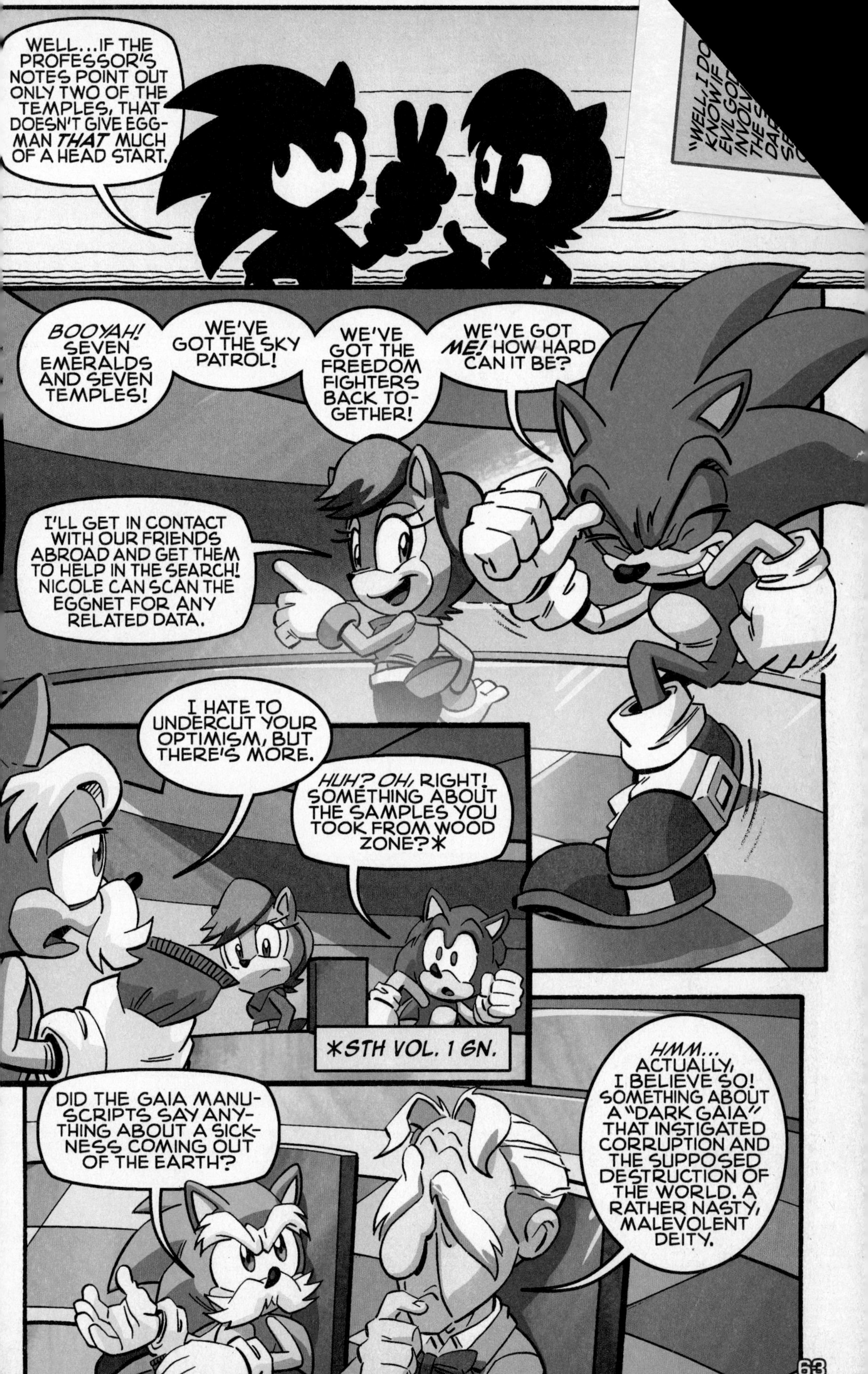

WELL...IF THE PROFESSOR'S NOTES POINT OUT ONLY TWO OF THE TEMPLES, THAT DOESN'T GIVE EGG-MAN *THAT* MUCH OF A HEAD START.

"WELL, I DO... KNOW IF... EVIL GO... INVOLV... THE S... DAR... SE..."

BOOYAH! SEVEN EMERALDS AND SEVEN TEMPLES!

WE'VE GOT THE SKY PATROL!

WE'VE GOT THE FREEDOM FIGHTERS BACK TO- GETHER!

WE'VE GOT *ME!* HOW HARD CAN IT BE?

I'LL GET IN CONTACT WITH OUR FRIENDS ABROAD AND GET THEM TO HELP IN THE SEARCH! NICOLE CAN SCAN THE EGGNET FOR ANY RELATED DATA.

I HATE TO UNDERCUT YOUR OPTIMISM, BUT THERE'S MORE.

HUH? OH, RIGHT! SOMETHING ABOUT THE SAMPLES YOU TOOK FROM WOOD ZONE?*

*STH VOL. 1 GN.

DID THE GAIA MANU- SCRIPTS SAY ANY- THING ABOUT A SICK- NESS COMING OUT OF THE EARTH?

HMM... ACTUALLY, I BELIEVE SO! SOMETHING ABOUT A "DARK GAIA" THAT INSTIGATED CORRUPTION AND THE SUPPOSED DESTRUCTION OF THE WORLD. A RATHER NASTY, MALEVOLENT DEITY.

63

...N'T ...ANY ...DS ARE ...ED, BUT ...STRANGE, ...RK ENERGY ...EPING OUT ...OF THE GROUND IS SOME **NASTY** STUFF!

"JUST A FEW SHORT TESTS PROVED IT WAS HIGHLY DANGEROUS, CORRUPTIVE, AND HAS INCREDIBLE MUTAGENIC PROPERTIES."

WE'RE TALKING THE POSSIBILITY OF TOTAL CELLULAR RE-WRITE.

?

I'M *FINE*, CHUCK. HONEST.

≶SIGH≶ ANYWAY-- BEFORE, WITH THE MINOR EARTHQUAKES, IT WAS SEEPING OUT, BUT THE CONCENTRATION SEEMED QUITE LOW.

WE'VE GOT TO FIX THINGS BEFORE WE REACH TOTAL GLOBAL SATU-RATION.

WITH THE WORLD AS IT IS, IT'S *POURING* OUT.

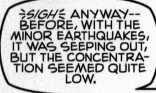

ON TOP OF THE WHOLE SHATTERED-WORLD THING.

HEY--IF ANYONE CAN HANDLE THIS KIND OF ADVENTURE, IT'S YOU.

WHY DO I FEEL LIKE YOU'RE PUR-POSEFULLY LEAVING ME OUT OF THE LOOP ON SOMETHING?

IT'S *NOTHING*!

REALLY! WE'VE GOT PLENTY OF OTHER STUFF TO WORRY ABOUT RIGHT NOW, SAL.

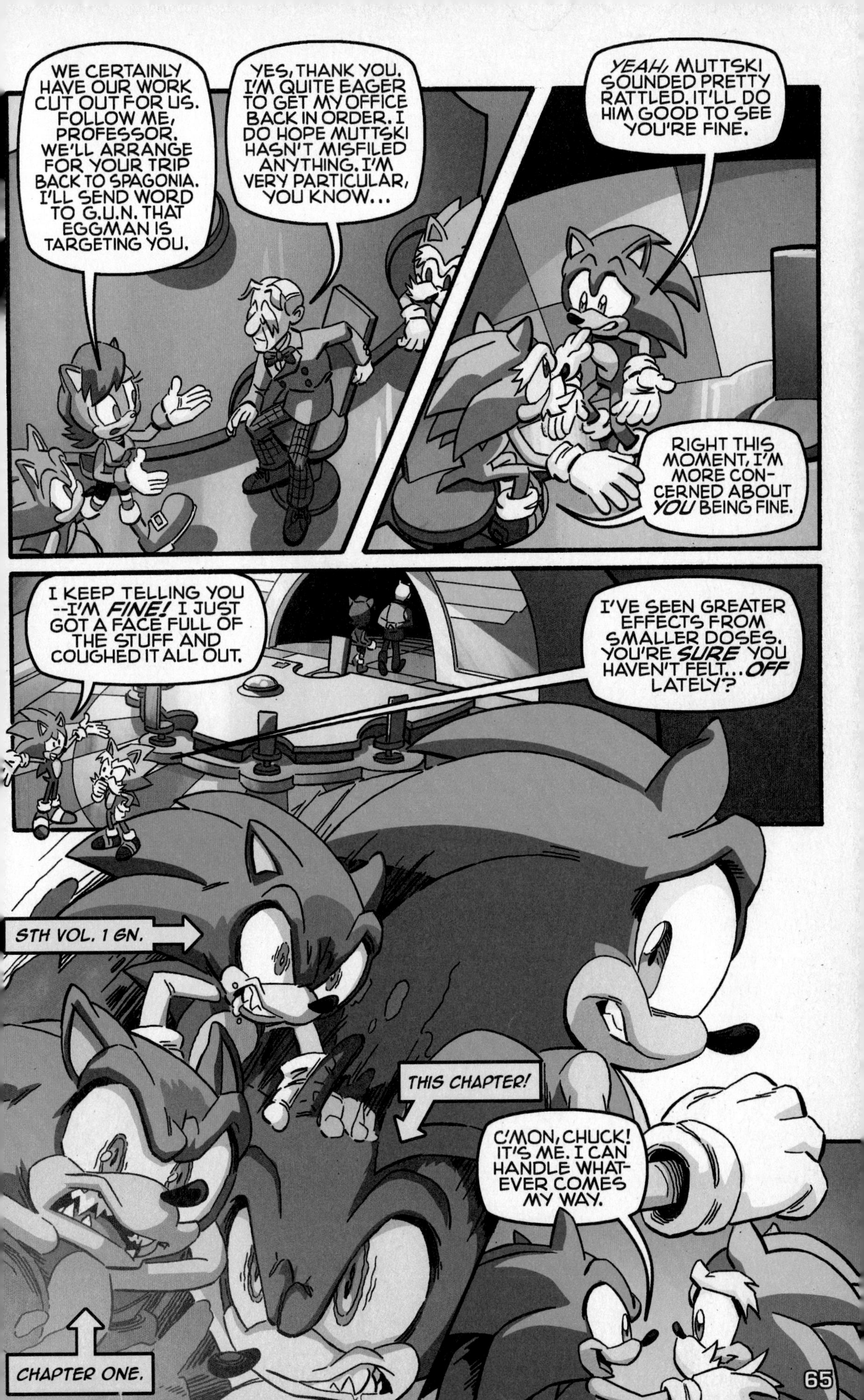
WE CERTAINLY HAVE OUR WORK CUT OUT FOR US. FOLLOW ME, PROFESSOR. WE'LL ARRANGE FOR YOUR TRIP BACK TO SPAGONIA. I'LL SEND WORD TO G.U.N. THAT EGGMAN IS TARGETING YOU.
YES, THANK YOU. I'M QUITE EAGER TO GET MY OFFICE BACK IN ORDER. I DO HOPE MUTTSKI HASN'T MISFILED ANYTHING. I'M VERY PARTICULAR, YOU KNOW...
YEAH, MUTTSKI SOUNDED PRETTY RATTLED. IT'LL DO HIM GOOD TO SEE YOU'RE FINE.
RIGHT THIS MOMENT, I'M MORE CON-CERNED ABOUT YOU BEING FINE.
I KEEP TELLING YOU --I'M FINE! I JUST GOT A FACE FULL OF THE STUFF AND COUGHED IT ALL OUT.
I'VE SEEN GREATER EFFECTS FROM SMALLER DOSES. YOU'RE SURE YOU HAVEN'T FELT...OFF LATELY?
STH VOL. 1 GN.
THIS CHAPTER!
C'MON, CHUCK! IT'S ME. I CAN HANDLE WHAT-EVER COMES MY WAY.
CHAPTER ONE.

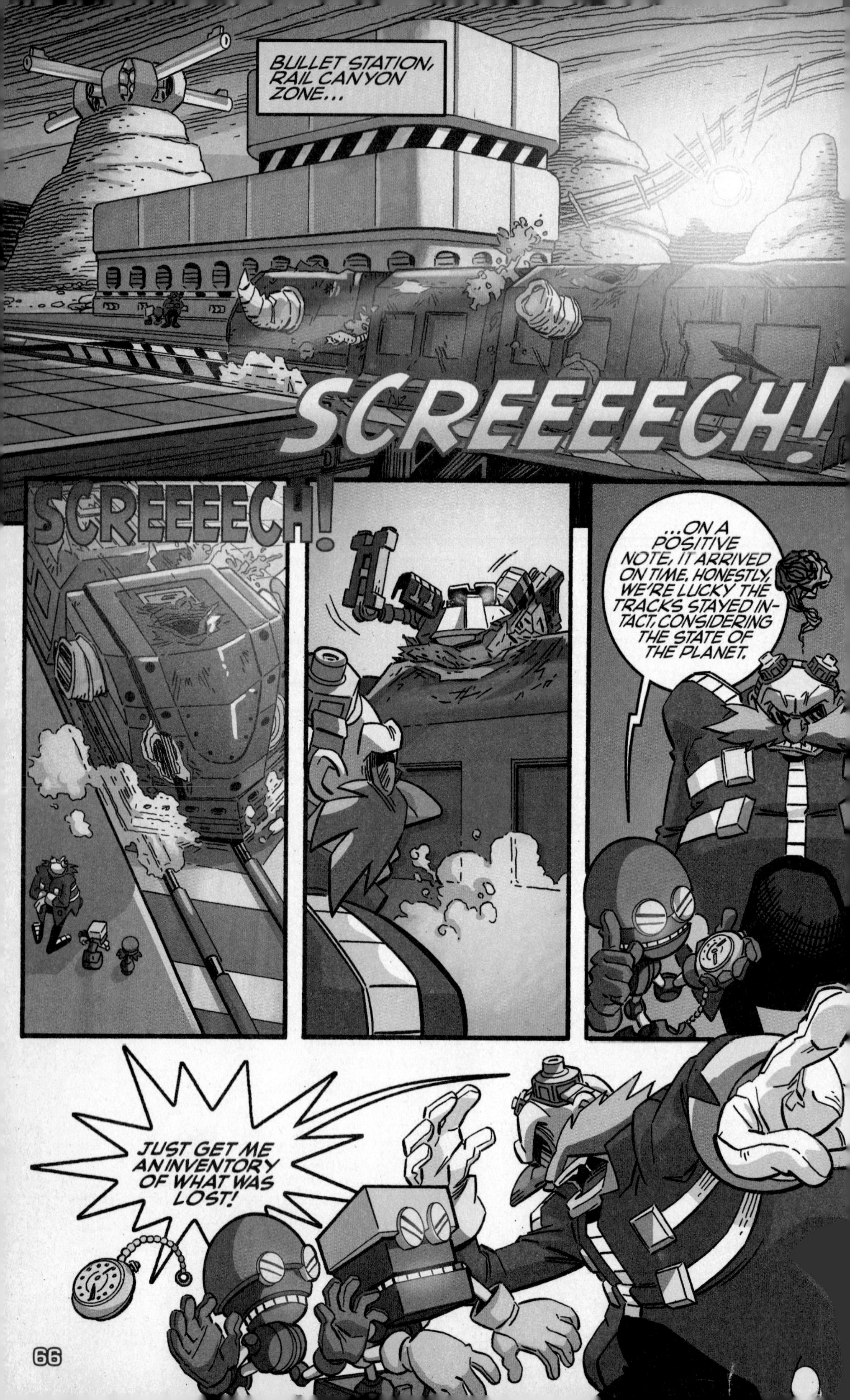
BULLET STATION, RAIL CANYON ZONE...
SCREEEEECH!
SCREEEEECH!
...ON A POSITIVE NOTE, IT ARRIVED ON TIME. HONESTLY, WE'RE LUCKY THE TRACKS STAYED INTACT, CONSIDERING THE STATE OF THE PLANET.
JUST GET ME AN INVENTORY OF WHAT WAS LOST!

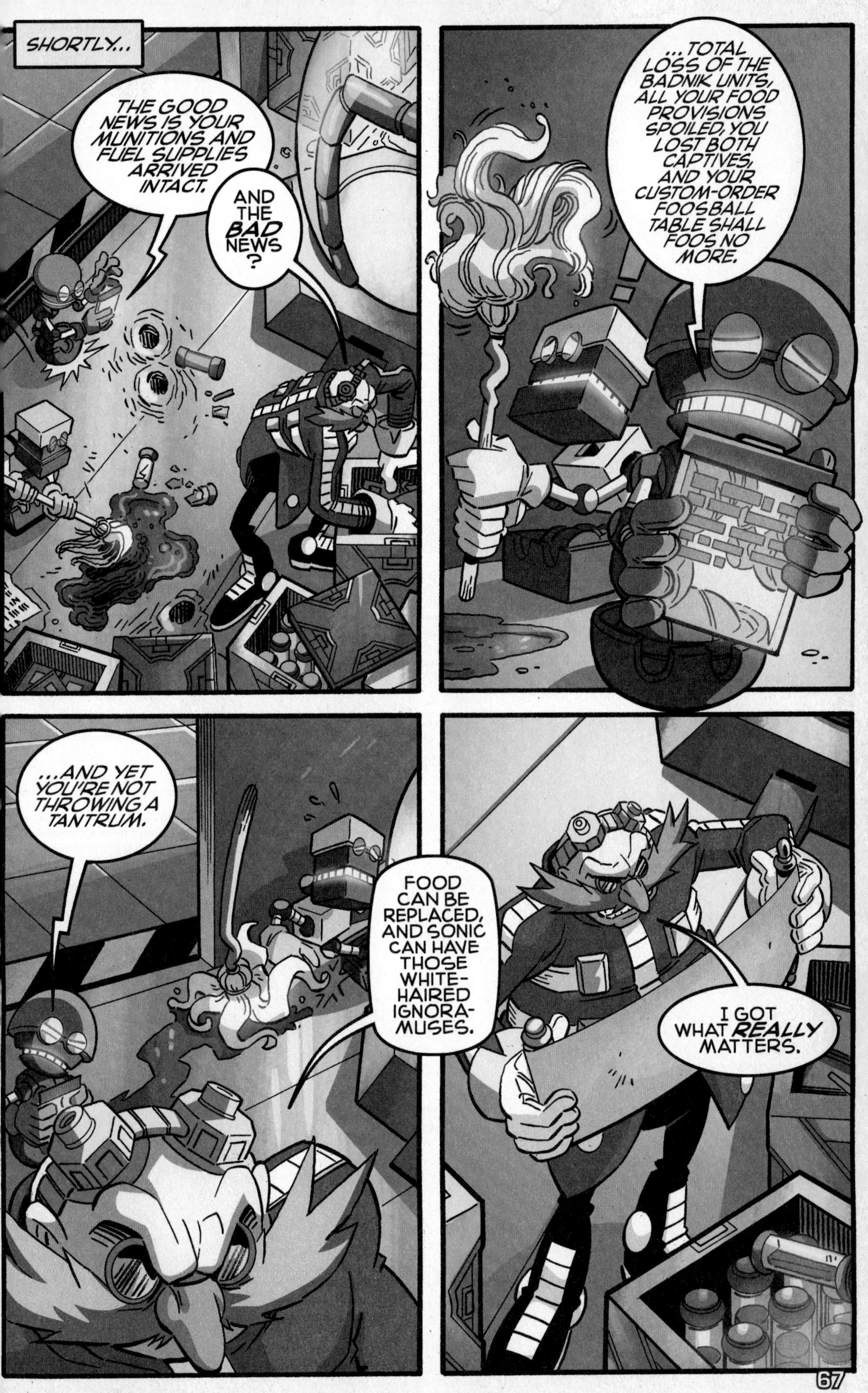
SHORTLY...
THE GOOD NEWS IS YOUR MUNITIONS AND FUEL SUPPLIES ARRIVED INTACT.
AND THE BAD NEWS?
...TOTAL LOSS OF THE BADNIK UNITS, ALL YOUR FOOD PROVISIONS SPOILED, YOU LOST BOTH CAPTIVES, AND YOUR CUSTOM-ORDER FOOSBALL TABLE SHALL FOOS NO MORE.
...AND YET YOU'RE NOT THROWING A TANTRUM.
FOOD CAN BE REPLACED, AND SONIC CAN HAVE THOSE WHITE-HAIRED IGNORA-MUSES.
I GOT WHAT REALLY MATTERS.

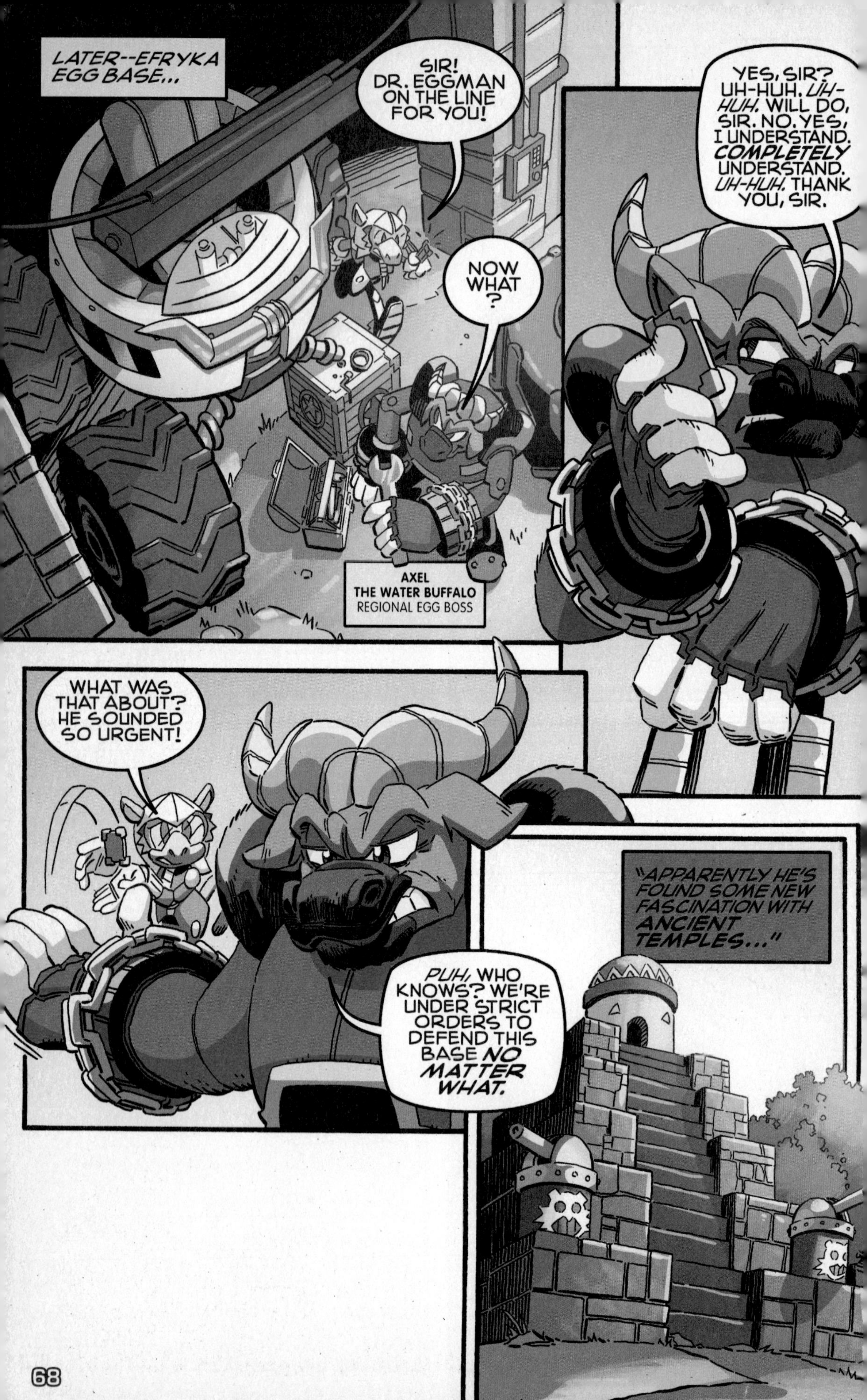
LATER--EFRYKA EGG BASE...
SIR! DR. EGGMAN ON THE LINE FOR YOU!
NOW WHAT?
AXEL THE WATER BUFFALO
REGIONAL EGG BOSS
YES, SIR? UH-HUH. UH-HUH. WILL DO, SIR. NO. YES, I UNDERSTAND. COMPLETELY UNDERSTAND. UH-HUH. THANK YOU, SIR.
WHAT WAS THAT ABOUT? HE SOUNDED SO URGENT!
PUH, WHO KNOWS? WE'RE UNDER STRICT ORDERS TO DEFEND THIS BASE NO MATTER WHAT.
"APPARENTLY HE'S FOUND SOME NEW FASCINATION WITH ANCIENT TEMPLES..."

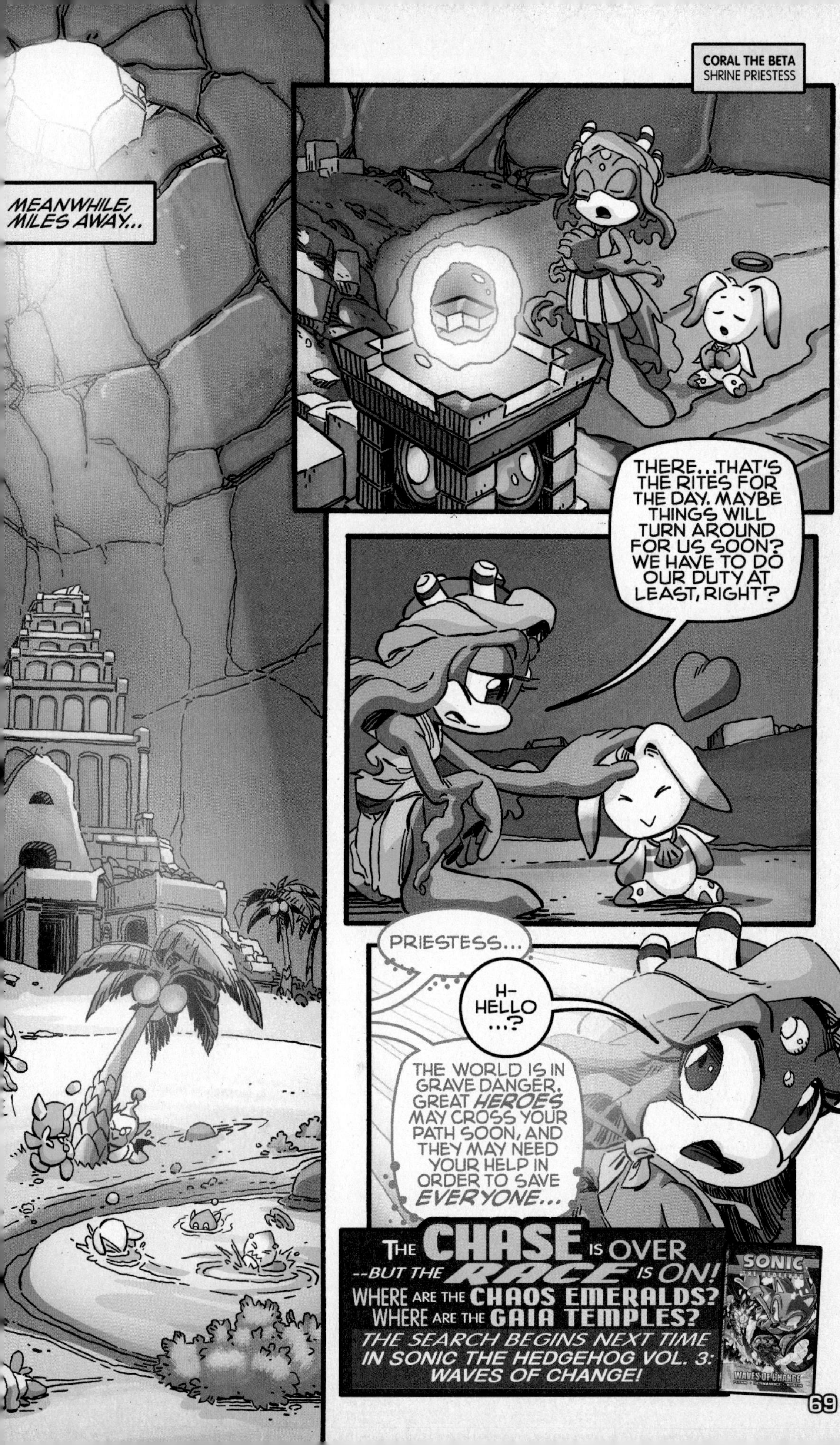
MEANWHILE, MILES AWAY...
CORAL THE BETA
SHRINE PRIESTESS
THERE...THAT'S THE RITES FOR THE DAY. MAYBE THINGS WILL TURN AROUND FOR US SOON? WE HAVE TO DO OUR DUTY AT LEAST, RIGHT?
PRIESTESS...
H- HELLO ...?
THE WORLD IS IN GRAVE DANGER. GREAT HEROES MAY CROSS YOUR PATH SOON, AND THEY MAY NEED YOUR HELP IN ORDER TO SAVE EVERYONE...
THE CHASE IS OVER
--BUT THE RACE IS ON!
WHERE ARE THE CHAOS EMERALDS?
WHERE ARE THE GAIA TEMPLES?
THE SEARCH BEGINS NEXT TIME IN SONIC THE HEDGEHOG VOL. 3: WAVES OF CHANGE!
SONIC
WAVES OF CHANGE

CHAPTER 4

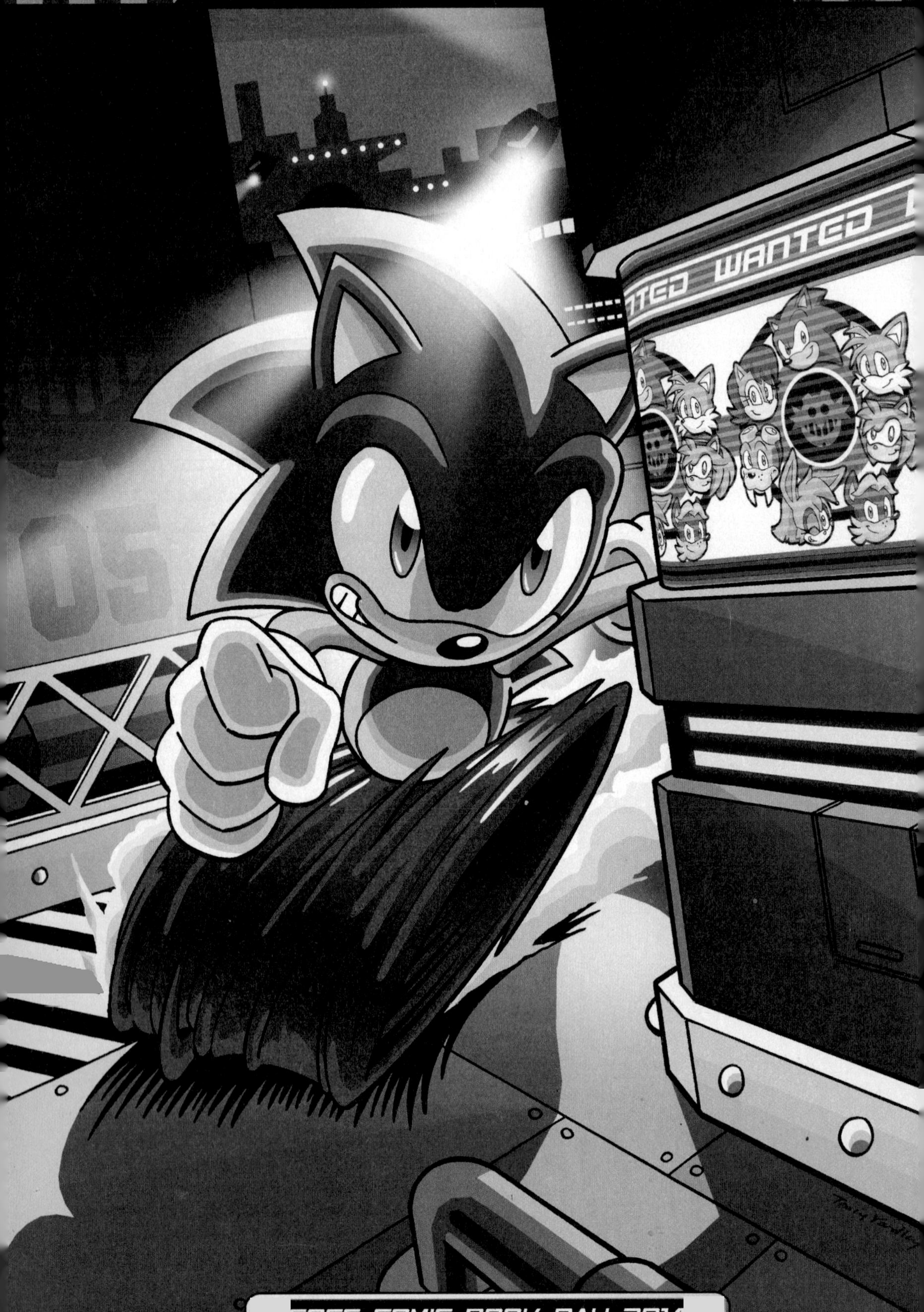
WANTED

FREE COMIC BOOK DAY 2014
COVER BY TRACY YARDLEY

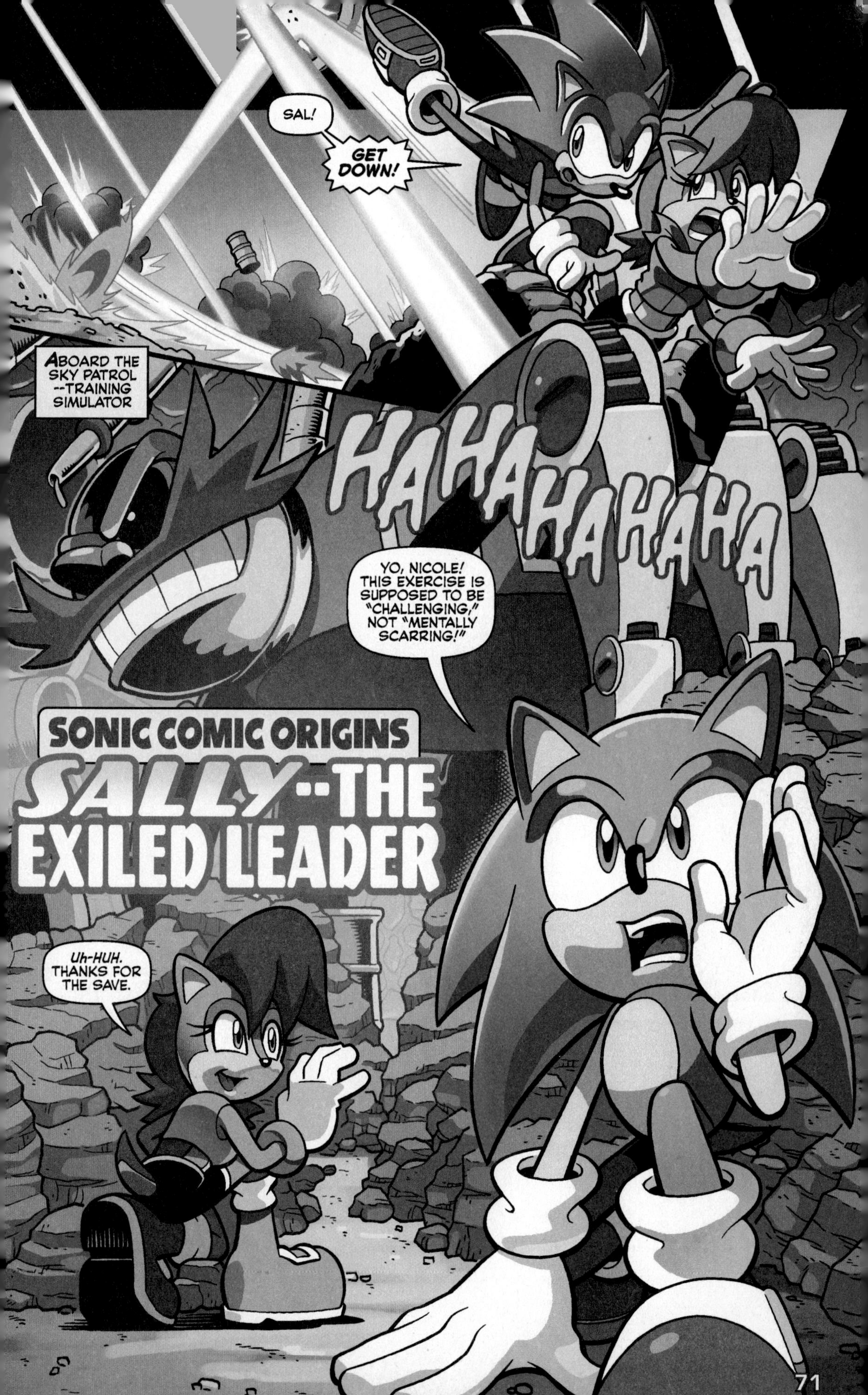

SAL!
GET DOWN!
ABOARD THE SKY PATROL --TRAINING SIMULATOR
HAHAHAHAHAHAHA
YO, NICOLE! THIS EXERCISE IS SUPPOSED TO BE "CHALLENGING," NOT "MENTALLY SCARRING!"
SONIC COMIC ORIGINS
SALLY--THE EXILED LEADER
Uh-HUH. THANKS FOR THE SAVE.

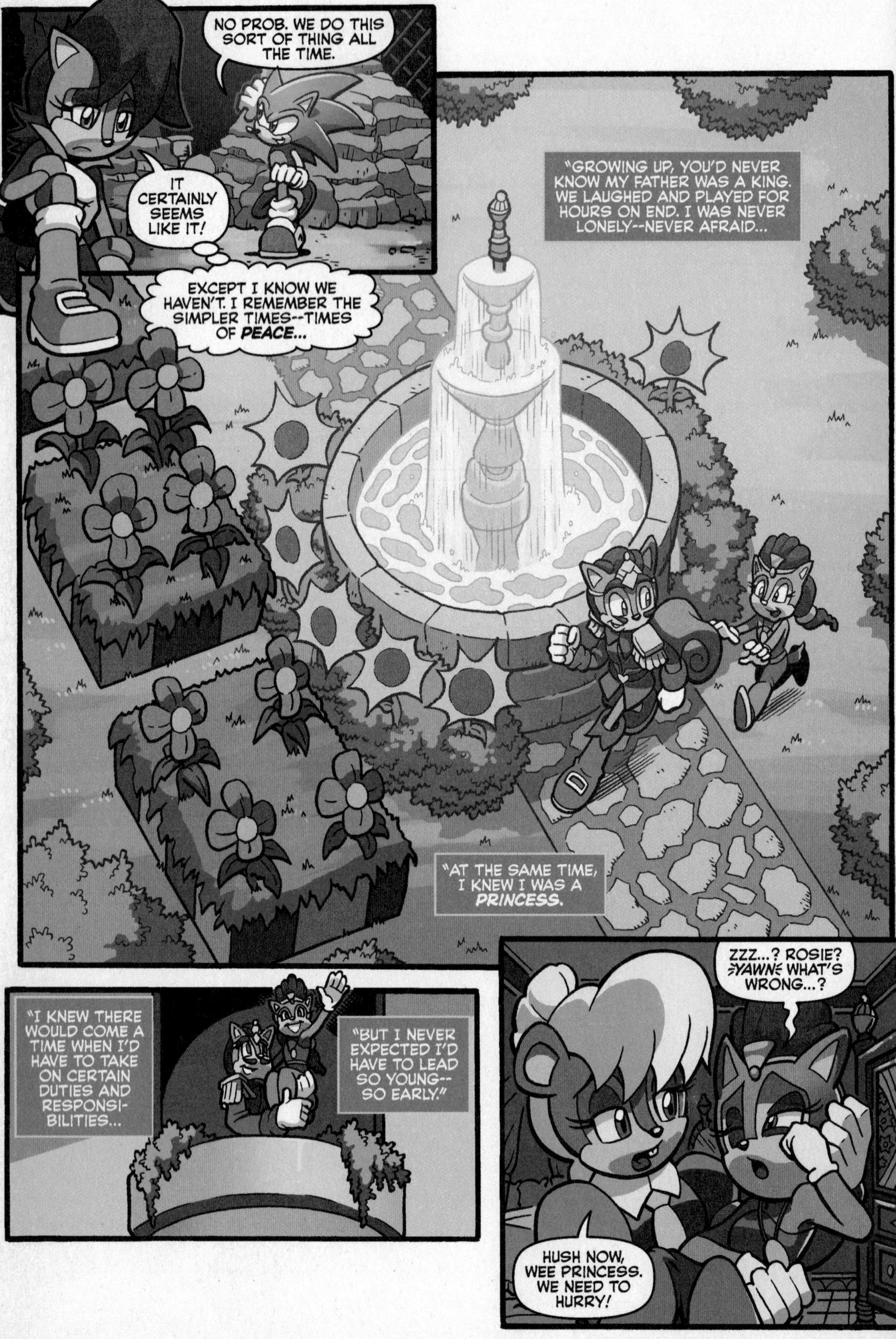
NO PROB. WE DO THIS SORT OF THING ALL THE TIME.
IT CERTAINLY SEEMS LIKE IT!
EXCEPT I KNOW WE HAVEN'T. I REMEMBER THE SIMPLER TIMES--TIMES OF PEACE...
"GROWING UP, YOU'D NEVER KNOW MY FATHER WAS A KING. WE LAUGHED AND PLAYED FOR HOURS ON END. I WAS NEVER LONELY--NEVER AFRAID...
"AT THE SAME TIME, I KNEW I WAS A PRINCESS.
"I KNEW THERE WOULD COME A TIME WHEN I'D HAVE TO TAKE ON CERTAIN DUTIES AND RESPONSIBILITIES...
"BUT I NEVER EXPECTED I'D HAVE TO LEAD SO YOUNG-- SO EARLY."
ZZZ...? ROSIE? ≶YAWN≶ WHAT'S WRONG...?
HUSH NOW, WEE PRINCESS. WE NEED TO HURRY!

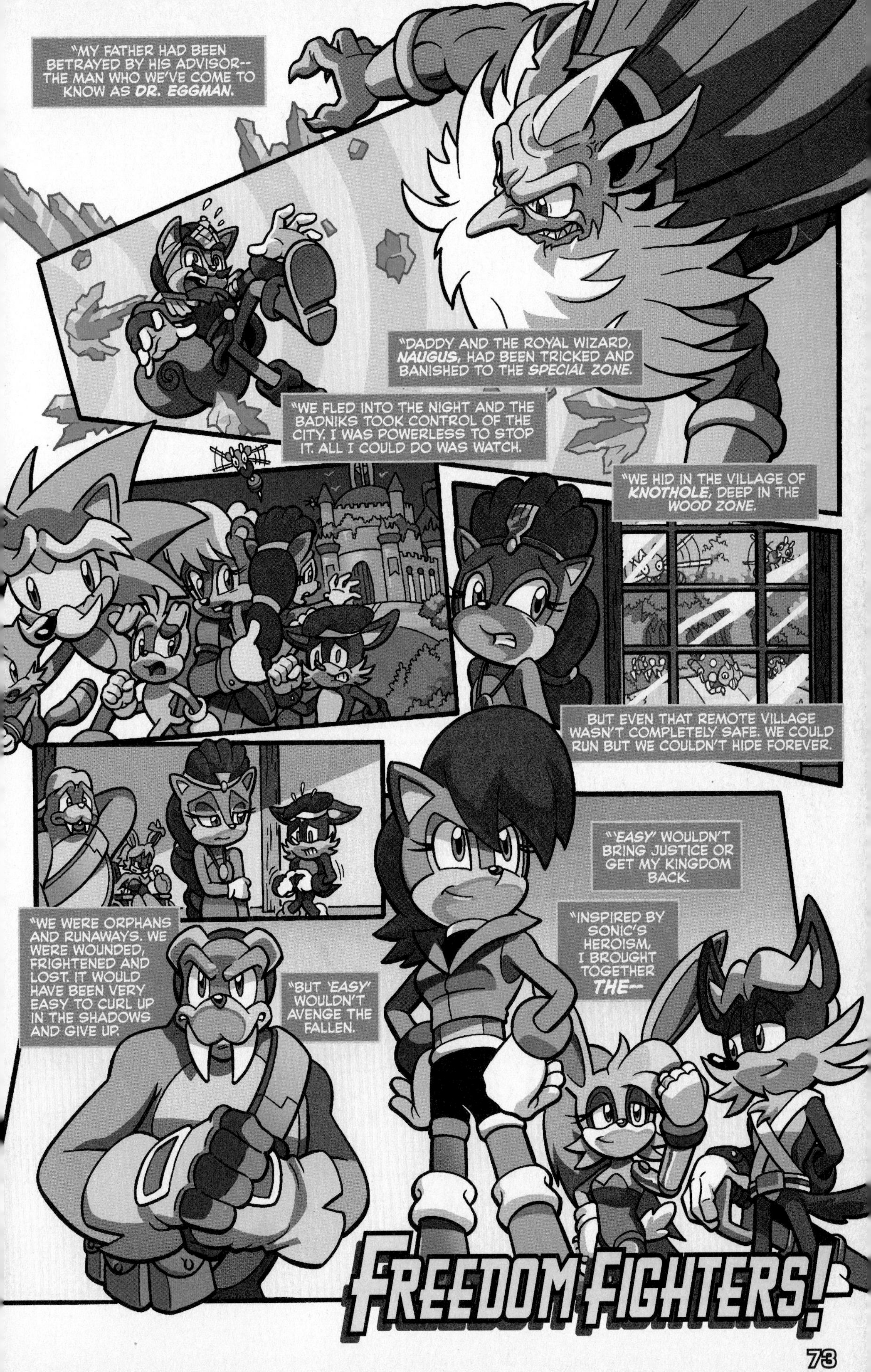

"MY FATHER HAD BEEN BETRAYED BY HIS ADVISOR-- THE MAN WHO WE'VE COME TO KNOW AS DR. EGGMAN.
"DADDY AND THE ROYAL WIZARD, NAUGUS, HAD BEEN TRICKED AND BANISHED TO THE SPECIAL ZONE.
"WE FLED INTO THE NIGHT AND THE BADNIKS TOOK CONTROL OF THE CITY. I WAS POWERLESS TO STOP IT. ALL I COULD DO WAS WATCH.
"WE HID IN THE VILLAGE OF KNOTHOLE, DEEP IN THE WOOD ZONE.
BUT EVEN THAT REMOTE VILLAGE WASN'T COMPLETELY SAFE. WE COULD RUN BUT WE COULDN'T HIDE FOREVER.
"WE WERE ORPHANS AND RUNAWAYS. WE WERE WOUNDED, FRIGHTENED AND LOST. IT WOULD HAVE BEEN VERY EASY TO CURL UP IN THE SHADOWS AND GIVE UP.
"BUT 'EASY' WOULDN'T AVENGE THE FALLEN.
"'EASY' WOULDN'T BRING JUSTICE OR GET MY KINGDOM BACK.
"INSPIRED BY SONIC'S HEROISM, I BROUGHT TOGETHER THE--
FREEDOM FIGHTERS!

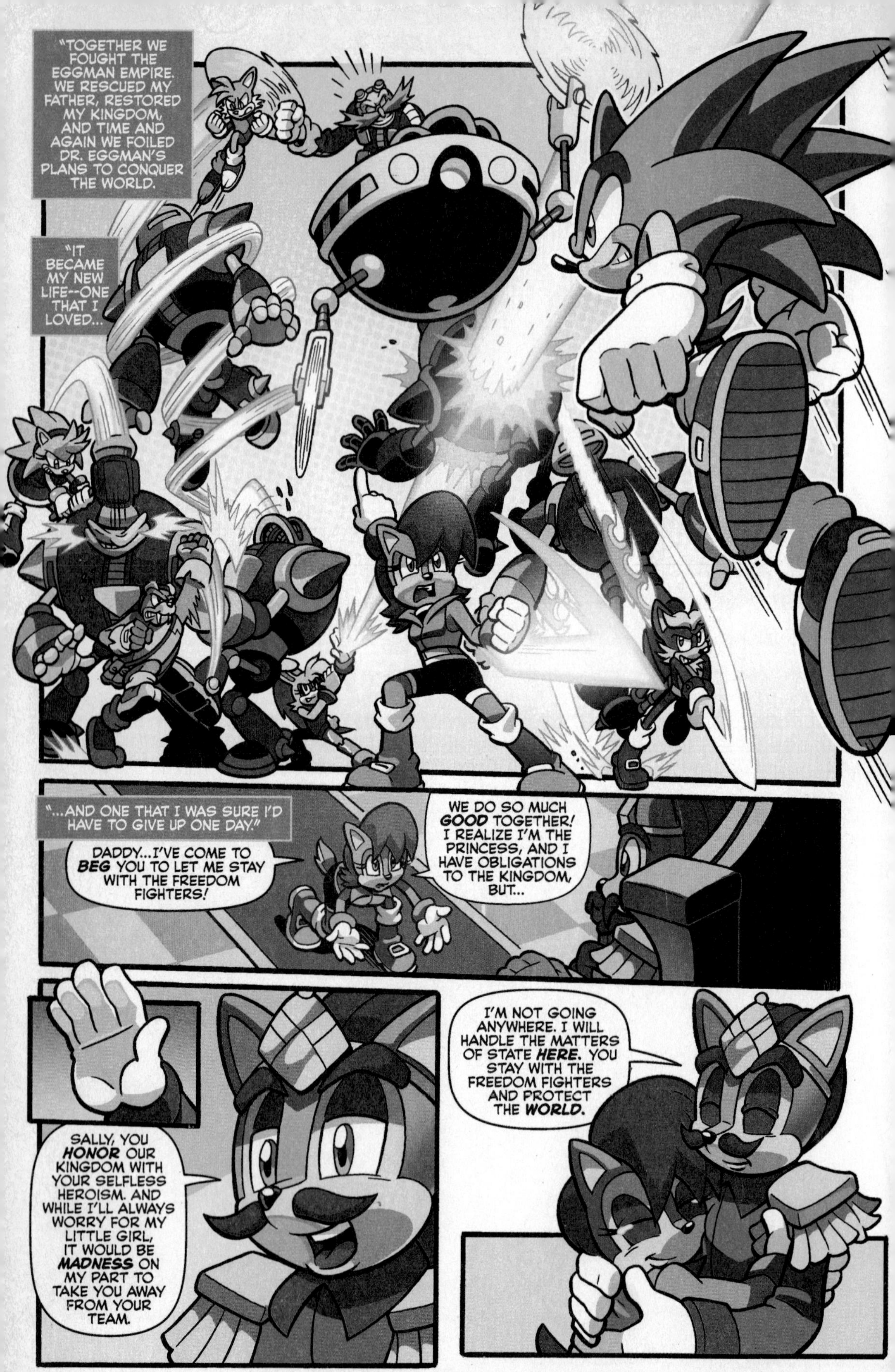
"TOGETHER WE FOUGHT THE EGGMAN EMPIRE. WE RESCUED MY FATHER, RESTORED MY KINGDOM, AND TIME AND AGAIN WE FOILED DR. EGGMAN'S PLANS TO CONQUER THE WORLD.
"IT BECAME MY NEW LIFE--ONE THAT I LOVED...
"...AND ONE THAT I WAS SURE I'D HAVE TO GIVE UP ONE DAY."
DADDY...I'VE COME TO BEG YOU TO LET ME STAY WITH THE FREEDOM FIGHTERS!
WE DO SO MUCH GOOD TOGETHER! I REALIZE I'M THE PRINCESS, AND I HAVE OBLIGATIONS TO THE KINGDOM, BUT...
SALLY, YOU HONOR OUR KINGDOM WITH YOUR SELFLESS HEROISM. AND WHILE I'LL ALWAYS WORRY FOR MY LITTLE GIRL, IT WOULD BE MADNESS ON MY PART TO TAKE YOU AWAY FROM YOUR TEAM.
I'M NOT GOING ANYWHERE. I WILL HANDLE THE MATTERS OF STATE HERE. YOU STAY WITH THE FREEDOM FIGHTERS AND PROTECT THE WORLD.

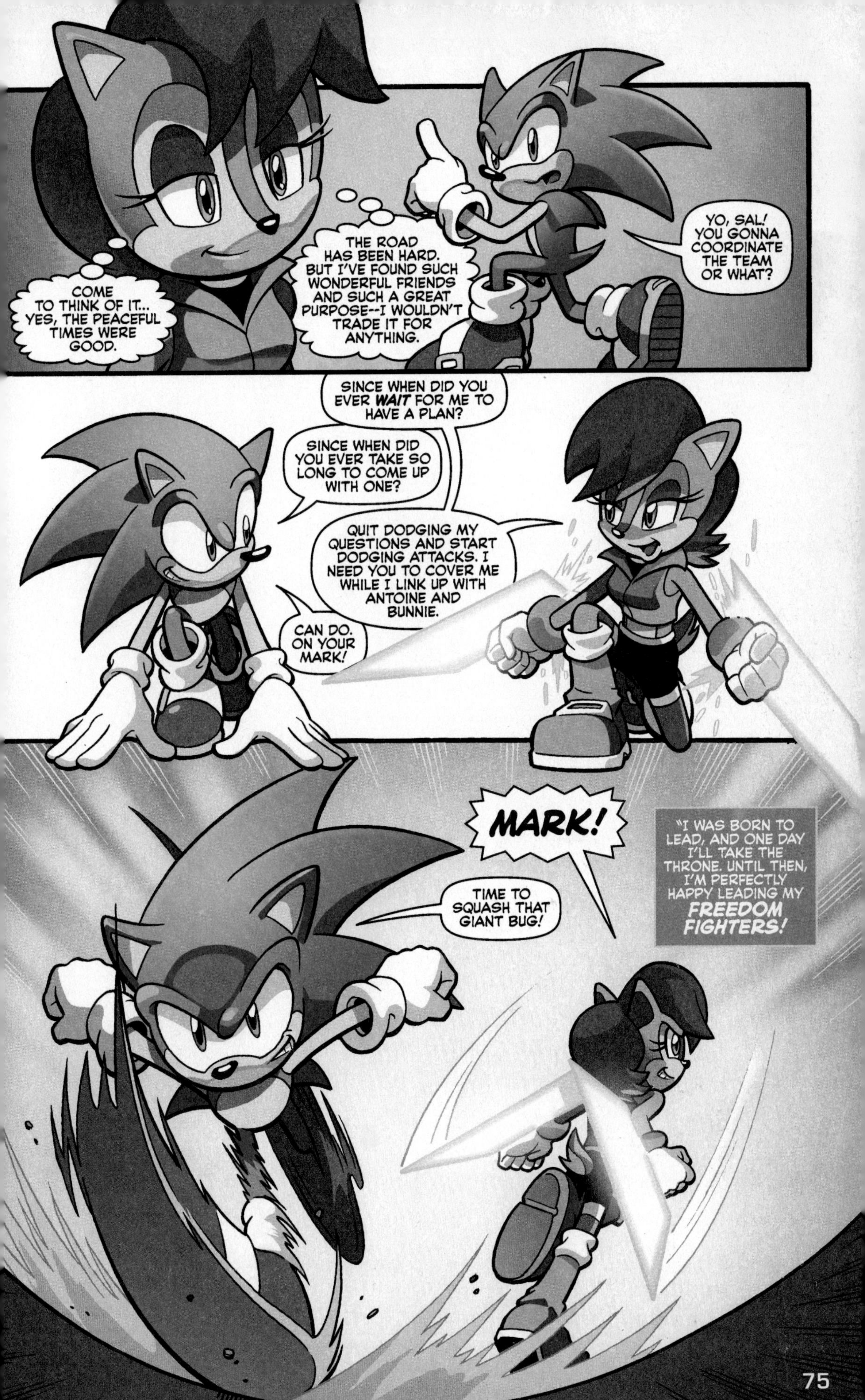
COME TO THINK OF IT... YES, THE PEACEFUL TIMES WERE GOOD.
THE ROAD HAS BEEN HARD. BUT I'VE FOUND SUCH WONDERFUL FRIENDS AND SUCH A GREAT PURPOSE--I WOULDN'T TRADE IT FOR ANYTHING.
YO, SAL! YOU GONNA COORDINATE THE TEAM OR WHAT?
SINCE WHEN DID YOU EVER WAIT FOR ME TO HAVE A PLAN?
SINCE WHEN DID YOU EVER TAKE SO LONG TO COME UP WITH ONE?
QUIT DODGING MY QUESTIONS AND START DODGING ATTACKS. I NEED YOU TO COVER ME WHILE I LINK UP WITH ANTOINE AND BUNNIE.
CAN DO. ON YOUR MARK!
MARK!
TIME TO SQUASH THAT GIANT BUG!
"I WAS BORN TO LEAD, AND ONE DAY I'LL TAKE THE THRONE. UNTIL THEN, I'M PERFECTLY HAPPY LEADING MY FREEDOM FIGHTERS!

CHAPTER 5

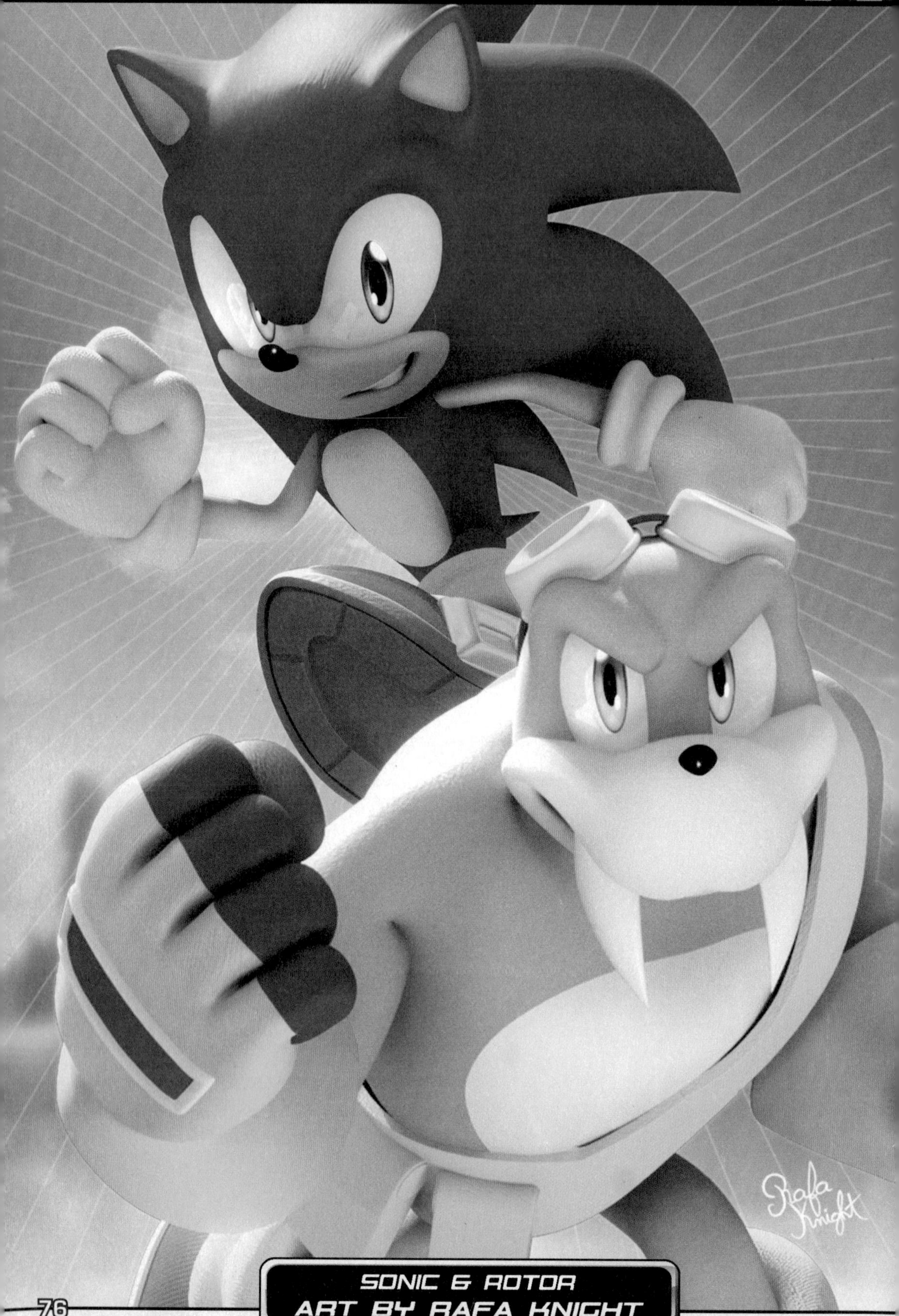
Rafa Knight

SONIC & ROTOR
ART BY RAFA KNIGHT

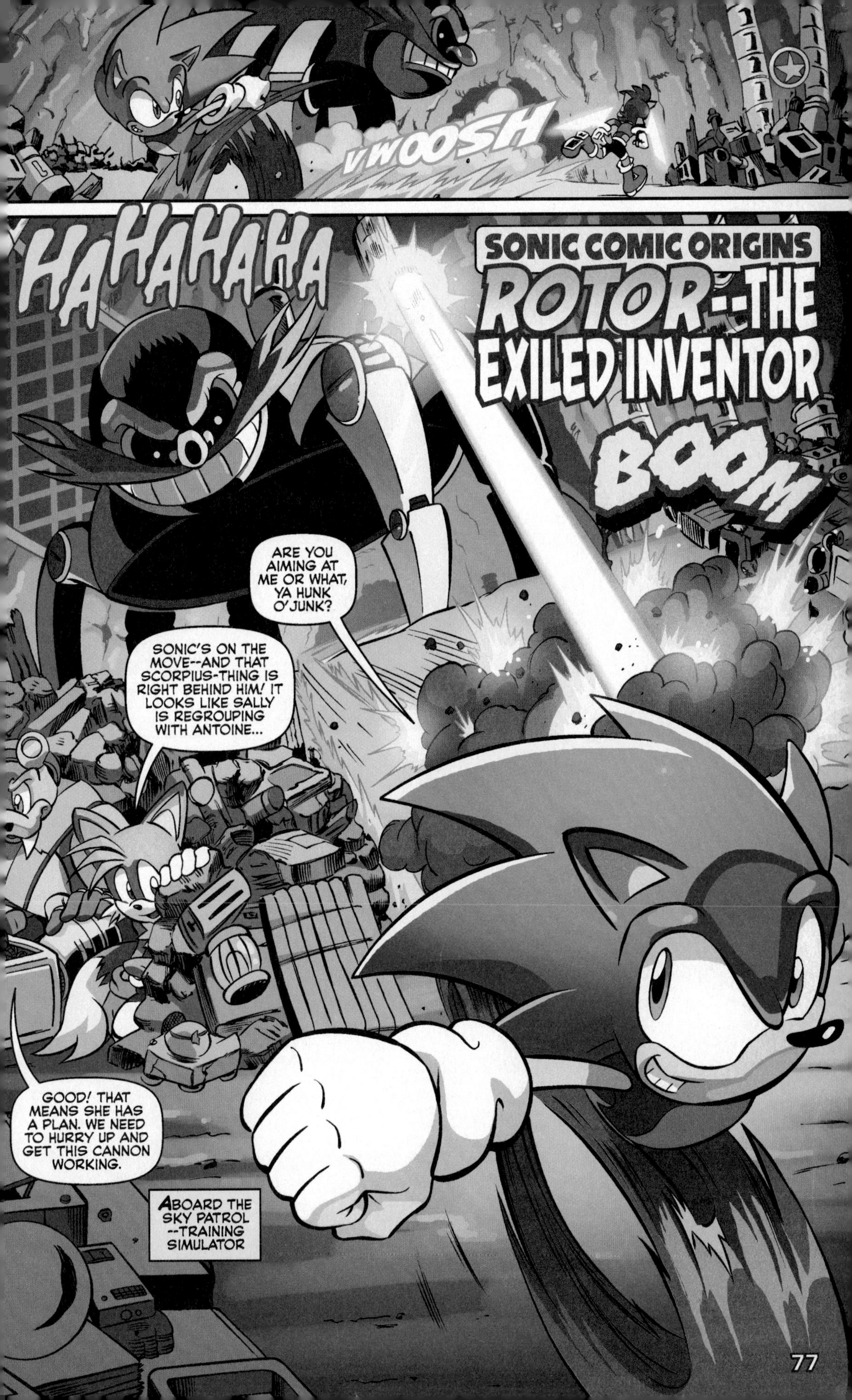
VWOOSH
HAHAHAHA
SONIC COMIC ORIGINS
ROTOR--THE EXILED INVENTOR
BOOM
ARE YOU AIMING AT ME OR WHAT, YA HUNK O' JUNK?
SONIC'S ON THE MOVE--AND THAT SCORPIUS-THING IS RIGHT BEHIND HIM! IT LOOKS LIKE SALLY IS REGROUPING WITH ANTOINE...
GOOD! THAT MEANS SHE HAS A PLAN. WE NEED TO HURRY UP AND GET THIS CANNON WORKING.
ABOARD THE SKY PATROL --TRAINING SIMULATOR

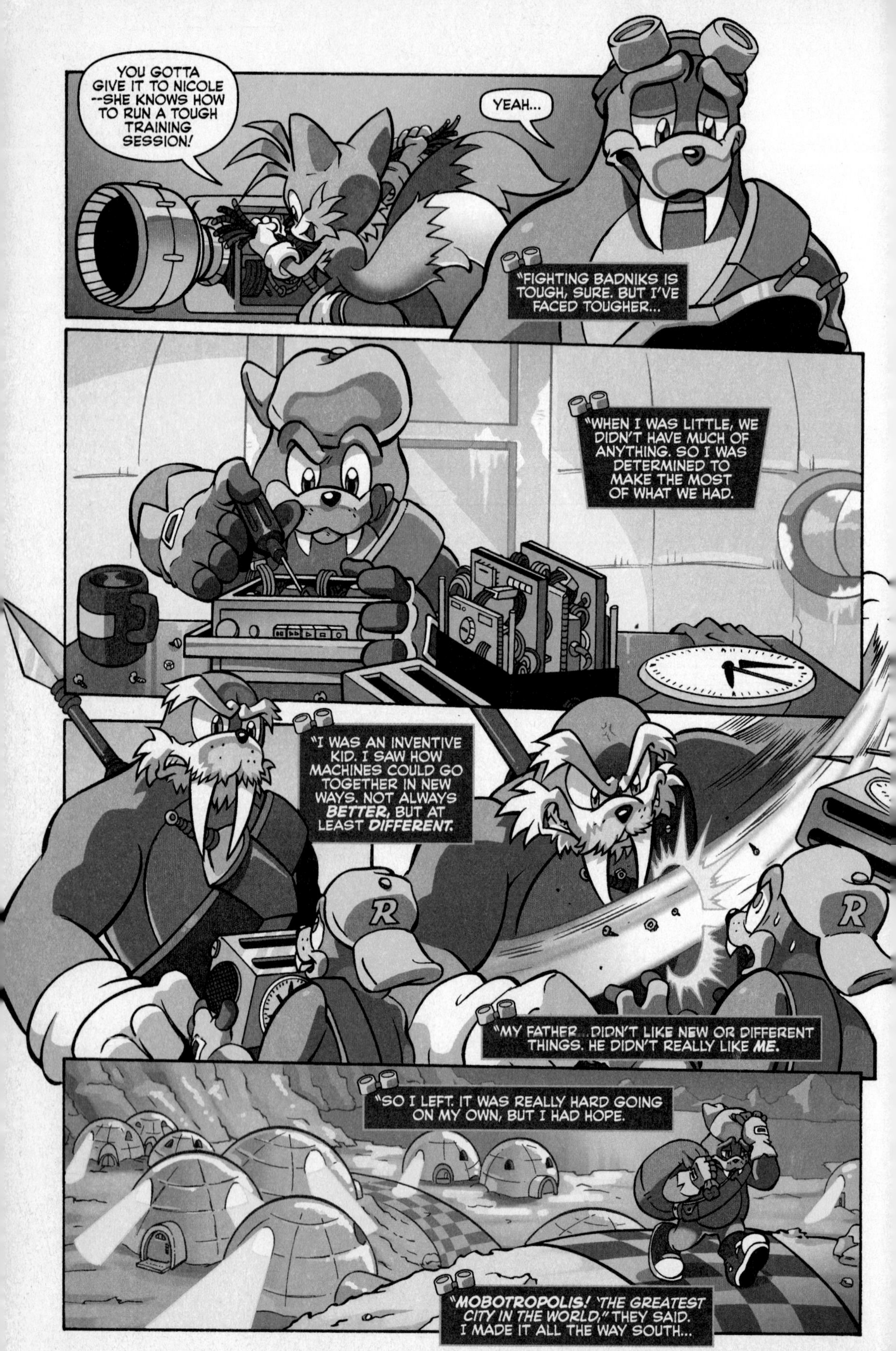
YOU GOTTA GIVE IT TO NICOLE --SHE KNOWS HOW TO RUN A TOUGH TRAINING SESSION!
YEAH...
"FIGHTING BADNIKS IS TOUGH, SURE. BUT I'VE FACED TOUGHER...
"WHEN I WAS LITTLE, WE DIDN'T HAVE MUCH OF ANYTHING. SO I WAS DETERMINED TO MAKE THE MOST OF WHAT WE HAD.
"I WAS AN INVENTIVE KID. I SAW HOW MACHINES COULD GO TOGETHER IN NEW WAYS. NOT ALWAYS BETTER, BUT AT LEAST DIFFERENT.
"MY FATHER...DIDN'T LIKE NEW OR DIFFERENT THINGS. HE DIDN'T REALLY LIKE ME.
"SO I LEFT. IT WAS REALLY HARD GOING ON MY OWN, BUT I HAD HOPE.
"MOBOTROPOLIS! 'THE GREATEST CITY IN THE WORLD,' THEY SAID. I MADE IT ALL THE WAY SOUTH...

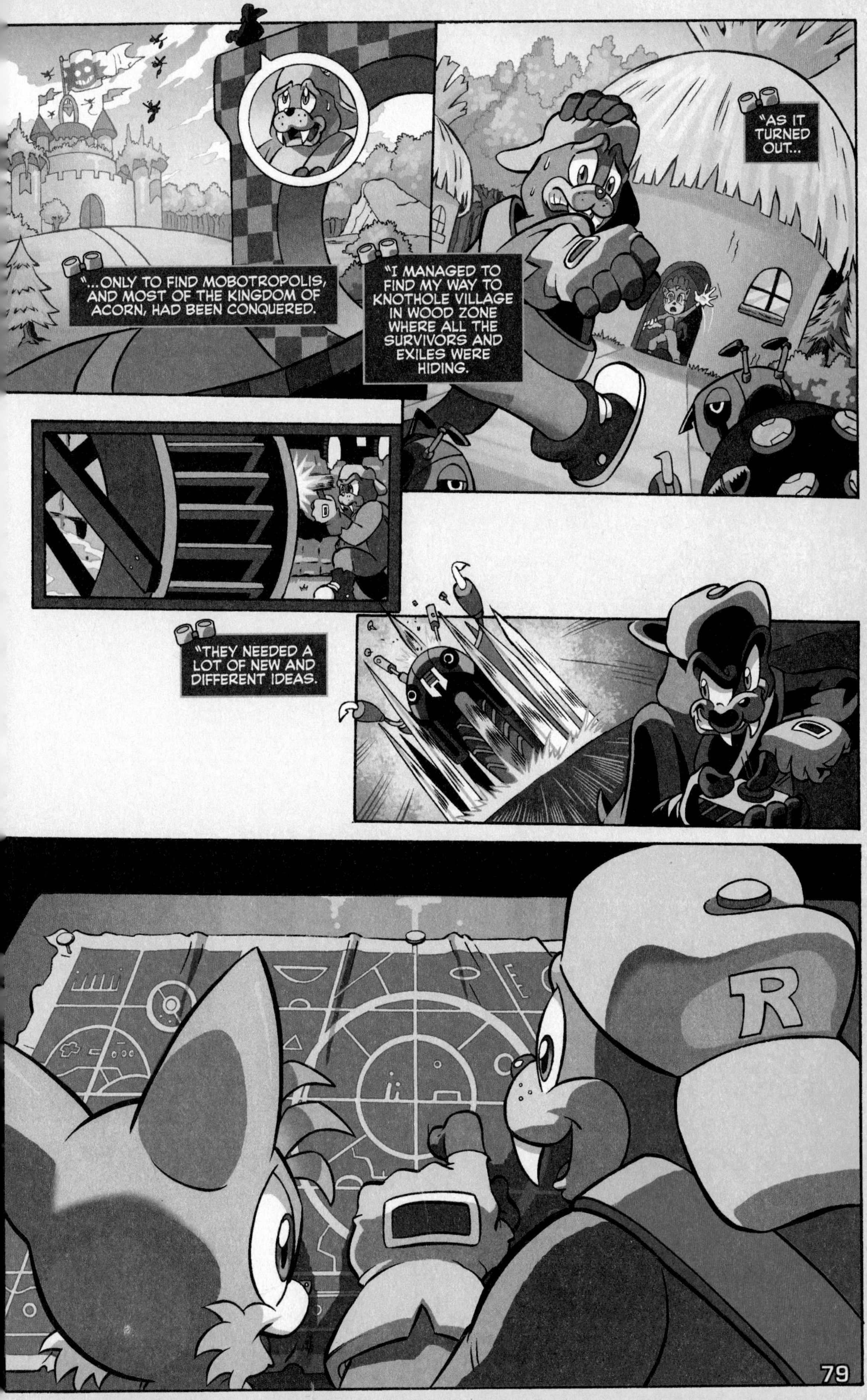
"...ONLY TO FIND MOBOTROPOLIS, AND MOST OF THE KINGDOM OF ACORN, HAD BEEN CONQUERED.
"I MANAGED TO FIND MY WAY TO KNOTHOLE VILLAGE IN WOOD ZONE WHERE ALL THE SURVIVORS AND EXILES WERE HIDING.
"AS IT TURNED OUT...
"THEY NEEDED A LOT OF NEW AND DIFFERENT IDEAS.
R

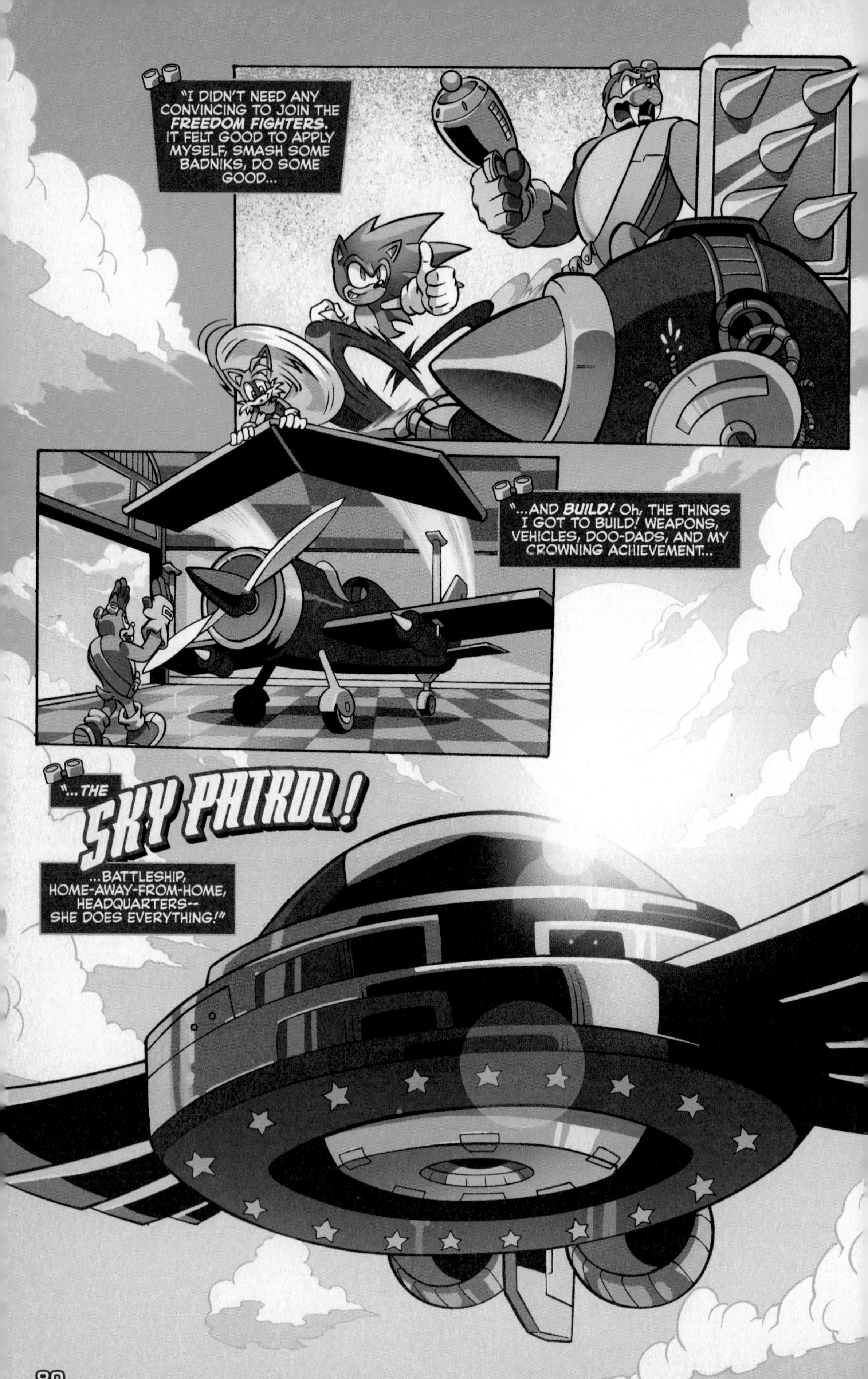
"I DIDN'T NEED ANY CONVINCING TO JOIN THE FREEDOM FIGHTERS. IT FELT GOOD TO APPLY MYSELF, SMASH SOME BADNIKS, DO SOME GOOD...
"...AND BUILD! Oh, THE THINGS I GOT TO BUILD! WEAPONS, VEHICLES, DOO-DADS, AND MY CROWNING ACHIEVEMENT...
"...THE SKY PATROL!
...BATTLESHIP, HOME-AWAY-FROM-HOME, HEADQUARTERS-- SHE DOES EVERYTHING!"

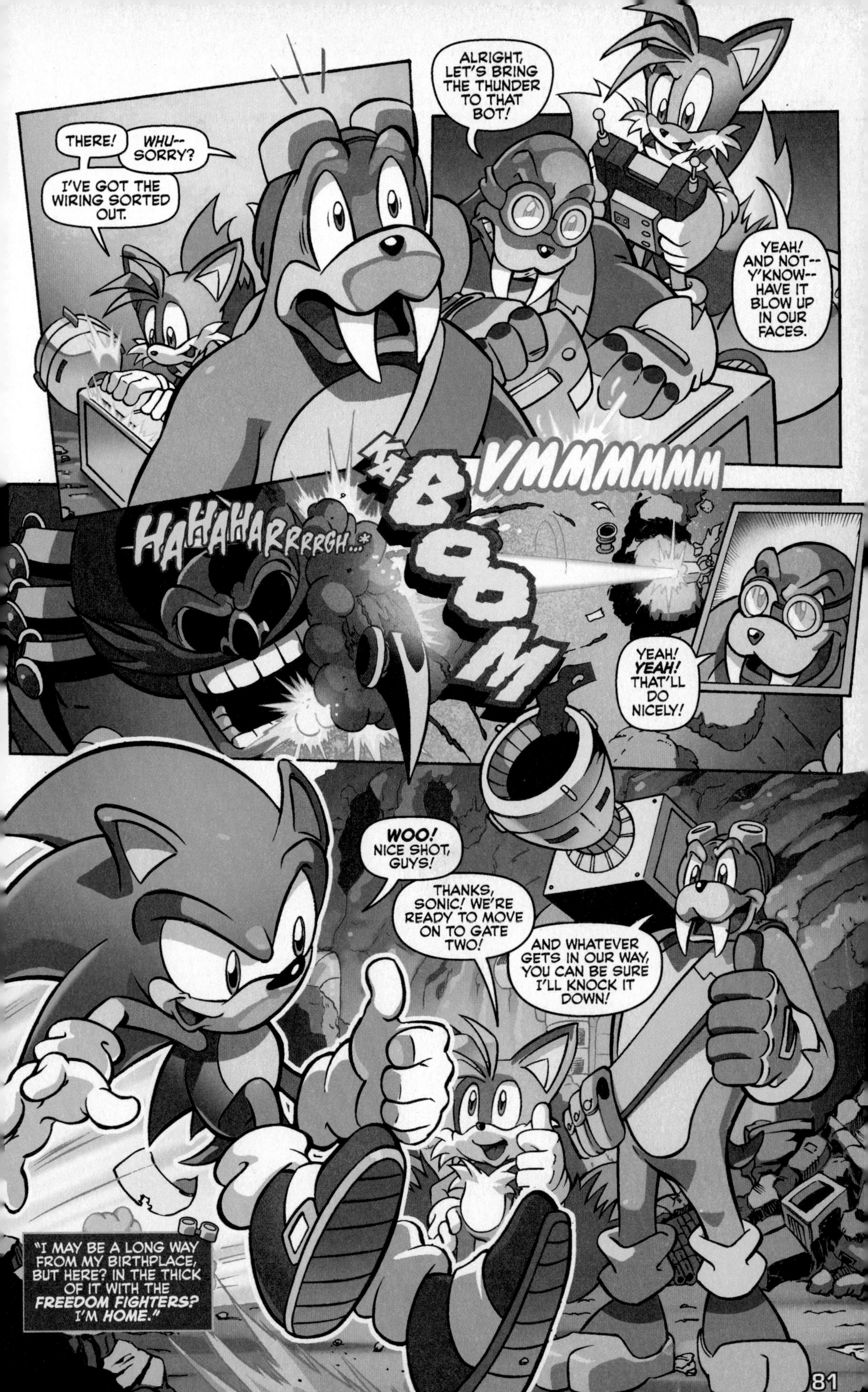
THERE!
WHU-- SORRY?
I'VE GOT THE WIRING SORTED OUT.
ALRIGHT, LET'S BRING THE THUNDER TO THAT BOT!
YEAH! AND NOT-- Y'KNOW-- HAVE IT BLOW UP IN OUR FACES.
VMMMMMMM
KA-BOOM
HAHAHARRRRGH...*
YEAH! YEAH! THAT'LL DO NICELY!
WOO! NICE SHOT, GUYS!
THANKS, SONIC! WE'RE READY TO MOVE ON TO GATE TWO!
AND WHATEVER GETS IN OUR WAY, YOU CAN BE SURE I'LL KNOCK IT DOWN!
"I MAY BE A LONG WAY FROM MY BIRTHPLACE, BUT HERE? IN THE THICK OF IT WITH THE FREEDOM FIGHTERS? I'M HOME."

CHAPTER 6

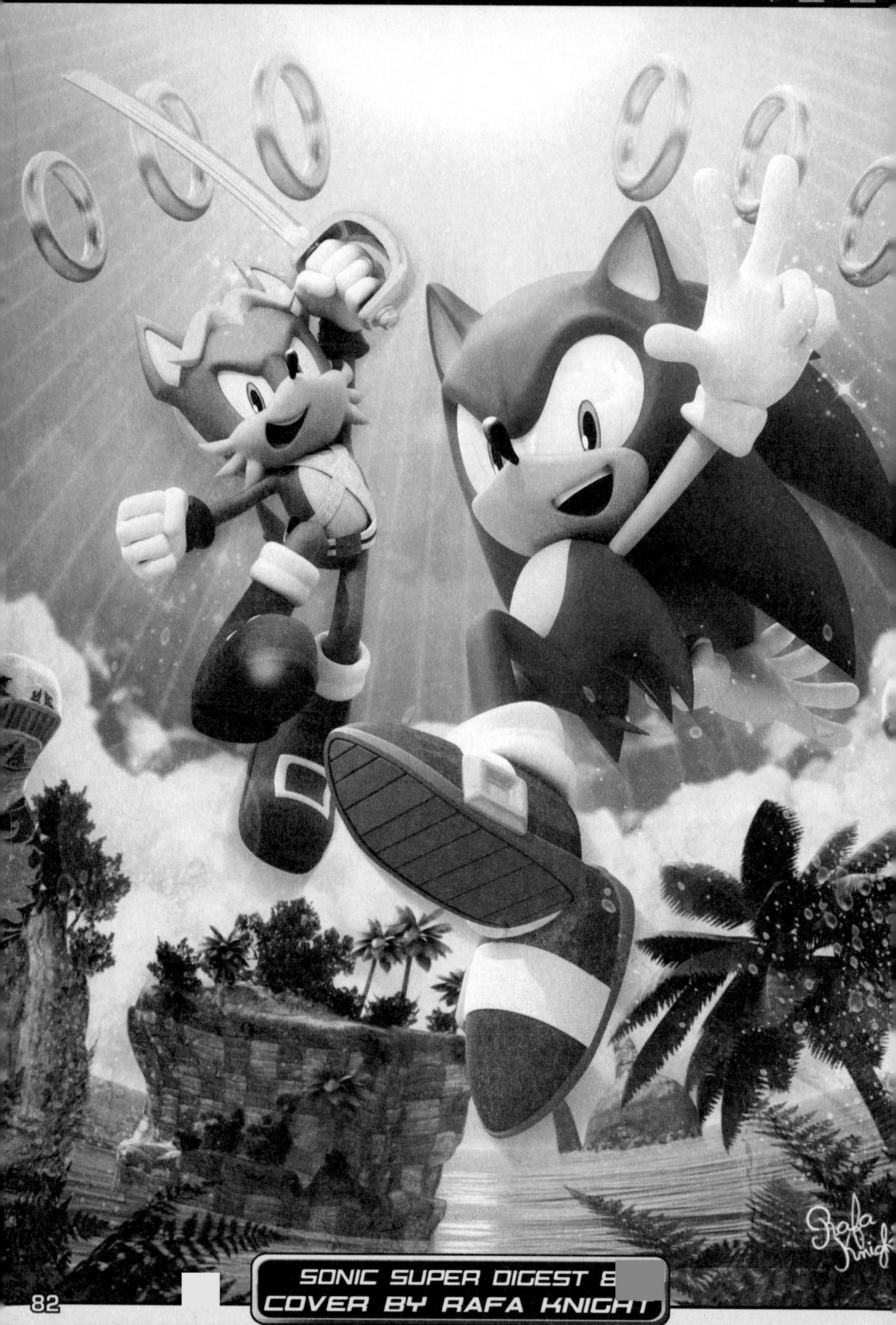
Rafa Knight

SONIC SUPER DIGEST
COVER BY RAFA KNIGHT

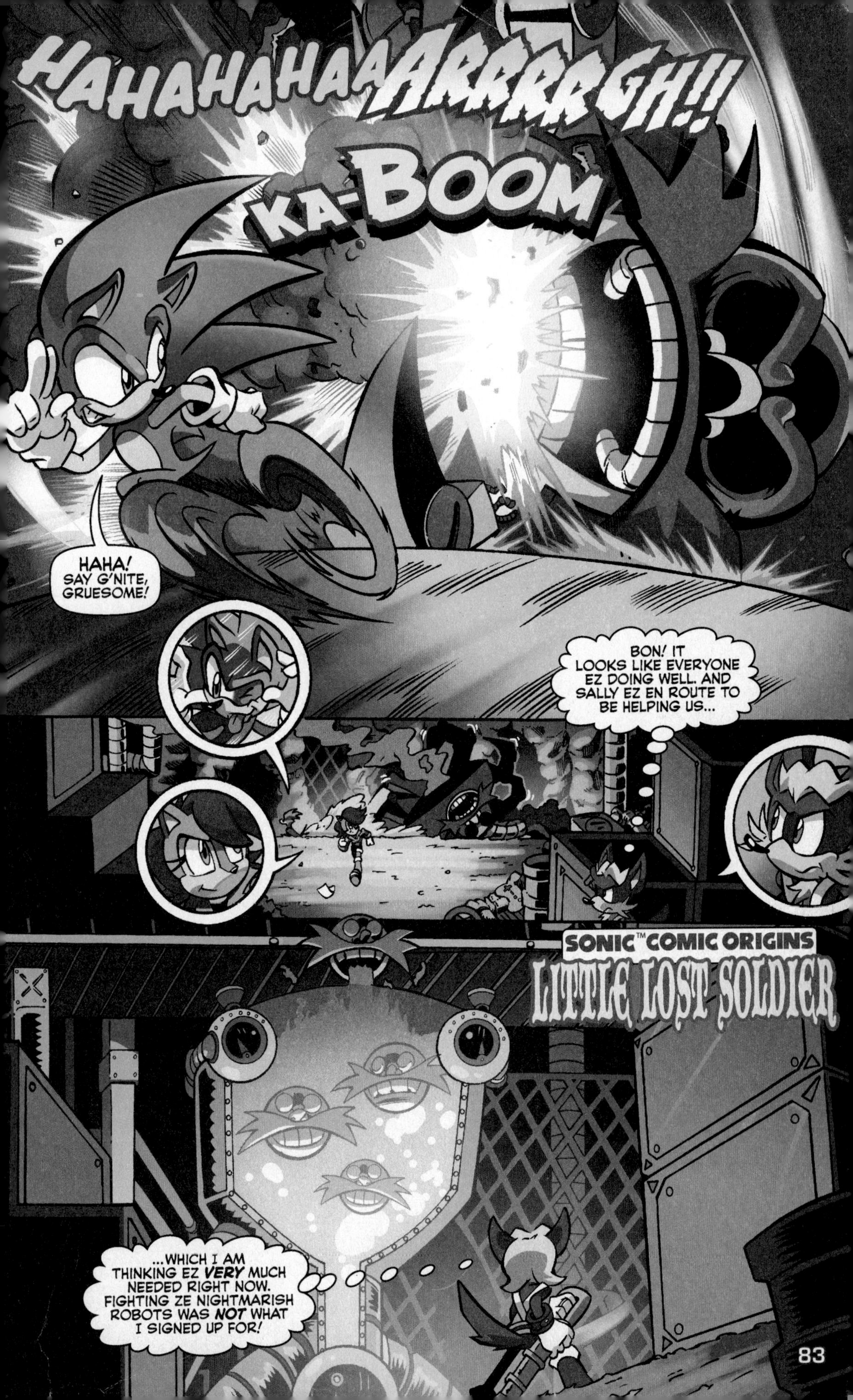
HAHAHAHAAARRRRRGH!!
KA-BOOM
HAHA! SAY G'NITE, GRUESOME!
BON! IT LOOKS LIKE EVERYONE EZ DOING WELL. AND SALLY EZ EN ROUTE TO BE HELPING US...
SONIC™ COMIC ORIGINS
LITTLE LOST SOLDIER
...WHICH I AM THINKING EZ VERY MUCH NEEDED RIGHT NOW. FIGHTING ZE NIGHTMARISH ROBOTS WAS NOT WHAT I SIGNED UP FOR!

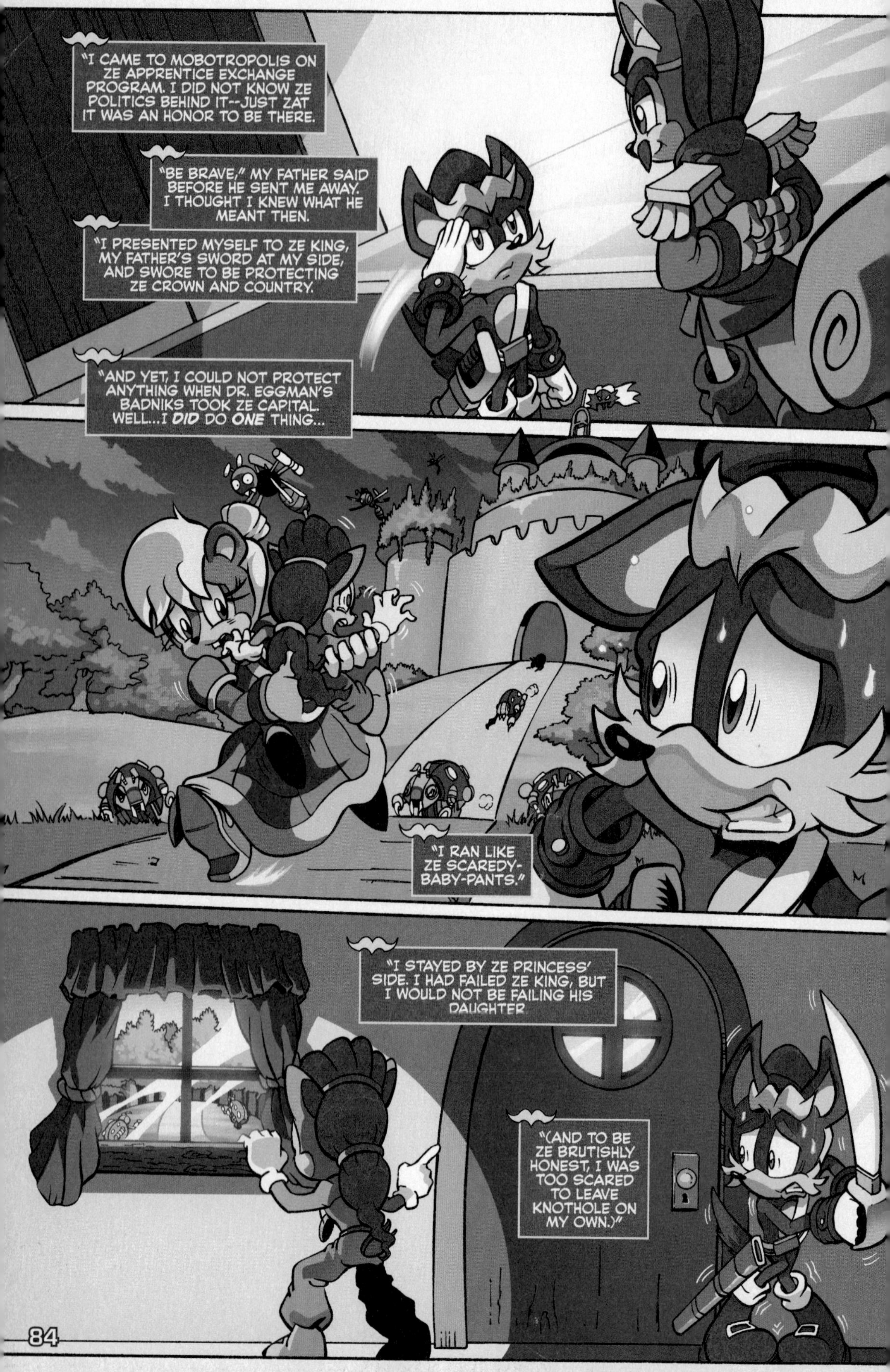
"I CAME TO MOBOTROPOLIS ON ZE APPRENTICE EXCHANGE PROGRAM. I DID NOT KNOW ZE POLITICS BEHIND IT--JUST ZAT IT WAS AN HONOR TO BE THERE.
"BE BRAVE," MY FATHER SAID BEFORE HE SENT ME AWAY. I THOUGHT I KNEW WHAT HE MEANT THEN.
"I PRESENTED MYSELF TO ZE KING, MY FATHER'S SWORD AT MY SIDE, AND SWORE TO BE PROTECTING ZE CROWN AND COUNTRY.
"AND YET, I COULD NOT PROTECT ANYTHING WHEN DR. EGGMAN'S BADNIKS TOOK ZE CAPITAL. WELL...I *DID* DO *ONE* THING...
"I RAN LIKE ZE SCAREDY-BABY-PANTS."
"I STAYED BY ZE PRINCESS' SIDE. I HAD FAILED ZE KING, BUT I WOULD NOT BE FAILING HIS DAUGHTER.
"(AND TO BE ZE BRUTISHLY HONEST, I WAS TOO SCARED TO LEAVE KNOTHOLE ON MY OWN.)"

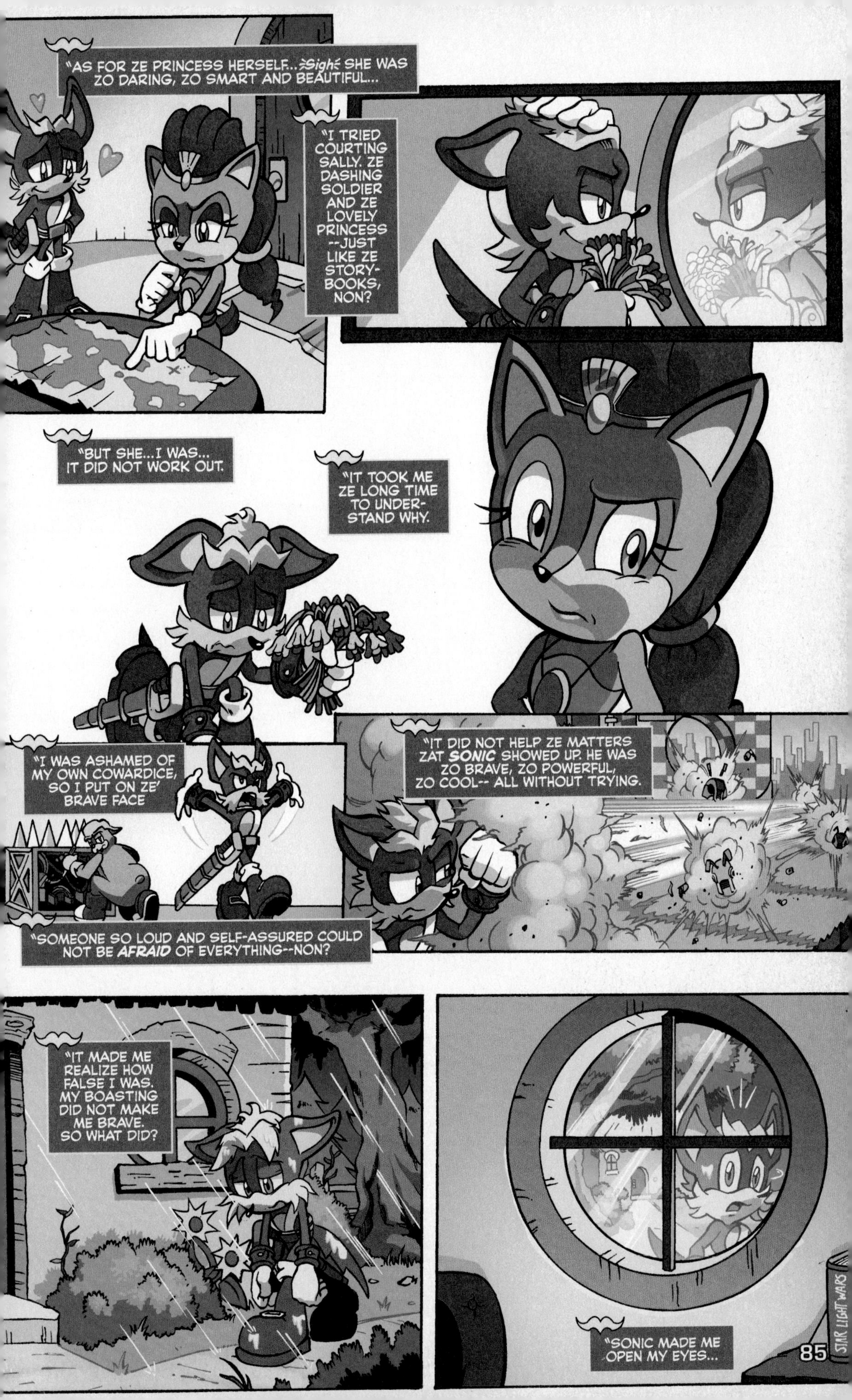
"AS FOR ZE PRINCESS HERSELF... *Sigh* SHE WAS ZO DARING, ZO SMART AND BEAUTIFUL...
"I TRIED COURTING SALLY. ZE DASHING SOLDIER AND ZE LOVELY PRINCESS --JUST LIKE ZE STORY-BOOKS, NON?
"BUT SHE...I WAS... IT DID NOT WORK OUT.
"IT TOOK ME ZE LONG TIME TO UNDER-STAND WHY.
"I WAS ASHAMED OF MY OWN COWARDICE, SO I PUT ON ZE' BRAVE FACE
"IT DID NOT HELP ZE MATTERS ZAT SONIC SHOWED UP. HE WAS ZO BRAVE, ZO POWERFUL, ZO COOL-- ALL WITHOUT TRYING.
"SOMEONE SO LOUD AND SELF-ASSURED COULD NOT BE AFRAID OF EVERYTHING--NON?
"IT MADE ME REALIZE HOW FALSE I WAS. MY BOASTING DID NOT MAKE ME BRAVE. SO WHAT DID?
"SONIC MADE ME OPEN MY EYES...
STAR LIGHT WARS

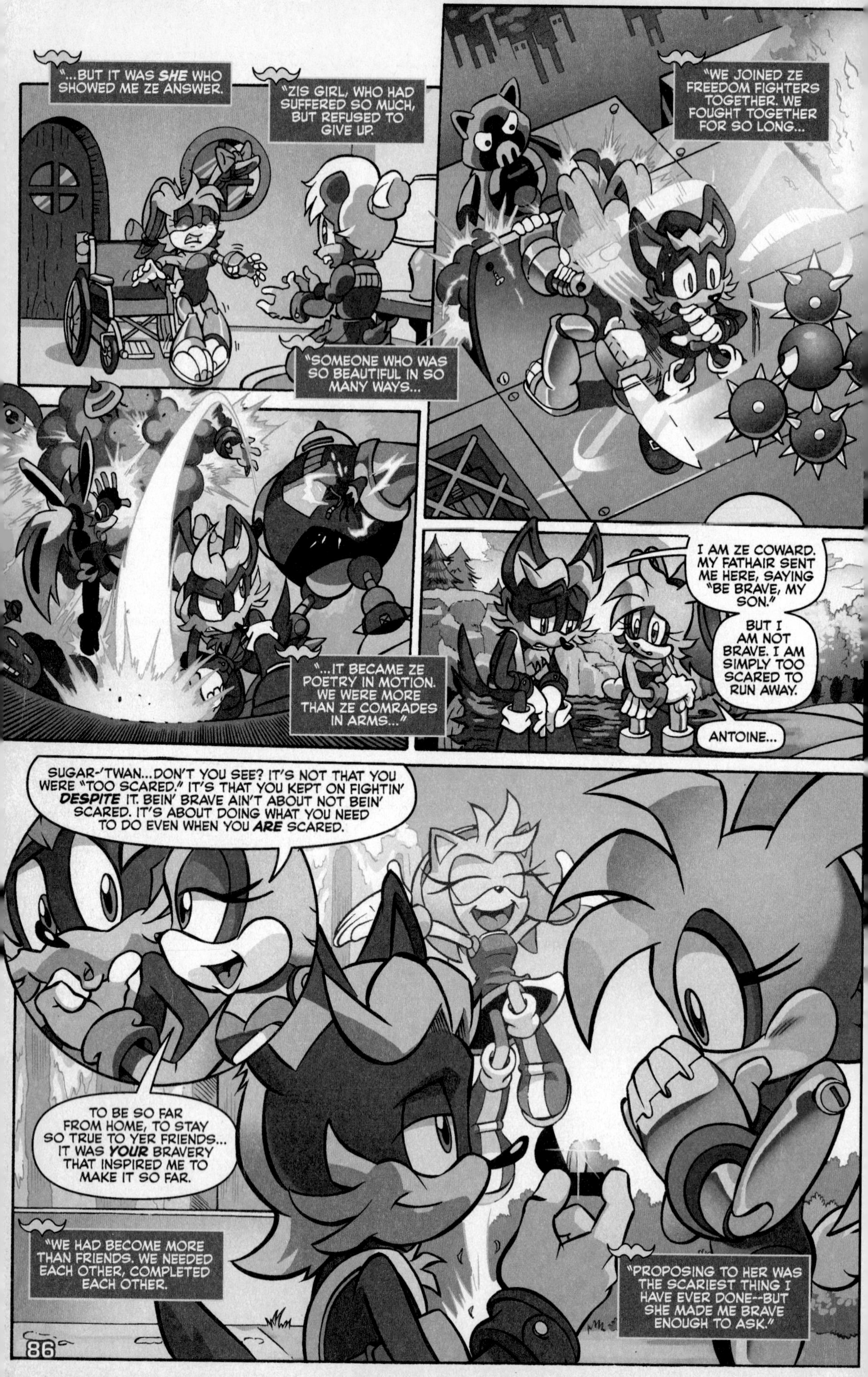
"...BUT IT WAS SHE WHO SHOWED ME ZE ANSWER.
"ZIS GIRL, WHO HAD SUFFERED SO MUCH, BUT REFUSED TO GIVE UP.
"SOMEONE WHO WAS SO BEAUTIFUL IN SO MANY WAYS...
"WE JOINED ZE FREEDOM FIGHTERS TOGETHER. WE FOUGHT TOGETHER FOR SO LONG...
"...IT BECAME ZE POETRY IN MOTION. WE WERE MORE THAN ZE COMRADES IN ARMS..."
I AM ZE COWARD. MY FATHAIR SENT ME HERE, SAYING "BE BRAVE, MY SON."
BUT I AM NOT BRAVE. I AM SIMPLY TOO SCARED TO RUN AWAY.
ANTOINE...
SUGAR-'TWAN...DON'T YOU SEE? IT'S NOT THAT YOU WERE "TOO SCARED." IT'S THAT YOU KEPT ON FIGHTIN' DESPITE IT. BEIN' BRAVE AIN'T ABOUT NOT BEIN' SCARED. IT'S ABOUT DOING WHAT YOU NEED TO DO EVEN WHEN YOU ARE SCARED.
TO BE SO FAR FROM HOME, TO STAY SO TRUE TO YER FRIENDS... IT WAS YOUR BRAVERY THAT INSPIRED ME TO MAKE IT SO FAR.
"WE HAD BECOME MORE THAN FRIENDS. WE NEEDED EACH OTHER, COMPLETED EACH OTHER.
"PROPOSING TO HER WAS THE SCARIEST THING I HAVE EVER DONE--BUT SHE MADE ME BRAVE ENOUGH TO ASK."

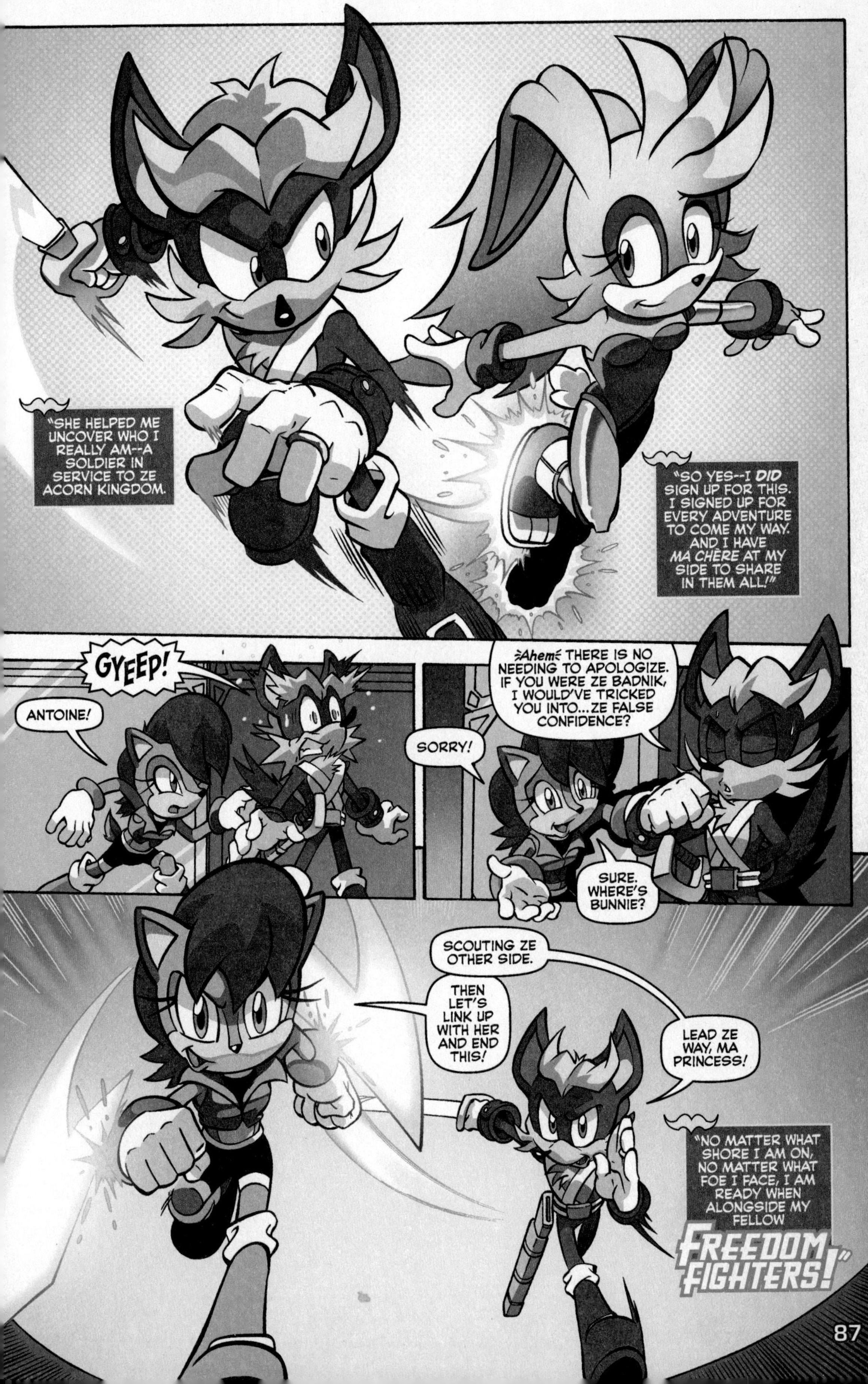
"SHE HELPED ME UNCOVER WHO I REALLY AM--A SOLDIER IN SERVICE TO ZE ACORN KINGDOM.
"SO YES--I DID SIGN UP FOR THIS. I SIGNED UP FOR EVERY ADVENTURE TO COME MY WAY. AND I HAVE MA CHÈRE AT MY SIDE TO SHARE IN THEM ALL!"
GYEEP!
ANTOINE!
SORRY!
Ahem THERE IS NO NEEDING TO APOLOGIZE. IF YOU WERE ZE BADNIK, I WOULD'VE TRICKED YOU INTO...ZE FALSE CONFIDENCE?
SURE. WHERE'S BUNNIE?
SCOUTING ZE OTHER SIDE.
THEN LET'S LINK UP WITH HER AND END THIS!
LEAD ZE WAY, MA PRINCESS!
"NO MATTER WHAT SHORE I AM ON, NO MATTER WHAT FOE I FACE, I AM READY WHEN ALONGSIDE MY FELLOW FREEDOM FIGHTERS!"

CHAPTER 7

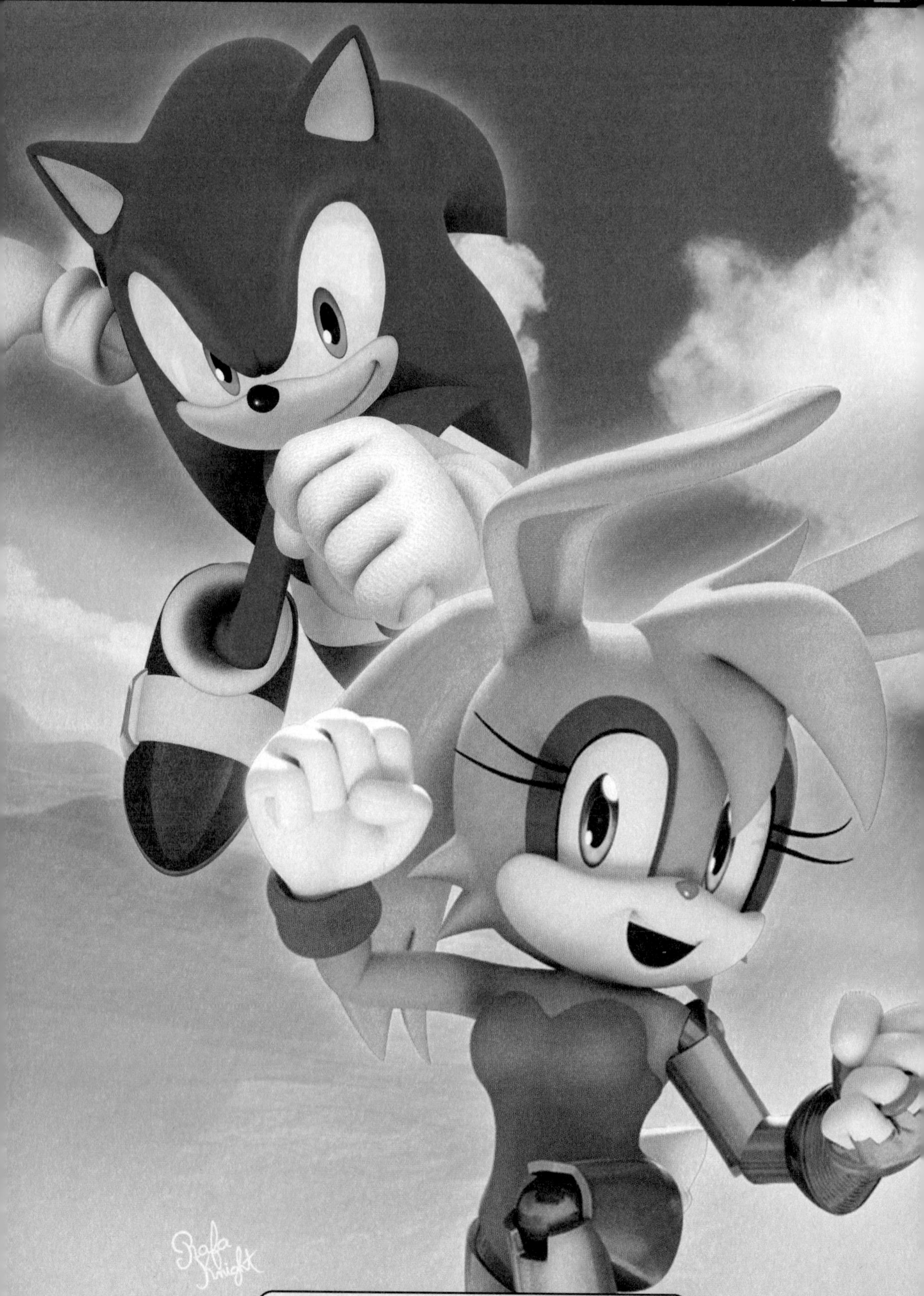
Rafa Knight

SONIC & BUNNIE
ART BY SEGA & RAFA KNIGHT

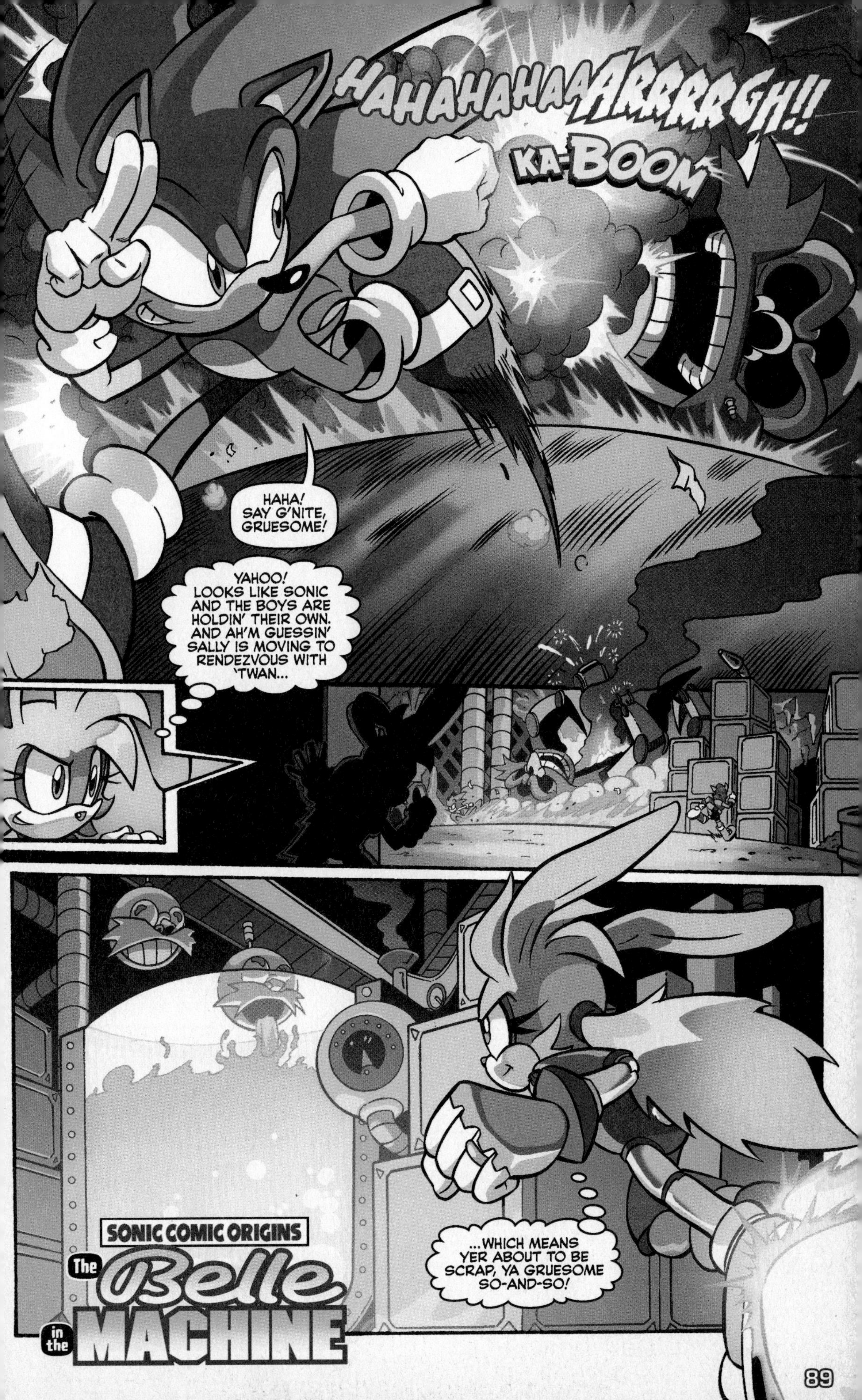
HAHAHAHAAARRRRGH!!
KA-BOOM
HAHA! SAY G'NITE, GRUESOME!
YAHOO! LOOKS LIKE SONIC AND THE BOYS ARE HOLDIN' THEIR OWN. AND AH'M GUESSIN' SALLY IS MOVING TO RENDEZVOUS WITH 'TWAN...
...WHICH MEANS YER ABOUT TO BE SCRAP, YA GRUESOME SO-AND-SO!
SONIC COMIC ORIGINS
The Belle in the MACHINE

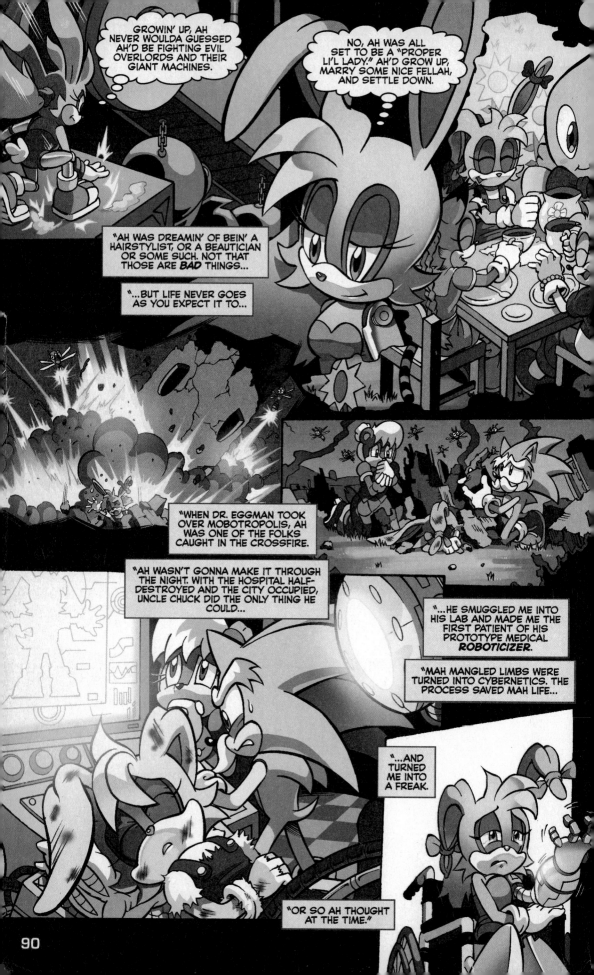

GROWIN' UP, AH NEVER WOULDA GUESSED AH'D BE FIGHTING EVIL OVERLORDS AND THEIR GIANT MACHINES.

NO, AH WAS ALL SET TO BE A "PROPER LI'L LADY." AH'D GROW UP, MARRY SOME NICE FELLAH, AND SETTLE DOWN.

"AH WAS DREAMIN' OF BEIN' A HAIRSTYLIST, OR A BEAUTICIAN OR SOME SUCH. NOT THAT THOSE ARE *BAD* THINGS...

"...BUT LIFE NEVER GOES AS YOU EXPECT IT TO...

"WHEN DR. EGGMAN TOOK OVER MOBOTROPOLIS, AH WAS ONE OF THE FOLKS CAUGHT IN THE CROSSFIRE.

"AH WASN'T GONNA MAKE IT THROUGH THE NIGHT. WITH THE HOSPITAL HALF-DESTROYED AND THE CITY OCCUPIED, UNCLE CHUCK DID THE ONLY THING HE COULD...

"...HE SMUGGLED ME INTO HIS LAB AND MADE ME THE FIRST PATIENT OF HIS PROTOTYPE MEDICAL *ROBOTICIZER.*

"MAH MANGLED LIMBS WERE TURNED INTO CYBERNETICS. THE PROCESS SAVED MAH LIFE...

"...AND TURNED ME INTO A FREAK.

"OR SO AH THOUGHT AT THE TIME."

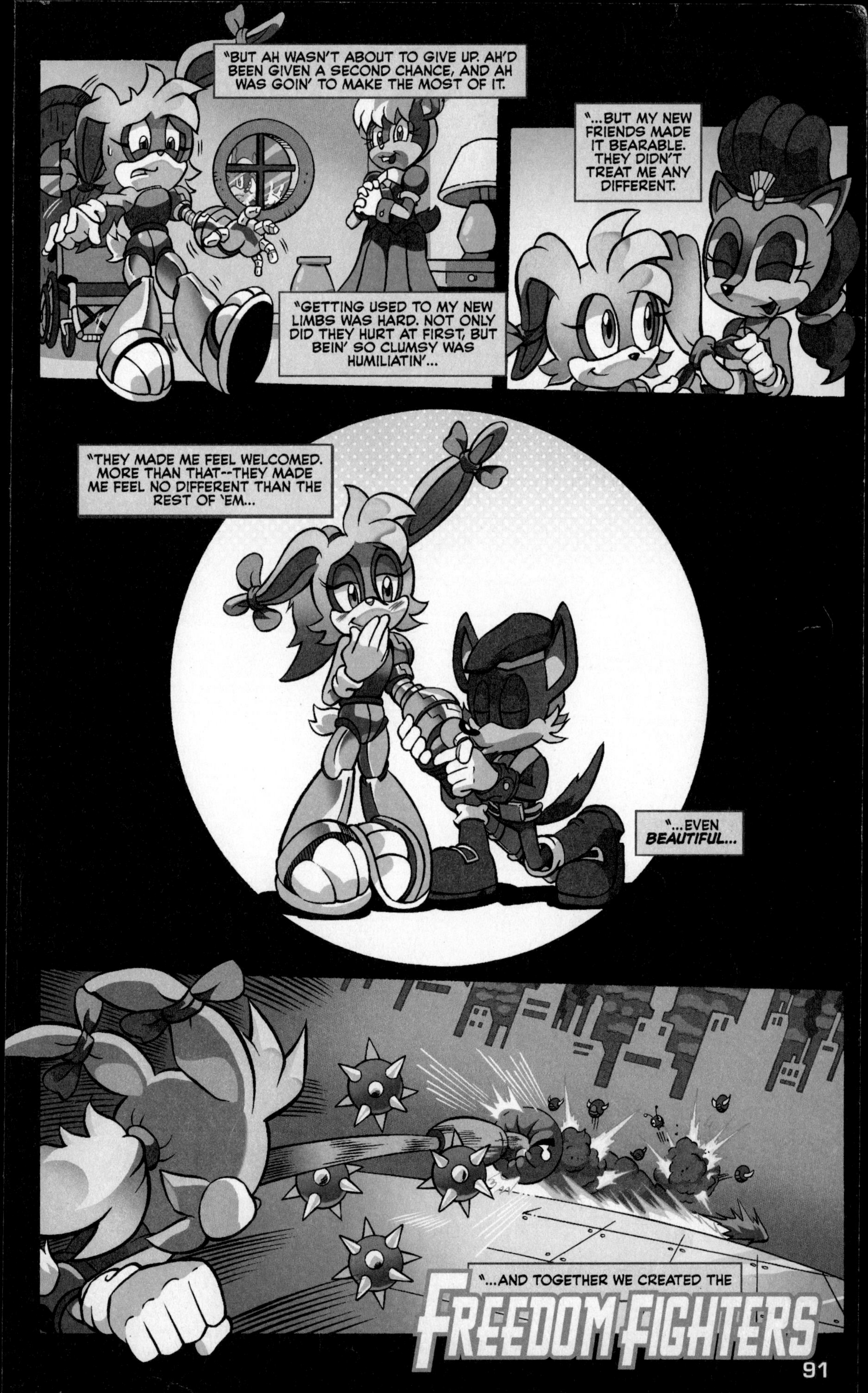
"BUT AH WASN'T ABOUT TO GIVE UP. AH'D BEEN GIVEN A SECOND CHANCE, AND AH WAS GOIN' TO MAKE THE MOST OF IT.
"GETTING USED TO MY NEW LIMBS WAS HARD. NOT ONLY DID THEY HURT AT FIRST, BUT BEIN' SO CLUMSY WAS HUMILIATIN'...
"...BUT MY NEW FRIENDS MADE IT BEARABLE. THEY DIDN'T TREAT ME ANY DIFFERENT.
"THEY MADE ME FEEL WELCOMED. MORE THAN THAT--THEY MADE ME FEEL NO DIFFERENT THAN THE REST OF 'EM...
"...EVEN *BEAUTIFUL*...
"...AND TOGETHER WE CREATED THE
FREEDOM FIGHTERS

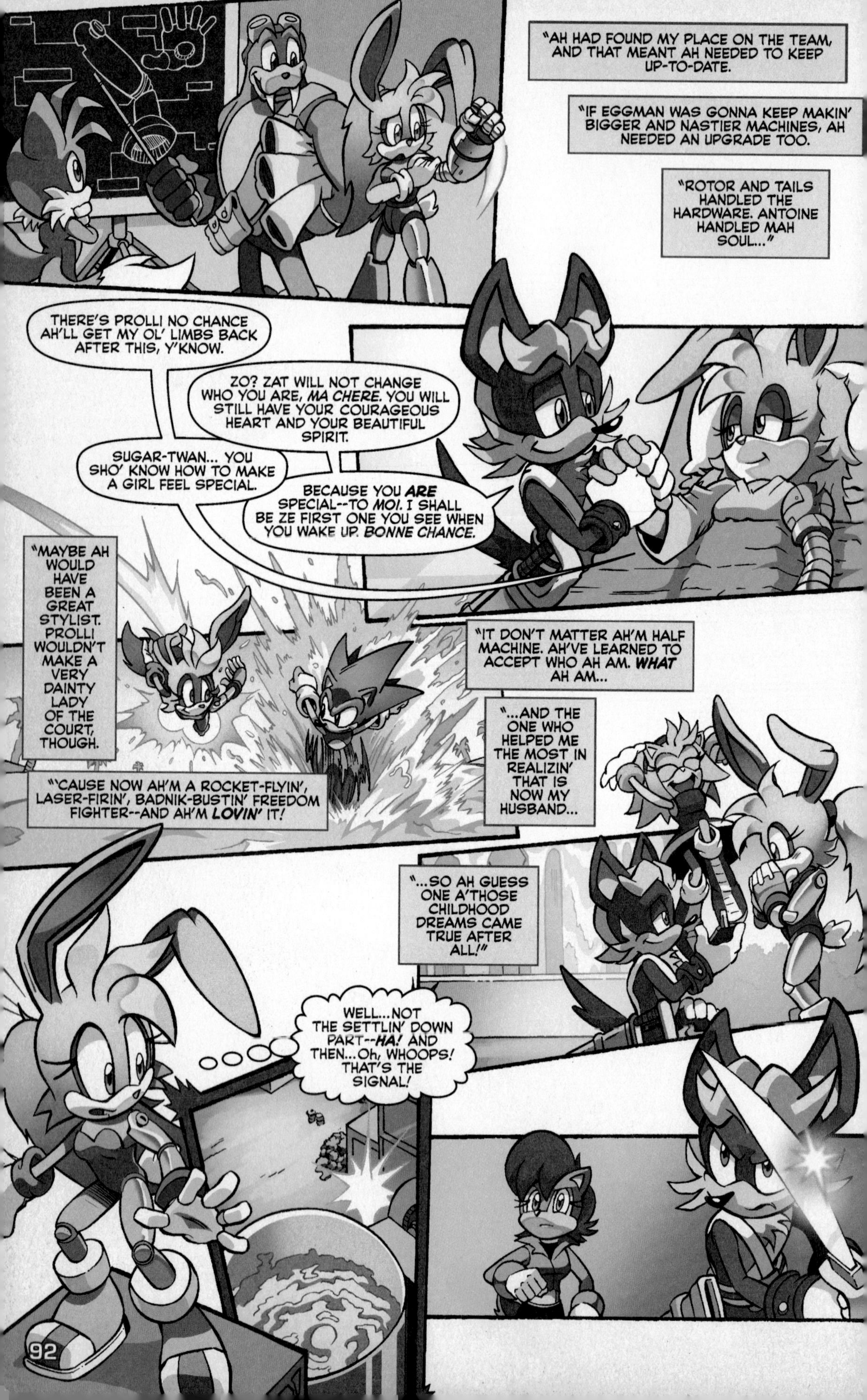
"AH HAD FOUND MY PLACE ON THE TEAM, AND THAT MEANT AH NEEDED TO KEEP UP-TO-DATE.
"IF EGGMAN WAS GONNA KEEP MAKIN' BIGGER AND NASTIER MACHINES, AH NEEDED AN UPGRADE TOO.
"ROTOR AND TAILS HANDLED THE HARDWARE. ANTOINE HANDLED MAH SOUL..."
THERE'S PROLLI NO CHANCE AH'LL GET MY OL' LIMBS BACK AFTER THIS, Y'KNOW.
ZO? ZAT WILL NOT CHANGE WHO YOU ARE, MA CHERE. YOU WILL STILL HAVE YOUR COURAGEOUS HEART AND YOUR BEAUTIFUL SPIRIT.
SUGAR-TWAN... YOU SHO' KNOW HOW TO MAKE A GIRL FEEL SPECIAL.
BECAUSE YOU ARE SPECIAL--TO MOI. I SHALL BE ZE FIRST ONE YOU SEE WHEN YOU WAKE UP. BONNE CHANCE.
"MAYBE AH WOULD HAVE BEEN A GREAT STYLIST. PROLLI WOULDN'T MAKE A VERY DAINTY LADY OF THE COURT, THOUGH.
"'CAUSE NOW AH'M A ROCKET-FLYIN', LASER-FIRIN', BADNIK-BUSTIN' FREEDOM FIGHTER--AND AH'M LOVIN' IT!
"IT DON'T MATTER AH'M HALF MACHINE. AH'VE LEARNED TO ACCEPT WHO AH AM. WHAT AH AM...
"...AND THE ONE WHO HELPED ME THE MOST IN REALIZIN' THAT IS NOW MY HUSBAND...
"...SO AH GUESS ONE A'THOSE CHILDHOOD DREAMS CAME TRUE AFTER ALL!"
WELL...NOT THE SETTLIN' DOWN PART--HA! AND THEN...Oh, WHOOPS! THAT'S THE SIGNAL!

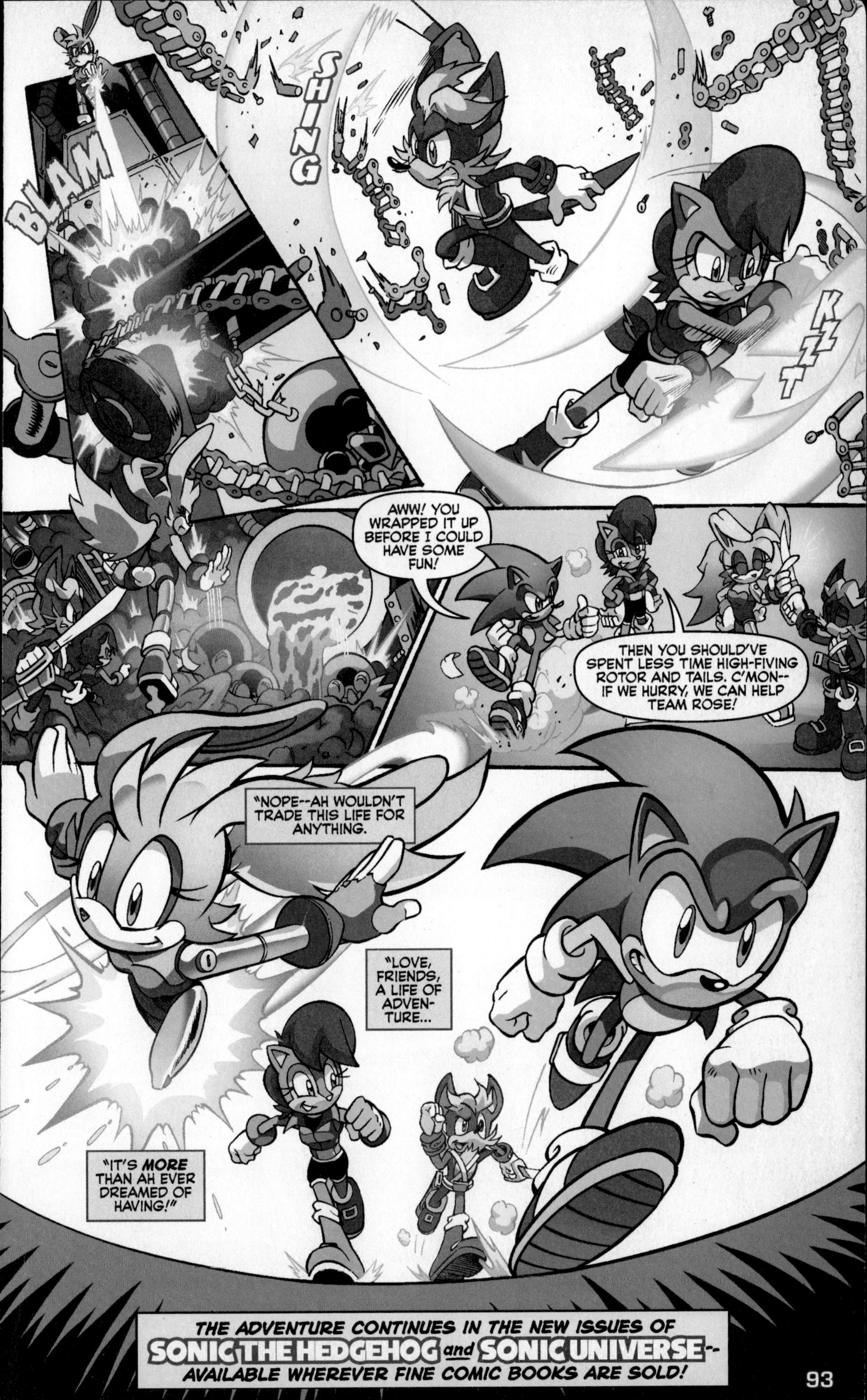
BLAM
SHING
KZZT
AWW! YOU WRAPPED IT UP BEFORE I COULD HAVE SOME FUN!
THEN YOU SHOULD'VE SPENT LESS TIME HIGH-FIVING ROTOR AND TAILS. C'MON-- IF WE HURRY, WE CAN HELP TEAM ROSE!
"NOPE--AH WOULDN'T TRADE THIS LIFE FOR ANYTHING.
"LOVE, FRIENDS, A LIFE OF ADVEN-TURE...
"IT'S MORE THAN AH EVER DREAMED OF HAVING!"
THE ADVENTURE CONTINUES IN THE NEW ISSUES OF
SONIC THE HEDGEHOG and SONIC UNIVERSE--
AVAILABLE WHEREVER FINE COMIC BOOKS ARE SOLD!

WHAT'S OLD IS NEW!

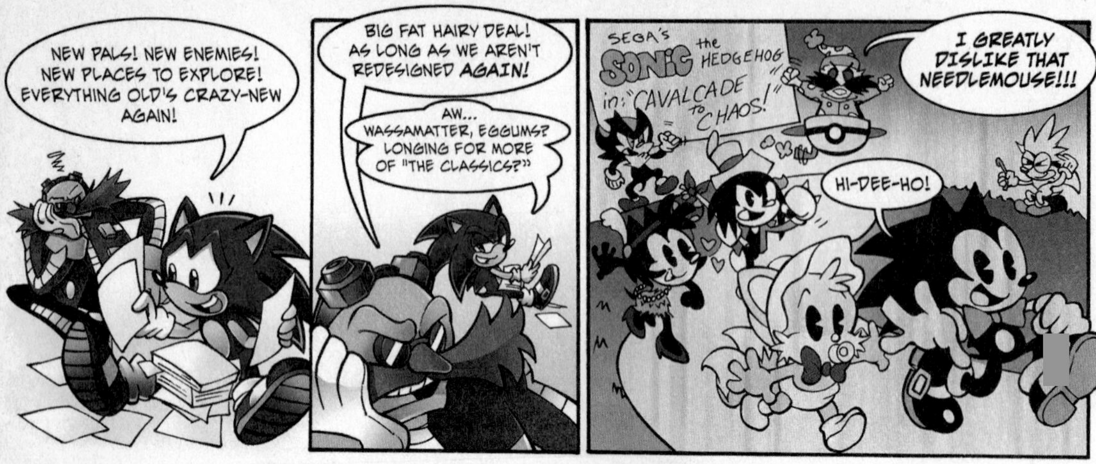
NEW PALS! NEW ENEMIES! NEW PLACES TO EXPLORE! EVERYTHING OLD'S CRAZY-NEW AGAIN!
BIG FAT HAIRY DEAL! AS LONG AS WE AREN'T REDESIGNED AGAIN!
AW... WASSAMATTER, EGGUMS? LONGING FOR MORE OF "THE CLASSICS?"
SEGA's SONIC the HEDGEHOG in: "CAVALCADE to CHAOS!"
I GREATLY DISLIKE THAT NEEDLEMOUSE!!!
HI-DEE-HO!

QUITE THE PICKLE

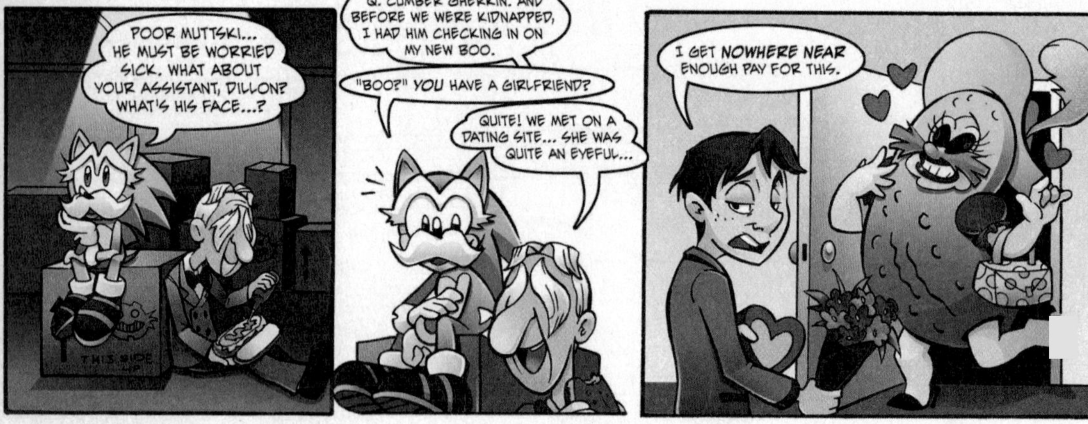
POOR MUTTSKI... HE MUST BE WORRIED SICK. WHAT ABOUT YOUR ASSISTANT, DILLON? WHAT'S HIS FACE...?
Q. CUMBER GHERKIN. AND BEFORE WE WERE KIDNAPPED, I HAD HIM CHECKING IN ON MY NEW BOO.
"BOO?" YOU HAVE A GIRLFRIEND?
QUITE! WE MET ON A DATING SITE... SHE WAS QUITE AN EYEFUL...
I GET NOWHERE NEAR ENOUGH PAY FOR THIS.

GETTING ON TRACK

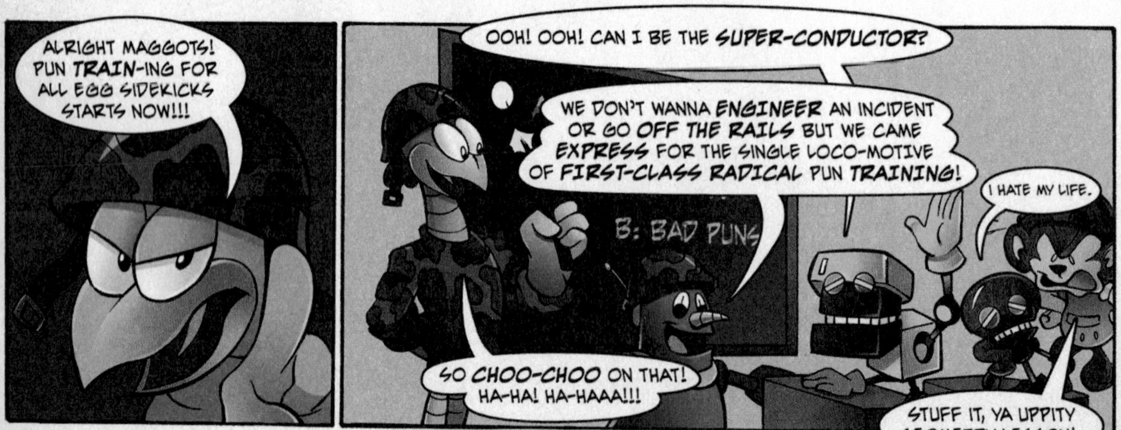
ALRIGHT MAGGOTS! PUN TRAIN-ING FOR ALL EGG SIDEKICKS STARTS NOW!!!
OOH! OOH! CAN I BE THE SUPER-CONDUCTOR?
WE DON'T WANNA ENGINEER AN INCIDENT OR GO OFF THE RAILS BUT WE CAME EXPRESS FOR THE SINGLE LOCO-MOTIVE OF FIRST-CLASS RADICAL PUN TRAINING!
B: BAD PUNS
I HATE MY LIFE.
SO CHOO-CHOO ON THAT! HA-HA! HA-HAAA!!!
STUFF IT, YA UPPITY GEOMETRY LESSON!

SCRIPT: JONATHAN H. GRAY PENCILS: JENNIFER HERNANDEZ INKS: RICK BRYANT COLORS: ALEAH BAKER

SONIC THE HEDGEHOG 257
VARIANT COVER

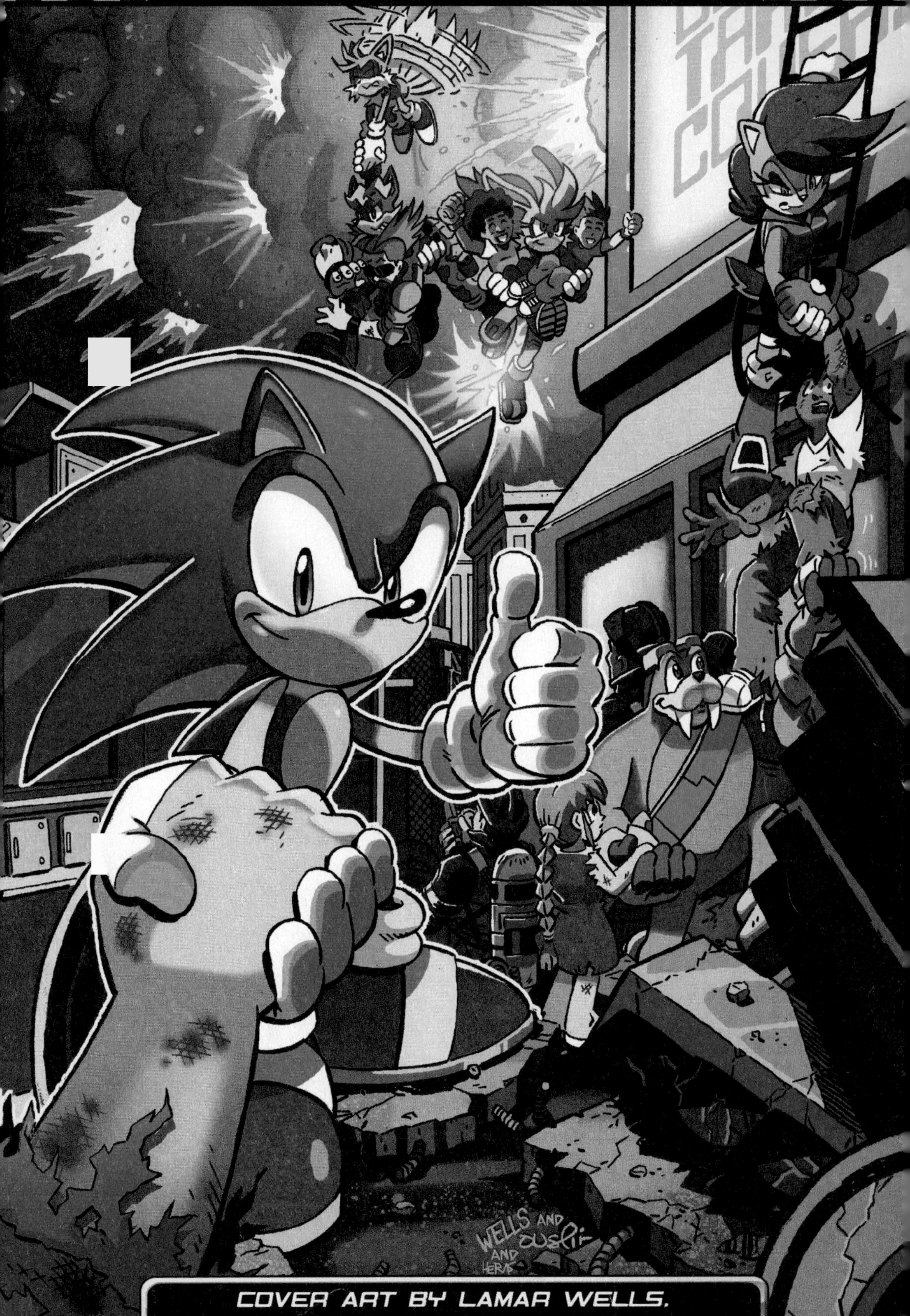

COVER ART BY LAMAR WELLS, TERRY AUSTIN & MATT HERMS

SONIC THE HEDGEHOG 258 VARIANT COVER

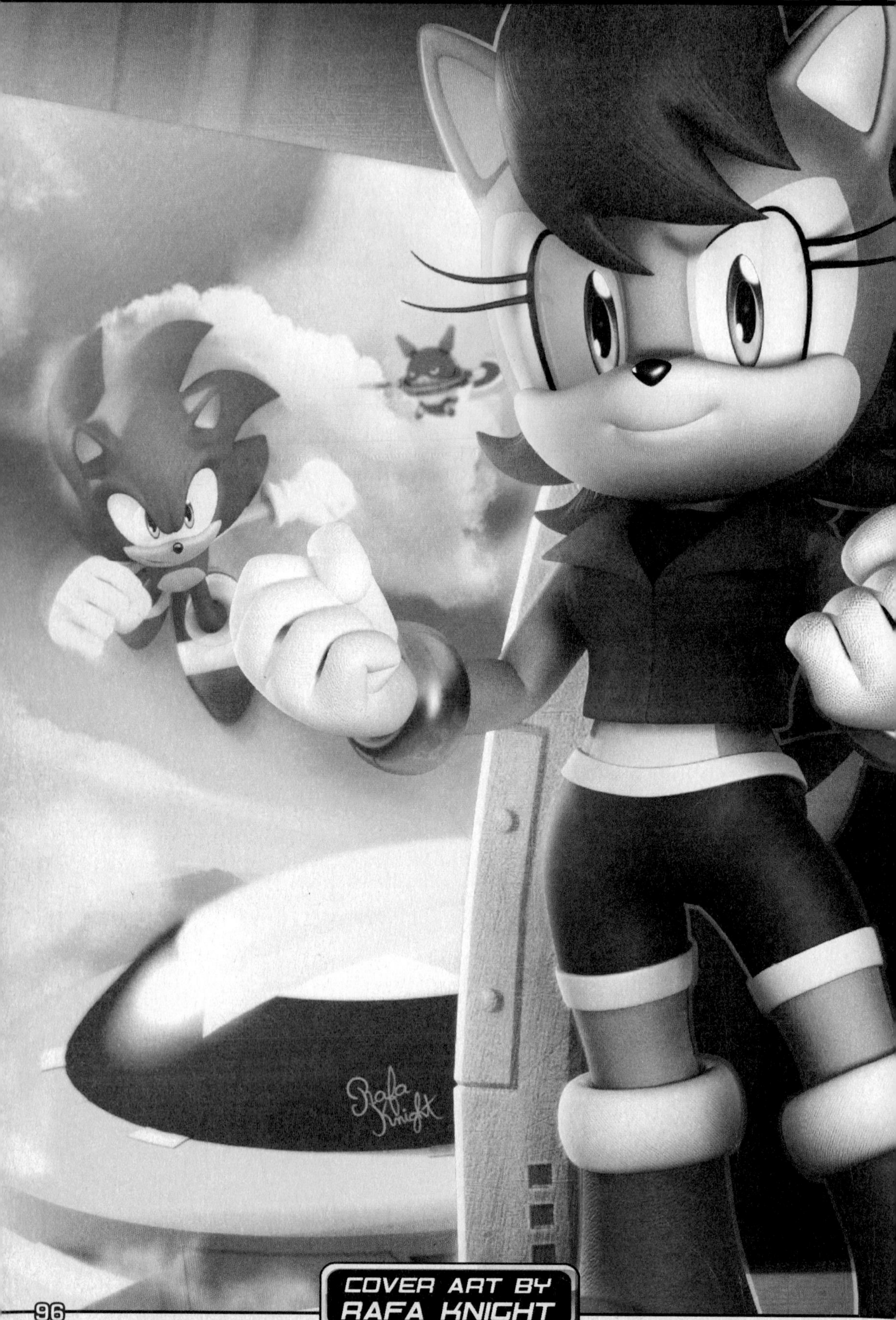
Rafa Knight

COVER ART BY
RAFA KNIGHT

SONIC THE HEDGEHOG 259
VARIANT COVER

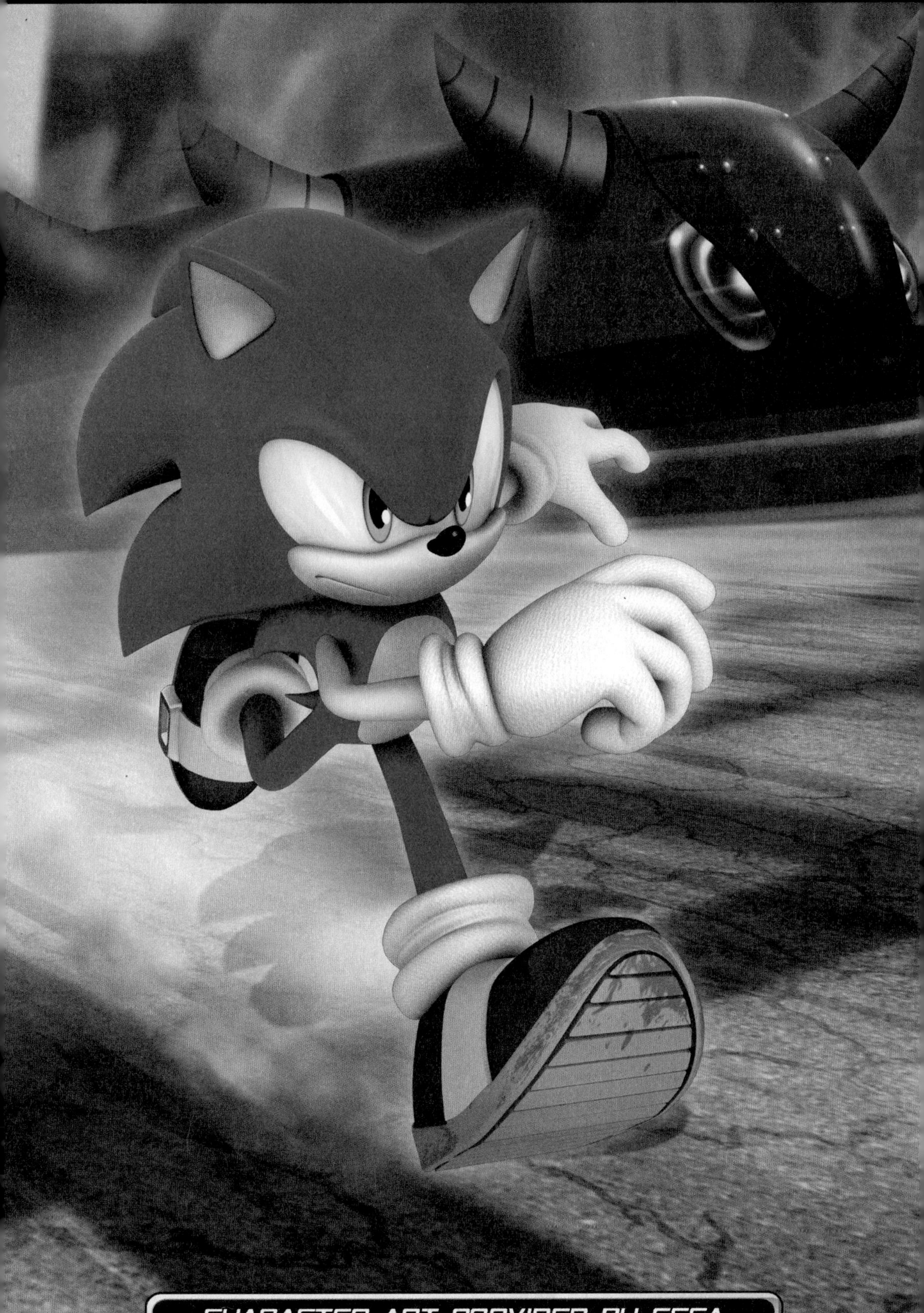

CHARACTER ART PROVIDED BY SEGA
BACKGROUND ART BY VINCENT LOVALLO

SONIC SUPER DIGEST 7

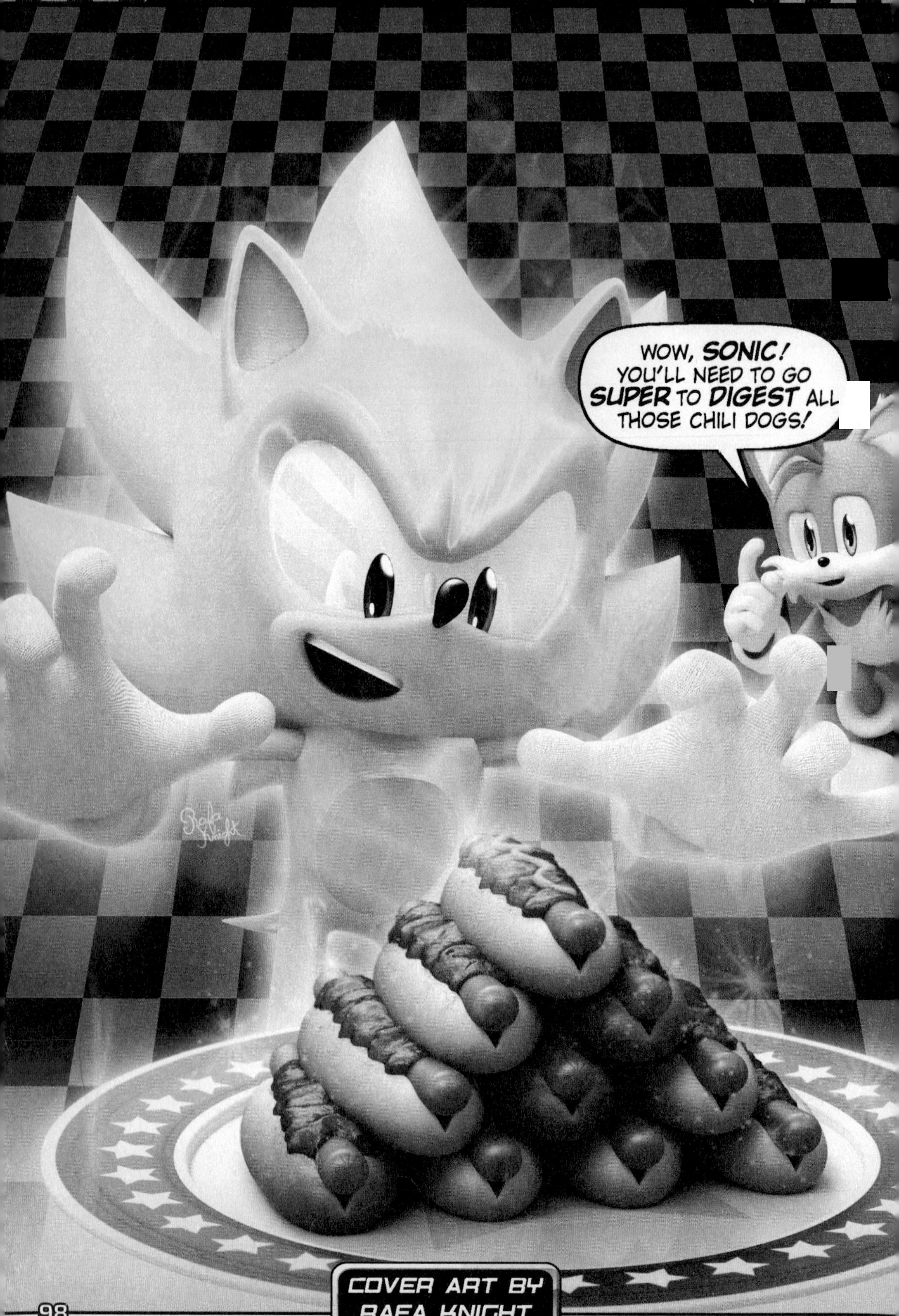
WOW, SONIC! YOU'LL NEED TO GO SUPER TO DIGEST ALL THOSE CHILI DOGS!
Rafa Knight

COVER ART BY RAFA KNIGHT

PENCIL SELECTIONS FROM CHAPTER 2 BY EVAN STANLEY

PAGE 28

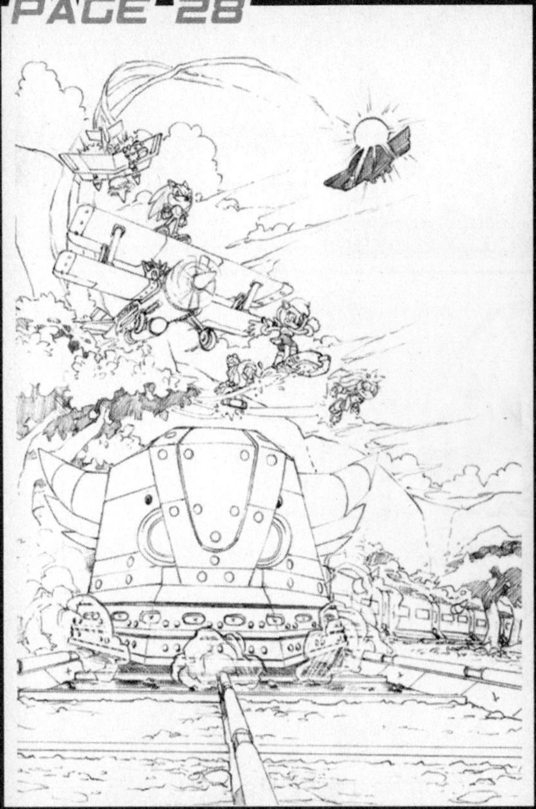

PAGE 29

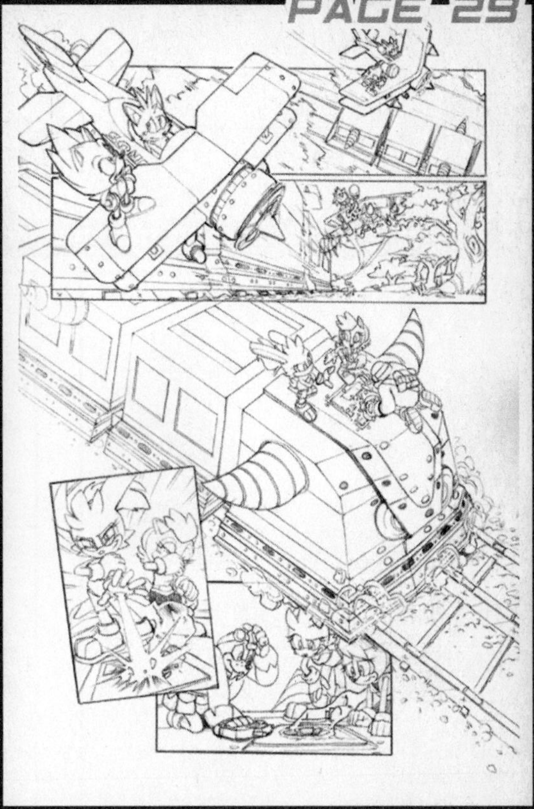

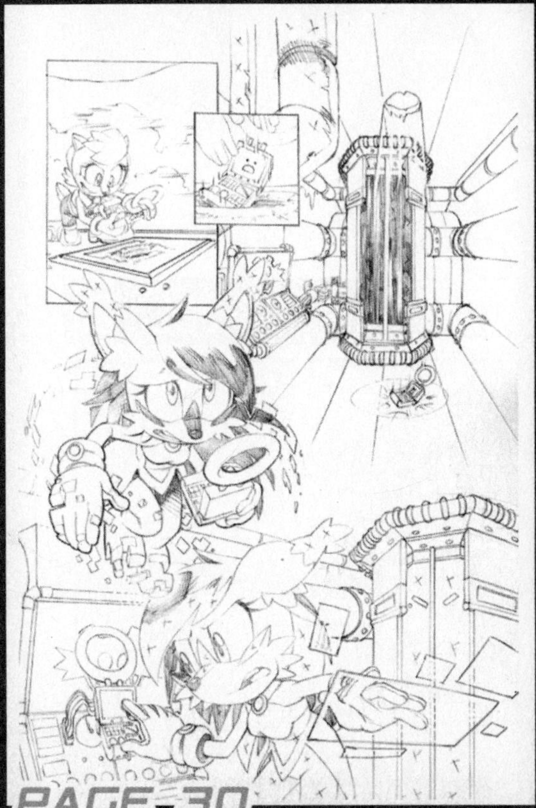

PAGE 30

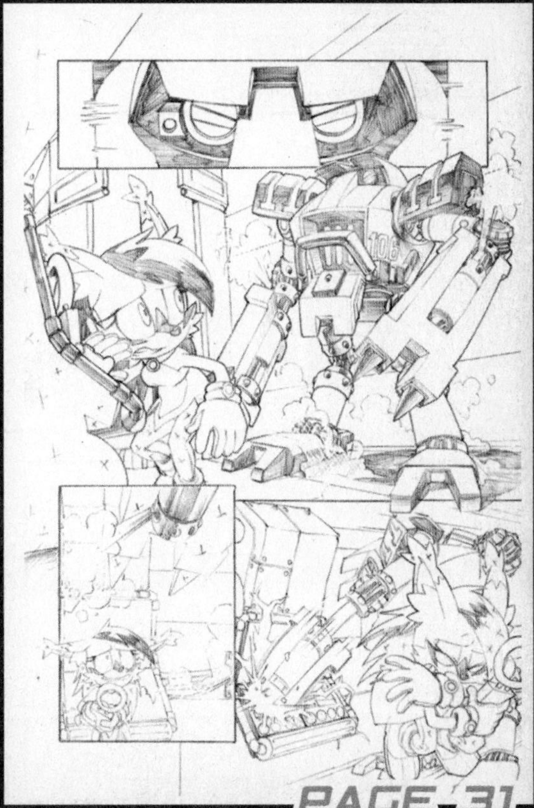

PAGE 31

PRODUCTION ART:
DESIGNING THE FREEDOM FIGHTERS!

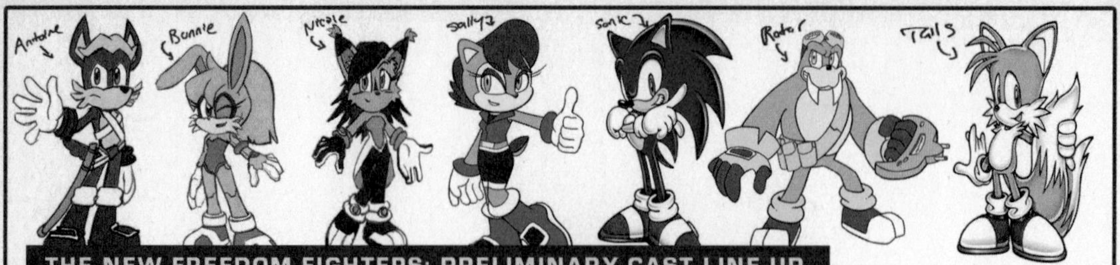
Antoine
Bunnie
Nicole
Sally
Sonic
Rotor
Tails

THE NEW FREEDOM FIGHTERS: PRELIMINARY CAST LINE-UP

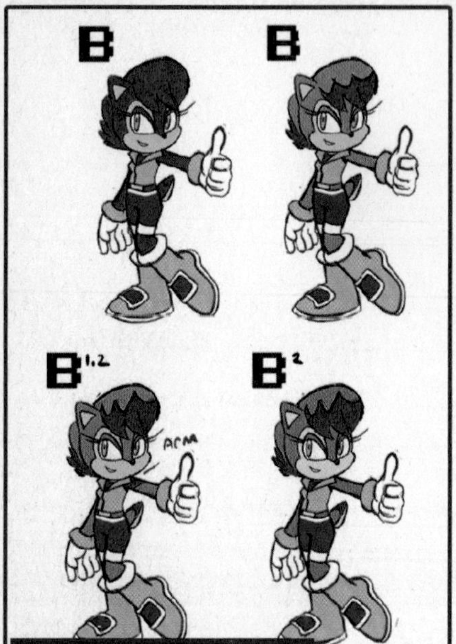
B
B
B1.2
B2
arm

SALLY ACORN ART
BY RYAN JAMPOLE

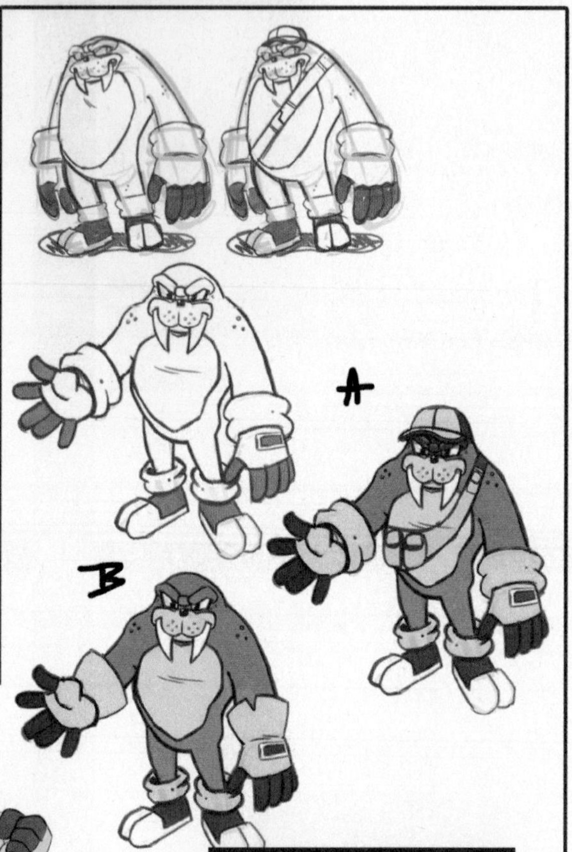
A
B

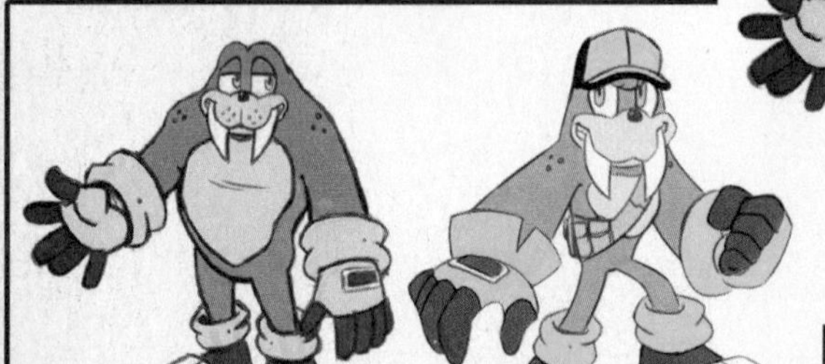

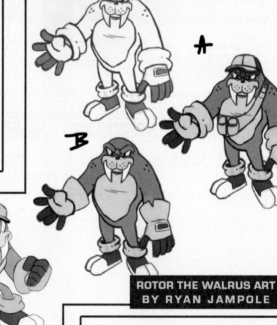

ROTOR THE WALRUS ART
BY RYAN JAMPOLE

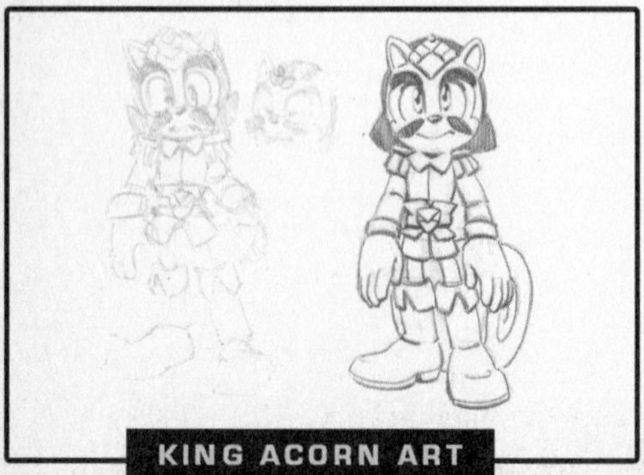

KING ACORN ART
BY EVAN STANLEY

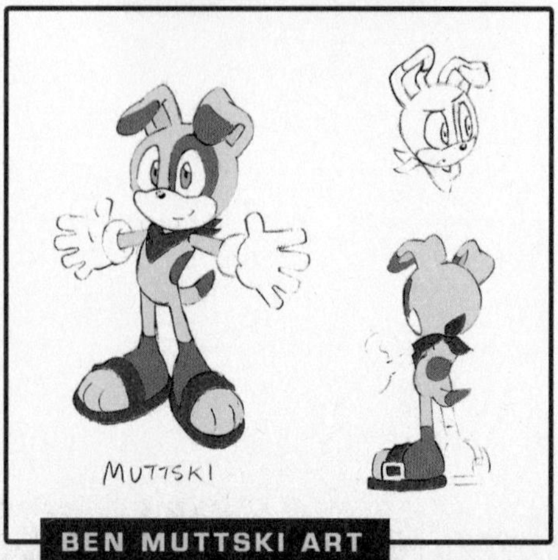
MUTTSKI

BEN MUTTSKI ART
BY TRACY YARDLEY

PRODUCTION ART:
DESIGNING THE SKY PATROL!

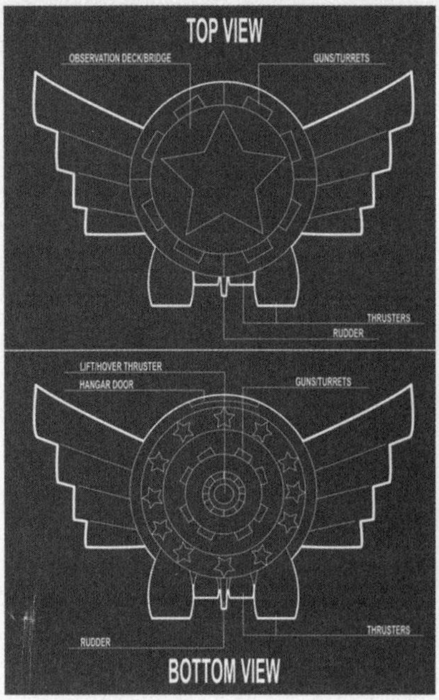
TOP VIEW
OBSERVATION DECK/BRIDGE
GUNS/TURRETS
THRUSTERS
RUDDER
LIFT/HOVER THRUSTER
HANGAR DOOR
GUNS/TURRETS
RUDDER
THRUSTERS
BOTTOM VIEW

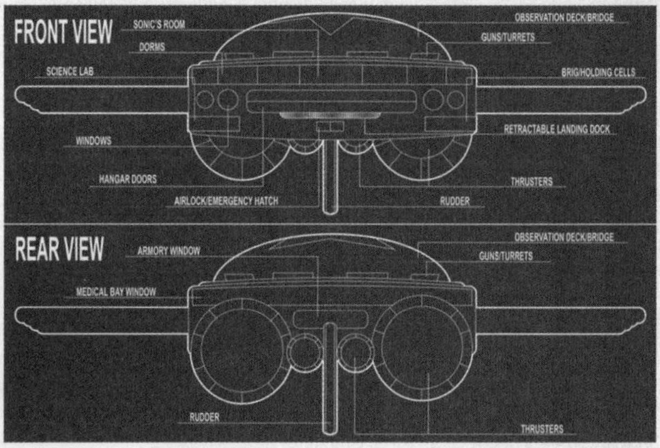
FRONT VIEW
SONIC'S ROOM
DORMS
SCIENCE LAB
WINDOWS
HANGAR DOORS
AIRLOCK/EMERGENCY HATCH
OBSERVATION DECK/BRIDGE
GUNS/TURRETS
BRIG/HOLDING CELLS
RETRACTABLE LANDING DOCK
THRUSTERS
RUDDER
REAR VIEW
ARMORY WINDOW
MEDICAL BAY WINDOW
OBSERVATION DECK/BRIDGE
GUNS/TURRETS
RUDDER
THRUSTERS

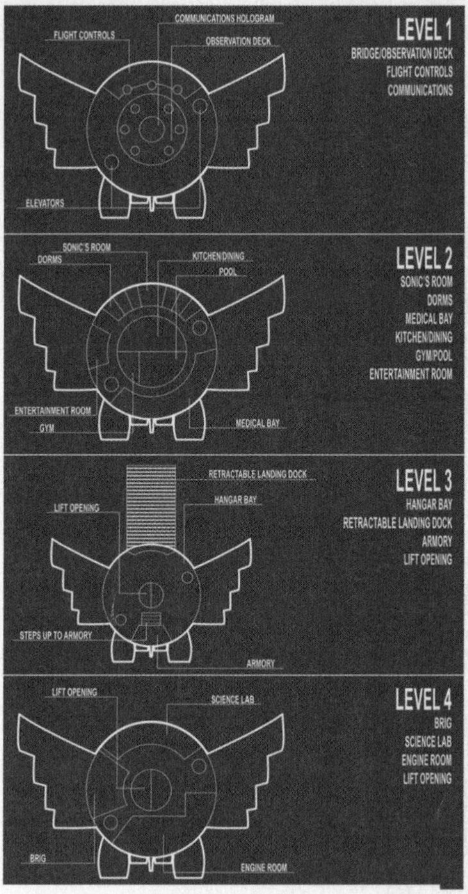
COMMUNICATIONS HOLOGRAM
FLIGHT CONTROLS
OBSERVATION DECK
ELEVATORS
LEVEL 1
BRIDGE/OBSERVATION DECK
FLIGHT CONTROLS
COMMUNICATIONS
SONIC'S ROOM
DORMS
KITCHEN/DINING
POOL
ENTERTAINMENT ROOM
GYM
MEDICAL BAY
LEVEL 2
SONIC'S ROOM
DORMS
MEDICAL BAY
KITCHEN/DINING
GYM/POOL
ENTERTAINMENT ROOM
RETRACTABLE LANDING DOCK
HANGAR BAY
LIFT OPENING
STEPS UP TO ARMORY
ARMORY
LEVEL 3
HANGAR BAY
RETRACTABLE LANDING DOCK
ARMORY
LIFT OPENING
LIFT OPENING
SCIENCE LAB
BRIG
ENGINE ROOM
LEVEL 4
BRIG
SCIENCE LAB
ENGINE ROOM
LIFT OPENING

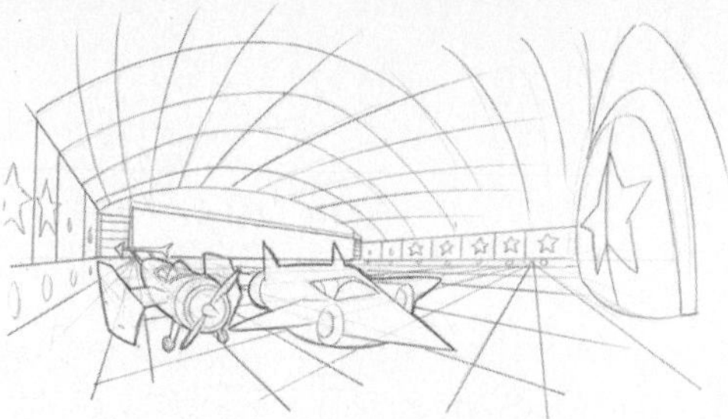

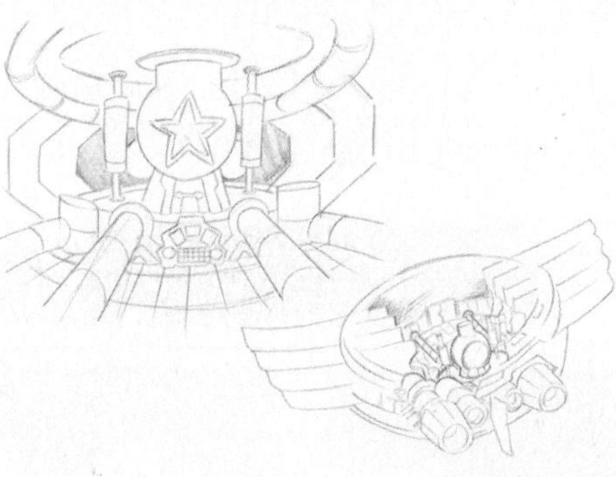

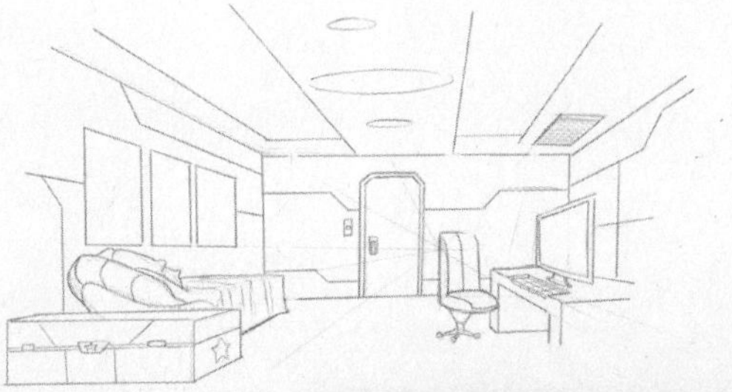

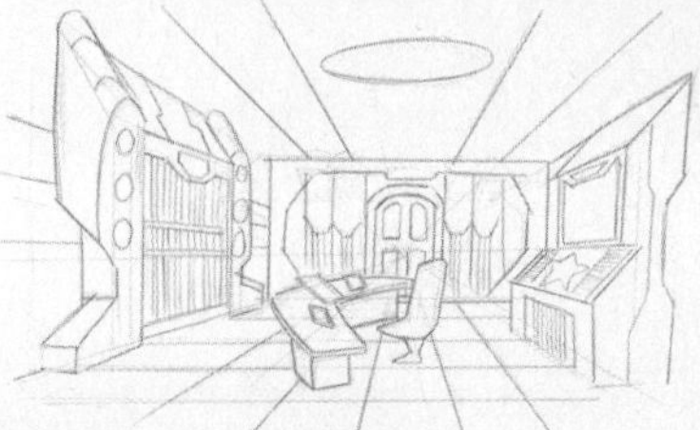

SKY PATROL ART BY JERRY GAYLORD

COVER CONCEPTS

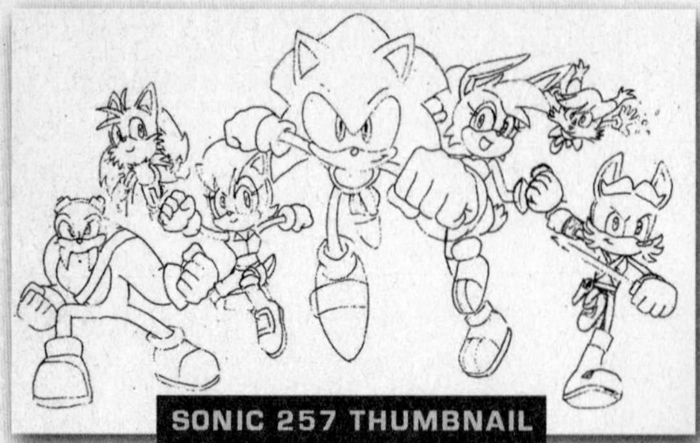

SONIC 257 THUMBNAIL
BY VINCENT LOVALLO

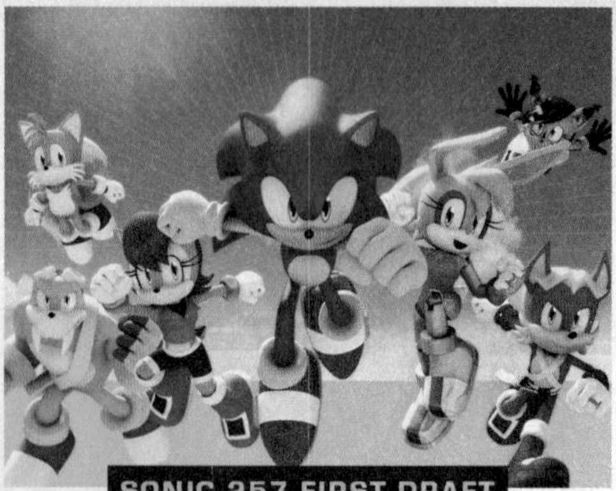

SONIC 257 FIRST DRAFT
BY RAFA KNIGHT

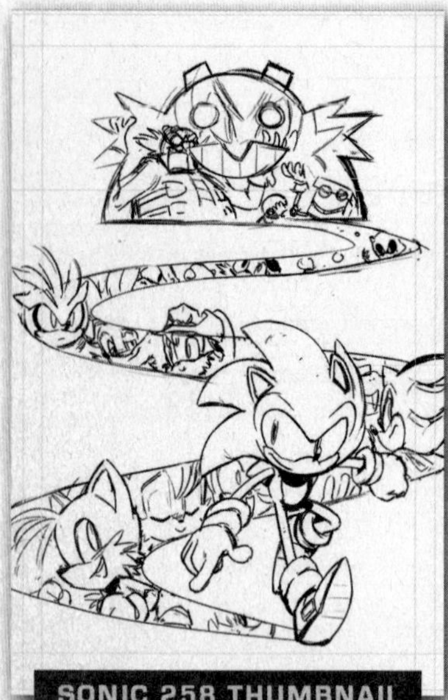

SONIC 258 THUMBNAIL
BY TYSON HESSE

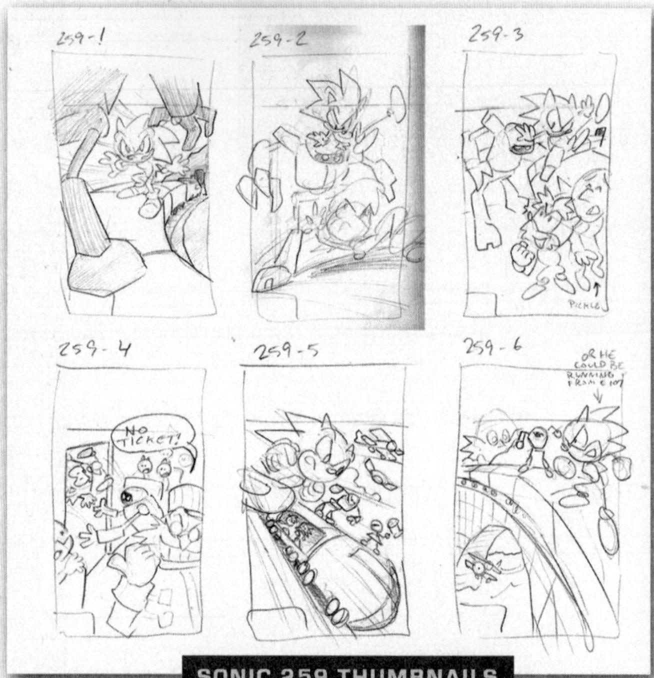
259-1
259-2
259-3
PICKLE
259-4
NO TICKET?
259-5
259-6
OR HE COULD BE RUNNING FROM E 107

SONIC 259 THUMBNAILS
BY TRACY YARDLEY

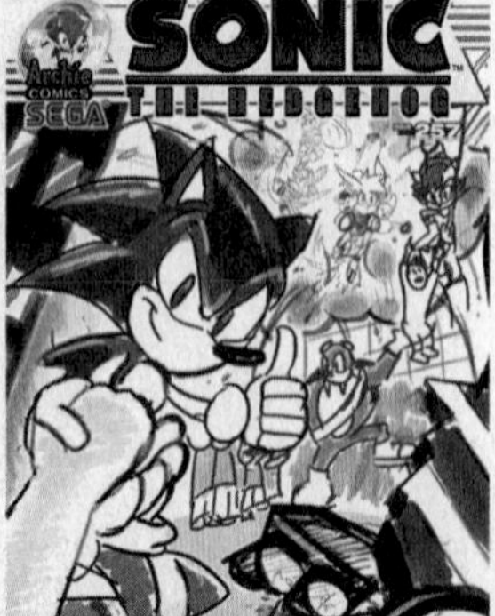
STATION SQUARE RESCUE MISSION!
SONIC
THE HEDGEHOG
Archie COMICS
SEGA

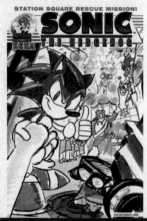

SONIC 257 VARIANT THUMBNAIL
BY VINCENT LOVALLO

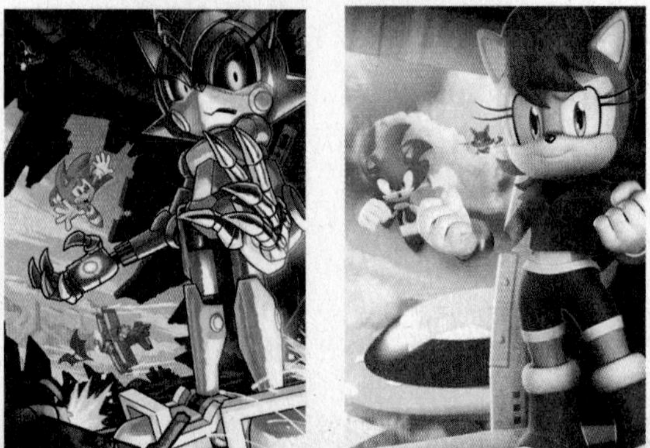

SONIC 258'S VARIANT COVER IS MODELED
AFTER THE REGULAR COVER TO SONIC 231